RISE OF THE
RENEGADES

Book Seven in the Pantracia Chronicles

RISE OF THE RENEGADES

Amanda Muratoff & Kayla Hansen

www.Pantracia.com

Cover design by Andrei Bat.

ISBN: 978-1-9995797-4-6

February 2024

We dedicate this book to those who have lost their way.

May you always find the light.

The Pantracia Chronicles:

Visit www.Pantracia.com for our pronunciation guide
and to discover more.

Chapter 1

Autumn, 2611 R.T. (recorded time)

DUST PLUMED AROUND RAE AS her back hit the ground, all the air leaving her lungs.

Jarrod pinned her, huffing a growl as he wrenched her wrists to her sides. His amber eyes bored into her.

She squirmed, wrapping her legs around one of his, but failed to displace his weight. Twisting her wrist, she freed it from his grip and threw a punch at his ribs.

He laughed. "That tickles."

"You're an ass." Rae punched him again, harder.

Jarrod cringed, grunting and falling off her in a dramatic show of defeat.

Propping herself up, she caught her breath while glaring at him. "I'm not sparring with you anymore. It's not even fair. Where's Corin? I bet I can beat him."

The captain snorted from the doorway as he entered the ruined arena. "I'd like to see you try." He paused, leaning on the open steel door's frame. He eyed Jarrod up and down. "Maybe you should pick on someone your own size, Martox."

The proxiet stood, his breath even, and offered Rae a hand. "Believe it or not, she bested me once or twice back in the day. Feisty little thief."

Rae frowned and slapped the offered hand before getting up on her own, brushing off her pants. She looked at Corin. "Next time, it's you and me. I'll probably still lose, but at least I have a chance. Damien refuses to fight me."

"Some self-righteous reason, I'm sure." Corin took a step from the wall as his face grew serious. His soft brown eyes met Jarrod's. "Liala's back. The Herald is waiting for us in Serityme."

Something churned in Rae's chest. She hadn't seen Andi since she'd disembarked her ship with Damien in Porthew.

A week ago, Jarrod had sent his hawk to request the captain's aid in transporting him and his husband home to Lazuli.

Still not sure how it'll go when he arrives at the Lazuli docks on a wanted privateering vessel.

Captain Andirindia Trace's galleon would be recognized.

"I'm coming with you." Rae blurted out the words before she could rethink them.

Jarrod and Corin looked at her, and the proxiet's brow furrowed. "To Lazuli?"

"No. Just to the Herald. To see Andi."

"Damien doesn't need you here? I mean, he all but bit off my head when I tried to tell him about Liala a moment ago. Some *delicate, mind-numbingly difficult spell* or something."

"He's working on the dagger we need to house the power of the Berylian Key." Rae rolled her eyes, mimicking a serious tone with the phrase she'd grown sick of hearing. "He needs me to fetch his tea, but that's all. He probably won't even notice I'm not here." She held out a hand. "I'll tell him, of course. Just saying..."

Jarrod shrugged. "I'm sure Andi would love to see you."

Corin stepped closer, lowering his voice. "Are we sure Damien's not getting too deep into this Rahn'ka shit right now? He's got to focus on what we're about to do in Helgath. The deadline for Dannet support is only weeks away." He put a hand on his husband's shoulder. "He's your personal advisor. We're going to need him."

Rae sighed, already planning what she should pack for the week's travel to and from the coast. "You can tell him that. Gods know I've already tried." Walking to the exit, she paused next to the men. "Meet you out front in a bit? Don't you dare leave without me."

She left after Jarrod nodded, returning to the room she shared with Damien. Packing her bag, she grabbed it and her bow and headed for the altar where the Rahn'ka worked. At first, they'd conspired together in the plan to separate the power of the Berylian Key from Amarie, whom they'd still hadn't even met. But Damien, on discovering the complexities of the weapon required to kill the woman and steal her power, became reclusive and secretive with the process.

Approaching quietly, she hesitated in the archway and leaned against the half-crumbled wall.

The surrounding mountains hid the circular cutout of the ruins while also lessening the amount of rainfall the area received. Two monoliths of vine-covered stone marked the narrow gorge entrance, a large courtyard of spiraled stone and grass spanning between two buildings still partially intact after thousands of years.

Damien sat cross-legged, balanced on the short stone pillar at the center of the courtyard. His hands rested in his lap and his loose cream shirt caught on the autumn breeze. The runes of the Rahn'ka, normally a navy tattoo just visible above his shirt collar, blazed with rich light. A tangle of energy passed down his left arm, where she could imagine the pattern extending to his wrist, little swirls of his Art ebbing from him into the obsidian blade in his hands. It pulsed into streams of silver embedded within the glassy stone.

The power coursing from the Rahn'ka's body stopped, leaving a void in the surrounding fabric. The weaves of Damien's energy settled into the guardless dagger.

His back straightened as he opened his eyes. They landed on Rae with no hesitance. Looking her over, he frowned when he saw the bag. "What's that for?"

Rae walked towards him, slinging the pack over her shoulder. "I'm going with Jarrod and Corin." Her heart beat sped, and she motioned to the blade. "Finally finished?"

Damien's brow furrowed as he slipped off the altar onto his bare feet. The ground beneath him emanated a faint glow as the grass quivered away from him. Without looking, he placed the obsidian dagger on the altar. "Mostly. But you're leaving with them? I thought..."

"I just want to see Andi, but I'll get off the Herald before she disembarks. I'll be gone maybe a week."

He relaxed and walked towards her. "All right. But I'll miss you while you're gone."

That's it? No resistance to his wife making a three day journey home all by herself in the middle of a brewing civil war?

Rae swallowed. "Sure. I'll miss you, too."

Damien tilted his head, his hazel eyes focusing the way they usually did when he listened to the voices of the souls around him. Except this time, he aimed it at her. "Did I say something wrong?"

Softening, she shook her head and lowered her voice. "No. It's me. I think I need—"

"You're finally getting rid of us. Aren't you ecstatic?" Jarrod's voice echoed behind her before the proxiet paused. "Am I interrupting?"

"No." Rae gave Damien a quick kiss. "I'll see you in a week. Try to remember to eat and sleep, would you?" She forced a smile, and Damien slipped his right hand into her left. Their wedding bands touched, sending a little vibration through her.

"Be safe," he whispered before turning towards Jarrod. He gave the proxiet a wide smile and patted him on the shoulder. "I'm just glad you're finally back to yourself. Are the chains restraining the wolf in your head holding up? You remember how to keep reinforcing them?"

Jarrod nodded as Neco raced into the courtyard from the forest, his sleek black form little more than a blur. "Aye. I remember. They're doing fine." He gave the valley wolf a stern look before smiling at Damien. "And I'd hardly say I'm back to myself, but I suppose it's close enough. Don't be long here. I'll need you soon."

"I'll try."

Rae walked around them, patting Neco's head as she made her way out of the courtyard towards a paddock within the sanctum where they kept the horses. She blocked out the rest of their conversation, not wanting to hear Damien's excuses again for why he needed to stay.

She tacked the buckskin mare she usually rode and strapped her bow to the saddle. The fresh air and blue sky called to her, and she nudged the horse through the monolith-rimmed gorge towards the forest beyond.

The boys will catch up.

"You rode all the way here just for a drink with me?" Andi settled into one of the overstuffed chairs in her quarters. "And you even brought the whisky."

The ship swayed with the waves, bumping against her mooring. An early winter storm brewed off the Olsa coast, bringing winds and delaying the cast off towards Lazuli.

But for Rae, that meant more time with her friend and finally having someone to talk to.

Andi brought the amber liquid to her lips, savoring the scent wafting from the crystal glass before she took a slow slip. She hummed and sank further into the chair, crossing one of her legs over the other. Tugging her chestnut braid from behind her, she draped it over her shoulder. Her deep blue irises glittered in the dim lantern light, a slight reflection like a cat's catching the crescent pupil of her eye.

"How could I forget the whisky?" Rae leaned back in her seat, sighing. "Thank you. For everything you did to help Jarrod and Damien find me in Eralas."

Andi frowned. "I wish I could have stayed to see them get you away from the auer. But I couldn't risk the ship or my crew missing the trade season. I thought they had it handled, and you didn't need another person fawning over your safety."

Rae shook her head with a smile. "I wouldn't have expected you to, but I wanted to thank you in person. I couldn't stay in Jacoby knowing you were coming here. Definitely worth the journey." She raised her glass to meet Andi's before taking a long drink.

Nymaera, it's been too long since I had a drink. I need to bring a few bottles back to the sanctum.

"So, when are we going to talk about *that*?" Andi smirked, nodding her head towards Rae's left hand. "Changed your mind?"

Looking at the wedding band on her middle finger, Rae's shoulders slumped. She downed the rest of her glass and popped the bottle's cork to top it up.

"Uh oh." Andi lifted her glass to her lips and let it hover there as she watched Rae. "Troubled waters? He being an idiotic Lanoret again?"

"No." Rae laughed without mirth. "Maybe..." She studied the drink in her hand. "I don't know. Maybe marrying him has nothing to do with how things are. I did change my mind, and I was so excited to marry him. But... It's all books and research and politics now. It's like he got what he wanted and..."

"He's just distracted." Andi waved a hand as she leaned forward, her knee-high boots thunking on the deck.

Rae quirked an eyebrow. "Coming to his defense? Not what I expected."

"Not defense. The boy needs to realize his priorities. And I think he will, given the right motivation." She poured herself more whisky. "And you *are* the right motivation. Give it time?"

Nodding, Rae sipped. "You're probably right. But it seems like everyone is moving forward except me. This isn't where I imagined my life. Damien is busy and Jarrod, gods, he's going to be king. Can you even believe that?"

The captain scoffed. "King." She shook her head and took another long drink. "That boy could hardly hold a knife when I met him. And now... And Helgath. Will be a rough job fixing that hell-hole of a country. You are all crazy."

Rae chuckled under her breath. "Right again. Are you sticking around in Lazuli to take the boys to their next destination? I have a feeling they won't be hunkering down at home for long."

"Only if that future king of yours is paying the way. Spring's coming and a war in Helgath doesn't stop trade for the rest of Pantracia. Have half a mind to go up to the Trytonia Strait and make my business there." She settled into the chair again, tugging on her blue corset vest. "Jarrod better be coughing up hazard pay."

"I think he's prepared to pay you whatever you want." Rae smirked. "Some deep pockets there. I bet he'll dictate your schedule all spring if you let him."

"Gods, he would, wouldn't he? But politics..." She wrinkled her nose and tipped her glass, downing the rest of it.

"I know. You're talking to his political strategist, remember?"

"Then you're the larger fool in this room."

"At least that hasn't changed." Rae downed her whisky, her mind blurring at the edges.

Andi lifted her glass after filling it, holding it towards Rae. "I'll happily remain on the outside of all this madness so I may continue to remind you."

Rae laughed. "On the outside? Now *you're* the fool. You may as well swap your flag for House Martox's crest right now, because you are so far on the inside you can't even see the outside anymore."

Andi choked, making a face as she swallowed. "I ain't flying a Helgath flag on this ship. The Herald is a free spirit, but she sure as shit ain't Helgathian, even in pretense!"

"We'll see about that. You got the future king aboard, remember?"

Andi's frown deepened. "And I'll throw that fancy king ass of his overboard if he tries to make me." Her eyes had glazed in the amount of alcohol they'd enjoyed, and she set her half-full glass on the table between their chairs. "But enough about politics. Why didn't Damien come with you? I didn't think that boy would be further than three feet from you after getting you back."

Rae sloshed her alcohol in a circular motion while staring at it. "We've been apart a few times already, though he protested the other times. He's all wrapped up in other stuff right now."

"It might be a good thing? The learning to be apart from you? You can't always be in the same place, and it's going to get worse when Jarrod takes the throne."

Rae rolled her lips together. "Maybe it is a good thing. I kind of sprung this little trip on him last minute and he didn't even bat an eye that I'd be traveling back to him alone."

"What has him so distracted? Must be important..."

"You wouldn't believe me if I told you. Just Art-related issues involving the fate of all Pantracia. Nothing huge."

The captain lifted her eyebrows. "I'll take your word for it, then. But sounds like it might be worth his attention. The world doesn't revolve around Helgath, even though it might feel like it right now."

Nodding, Rae sipped her drink. "Oh, I know it's important. I can't fault where his attention is, I just..." She grinned, sighing and pouring herself more whisky. "Just need a drink with an old friend. Can we meet again a little sooner next time?"

Andi laughed. "Assuming I'm not shipping cargo in the Trytonia Strait?" She gave a wry smile. "But I would like that.

And I'm very glad to see you're safe and well, despite your husband's distraction."

"Husband. Still strange to hear it. You're not departing until morning, right? I might borrow a cot." Rae ran a hand over her face, but it felt numb.

Andi gestured with her head at the four-poster bed against the far wall. "I don't sleep much at night, so help yourself. I ain't putting you down with the crew. And that future king already took up the guest quarters with *his* Lanoret." She narrowed her eyes at her glass before she picked it up and sipped again. "All that time, I swore he was trying to get you back. But you knew the whole time, didn't you?"

Rae eyed the bed. "I did tell you he didn't want to be with me."

Andi snorted. "True. But I could have sworn I caught him staring at my ass more than one time, and now I guess it was all a show. I wish he'd felt comfortable enough to tell me. But... glad he is now. And the whole damn country will know it." She paused, rolling her lips. "Won't be easy without a blood heir."

Taking a deep breath, Rae closed her eyes to will the room to stop spinning, but it only made it worse. Focusing on Andi, she shook her head. "He can have a blood heir. We will help him."

"I don't think Corin's body works that way."

Rae choked on her drink, coughing. "No. No, that's not what I meant. Damien's Art has to do with souls, and he might be able to..." She waved her hand around in front of her before patting herself in the abdomen. "You know."

"Fucking Art." Andi eyed Rae's stomach. "And you'd carry it? A child? Ain't all primrose and tulips, you know."

Rae scowled. "I'm not heartless. Of course I would. Unless you want to?"

Andi's face contorted in horror. "Fuck, no. All yours."

Rae watched the Herald sail east towards the rising sun. Her head pounded as she tried to remember everything they'd discussed the night before.

Did we talk about babies?

Shaking her head, she walked into town and retrieved her horse.

As she rode out of Serityme, she passed by a box cart, but didn't look at it. It sent a shudder down her spine, flashes of Rynalds pulling her from the back of the prison cart towards the docks. She pushed away the memories, riding out the gates of the small port city.

The north road forked, and she stopped.

The sky above Jacoby hung with dark clouds, preparing for the snows of winter. To the east, it shone with the morning sun, clear and candy-colored with desert clouds. She envisioned the city she'd called home since she was twelve and considered if she could really call it that anymore.

Mirage will always be home. Sarth would accept me back.

Her gaze returned to the storm-riddled north, and she imagined snow falling on the sanctum ruins. Damien sitting, as he usually did, on the altar.

But Damien needs me, whether or not he knows it.

She nudged her horse to take her north.

Chapter 2

"IT'S STRANGE BEING OUT OF that place." Corin leaned against the banister of the Herald's main deck, the ocean breeze making his cheeks rosy. "Got used to being in those ruins after three seasons."

Jarrod rolled his shoulders, eyeing the hazy shape of Helgath's coast through the hanging fog. "Doesn't feel as long for me. Perk of not remembering most of it, I suppose." He looked down at the gold wedding band on his finger.

How can I fight for a throne when I couldn't even win a battle in my own head without help?

Neco lay curled up at the bow of the ship, fast asleep.

Corin's hand closed over top of Jarrod's, the silver partner to his wedding band on the soldier's middle finger. "Now that we're on our way back to Lazuli, I need to fill you in on everything. There's a lot that's happened since you sent your declaration to Iedrus, stating your claim to the throne. The deadline for the other Dannet families is coming soon. Martox has only gained the support of House Cortise."

Clenching his jaw, Jarrod willed his nerves to calm. "Maybe we're making a mistake."

"We're not making a mistake." Corin touched his shoulder, turning him towards him. "Fighting for the people of *our* country is not a mistake. With everything we've seen..." He touched Jarrod's jaw, running his thumb over the old scar on the proxiet's chin. "Where's this doubt coming from?"

Jarrod sighed and took Corin's hand, kissing his knuckles. "I don't know. Just think the country can do better than a mad king."

"You're not crazy. None of that was you, and it's under control now. Besides, the term *wolf king* has been great for rallying support."

The proxiet huffed. "You're still encouraging that?"

He smiled playfully. "Of course. It's been a delicate process trying to combat Iedrus's slander. Those who witnessed you saving those two kids from the gallows only needed minor encouragement. The good people of Lazuli have been passing on the word of who *you* are and the great king you will be."

Anxiety knotted in Jarrod's gut. "Saving a couple kids is different than fixing a country. And what do you mean, Iedrus's slander?"

"We both knew it would come."

"Let me guess. I'm an heirless thief who doesn't know the first thing about ruling a country."

"It's like you wrote the propaganda yourself..."

Jarrod scowled. "Well, the best slander must run close to the truth. They've done it well." He looked at Corin, finding comfort in his steady gaze. "Too bad it won't be enough."

I hope.

"No. It won't be. We'll sway Belarast and Oraphin's Houses in time. We just need to flex our power. I thought it would make sense to ask Sarth and the Ashen Hawks to go to Xaxos to confront Belarast. It's time to show the support we have from the guild. And Oraphin, as corrupt as they are, will back down at the proper show of force. Plus, I think it's time the people see you again." Corin touched Jarrod's cheek.

Jarrod nodded, letting Corin's advice sink in. "It's a good call, sending the Hawks to Xaxos. This is why you're my master of war. If Oraphin needs a show of strength, then we should rally Eralas's army and head to Rylorn. With any luck, the auer can make an appearance and sway the house. Though, this reminds me..." He patted Corin's arm where the army brand had been tattooed. "Gotta update your ink."

Corin shrugged. "I guess I do. Maybe seeing it there will make all this feel more real." He glanced towards the Helgathian coast, heaving a sigh. "I'm still reeling from the fact that you married me, especially with everything else. In hindsight, it was pretty crazy of us... Impulsive."

"You're wondering if the wolf influenced me."

Corin chewed on his lower lip. "A little. It feels so long ago now, and it's hard to pinpoint which things were the wolf instead of you sometimes." He shook his head. "I'm sorry, I shouldn't be bringing this up. There's enough to deal with."

"Aye, but you need to bring these things up." Jarrod took his husband by the shoulders. "I can't calm a storm I don't know about. Marrying you was all me, I promise. I made some big mistakes in the last year, but that wasn't one of them."

Corin's eyes softened, and he touched Jarrod's wrist. "I flipped everything upside down for you when we met in that meadow outside Quar. I'm surprised you don't hate me."

A grin spread over Jarrod's face. "I think upside down is a bit of an understatement, but I wouldn't have it any other way. I could never hate you for anything."

"Then I maintain that I'm the luckiest man in Pantracia." He leaned in, placing a kiss on Jarrod's lips. "And I will support you in whatever ways possible. You just tell me what you need, and you know I'll do it."

"As my master of war or as my husband? Because now you've got me thinking..."

Corin laughed. "Both. Which part would you like me to play right now?"

"Definitely husband."

"Most happily." Corin leaned close again, kissing him more deeply.

Boots tapped over the wooden deck, and Andi's scent wafted over the breeze. "It's a good thing I'm not a gambling woman, or I'd have lost good coin betting on your relationship with Rae."

Pulling away from Corin, the proxiet smirked at the Herald's captain. "Well, I was technically chasing Rae, so I can understand the confusion. Did you have a pleasant evening last night with her?" He breathed deeply, catching the hint of whisky. "Are you sober yet?"

Andi squinted, touching the back of her head. "Not quite. Which is why Keryn is still in command of my ship." She eyed Corin. "Sober enough to still question my sanity for allowing yet another Lanoret on my ship. Last one nearly sank it."

Jarrod let go of his husband to lean against the banister. "I thought Lanorets were permitted with a Hawk escort?" He quirked an eyebrow as Neco trotted over to join them. "And didn't the last Lanoret solve your *dog* allergy?"

The black wolf stopped next to Andi, his back as tall as her hips, and leaned against her. His tongue lolled out the side of his mouth when the ship captain begrudgingly scratched his ears.

"Fur ball is growing on me, too. Long as he doesn't hunt down the mouser in our cargo hold. Our cook is rather fond of our whiskered crew member, and I'd never hear the end of it."

Neco's voice echoed in Jarrod's head. *The cat bit me.*

Anxiety bubbled in Jarrod's gut, and he refused to answer or acknowledge Neco's complaint. Damien told him it was safe to communicate with the animal again, but it did little to ease his fear of the bond.

"Neco will behave." Jarrod looked at the wolf. "I'll keep him fed, so he doesn't think about it." He focused on the captain again. "How long until Lazuli?"

"Winds are in our favor. Should be there before sunset tomorrow. Though we will hoist sail before that to disguise the ship. Royal ass aboard or not, Helgath won't act kindly to our flag flying into harbor."

Jarrod shook his head. "That won't be necessary. You can dock at my family's port and no one will give you trouble. In fact, I can get our naval commander to provide you with a Martox flag for while you're in Helgathian waters."

Andi made a face like a foul stench had reached her nose. "Hells, no. I will do no such thing."

Frowning, Jarrod crossed his arms. "What? My family crest not good enough for your ship?"

Andi rolled her eyes. "Ain't got anything to do with your family. The Herald won't be flying Helgath colors."

"You're transporting a Helgathian proxiet. Don't you think it might be worth it to avoid potential complications?"

"I'm transporting a *friend* because he's *paying me*. Don't give a rat's ass about your title. I can still shove you overboard just as well as any other twat."

Jarrod smirked. "But he can pay you a lot *more* if you fly the flag."

Andi grimaced and narrowed her eyes. "Fuck you, Martox. Not enough."

"I don't know, I'm kind of with the captain on this one..." Corin pursed his lips. "I mean, I can't blame her for being scared of flying the colors." He leaned back next to Jarrod, subtly poking his ribs.

The proxiet nodded. "You have a point. Besides, I think my father has faster ships for getting us to Eralas and Rylorn."

Andi's back straightened, her fingers twitching on the hilt of her sword. "Ain't scared, Lanoret. I got my reasons. And there isn't a ship faster than the Herald, and *you* know that, *your royal pain-in-the-ass-ness.*"

Jarrod shrugged with a smile. "Maybe not faster, but fast enough. A royal vessel will be more intimidating in Rylorn's harbor, anyway."

She huffed, pursing her lips. "I see right through you. I know what you're doing. I ain't flying the Martox flag on *my* ship."

Jarrod nodded. "Suit yourself, Captain. It's not like you want Helgath's future king to owe you a favor. Who, by the way, could lift the bounty on privateering vessels."

"Pardon all those held as enemies during the Dul'Idur Wars?" Corin furrowed his brow. "I mean, that would clear the name of a number of particularly infamous pirates." He looked at Andi, whose cheeks flushed as she rubbed her head.

"Fuck the both of you. I'm still too drunk for this." Andi sighed, licking her lips. "Fine. Get me the fucking flag and I'll fly it under your *guarantee* that you call off the hunt for not only the Herald, but all privateering vessels that acted *rightfully* within a time of war between Ziona and Helgath. *And...* you make sure the fourth war we all know has been hovering doesn't happen."

"Ziona is the enemy of King Iedrus." Jarrod stood from the banister, taking on a serious tone. "Not my enemy. Let me hire the Herald for the coming weeks as my ship and you have a deal. There's no other captain I trust with our lives." He extended his hand. "You will be paid exceptionally well."

Andi glared at his hand before she grabbed it and squeezed hard. "Don't disappoint me, Martox."

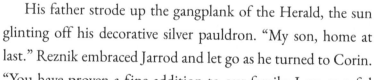

His father strode up the gangplank of the Herald, the sun glinting off his decorative silver pauldron. "My son, home at last." Reznik embraced Jarrod and let go as he turned to Corin. "You have proven a fine addition to our family. I am grateful for all your correspondence since your departure."

Corin nodded, holding out his hand to greet Reznik. "I wish I could have done more. You've certainly carried the greater burden through it all. But it's almost over, one way or another, isn't it?"

Reznik huffed, taking Corin's hand and pulling him into a hug. "I hope so. Without a civil war, ideally. Where are Damien and Rae?" Straightening, he smoothed his formal maroon coat. The joy lines at the corners of his eyes faded as he looked down at Neco.

The proxiet could see himself in his father's face, noting the suspicion in his dark eyes.

"They will join us as soon as they can." Jarrod patted Neco's head. "What's important is that I'm... better, now. Where is Mother? I'm surprised she didn't come to berate my return."

His father shook his head, tearing his gaze from the wolf. "She isn't here. Not good for her *mind*. So she's gone to live with her sister in Galestrom."

Jarrod relaxed. "For how long?" He tried not to sound hopeful, but even Corin's lips twitched.

"Indefinitely." Reznik smiled. "It's better for everyone. Come, we have some paperwork to deal with before you continue your journey. And I'll see to a flag being provided for your... new vessel. Are you sure you don't want one of our ships?"

The proxiet smirked and took Corin's hand as they started down the gangplank. "With all the chaos, there's no ship I trust more than the Herald."

"Ashen Hawks, pirates... When all this is over, son, you need to fill me in on the years of your life I missed."

Corin squeezed Jarrod's hand, giving him a small smile before looking to Reznik as they walked down the dock. "What is the state of our communications with Eralas? Did you have the opportunity to ask for their aid in making a show of strength in Rylorn?"

Reznik grunted. "We've filled them in on the situation and they're prepared for your arrival in Quel'Nian. But they made it clear the council will only discuss details with Jarrod in person." He glanced at his son. "It seems your absence was noticed by more than just our people."

"We shouldn't delay and make our way to Eralas as soon as possible." Corin eyed the sunset. "Maybe set sail again tonight if we can."

"Tomorrow." Jarrod caught his gaze. "We'll leave in the morning. The Herald's crew needs to rest and restock. Half a day won't make the difference. Best to make sure everything is in order without rushing. We also need formal attire for when we arrive in Rylorn and I'd rather not spend the night getting poked with the tailor's needle because he's tired."

"If we can even convince Lord Oraphin to see us... Any luck with house messengers being accepted into their castle?"

Reznik shook his head. "Not yet. But they might if it's Jarrod himself."

"Hope the surprise of his first public appearance in months is enough..." Corin rubbed the back of his head. "But I suppose a proper bath tonight would be a welcome way to ease back into this political game."

Jarrod chuckled. "It's no Mirage hot springs, but it'll do."

Chapter 3

HOW MANY TIMES ARE YOU going to read that same tome?

Damien growled, slamming the book in his lap closed. Placing it on the top of the precarious stack he'd brought to the warmest room of the sanctum, he eyed the failing fire. Late afternoon sunbeams strayed through the thick curtains above the cot fashioned into a lounge, but he'd ignored the comfort for the light and heat of the fire.

"It's ridiculously difficult to focus on it when you keep interrupting me." Damien picked up the iron poking rod and stoked the fire back to life with a dry log.

Sindré shimmered into view in the corner near the door. Their faint blue figure stood far taller than Damien, even more daunting with him sitting. Their indistinct robe flowed against the dirty stone floor as they stepped forward. They knelt, their head wreathed with antlers and nose upturned like a deer.

I had hoped that with the loss of human distraction, you would refocus on broadening your knowledge. Not lingering on the same.

"I still have a lot to figure out about this whole Uriel thing." Damien waved a hand at the stack of books. "About Shades, about the Mira'wyld and how she'll fit into all this. The abandoned host..." Damien glowered at the spirit. "And you aren't offering a lot of insight."

It is not my place. Sindré stood back up, crossing their arms over their flat chest. *I am only to—*

"I've heard the speech enough times." Damien ran his hand through his short hair, wincing at the growing headache. He heaved a breath. "Kin's been getting better. At least I'm getting him outside now. But it feels like separating him from his master is going too slow. The withdrawals are lasting too long."

Perhaps he is not a suitable candidate for redemption.

"I won't make that kind of call. Everyone deserves a chance."

Your naivety clouds your judgment.

"Now you sound like Yondé. I'm sure the next thing you'll say is that I should kill him."

He is an infection—

"Gods, I wish you were less predictable sometimes." Damien shoved the log with the iron poker again and the ash beneath collapsed, sending a wave of embers into the air. "I'm not giving up on Kin. It's too much of a coincidence that he provided me with information to find the Berylian Key. If I can save him, I will."

And how has rereading the same tomes over and over helped you with this?

"I'm sure I'm missing things. I haven't been able to focus, too much is swimming around in my mind." He scooted to lean against the cot and brought his knees to his chest. "It helps when I have Rae here to sort through the ideas with me. But she—"

I am here. Sindré's eyes darkened as they bowed their head towards him. *Am I not as helpful as she?*

"You're kidding, right?" Damien lifted his eyebrows. "You just tell me how everything I'm focusing on is wrong. You really think that's being helpful?"

Sindré snorted.

"I just need to talk to Rae about everything again. When she gets back—"

She is back. She arrived in the sanctum this morning.

Damien frowned. "What?" He stood and pulled the curtain aside, glaring outside. "Why didn't she come tell me she was back? It's almost twilight."

I do not pretend to understand the emotions of mortals.

Damien rolled his eyes, loosening his hold on his senses to seek Rae. To avoid interruption, he'd locked them down while studying. Before he could focus on her, however, something else caught his attention.

"Dammit." Walking to the door, he pulled it open with a frustrated sigh. He made his way down the hall towards the arena, turning into the deeper section of ruins where he'd sequestered Kin.

The Shade had unfortunately caught onto Damien's ability to read his emotions. He couldn't be sure if the summons Kin's ká sent to the Rahn'ka was subconscious or purposeful.

Kin sat on the edge of his cot, his head nestled between his hands. He'd pushed the single candle in the room as far back on his table as possible, leaving a black soot mark climbing the wall behind the flame. The Shade's face hid in shadow, made darker by the thick stubble on his chin. He radiated pain.

"Good." Kin's voice barely reached Damien. "You're here. My head feels like a dire wolf is digging into it."

Damien sighed. "We both know these headaches won't go away anytime soon. Your body is still adjusting." He closed the door and moved to the desk, investigating the essentials he'd left for the man. The plate of fruit and bread was still half eaten, just as it had been that morning. But the water pitcher was empty.

Damien glanced behind him to see the tin cup also empty on the floor beside Kin. "Only thing I can do is get you more water."

"I'm sorry." Kin's voice cracked, making Damien pause.

"For what?"

"Everything." The shade straightened, but winced and curled his back again. "But more specifically, I'm sorry for what happened with Bellamy. I can only assume it is your wife who cared for him, and it's my fault he died. I could've been a better person. I could've helped him."

Damien stiffened, watching as Kin braced his hands around the back of his neck, pulling his head down lower. Thinking of the Shade, of Bellamy, who'd been Rae's only friend while held captive by Helgath, sent a wave of regret through the Rahn'ka's chest. He drowned it with anger for Kin, who'd been the Shade tasked with hunting down the wayward Bellamy. "You're right. You could have done something, but instead you fed that poor boy to your master."

Kin's body twitched. "It was my task. I had to. If I didn't... But I'm sorry. I'm so sorry. Would you tell your wife?"

Damien sighed. "I'm not sure how much that would help, but I'll try. Ultimately, Bellamy made his own choices, and I hope the help he provided my wife granted him access to Nymaera's afterlife. Rest easy, my friend. If it hadn't been you, it would've been another."

Fetching water for Kin turned into several more tasks, along with Sindré once again requesting his presence in the library to draw his attention to different tomes of knowledge.

Before Damien could pull himself away, the sun was long gone, and he'd summoned a small orb of blue light to follow him through the sanctum as his lantern.

I can't keep doing this.

His entire body ached, his eyelids heavy while he pushed the door to his bedroom open. He knew Rae was there, even before the soft beams of his Art-crafted light touched her slumbering features.

She lay on her side in their bed, a stuffed mattress on the stone floor. She'd curled up beneath several woolen blankets, her bow within reach beside her. Her left hand rested near her head, fingers touching her wedding band, removed and resting on the bedding.

A knot tightened in his stomach, a voice in the back of his head suddenly afraid.

I've been so terrible to her lately.

Damien crossed the room and crouched beside her. Taking her hand, he picked up the ring. It felt oddly heavy, like something so much more. A trickle of his power ebbed around the metal, lingering from the previous energies he'd channeled into it. Looking at Rae, he kissed her hand and slid the ring onto her middle finger.

She hummed and shifted her feet, sighing before stilling once again.

He smiled, tucking a strand of her hair behind her ear as he leaned to kiss her temple. "I'm sorry, Dice. But I promise things will get better soon."

Chapter 4

Three weeks later...
Winter, 2611 R.T.

THE MARTOX FLAG WHIPPED AT the top of the Herald's mast, just visible through the sheer curtains framing the harbor-facing balcony of the meeting hall. The mansion, typically reserved for visiting Dannet family members, had been the only courtesy Oraphin extended to House Martox on their arrival in Rylorn.

Squinting at the northern horizon, Corin wished the Eralasian ships would arrive, round the peninsula, and end the foolishness of Oraphin's resistance.

This whole damn city makes me uneasy.

The docks of Helgath's armada loomed through the clouds of smoke, settled in the lower valley of the piers. Their skeletal masts reminded Corin how much of Iedrus's power rested in Rylorn and its most trusted Dannet family. House Oraphin had always been blindly loyal, and their influence in the city left Corin feeling like his back was exposed.

Leaning against the wood-paneled wall a few feet away, Jarrod stared at the plate of fresh-baked goods on the table. "Does poison have a smell? I don't remember sniffing any of the vials the Hawks use."

"Don't eat it. Gods know what might be in it." Corin rolled his shoulders as he turned back to the long table. "We'll sneak out later and get something in the city."

He and Jarrod were alone, but he didn't expect it to last long. Word of their arrival would spread, and Corin had discreetly paid several of the Herald's crew to deliver letters to their rebel allies within the city.

Neco whined at Jarrod's feet and the proxiet patted the wolf's head while covering the plate with the domed steel lid.

"Probably a good—" Jarrod's head twitched to the side, his pupils dilating as he and Neco stilled. His brow furrowed. "Someone new just came into the mansion."

"I positioned three of our guards at the front doors and dismissed the Oraphin ones. Probably a messenger." Corin waved his hand as he crossed to the table and leaned over the map of the bay spread across it.

If we position Eralas here...

Walking towards the hallway off the meeting room, Jarrod paused at the archway and lowered his voice. "No, not from the front doors. From somewhere else. They're *really* quiet."

Corin looked up, his shoulders tensing. "Oraphin isn't wasting any time." His palm closed over the cold metal hilt of his sword, which hadn't left his hip since entering the city.

Neco growled at the balcony, and Jarrod changed his focus to match the wolf's. "Another."

Soft footsteps sounded from the direction of the stairs at a fast pace while a hooded form dropped onto the balcony from the roof.

"Do we have any guards inside?" Jarrod backed towards Corin, Neco prowling in front of him.

"Nope." Corin withdrew his sword and the familiar weight felt comforting.

Been too long since I've swung it, anyway.

The figure on the balcony knocked on the glass with a gloved hand.

Huh?

Before either of them could move, the first intruder burst through the archway from the hall, panting. She pulled her hood down and laughed, pointing at the person on the balcony. "Beat you!"

Jarrod relaxed, Neco doing the same shortly after. "Couldn't you have knocked at the front door like normal people?" Irritation tainted the proxiet's tone as he approached the balcony door.

Studying the woman's face, Corin tried to figure out why she looked so damned familiar. It'd been dark in the tunnels beneath Veralian and, in his wretched state, he'd nearly forgotten about the twin Hawks who'd participated in saving him from the executioner's block.

Corin lowered his sword and turned to put it on the table across the map. "Damn thieves."

Jarrod opened the balcony door, and the other twin danced inside.

"I got here before you."

In a dry tone, the proxiet addressed them both. "Keema, Meeka, you remember Corin..."

"Yes, boss." They answered him in unison, hands at their backs.

One elbowed the other. "But I got *in* the room first."

"Any other Hawks going to make this meeting?" Corin looked back and forth between the identical women. The only difference between them was Keema's scar that ran across her mouth.

Or maybe that's Meeka.

Neco loped over to the balcony and curled up by the door.

"We're the only Hawks for today, but there are two... *soldiers* headed towards the mansion."

"City guards have been finicky with people wearing cloaks and hiding their faces in town. So no Hawk with a poster is allowed out of the safe house. We're just sneaky enough to make it without being caught."

"Yes, sneaky." Meeka stalked towards Corin and took his left hand, staring at the wedding band. "Off limits, then?" She smiled at him, one eyebrow rising.

Corin suppressed an amused smile. "Taken now, officially. Looks like you lost out on your opportunity, sweetheart. Sorry."

"Congratulations." She stuck out her bottom lip. "Another handsome Lanoret, taken by a thief. Do you have any cousins, perhaps?"

"Not that I still talk to. Us Lanorets seem to be the only traitors in the extended family." Corin took his hand back from her, slipping it to his belt to confirm his money purse was still in place. "Thank you, Meeka. I'm a lucky man."

The thief curtsied while the other rolled her eyes. "You're welcome, your future highness, sir. Or do we call him boss now, too?" She looked at Jarrod, who sighed.

Keema sauntered over to the map on the table, shoving Corin's sword out of the way. "He's not a Hawk. Not our boss. But I think *future highness* has a certain ring to it."

"Better get used to calling Lykan that too, then." Corin watched Jarrod as he called him by his Hawk moniker, and the proxiet raised one eyebrow.

The twins frowned at each other and then both spoke. "King Lykan."

It sent them into a flurry of laughter.

Jarrod approached and took Corin's hand from next to his coin purse. "They take some getting used to, but you can trust them."

Neco rose from his spot and trotted over to Jarrod with his head low.

"Lord Martox?"

Corin and Jarrod faced the archway.

I guess I've learned to answer to that name, too.

He squeezed Jarrod's hand, entwining their fingers, but quelled the desire to kiss his knuckles.

The greying Martox guard narrowed his eyes at the two women, back stiffening beneath his decorative armor. He opened his mouth as if to question, but then shook his head and looked at Corin. "Two soldiers have arrived and are requesting entrance. Corporal Remmy Pickford and Captain Belladora Septal."

"Corporal? Looks like Remmy got himself a promotion. Send them up, please, Auster." Corin slid the sword off the table and sheathed it.

"Remmy?" Jarrod watched Corin as the guard disappeared. "From the blockade when we were after Rae?" He patted Neco's head and the wolf huffed.

Corin nodded. "Surprised you remember him."

"How could I forget? You spilled my name that night." The proxiet's eyebrow quirked.

"Not on purpose." He smirked. "Not my fault that old windbag Ermel recognized you."

Two new figures appeared in the doorway, shrouded in heavy cloaks with hoods pushed back. Neither wore the traditional uniforms of their positions within the military, except the insignia on their left shoulder. The gold emblem hid beneath their cloaks, only partially visible from the opening in front.

The male soldier stepped forward first. His shoulders had filled out, no longer the scrawny youth from the blockade. His wiry black hair stuck out in spots where the hood of his cloak had disheveled it. "Captain!" He held out his hand to Corin, who took it.

"Good to see you, *Corporal.*" Corin squeezed Remmy's hand a little harder. "Congratulations. And thank you for your continued hard work."

Remmy straightened, his chest rising with pride. His eyes passed over Corin's shoulder, and he couldn't be sure which sight made his face harden more, Jarrod, the twins, or Neco.

The proxiet stepped forward next to Corin, Neco beside him, and offered Remmy his hand. "Thank you again for your assistance at the blockade."

"Sir. I mean, my lord." Remmy stiffened, but took the offered greeting from Jarrod. He cleared his throat, glancing at the wolf. "Gods, it wasn't an exaggeration then, the whole *wolf king* thing."

Jarrod released his hand, a smirk twitching the corner of his lips. "Not an exaggeration. This is Neco."

The big black wolf sat next to the proxiet and barked a howl.

Remmy eyed Neco before he looked back at Jarrod and pushed his fist to his chest in salute. "Ready to serve, my king."

Instead of shrugging off the formality like Corin expected, the proxiet clapped his own fist to his chest. The chains on his formal Martox coat jangled with the motion, and Corin took a moment to examine his husband. He looked the part of a king, his regal attire tailored perfectly to his muscled body. The thief he'd met outside of Quar was still there, in the little smirks and subtle twitch of his fingers towards his coat where he hid his dagger despite the tailor's protests. But acceptance warmed his amber eyes now.

Knowing.

He'll fully look and play the part of a king soon.

The female soldier stepped up beside him and batted Remmy's shoulder, a crooked smile on her wine-colored lips. A set of tight braids contained her blond hair, ending in a bun at the base of her neck. "Apologies for my companion, my lord. He's been blathering about meeting you again the entire walk from the barracks." The woman squared her broad shoulders and held out her hand to Jarrod, who took it. "Captain Belladora Septal. I understand you may have met my wife, Willow. She was at the blockade with Remmy here."

"Aye, I did. Is she not stationed in Rylorn with you?" Jarrod let go of her hand.

Belladora shook her head. "Doing the rebellion's work in Xaxos now. Fancies herself a bit of an Ashen Hawk, and I believe that to be your doing too, sir." She gave another teasing smile before her eyes passed over the twins.

Jarrod chuckled and waved the two Hawks over to join them. "May I introduce Keema and Meeka."

Neco trotted back to the balcony door at a look from his handler, curling up again on the floor but keeping his eyes open.

The twins curtsied after their approach, Meeka slinking a little closer to Remmy, whose hand slipped discreetly to the sword hilt beneath his cloak. "Young for a Corporal." She lifted her chin and reached towards Remmy's smooth face. "How old are you?"

Remmy stammered, his jaw flexing. "I... uh... twenty."

Corin felt a familiar pinch in his gut.

So young to be risking everything.

Meeka ran a finger down Remmy's neck, his arm, all the way to where his hand touched his hilt. She stepped closer and lowered her voice. "Are you going to use that?"

The young soldier swallowed, his eyes wide. "I... uh..."

"Ease up, Meeka." Corin managed not to laugh at the poor corporal's perplexed face. "She's not a threat, Remmy. At ease."

"Sir?" Remmy's body tensed even more as Meeka's face inched closer to his, though his training stopped him from retreating.

Jarrod chuckled. "*Meeka.*"

"What?" Meeka let go of Remmy and stepped backwards, keeping eye contact with the soldier. "He's cute."

Finally unable to hold it in, Corin chuckled, shaking his head. "Better check your pockets, Corporal. I hear Ashen Hawks love leaving stuff behind as much as taking it." He gestured with his head towards the table where Keema remained intent on the maps. "Can we get to work? I need to know how recruitment is going."

Remmy pulled on his cloak, the red on his cheeks starting to fade. He moved slowly, watching Meeka as she waited for him to approach the table first.

"What do you have for me, Corporal?" Corin prompted, making Remmy jump slightly.

Remmy reached into his cloak, his eyes widening as he rapidly dug his hand deeper, fervently patting his pockets

Meeka held up a scroll. "This! I'm assuming it's important."

Letting out a sigh, Remmy's shoulders relaxed. "Gods. Don't do that." He reached for the scroll, but she teasingly pulled it away.

Corin cleared his throat as Remmy scowled.

At his gesture to hand it over, Meeka rolled her eyes. "Fine." She huffed as she tossed it across the table at Corin.

"Talk, Remmy." The master of war caught the parchment, spreading it before him and Jarrod.

"It's all the names I could collect, which is hard when you've been trying to keep something secret. Whole point is to not have a record." He glanced sideways at Meeka as she skipped to stand close to him.

Her eyes danced over his face and down his body.

Poor kid, gonna have his hands full. Soldiers and Hawks apparently make excellent pairs.

Securing the map with an inkwell in the corner, Corin read over the list of names, some more familiar than others.

"Recruitment's been easy." Belladora leaned on the table, removing her worn grey cloak and draping it over an open portion of the table. "Word has spread about House Martox's challenge for the throne and it's getting hard to keep the rebellion secret from the superiors. Though, some of them have signed on, too."

"Won't have to keep it secret much longer." Jarrod eyed Belladora. "What about talk outside the rebels? What are the rest saying about my challenge?"

Belladora lifted her eyebrows. "Nothing out loud in support. The loudest of the opinions are obviously against, because the generals are still under Iedrus's thumb. Everyone's afraid to talk because arrests and executions are double what they were a month ago. Heard you made it illegal in Lazuli, but every other city ramped it up."

"The deadline is probably pushing Iedrus to eliminate all your support. To weaken your show of force." Corin looked at Jarrod, examining the focused lines of his face.

"Ain't just rebels, either. Hawks, too." Keema rocked against the table, elbowing her sister. "They're arresting anyone with hoods up in the streets nowadays, boss."

The proxiet's jaw clenched. "This has to end. And that only happens when Iedrus falls. Tell me honestly..." He looked at the two rebels. "What is the consensus within the rebellion itself? Are they supportive of my challenge for the throne?"

Belladora and Remmy exchanged a glance.

"It might have been rocky at first, sir. Some thought you were stepping in on something you hadn't started when word first spread." Belladora shrugged. "The rebellion began with Lanorets, and I suppose that's where it still lies. But you have both of them at your side, so trust is building."

"Lieutenant Damien Lanoret's position as your personal advisor, assuming that is true, will solidify support from the early rebels, and the captain... excuse me, War Master Corin Lanoret's position catches the rest." Remmy glanced towards Corin's right hand, positioned on the table. He motioned his chin. "Among another union. Since those rumors seem to be true, too."

Jarrod twisted his wedding band. "All choices not made for political reasons, yet affecting politics." He looked at Corin, something deeper in his expression. "I hope, one day, the support grows beyond those I keep by my side."

Belladora's expression turned serious. "The best way to do that is to avoid war." She rubbed her jaw. "The rebels are ready to fight for you, sir, but to be frank, would rather not kill their compatriots."

The proxiet nodded. "I understand and, while I appreciate the willingness, I'll do everything in my power to prevent a civil war."

"How?" Remmy ran a hand through his messy hair. "All due respect, but the deadline for the Dannets is approaching and if Oraphin doesn't sway, civil war will be the only way for your ascent to the throne—"

"Oraphin will sway." Jarrod straightened.

"If they'll ever see us," Corin grumbled, gesturing his head towards the silver-domed food plate they'd provided. "Or stop trying to kill you."

Jarrod waved a hand in front of him. "Attempts to kill me won't stop until Iedrus is dead, but Oraphin doesn't need to see me personally to realize the error of their loyalties. When the armies arrive, the harbor will be so full that Lord Oraphin will be lucky if he doesn't shit himself."

"Armies?" Remmy's eyes widened. "You've gained outside support?"

The proxiet chuckled. "Aye. We have Eralas on our side."

The room fell perfectly silent until a distant scuttling pierced the air, an eerie wheeze and growl almost like a breeze.

Neco's ears pricked, and Jarrod faced the balcony.

Remmy whistled.

"Quiet." Corin held up his hand, and the corporal stiffened.

Neco leapt to his feet and snarled.

"Just rats."

"It's not rats," Jarrod growled, drawing his sword and meeting Corin's gaze. "I sure hope this isn't what I think it is, but it sounds like—"

A blackened beast crawled over the railing, bright eyes locking on the proxiet. Its forked tongue lashed out of the canine maw.

Corin's breath caught as images flooded his mind of Jarrod nearly dying after the last time they fought the unnatural beasts.

"Corrupted."

Chapter 5

RAE LAUNCHED FROM THE TOP of one ruin wall to the next, making it over the gap with ease. Sweat ran down her back even with the winter air chilling her skin. She kept running, balancing along the narrow wall until she jumped, catching the edge of the next level. Pulling herself up, the stone crumbled from beneath her grip, and she yelped.

Landing on the narrow wall, she tried to regain her footing, but the slickness of the icy stone gave her no opportunity. She fell, hitting the ground beside the wall and rolling down the steep slant until she collided with another ruin wall.

Groaning, she opened her eyes and gasped.

The stonework broke, rocks thundering down towards her head.

She braced for the impact, shielding her head, but the crushing blows didn't come.

Peeking one eye open, she met Sindré's disapproving gaze.

The guardian spirit stood in their human-like shape, waving a hand at the failing wall. Motes of faint blue light tangled with the stone, making it pulse with invisible runes before they righted themselves and slid back into place. The guardian's navy skin and long flowing robes of nearly white made Sindré appear perfectly in place amid the snowy sanctum.

Rae crawled away from the wall before standing, trying to catch her breath. "Thank you."

Gods, I miss the arena in Mirage. Nothing ever tried to kill me there.

"I did not restore the wall for you, auer. But for me." Sindré's voice sounded like several speaking together. They tilted their antler-crowned head towards Rae. "Why do you insist on damaging my sanctum?"

"The wall was half-ruined, anyway, and I need to... you know, blow off steam sometimes."

"Irrelevant. This wall has been like this for two hundred years. I've grown... accustomed to the structure as it is. And your need to *blow off steam* is hardly my concern."

Rae turned away, walking down the hill towards the main area of the sanctum. "Whatever. Keep your stones, then." She brushed her hands off on her pants, shivering as her adrenaline faded.

Sindré followed. "I tolerate your presence only because you are the mate of our Rahn'ka."

"*Yippee.*" She rolled her eyes.

"Yet his incompetence and arrogance have only been growing worse. I accept that he is no longer interested in listening to me and instead... hope perhaps you can provide persuasion?"

Rae scoffed without pausing her pace. "He won't hear anything I say, either. I don't even know why I'm still here." She cringed, wiping her forehead with her forearm. "He doesn't need me." She hissed, eyeing the small streak of red left behind on her arm, which donned several scrapes of its own. "Damn it."

Damien had been painfully absent in the weeks following her visit with Andi. Always occupied with books or Kin. He'd spoken to her so little that she wondered if he even realized she was still there. It bore a hole in her heart, doubts running rampant.

Is it because we got married?

Sindré tilted their head, the dark pits of their eyes unreadable. "Are you not his mate?"

"Of course I'm his *mate*." She held up her hand, displaying her ring. "Just... Nevermind. It doesn't matter."

"It does matter if your continued frustration puts my sanctum in danger. But I also admit the Rahn'ka has been remarkably distracted. It's infuriating."

For once, Rae couldn't have agreed more with the guardian. "Infuriating. Yep, that sounds about right."

"I continue to point him in the correct direction for guidance, for learning and expanding his knowledge, but he refuses and rereads the same texts. He is limiting himself, and I believe it's becoming deliberate to spite *me*."

Reaching the bottom of the slanted walkway, Rae collected her cloak and pulled it over her shoulders. "He doesn't realize a lot of things that are happening." She frowned, pulling the material tight. She looked around at the ruins, swallowing. "Ruins. Texts. Shades. Who *am* I?"

Sindré scrunched their nose. "You are Raeynna Lanoret, Mira'wyld of the auer people, despite a muddled bloodline." They shook their head, like a deer shaking its antlers. "Chosen mate of the Rahn'ka, and thus the hope for our people, despite it all."

Rae laughed. "The hope for your people. How ironic. Sometimes I forget that I'm a Mira'wyld. I mean, I don't *forget*, but I forget what it means for me and not some grand overall picture. I wish I knew more. They had more books in Eralas, but I left before I got to read them."

"I thought you had a distaste for books..." Sindré gestured towards the north end of the ruins, where the half-reconstructed roof sloughed off snow, protecting the tomes within. "This sanctum is intended for knowledge, including wisdom about our enemy."

"You mean you have texts about the auer?" Rae stopped and looked at the guardian. "Or do you mean about the Mira'wyld, specifically?"

"Both. But I suspect those regarding the Mira'wylds before the Sundering may be of greater interest to you."

A weight lifted off Rae's chest. "You'd let me see them?" Images of Damien reading flashed through her mind and her hope disappeared. "But I can't read the language."

Sindré paused. "I will teach you."

A smile twitched Rae's lips. "Really? Why would you do that?"

"Acceptance. You may not see it, but I do. The Rahn'ka would be worse if you were not present, and as I said before... you are the hope for our people. It seems only natural to allow you to learn our language so you may teach others."

Rae narrowed her eyes. "When you say *hope for our people*, what *exactly* do you mean by that?"

"Offspring." Sindré stepped closer to Rae, towering over her. "We guardian spirits cannot provide our power to more than one Rahn'ka. Procreation is the only way for our people to begin again."

"You mean there can be more than one Rahn'ka?" Rae gaped. "Meaning my children will be Rahn'ka?"

"Yes."

"Have you told Damien this?"

"He has not asked." Sindré walked around Rae, gliding towards the library ruins, a lingering frown on their lips. "The Rahn'ka before him showed little interest in such matters, and I did not want to overwhelm their minds still comprehending the power with more responsibility. None have taken a mate before, at least not... seriously enough to question our threat of infertility."

Rae fell silent, contemplating the information before chuckling. "An auer Rahn'ka. At least part auer. You guardians will love that."

"All Rahn'ka were auer once..." Sindré turned back to her. "There is much history behind the loathing between our people. We suspect you may learn as you study the Mira'wyld. Most of the texts were written during the war."

Nodding, Rae rolled her lips together. "Teach me."

Sindré fell silent as they led Rae into the library, gesturing to a stack of books. The power of the ruins surged, knocking several away before a tome lifted into the air on a swirl of fine mist. It opened, pages flipping with a gesture of Sindré's hand. The book tumbled through the air into Rae's waiting hands, the ink on the pages glowing in a pulse of power. A dizzying haze of voices entered Rae's mind, each whispering meaning behind the symbols.

"Whoa." She looked at the symbols, the corresponding word echoing in her head in Common. "Is this similar to what Damien hears?"

Her heart twisted at the thought of him and how much she missed him, but she pushed it away.

"If you multiply it many times, perhaps." Sindré shrugged with a smile. "You are merely hearing the remnants of ká still attached to the texts by the writers."

"It's effective." She drew a finger down the page, scanning the information for mention of her genetic disposition.

"It's necessary to learn quickly here. You may also ask questions. I, as the guardian spirit of these tomes, retain the knowledge myself. But reading will give you direction."

And Damien says Sindré isn't helpful.

"I've learned so much from the auer, but I think reading these will help me reconnect with the basics of who I am." Rae skimmed a paragraph explaining the different ways the power reacted to each element. "My power used to be unrestrained, doing whatever it wanted."

"Dangerous." Sindré settled to the ground, crossing their legs beneath their robe.

Rae shook her head, sinking onto a bench seat. "Maybe, but it protected me."

"The Art is instinctual in many ways. More so after the Sundering, as it became more prevalent and easier to access. Intentionally and unintentionally." Sindré sorted through the next stack of tomes with their power, attention vaguely on Rae. "How did it manifest for you?"

"Fire." Rae paused her reading. "Usually fire. But the first time I used it intentionally, I called lightning from the sky. Right after that, it saved me by not letting me drown."

Sindré paused, the tomes within their power hovering in a frozen position for a moment. "Mira'wylds cannot breathe underwater."

Shaking her head, Rae set the book, still open, aside. "Well, humans don't, but I still breathed. At least, I held water in my lungs and didn't die. Whatever my power did, it saved me."

Sindré didn't move, but their attention turned to a different corner of the room. Wisps of power circled through the air, tangling around the spine of a book shoved to the back of a shelf. It popped out, displacing several others in the process before weaves of Sindré's energy replaced them. The tome bumped into Rae's shoulder before it plopped into her lap and a new wave of words, spoken in different voices, accosted her mind.

"Alcans?" Rae looked up at the spirit. "What does this have to do with being a Mira'wyld?"

"Nothing." Sindré flicked a finger, and the book opened to the first few pages. "But your ká is not purely auer and human. This may hold some answers for you. However, I do not know the mating rituals of our sea-dwelling brethren."

Huh?

Rae shook her head again, ignoring the book in her lap. "Are you saying I'm part alcan? That's impossible. My father is half auer and my mother is human."

Sindré shrugged. "Human lives are short and difficult to record accurately. Our direct contact with alcans is limited, but our knowledge suggests the origin of your ká to be equally auer as it is alcan."

Nerves built in Rae's chest, and she swallowed. "How... How could I not notice one of my parents is half alcan? Have you known this whole time?"

Does Damien know?

Sindré blinked. "Yes. I assumed you did as well. Alcan traits are often recessive."

Rae ran a hand over her braided hair. "Andi will lose it when she finds out I'm like her."

Sindré tilted their head, snow outside the windows of the library falling in big white clumps.

Standing, Rae set aside the book. "I'll be back in a few minutes, I need to share this with Damien." She jogged out of the room, contemplating all the things her heritage might mean as she wove through the ruins to where her husband spent most of his time.

She found him sitting on the ground outside Kin's room, an open book in his lap.

"You'll never guess what I just learned. I was in the library with Sindré and we were talking about my *muddled* bloodline and..." Rae paused, waiting for him to acknowledge her. "Damien?"

"Hm?" He glanced up, but looked right through her. His gaze returned to the book. "Sorry, Dice. What was that?"

A knot tightened in her stomach. "I was in the library with Sindré. We were talking about my bloodline and I made a crazy discovery."

"Mhmm." He ran his finger over the page he was reading. He blinked a moment later and glanced up again. "Could we talk about it later? I'm still trying to figure all this out." He gestured at the book before he started reading again.

Rae's shoulders slumped. She stood silent for a breath before turning away. Rounding the corner, she stopped with her back against the wall. Her eyes burned as she shut them.

Chapter 6

GLASS SHATTERED AS THE CORRUPTED barreled through, tongue flicking and fangs dripping with grey saliva.

Jarrod clenched his jaw, spinning the sword in his grip.

Not this again.

Neco lunged, tackling the Corrupted mid-air as more decrepit beasts scurried over the balcony railing.

Their dark shapes moved unlike any animal, sending a jolt of fear through Jarrod.

"Go for their necks! The spine." Corin's sword scraped from its sheath as clattering armor and screams sounded from the foyer of the mansion where the Martox guards watched the front door.

The twins raced forward in tandem, flanking a large beast with a spiny back as it lumbered across the broken glass from the balcony's windows.

An icy gale whipped the curtains back.

A small Corrupted, with fangs longer than its tongue, leapt onto the meeting table. Its claws dug into the wood, scattering the maps as it darted for Jarrod's side.

The proxiet sliced his blade through the air, decapitating it before turning to Neco and the Corrupted attacking the wolf.

Corin rammed his sword through the back of the first creature's neck, avoiding Neco, then kicked the body free from the wolf. "Watch Jarrod's back, boy." He dodged a charging cat-beast. It extended its claws as it flung past him, but he narrowly avoided them and caught the thing's back leg with his blade.

The creature howled, a bubbling leonine roar reverberating through the entire room.

More glass shattered as inky shapes surged forward.

"What in the hells..." Remmy had drawn his sword and flung off his cloak. He positioned himself beside Belladora, who held a pair of wicked axes that'd been secured at her belt.

Jarrod scowled. "At least this is less offensive than trying to poison me." He stalked towards another Corrupted, but Belladora stepped in front of him. He glared at her. "If you're about to tell me to take cover and let you all handle this, then you need to learn a thing or two about me."

Belladora glowered, her attention shifting to the archway where a lumbering shape crossed the threshold. The mottled fur of the bear, merged with the body of a lizard, smelled burned. Its fangs dribbled blood and saliva onto the fine tile floor of the meeting hall.

Jarrod focused on it, letting his senses take over for the first time since he'd regained control from the wolf. A haze of scents darkened within the room, and he could hear the bear-creature's chaotic heartbeat. When it charged at him, everything moved in slow motion.

A Corrupted slipped past Remmy, plowing him to the ground and lunging towards Belladora. She lifted one axe in time to catch its jaw, swinging her other at its gut, but it left her open to the encroaching bear.

Jarrod darted around her, lifting his sword to block the oncoming teeth, but landed on his back with the massive bear pinning him. Its serpentine tails lashed to the side, sweeping one of the twin's feet out from under them.

Neco howled, slamming into the front legs of the creature and unbalancing him enough to let Jarrod roll free.

The proxiet plunged his sword up into the bear's middle, but it did little to slow its movement. Its heart thundered in Jarrod's ears, the stench of decay overwhelming anything else.

Opening channels he'd sought to block, he allowed his thoughts to flow into Neco, who responded with giddy energy.

Awareness of the wolf's planned movements flooded Jarrod's mind.

Neco bit the bear's legs, dodging each swipe of talons before doing it again. With every attempt, Jarrod slashed the beast with his sword, drawing black ooze to the surface.

With a roar, the Corrupted whirled on Jarrod, knocking him sideways and sending his sword rolling across the floor. As it charged, the proxiet gasped and shirked to the side in time to avoid the gaping jaws. He locked an arm around the creature's neck, wrestling it to the floor. Its tails caught Neco as he dove in for its neck, sending the wolf across the room into the wall.

A flash of metal slammed down into the bear's skull.

"Move!" Corin lifted his blade again and Jarrod released the creature's neck, rolling away. Corin's blade whizzed through the air and slashed through its spine, severing the head in three blows. Black and red blood splattered his exposed arms, where his sleeves, like Jarrod's, had been pushed up to free his movements. The decorative pauldron was gone, torn free just as Jarrod's had been in the fighting. Sweat coated Corin's brow, and he heaved his sword up from the stone floor as if it weighed much more than it did.

"Think that'll count?" Corin huffed, a tight smile on his lips. "As wrestling a bear for the throne?"

"It'd better." Jarrod's heart jumped in his chest when a lean Corrupted soared through the air towards Corin's back. "Behind you!"

As his husband spun around, one of the twins dove and intercepted the Corrupted. She lifted a blade, but wings sprouted from its back and it dodged the parry. Blood sprayed as claws met flesh and Jarrod scrambled to his feet in time to see his ally fall with a gaping wound at her throat.

The Corrupted launched from her body, soaring to the wall where it dug its claws in and hissed at Jarrod through its beaked mouth.

"Fuck." Corin caught Keema, preventing her from crashing to the floor. Pressing his hands to her throat, he dropped his sword, and it clattered to the ground.

Belladora cried out and a whistling sound cut through the air as her axe flew. It collided with the wall and the creature with a satisfying reverberation, burying itself into the wooden paneling. The small Corrupted's head plopped to the ground while the body wriggled against the embedded axe before falling still.

With it, everything else grew quiet except for labored breathing, and boots thundering from the front foyer.

Auster slid to a stop in the archway, holding one arm stained with blood. Crimson splattered his salt and pepper beard, his eyes wide. He nearly tripped over the body of the bear, its black blood coating the floor. "My lord? We couldn't hold that one back."

Jarrod lifted a bloodied hand. "I'm fine. Get the medical supplies." The proxiet glanced at the other side of the room, where Remmy sat on the floor with his back to the wall. Blood coated the corporal's left side, but he looked stable, prompting Jarrod to kneel beside Keema instead.

Corin met his eyes, his hands covered in the mess of her blood, still trying to hold her throat together.

Meeka crashed to the floor beside them, fumbling to help Corin.

Her sister stared at the ceiling, blood oozing from her lips as she choked.

"No, no, no..." Tears raced down Meeka's cheeks in a show of emotion Jarrod had never seen from her before. "Don't die. Please don't die."

Auster raced back into the room with gauze in hand.

Jarrod met his gaze and subtly shook his head, motioning with his chin towards the bleeding Remmy. He looked down at the thief, emotion tightening his throat as she stopped struggling, her body going limp.

Corin watched Meeka, his brow furrowed before he removed his hands from Keema. "I'm sorry," he whispered.

Meeka cried out, taking the place of Corin's hands with hers, but the blood had stopped flowing. "No. I need you." She leaned forward, lowering her forehead to her sister's chest as she sobbed.

Corin wiped one hand on his pants, then used it to close Keema's staring eyes.

Placing his hand on Meeka's shoulder, all the proxiet could imagine was if Corin had been in Keema's place.

She saved him.

"May the gods bless your path to Nymaera's arms, Keema." Corin rocked back onto his feet and looked at Jarrod. He touched his arm, pursing his lips. "I need to check on Remmy. I'll be right back." He stood, his boots crunching in the shattered glass as he made his way to where Auster was wrapping Remmy's wound.

Belladora crossed the room to her axe, still stuck in the wall, and yanked it free with a grunt. She nudged the fallen Corrupted with her boot, her lips parting as if about to ask something. Her mouth closed with a glance at Meeka, still crouched over her sister's body.

Neco whined, limping towards Jarrod.

"You did good, boy." The proxiet patted the wolf, urging him to lie down and be still.

Jarrod stood, anger speeding the tempo of his heart as he looked over the gore of the room.

Their maps lay scattered, soaking up pools of black blood, the furniture splayed about.

His gaze landed on the bear's severed head, and he growled. Stomping over to it, he lifted it by the fur.

Oraphin is gonna pay for this.

"Jarrod?" Corin stood from Remmy's side.

"I'm going to pay Lord Oraphin a visit." Jarrod picked up

his sword and sheathed it, taking the bear's head with him as he exited through the archway into the hall.

Corin chased him. "Slow down." He caught Jarrod's sleeve, his hand still caked with Keema's blood. "Now? You want to go now? Like this?" He gestured up and down his body, and pursed his lips. "Are you sure?"

Jarrod spun on Corin. "Oh, I'm sure. If Oraphin thinks he can use *Corrupted* to kill me and my allies, he's got another thing coming. That thing almost *killed* you." He grabbed Corin's upper arm and lowered his voice. "And he's lucky it didn't, otherwise his head would join this bear's and his home would *burn*."

Corin's eyes hardened, and he grabbed Jarrod's wrist. "But this is *you* making this decision, right? I'm not trying to justify what Oraphin has done, but don't we need to play this smart? With everything at stake..."

Jarrod took a step back, doubt resurfacing. "You don't think this is me? Who else would it be?"

Corin heaved a sigh, his gaze dropping to Jarrod's chest where his clean hand tugged on the buttons of his coat. "I think it's you... But I worry." He chewed his bottom lip and met his eyes. "You're not going alone."

Seeking to banish the images his mind still raged with, Jarrod stepped into Corin and kissed him hard before pulling away. "I know better than to think you'd let me. But following the rules won't shake Oraphin out of his comfortable seat. I need to show him something a little bloodier, and maybe he'll think twice about the next assassination attempt."

Boots thumped on the floor behind them, but Corin didn't let go, still studying him.

"Oraphin could be unaware of this attack." Belladora latched the thong that held one of her axes to her side as she approached. "There have been orders coming from the capital that are bypassing the local constabulary. Straight to the academies. In fact, the rumor is the chief vizier is in town."

Son of a bitch Iedrus.

"All the more reason to go to Oraphin now and open his eyes to what his *king* sanctions." Jarrod watched Belladora. "Is Remmy all right?"

"Flesh wound. He'll be fine." Belladora eyed the bear's head in Jarrod's hand.

"Good. Please stay with him and Meeka."

She pursed her lips. "All due respect, sir. No. I'm coming with you. Your personal guard is down and you'll need support. And I speak for a battalion within Oraphin's own military."

Jarrod ground his teeth, unable to argue her logic. "Fine."

"Lord Martox, with all due respect, you can't just walk—"

"Do you know what this is?" Jarrod lifted the severed head.

Black ooze, mixed with blood, dripped from the bear's head

onto the polished floor, drawing the guard's horrified gaze. He shook his head rapidly back and forth. "Sir, I can't let you—"

"This is a Corrupted. Or at least, it was. One of the many involved in an assassination attempt. Either your lord is behind it or is next on the list. So you'll let me through so we may settle this. Unless you'd prefer I bring my soldiers and we force our way in?"

The guard gulped and shook his head again as he stepped out of their way.

Jarrod, with Corin and Belladora at his side, climbed the stairs to the dining hall, leaving a trail behind them on the lush carpets. When he reached the double height doors, he glared at the guards, who scrambled to open them.

The three entered the private dining area, one wall crowded with banners and the other draped with sheer-curtained windows overlooking the bay, the sky bright with the orange sunset.

Four people sat at the long dining table overflowing with more food than they could possibly eat. Their eyes lifted at the entrance and Lord Oraphin stood from his position at the end, his high-backed chair grinding over the floor.

"Lord Martox." His mouth hung open, eyes landing on the head still oozing black muck. "What is..."

Jarrod heaved the bear's head across the table, where it tumbled into the towers of food and landed in a pie at the far end.

Everyone jumped up from their seats and one of Oraphin's sons gagged loudly before covering his mouth.

"Did you send the order to have me killed or did it come from over your head?" Jarrod walked farther into the room, trying not to listen to the sound of the son's stomach lurching.

The Corrupted's head sank deeper into the pie, the mix of blood and fruit filling splattering to the table.

Corin stayed close behind him, his hand resting on the hilt of his sword, while Belladora stopped in the doorway.

The Oraphin proxiet dry heaved again, and his brother shot him a disapproving look.

"Father?" The more collected of his sons faced the silver-haired lord. He stepped to get a better look at the creature's head, curiosity in his eyes. "What is this?"

Lord Oraphin cast a wary glance at the head, then met Jarrod's eyes. "How dare you enter my home and accuse me of such treachery, boy!"

Rage ignited in Jarrod's veins and he slammed his fist onto the table, careful not to splinter the wood. "Don't insult me by pleading ignorance! You know Iedrus has been using the academies to summon Corrupted. This isn't the first time he's sent them after me, so I have a difficult time believing his *lap dog* knew nothing about it."

"How dare you..." Lord Oraphin's face reddened.

"How dare I? How dare *you*. Refusing to see me and hiding up here in your castle while Iedrus tries to kill me. I am acting according to the law set forth by our ancestors." Jarrod rounded the table on the windowed side, fists still clenched. "You disgrace your house by following that tyrant."

"You disgrace yours by being foolish enough to challenge the king. And by entering these halls in such a barbaric fashion. Your father is a great man, but he failed in teaching you the proper ways of society. Perhaps that is to be expected, though, having been raised by criminals." Lord Oraphin threw his napkin over the head of the bear as he stepped around his wife towards Jarrod. A pair of guards entered from the back hall, but froze with a gesture from their lord. "Tell me, boy. How do you intend to fight a king with not only the might of the Helgathian military but also monsters at his beck and call?"

Jarrod crossed his arms, wrinkling his nose at the scent of fear drifting through the room. "I have the means to fight him and you'll want to be on the right side when the time comes." His eyes flickered to the window, where the first of the Eralasian ships entered the bay.

Better late than never.

Lord Oraphin scoffed. "The right side. Such a noble thought. I'll settle for the winning side." He turned his back to Jarrod. "You have nothing but criminals. Rebels, pirates, and thieves. You might be able to flex what strength your father's blood gives you, but it's not enough to rule a country. To rule *this* country."

"With the support of the Dannet families, I have all I need. Last I checked, Lord, your ships all flew Iedrus's flag." Jarrod rolled his shoulders back and lifted his chin. "Or am I mistaken?"

Lord Oraphin narrowed his eyes, turning to the windows. He glared through the sheer material before he stepped forward and pulled it aside.

"Oh, that's right." Jarrod nodded. "Those are for *me.*"

A fleet of Eralasian ships rounded the peninsula of Rylorn, their translucent sails glittering like rubies in the fading sunlight. At first glance, Jarrod counted twenty ships, but more kept coming. Positioned at the banister of each ship were rows of Eralasian soldiers, their silver armor shimmering. Ship after ship appeared, spanning the entire width of the bay.

"The auer?" Lord Oraphin let out a long breath, eyeing Jarrod from the corner of his gaze. His jaw tightened with every new arrival of the Eralasian armada.

"You might want to rethink which side will be the *winning* one."

"Iedrus won't go down without a fight, you know that. Regardless of ancient traditional agreements to pass power when the right steps are observed. He won't hand you the throne without war."

"Aye. And if that's what he wants, we'll give it to him."

Chapter 7

"SON OF A BITCH IEDRUS." Damien crumpled the parchment Liala delivered.

The hawk tilted her head at him with a chitter.

He sighed, rubbing his neck. Tilting his head, he peered up at the grey sky through the bare branches of the trees above the sanctum. The cold stone of the half-collapsed wall he sat on permeated his breeches, eliciting a shiver up his spine. His mind filled with images of the Corrupted, envisioning them tearing apart his brother and Jarrod. Their blood coating the floor.

I should have been there.

"But they're alive." Damien looked at the light brown bird, and the animal ruffled her wings, cooing as he scratched her cheek.

Rae appeared in his peripheral vision at the north end of the sanctum, but she spun on her heel to go back the way she'd come without a word.

Damien furrowed his brow and looked again at Liala. "What was that about, you think?"

It's getting worse between us. She doesn't even steal from me anymore.

Liala lifted a wing and preened the feathers beneath, her ká dismissing his attempt at conversation.

Spreading the parchment on his thigh, he pressed out the wrinkles before he stood. Rae would never forgive him if he didn't fill her in immediately on the events in Rylorn or Jarrod's progress towards the throne.

And the death of a fellow Hawk.

A knot tightened in his stomach, and he swallowed. Speaking to Rae had become difficult with her apparent anger. He feared making it worse with each attempt. Her obvious avoidance of him didn't make the situation any more tenable.

Allowing his senses to mingle with the energies of the sanctum, he found Rae and identified her route. Standing, he crossed to the south edge of the ruins, closest to the monoliths which marked the entrance into the sanctum they'd called home for nearly a year. He positioned himself out of sight around the corner and waited.

Rae walked right past him, bow slung over her shoulder with her pack. Her ponytail swayed with each step, half braids and half loose hair.

"Headed to town?"

His wife jumped, spinning around with a few backward steps. "The hells, Damien."

"We need to talk."

She huffed, shaking her head. "Oh, so when you need to talk to me, it happens immediately."

He lifted the parchment.

"From Jarrod?" Rae frowned and stalked towards him, taking it and lowering it to read.

He watched her eyes dart back and forth over the letter.

Rae's brow knitted, and she lifted her hand to her mouth, turning away from him.

"I'm sorry." Damien stepped into her and placed a hand on her shoulder. Circling around her, he took the pack from her shoulder, along with her bow, and set them against a stone. "I don't know how else to say it other than I'm so sorry."

Tears brimmed in her eyes, and she shook her head. "They all could have died. And Keema..." She took a shaky breath.

Damien touched her jaw, his thumb brushing away a fallen tear. "I know."

Her fiery gaze met his, and she pushed the letter into his chest. "You *know*? You know they could have all died and you're fine sitting here babysitting a Shade?" She backed up. "Don't tell me you *know*. You know nothing."

"Whoa. That's hardly fair, Rae. I care about them as much as you do."

"Don't talk to me about fair and *don't* try to tell me you care about Keema at all, let alone as much as I do."

"That's true, I didn't know Keema, but I'm sorry for how you feel. I have a lot going on right now. And I don't want to fight with you." He tucked the letter into his pocket.

Rae rolled her eyes. "I *know*. But see, Damien, you don't have a *clue* what I have going on, because you're not even here."

"Then tell me. Tell me now. I'm here *now*." He opened his arms, backing away from her. "Let's get it all out in the air. Punch me, whatever you want, as long as you stop fucking avoiding me."

Her chin quivered, and she rolled her lips together, cringing. "Do you know how easy it is to avoid you?"

"Doesn't mean you have to do it... What did I do?"

"Nothing!" Rae threw her hands in the air. "Nothing, Damien, that's the whole point. Every time I came to you, you weren't there, so I stopped trying. I'm tired of being told we can talk about something later. I'm tired of coming second, third, fourth, to whatever it is you're doing. I'm tired of being *here* when I should be with those who actually *need* me."

Damien's chest tightened, and he winced. "That's fair. Except for the part about being needed here." He forced his body to relax, taking a calming breath as he controlled his tone. "I know it's hard to see, but I wouldn't be able to keep doing all this without you. But that's why we need to talk... I don't want you to feel like you're anything less than my first priority."

Rae laughed, but it held no mirth. "Well, I guess we don't always get what we want."

"Then let me fix it. What can I do? *Help me* fix it."

Her jaw flexed. "Is it broken because we got married?"

"What?" Damien couldn't breathe, and he froze. "Why...? No. It's because of all this Rahn'ka bullshit." He gestured behind him at the ruins.

Rae bowed her head, loose hairs falling free. She turned the silver band on her finger, shuffling her feet.

"Dice..." Damien stepped forward, holding out his hand to her. The sun shone on the silver wedding band around his middle finger. "Rae, I love you. Just as much today as any other day, if not a little more."

Her gaze lifted, landing on his hand before moving to his face. "You don't even know me anymore," she whispered, taking a step towards him. "I hardly know who I am."

He furrowed his brow. "What do you mean? You're still you, no matter what's happened. You're still Dice, still Rae.

Still the woman I married and would marry again. Just tell me how I can fix this."

Rae studied his face before slow steps brought her closer. She moved past his offered hand and touched his chest. Looking up at him, she slid her hand to his neck.

He wrapped his arms around her. She fit perfectly, as she always had, and he traced her spine at her lower back as she leaned on him. Resting his head against her hair, he inhaled the sweet scent.

"I miss you." Rae lifted her chin and kissed the side of his neck. "I need you sometimes, too, you know."

"I'm sorry." He kissed the top of her head. "I'm here, now. And I'm not going anywhere."

Her lips formed another kiss on his neck, and his breath hitched.

Warmth passed through him and he tilted his head as the kisses trailed closer to his jaw. His grip around her tightened with his body, responding to sensations it hadn't felt in far too long. Touching her jaw, he encouraged her mouth up, bringing it to meet his in a fevered kiss that made the knot in his stomach flutter.

Rae's fingers tangled in his short hair, holding him close as her tongue teased his. Breaking from the kiss, she nipped his bottom lip. "Maybe I need to find better methods of keeping your attention."

Damien groaned, smiling. "I like this method." He slipped his hand down her body and grabbed her backside, pulling her closer with a growl. "Please, elaborate, and I'll find the proper ways to apologize more thoroughly."

Lacing her arms over his shoulders, Rae bit her lip and jumped against him, wrapping her legs around his waist where he caught her. "And I do expect it to be *thorough*."

His chest rumbled, her body against his stoking the fire. He nibbled on her neck as he turned them towards the hallway to their room, his hand brushing beneath the layers of her tunic to touch her warm skin. His footsteps staggered as Rae's mouth found his earlobe, her hands already working at the buttons of his shirt.

Once inside their room, he couldn't bring his feet to move further. He turned, pushing her back against the stone wall beside the door frame, his touch playing down her side. He wove a tangle of energy into the rock behind her and felt her shiver against him as it heated.

Their mouths met as he unfastened the clasps of her tunic, the material cascading to the floor with her help. His joined hers a moment later as he shrugged it off.

Rae's hands trailed over his chest, and she met his gaze before glancing at where their bodies connected. "I miss dresses sometimes."

He smirked, rocking his hips despite the layers between them. Her grip on his shoulders tightened as he did it again before lowering his mouth to kiss her bare shoulder. "I've just missed this," he whispered, running his hand down her abdomen to unfasten her breeches. His mouth trailed to her neck.

"Me, too." Rae's voice grew breathy, and she ran her nails over his back.

Hips rocked again with the building pressure. He gripped her thigh, encouraging her legs down as she loosened her hold to let her feet touch the ground.

Damien's mouth kissed towards the button at the front center of her chemise. He traced her body before unfastening it. The material parted and his tongue followed. He responded to her sharp inhale, coupling it by taking the peak of her breast into his mouth, flicking his tongue against her nipple. Moving to her other, he slipped his hand down the front of her unfastened breeches, making her gasp.

Rae's back arched off the wall, her breath coming in quick inhales with each stroke of his fingers.

His free hand found her boots, removing them one at a time while his mouth lingered on her toned abdomen. Once she stepped free of her leather breeches, he knelt before her, his tongue tracing dangerously close between her thighs. She shivered as he lifted her leg, encouraging it over his shoulder. He met her gaze for the briefest of moments, the topaz and jade of her mismatched eyes hungry, before he brought his mouth against her.

Rae whimpered, her grip in his hair tightening as her head tilted back against the wall.

Listening to the tempo of her breath, Damien pulsed his tongue with each natural shift of her hips. Taking his time, he supported her weight as her legs quivered. When her pleasure peaked, she cried out, and he slowed his mouth with a hum.

I need more of her.

He took her thighs, lifting her as he stood, his mouth trailing kisses back up to her neck as she caught her breath.

Rae gripped hard at his back while he pushed his breeches down, bringing his mouth to hers. She moaned as he entered her, his body screaming in passion. Her hips moved with his, her heels pulling him deeper.

Everything in him roared as he thrust into her, her body tightening.

Her mouth left his, her head tilting back as she closed her eyes and whimpered.

The sight made his heart pound faster, his control slipping.

When she cried out again, an inferno ripped through him, and his cry joined hers. Burying himself in her with a final, desperate press of his hips, the world blurred.

As his senses returned, he carried her to their bed, removing his breeches entirely before crawling to join her.

She laid her head in the crook of his shoulder, draping herself half over him as he pulled a blanket up.

Running his finger in indistinct patterns on her bare hip, Damien caught her mouth for a passionate kiss before pulling back. He placed a gentler one on her forehead. "I love you."

She met his gaze and smiled. "And I love you." Kissing his chest, she sighed. "I'm happy we got married, but I want *this* again. The way we were before."

He squeezed her. "Getting married had nothing to do with this stopping. That was all me. And I was an idiot. My head is clearer now than it has been in months."

Rae bit him. "I could have tried harder to talk to you. Share things with you." She looked up at him.

He inhaled as he kissed her forehead again. "Share with me now?"

Propping herself on her elbow, she hovered her face above his, her hand on his chest. "Well. Sindré and I have gotten... kind of close, actually. I dare say we're friends."

Damien furrowed his brow, a wave of shock passing through him. "Sindré? Is that why they've been leaving me alone?"

Rae nodded. "They taught me to read Rahn'ka and showed me some books on Mira'wylds and... alcans, actually."

"Alcans?" He touched her shoulder, leaning to nibble on it. "And they're teaching you?" He laughed, pulling back. "I guess even the guardian spirits are full of surprises. What have you learned?"

"Lots. But for starters, I learned that Mira'wylds can't breathe underwater. They can drown just as any human or auer."

Damien paused, pursing his lips as he tried to remember the significance of such a statement. "But when the Helgathian ship sank..."

"I breathed. Sort of." Rae took a deep breath. "And apparently it has nothing to do with my power because I'm part alcan."

He quirked an eyebrow. "Huh." He smiled and touched her jaw. "I guess I have missed a lot." He leaned up and kissed her before settling back against his pillow. "But you're still you. Tell me more."

Rae's expression sobered, and she shook her head. "I've just been... struggling, I guess. With my role here and my role with the rebellion, a change in my heritage threw me harder than it should have. But I was thinking the other day that maybe we both aren't where we're supposed to be. If your Shade doesn't recover soon, we need another plan. And I think I have one."

An emotion different from what he expected filled him. Relief. "I agree. I should have been in Rylorn with them, and Jarrod made it clear in his letter that he wants me to join them soon. I'm open to suggestions for how to deal with Kin."

"Slumber."

His breath caught. "I'm not—"

Rae pressed a finger to his mouth. "Hear me out." She lowered her hand. "I've been through it, so I know. There's no pain and, while you're asleep, you're just that... Asleep. No terrors. He could heal through his withdrawals while sleeping, and when we wake him up later... In a few months, a year, two years, you can give him back his memories the same way you gave me mine."

He cringed. "Without all the mistakes this time, perhaps." He studied Rae's face, looking back and forth between her eyes. "You think it'd work?"

"I'm confident it will. And it would give us the time we need to be there for Jarrod and Corin. We can come back to all this bigger stuff later. It will also give us some time to figure out the rest of the puzzle required to defeat Uriel. If Kin isn't better soon, maybe bring it up and see how he feels."

Damien chewed his lip, then nodded. "You're right. I'll bring it up if things get worse again. But we're making progress, and he might not need it." He encouraged her down against him, embracing her and giving a warm kiss. "No matter what, I don't want to lose this."

Chapter 8

THE COLD WIND OF THE Lazuli beaches whipped Corin's hair back, stinging his eyes. Hooves pounded through the sand, his horse's nostrils expelling clouds with each breath. He leaned forward in the saddle as he glanced at Jarrod close behind.

He squeezed his calves, urging the horse a little faster as they neared the stone wall at the edge of the Martox property. It crumbled into the sand where the sea's tide had worn it down.

Corin tightened his hold, bracing as they jumped the low ridge of eroded rock. After the jump, he let up on the pressure, sat up, and guided his horse to slow. They turned, circling towards the ocean, bits of wet sand spraying behind him.

He grinned. "There, finally something I can beat you at."

The proxiet laughed, patting his gelding's neck. "Satisfied now?" He stopped his horse next to Corin's, amber eyes bright. "I didn't think it was that obvious when I let you win at sparring yesterday."

Corin rolled his eyes. "I can tell when you're holding back. Though I do appreciate when you stroke my ego." He brought his horse close to Jarrod's enough that they could almost touch. "Among other things." He gave a wicked smile.

A devilish smirk crossed Jarrod's features. "What? Do I not give you enough attention?"

"Politics are distracting. We both know I wish we could stay in that fancy bedroom and never leave some days." Corin stretched, lifting his arms above his head. "But today... it felt like we could both use some air."

"I agree. I get a little... restless after being inside all day." Jarrod turned his horse to continue at a walk down the beach. He glanced back as Corin followed, but his eyes glazed over.

He recognized the distant look on his husband's face.

He's been so resistant to talk about the bond.

Frowning, Corin hurried to ride beside him. "Tell me."

Jarrod refocused, rolling his shoulders with a smile. "Just Neco. He wanted to know if we were doing anything exciting."

"Big fur ball can have you later," Corin teased. "But everything feels normal with the connection? Nothing's changed?"

Quieting, Jarrod took a deep breath. "Is it that *you* think it's changing, or that you don't think I'd tell you if it was?" He eyed Corin. "You had these doubts in Rylorn, too."

Corin pursed his lips. "I'm just worried. Can't that be what it is? The excitement in Rylorn seemed the perfect opportunity for the wolf to establish some hold again. But you seem like you."

The proxiet nodded with a long exhale. "It is me. It's all me, temper included."

"So Lord Martox, future king of Helgath, threw a decapitated head across a Dannet lord's table. Though... the look on his son's face was worth it."

Jarrod laughed. "Aye. I threw a head on a table, but it got the point across, didn't it?" He paused, a muscle in his jaw flexing. "I have my own reservations about the bond. I'm reluctant to keep testing it. But even during the fight with the Corrupted, when I let Neco's consciousness fully interact with mine, I never lost control. I don't blame you for worrying, but I swear, husband, I will tell you at the first sign something isn't right."

"I still like hearing you say that." Corin took in a slow breath, his body tingling with the term. "Husband."

Jarrod met his gaze. "As you'll always be. Which, correct me if I'm wrong, but that also makes you the future king of Helgath. Maybe not the *ruling* one, but..."

Corin groaned. "Ruin the perfect moment, why don't you." He rolled his eyes, but smiled. "I'm proud to stand at your side and support you in all the ways I can, *my* king."

Stopping his horse next to a fallen log, Jarrod dismounted and looped the reins around a protruding branch. "It goes both ways, my love." He offered Corin his hand and gestured with his chin. "Come with me."

Corin dismounted without letting go of Jarrod's hand, tossing his reins around the same branch. Stepping beside him, their palms pressed pleasantly together, fingers entwined.

I love just holding his hand.

A strength lingered, even in the subtle embrace, and Corin's stomach fluttered in excitement. "Have a destination in mind? Or a walk?"

Jarrod motioned with his free hand to a boulder where the beach met the dense forest. Carved on the rock's surface was a small arrow, pointing into the trees. "We should investigate, don't you think?"

Corin grinned. "You're telling me you don't already know? When you grew up here?" He lifted one eyebrow.

Jarrod shrugged, a playful smile on his face. "If you aren't curious, we can always turn back..."

Corin sped his pace, tugging on Jarrod's arm. "Oh, I'm curious." He walked backward for a step before turning towards the stone. "Show me."

The arrow from the first boulder led them to a second, which sent them to find the third. After the sixth, they all looked the same.

"Lost yet?" Jarrod squeezed Corin's hand, leading him under yet another half-fallen pine.

"I was lost three arrows ago." He nudged Jarrod's shoulder with his own. "You could be leading me in circles and I wouldn't know it. Not that I mind."

Chuckling, Jarrod turned Corin around and they stepped into a small clearing.

On the far side, an overgrown wooden structure encompassed a tree trunk, equipped with a frayed rope ladder. A circle of rocks sat in the center of the area, perhaps once part of an old fire pit. Next to it, a tattered rug grew wild with moss and dried pine needles. A round, worn target adorned another tree, three rusted throwing blades still protruding from its surface.

Corin held tight to Jarrod, dragging him along as he inspected the structure and throwing board. He smiled, lifting Jarrod's hand to his lips, kissing the back of it. "Your hideaway?" He met the proxiet's eyes, then gestured to the throwing board. "Always had horrible aim, I see."

Grinning, Jarrod pulled him closer. "Ruthless. I was twelve. Maybe younger. I don't remember the last time I came here." He pulled the necklace from within Corin's shirt, touching the damaged signet ring adorning it. They had passed the whistle charm for Liala to Damien. "All this moving forward, sometimes I want to look back and remember how I got here."

Corin closed his hand around Jarrod's, tilting his chin to kiss his husband's cheek. "The past is what's made us who we are. I can understand that." He wrapped his arm around Jarrod's waist, holding him close. "Hells, I still see that teenager who fell off his horse in Degura when I look at you sometimes. And I'm still madly in love with him."

Jarrod kissed him, warmth swelling in Corin's chest. "The feeling is mutual. I've never been so grateful for falling off a horse."

Corin closed the distance again, savoring the taste of his lips. "Now I know where to come looking when you vanish from the castle for hours at a time."

The proxiet narrowed his eyes. "The only time I vanish for hours at a time is when I'm with you. But this place should stay confidential, no one else has ever been here."

"I fail to see why I would ever want anyone else to know, then. Besides... I can keep a secret. And I like being able to have you to myself." He ran his finger along the edge of Jarrod's collar. "Going to take advantage of it as often as I can, since I'm not sure how long the opportunities will last."

The proxiet's chest rumbled, and it sent a quiver through Corin's muscles. "Forever, that's how long."

"You know what I mean. With all this Iedrus shit going on. The politics. The war. It's quiet now, but once we get Belarast's support, it's all going to start rolling downhill." The soldier shook his head, damning himself for bringing up the topic he'd hoped to avoid.

But we have to talk about it. Iedrus's response could change everything, and the assassination attempts will grow more desperate.

Corin averted his gaze, looking at the exposed, umber skin of Jarrod's neck. "I'm sorry. I shouldn't have brought it up. Now isn't the time."

Leaning down, his husband caught his gaze. "My answer still doesn't change. There will always be time for us. Time for you. Even after we get Belarast's response, we will delay sending word to Iedrus. Lord Oraphin is right. Iedrus won't go down without a fight, and we need to put it off as long as possible. Give Damien and Rae time to join us. Eralas time to prepare the rest of their army."

Corin's jaw tightened. "War." He breathed. "I guess it really is coming. And you're ready for all this, aren't you?"

Jarrod nodded. "Only because I have you."

Corin shook his head with a weak smile. "You could have done it without me, but I'll admit I probably helped a little." He gave the proxiet a tender kiss on his clean-shaven jaw.

Smirking, Jarrod sighed. "You're delusional. Without your influence, I'd still just be a..." He looked up. "...Hawk."

Corin followed Jarrod's gaze towards the sky, barely visible through the dense pine trees.

The cry of the hawk signaled the creature's arrival before the massive red raptor soared into view.

How did he...

"You heard his wings, didn't you?"

"Maybe." Giving Corin a quick kiss, Jarrod released him and backed up, bringing two fingers to his mouth for a sharp blast.

The hawk descended, landing on Jarrod's outstretched arm. It screeched, hopping onto a nearby log after he retrieved the note from the iron cuff on the bird's ankle.

Red flapped his wings, a gust of air rushing over Corin's face. While expected, the messenger hawk's arrival was the final brick in the path towards civil war.

"Sarth just likes being flashy with that big ass hawk, doesn't she?" Corin gave the creature a wide berth, since Red had snapped at him on their last encounter.

Unrolling the parchment, Jarrod chuckled. "When you're the leader, you can be as flashy as you want." He started reading, eyes darting back and forth over the paper. "Remmy, Meeka and Belladora arrived safely in Mirage. And..." He pulled a second page of paper from behind the letter. "We have the support contract from Belarast."

Instead of relief, the bubble of anxiety doubled in Corin's gut. "So now we wait as long as we can to send word to Iedrus that they're to pass over the throne according to Helgathian law."

Jarrod nodded, still staring at the letter from Sarth. "You think Meeka and Remmy are getting along?"

Thinking back to the way Meeka had initially flirted with Remmy, then insisted on staying near his side as much as possible after his injury left plenty to the imagination. Of course, she'd been distraught over her twin's death, and caring for an injured rebel could have just been a distraction.

"Remmy looked like he wasn't sure if Meeka wanted to bite him or kiss him when we left them in Rylorn. Though, I think he liked the attention. Grunt in the military like him wouldn't get it much." Corin's experience as a lower-ranking soldier had been fraught with solitude before he worked his way into his promotions.

Jarrod nodded, his eyes distant. He ran a hand over where a scar marred his throat, letting out a breath.

Corin winced. "You're thinking about Keema now, aren't you?"

The proxiet's shoulders drooped. "I almost died the same way on your parents' ranch. She didn't need to die. If Damien had been with us..."

Touching his husband's jaw, Corin shook his head. "She saved my life, and I wish I could've done the same for her. I would have given anything to have my brother's Rahn'ka powers at that moment. Heal her like he healed you."

Damien's messages, delivered through Liala, had remained vague and uncommitted. Excuse after excuse why he couldn't leave the sanctum and the Shade he was trying to redeem.

I can't believe he's choosing a Shade over Jarrod in all this.

Corin couldn't help the anger rising in his chest. "We can't rely on my brother right now. The attempts made by Iedrus to kill you will only grow more frequent. We're not safe here. Martox castle is like a giant target for their assassins."

"Aye, and while I'm here, I'm putting my father and your parents at risk. But I can't go to Mirage and put all the Hawks in danger." Jarrod lowered the letter, pulling Corin closer. "Besides, I disappeared already for months. Now isn't the time to do it again. The people need to know I'm here to support them."

Corin grimaced. "I know." He looked at the treetops, rubbing the back of his head. "But we can't stay here. They'll send more Corrupted. Kill more of our people. Our family."

We can't hide, but somewhere Iedrus can't get to us.

A spiderweb caught in a breeze, a sunbeam shimmering across its surface like the sails of Eralasian ships in the Rylorn harbor.

"Eralas." Corin blurted, meeting Jarrod's gaze. "Make a public declaration that you're going to Eralas. Not hiding, but going to build power with your ally. It's political and safe."

Jarrod fell silent, his jaw working as he thought. "You must realize my first inclination is to say no." He took a breath and nodded. "But you're right. I don't want lives in jeopardy and going to Eralas is a good political move. But only temporarily."

"And here I was, worried about your safety most." Corin smiled, touching the scar on Jarrod's chin. "I don't like it either, but it makes the most sense. The auer chose to be part of this conflict, so they can shelter us for a little while."

Chapter 9

RAE PULLED BACK ON THE azure bowstring, aiming at marks in the ruin wall while balancing on a narrow ledge. She let the Art-laden arrow fly, drawing back for another without needing a quiver. In the span of a breath, four arrows hit their marks, and she grinned.

The extra silver rings on her hand hummed with the power of the Rahn'ka runes carved inside their bands. They glowed with a faint blue, matching the bow Damien had recreated for her as an apology. It looked the same as the one he'd assembled in a rush during the fight at his family ranch. But the permanent tattoo on her forearm, matching his, allowed her access with a mere thought.

The ink darkened to navy as she released her hold on the bow's power, letting it flow back into the rings.

This is ridiculously badass.

Hopping down from her perch, Rae eyed the hallway before turning down it.

Damien had been encouraging Kin out of his room even more often, increasing her need for vigilance. The Shade didn't know about her involvement in his care, and they wanted it to stay that way.

Entering the courtyard, she glanced at the footprints in the snow leading out.

Damien took him out of the sanctum today.

Hope blossomed.

Kin must be almost ready to be on his own.

She resisted the urge to follow the men and spy on their activities, heading back to her bedroom. Removing her cloak, the winter breeze made her shiver as she pulled on a long-sleeved tunic over her short-sleeved one. Replacing her cloak, she picked up her gloves.

Mid-step, a torrent of power struck her, heating her veins like they flowed with molten lava. Her skin blazed, and she gasped, dropping the gloves as she staggered forward. Clutching her chest, she braced a hand on a table, breathing in the aura's energy she'd only felt once before.

Nymaera's breath. The woman from Eralas.

Her mind raced as the power faded, less abruptly than when she'd experienced it in the gardens near the Sanctum of

Law. She hadn't told Damien about it, taking her vow of secrecy to the auer's arch judgment seriously.

But now isn't the time to keep that promise. He'd have felt it, too.

Rae picked up her gloves and hurried out of her room towards the courtyard, skidding to a stop when she heard footsteps approaching from outside. Jumping to the side, she hid with her back to a wall as Damien and Kin returned.

When she heard no voices, she peeked around, stomach knotting at the sight of her husband practically carrying the Shade.

Rae lingered in her spot until they passed and then followed behind. Once Kin was in his room and Damien had closed the door, she threw her hands up. "What happened?"

Damien sighed, rubbing his forehead. "Gods if I understand it exactly. You felt that wave of power, right? I mean, it was sure as hells hard to miss." His jaw flexed, his eyes focused somewhere behind her in the familiar look he gave when his mind filled with the voices his power granted him access to.

"I felt it. But why did it affect Kin?"

Damien glanced at the closed door. "It must have opened up some wounds, in a sense. Maybe because the power is something Kin is familiar with, and Uriel's infection is intelligent enough to recognize the Berylian Key, too."

"Wait. Are you telling me that was the Berylian Key's power? Did you talk to her? To Amarie?"

Damien's brow furrowed. "Yes, that was her, but she was still a mile away. Gods, I knew the Berylian Key had to be powerful, but *that*..."

"I know. I've felt it before."

"You what?" Damien gaped.

Rae struggled to process all the conclusions her mind threw at her. "The last time I was in Eralas. She was there. I saw her. We were all sworn to secrecy about it, but I didn't know it was the Key."

Damien collapsed back against the wall with a groan. He rubbed his temples. "Damn it. Kin was getting so close, but his ká is as bad as it was months ago now. And the Berylian Key is right there, running around with her power exposed. She's going to gain attention."

"If she gets picked up by the academies, or worse, Uriel, all our planning is going to go up in smoke." Rae ran a hand over her braids. "Gods, why is she being so reckless?"

"Kin kept saying that something was wrong, so this is unusual behavior for her. We can't let her keep running towards Helgath the way she is... It's suicide."

"I can go after her." Rae stepped closer to Damien, taking his hand. "She saw me, too, in Eralas. I might be able to use that to make her trust me."

Damien shook his head. "No, that's too dangerous. Besides, Jarrod and Corin..." He rubbed his temple harder, wincing. "Fuck, with Kin like this again, there is no option but Slumber now."

"Then you take him to Eralas." Rae touched Damien's face. "If I can convince Amarie to go, too, I will meet you there. She'll be safe from Helgath and Shades, plus we'll know where she is when it comes time to use the dagger."

Damien pulled the obsidian weapon from his belt, glowering at it. "This would be so much easier if I didn't have a conscience, and we just killed her now. But I can't go with you to bring her back. You're right, it'll have to wait."

Rae nodded, rolling her lips together. "If Amarie is safe in Eralas, there'll be no rush."

"Couldn't this have all happened after Jarrod is crowned king?"

Chuckling, she shrugged. "That would have been much more convenient."

Damien slipped the dagger back into his belt. "None of this will ever be convenient." He pulled her against him, leaning in to give her a gentle kiss. "While I don't like it, we can't risk Uriel finding her before we do. But maybe you should use a different name. Too many in Helgath know Raeynna Lanoret."

Rae smirked, still not used to hearing the name out loud. "I'll go by Mira. And don't worry, I'll be careful. If I create a bit of a snowstorm, it should ensure she doesn't leave Jacoby tonight."

He nodded and kissed her again. "I'll meet you in Eralas. As soon as we both can get there."

"I'll send you updates with Din."

Damien ran his hand over Rae's hair and kissed her hard a final time.

Amarie's power stood out like a lighthouse on a misty ridge, emanating from the tavern Rae first visited the night she met Damien. She'd returned many times since arriving back in Jacoby.

The place still looks the same as it did back when I knew him as Bastian.

Rae walked inside, pulling her hood down. She nodded at Thella, the barmaid, and worked her way through the crowds to find Amarie.

The Berylian Key's dark red hair, pulled back into a thick ponytail, helped separate her from the rest of the patrons in the packed tavern.

Hanging back to observe, Rae watched a regular try to spark a conversation with the tumultuous woman, ignorant of the power she radiated.

"You're a popular one tonight with the looks you're getting."

"Leave me alone." Amarie shrugged off his attempt, glancing behind her. Her gaze narrowed on a blacksmith Rae had purchased arrowheads from. A single father. The Berylian Key's power heated the room, dancing in Rae's veins as it readied to take on the harmless man who looked like he'd seen better days.

She's paranoid and angry.

Rae maneuvered between customers, stepping in front of Amarie just as the woman stood. Touching her elbow, she blocked her view of the blacksmith. "He's not what you think."

"Excuse me?" Amarie met her gaze and her blue eyes, tinted with beryl tones of purple and pink, widened. She backed up, bumping into her stool. "You."

Rae touched the shoulder of the man next to Amarie and leaned towards his ear. "Could I borrow your seat?" When he smiled and nodded, vacating the stool, she sat down facing the bar. "You remember me."

Amarie looked at the blacksmith again as his daughter clung to his leg, his mother embracing him. She looked down and rubbed her neck. "How did you know...?"

Rae gave her a sideways look. "That you thought he was your enemy? Your energy was boiling. I'm sure every practitioner within a block knew it. But he's a local with just enough power to make him noticeable to people like us."

Thella placed a mug of ale in front of Rae and she sipped, motioning for another for Amarie.

"You know who I am." Amarie tilted her head. Her eyes looked sunken, her youthful face worn with exhaustion. Nothing like the strength she'd emitted in Eralas.

Rae nodded. "I was there when you shared your power with the council. The council swore all witnesses to secrecy, but there's no rule against talking to you." She motioned with her chin to Amarie's meal. "You should eat. The food is good here. I'm Mira."

"Amarie." She stabbed a potato with her fork. "This can't be a coincidence. What do you want from me?"

"I recognized you the moment you came into town. Your timing couldn't be better." Rae sighed, mentally organizing the story she'd come up with. "I was hoping you'd help me."

Amarie shook her head. "Not interested. Just because you're auer doesn't mean I have to help you. And helping strangers hasn't gotten me far in the past."

"Is that why you're flaunting your power, now? To dissuade anyone from approaching you?"

If I can just learn why she's being so careless...

Rae cleared her throat. "You might want to reconsider being so blatant this close to Helgath..."

"I'm not afraid of Helgath."

Ease off.

Rae let Amarie eat in peace, occasionally chatting with

patrons she recognized and exchanging pleasantries.

"Do you know everyone here?" Amarie sounded annoyed.

"Yep." Rae smirked. "Is that a problem?"

"No. Why would it be?"

"How about you tell me?"

Amarie rolled her eyes and rose from her seat, pushing her empty plate away. Without another word, she headed for the door.

Rae exhaled slowly, focusing on the snow falling outside to encourage more before following the Key outside.

"Persistent, aren't you?" Amarie didn't even turn around.

"Yep. Is that a problem, too?" Rae jogged to walk next to Amarie, but when the woman didn't stop, she remembered her story. Any mention of a Shade would get Amarie's attention, considering her relationship with Kin. "Please, I really need your help."

"Why?"

"There's someone who keeps showing up, and he's got this strange power. Every time I get close to him, he just vanishes into shadows. I don't think I'm—"

Amarie stopped and faced Rae. "What did you say about shadows?"

Bullseye.

Rae's boots slid in the snow, and she almost bumped into Amarie. "I know it sounds ridiculous. Like the old myths. But it's true, I swear."

"Does he have a tattoo?"

Kin did, so let's go with that.

Rae pointed to her forearm, her own tattoo covered by her long sleeves. "Here. How did you—"

"Why would a Shade be following you?"

"I don't know. Maybe because I have the Art? I don't know what to do, where to go—"

Come on...

"Eralas. Go back to Eralas, they can't follow there."

"How am I supposed to get to Eralas alone?" Rae narrowed her eyes, not sure if Amarie was listening anymore. "And even if I did, he could follow me and attack, and then what would I do? I wouldn't be able to—"

"I'll take you." Amarie refocused on her.

Jackpot.

"Can you leave first thing tomorrow?"

Rae nodded. "Of course. Thank you."

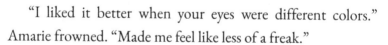

"I liked it better when your eyes were different colors." Amarie frowned. "Made me feel like less of a freak."

"If you put your power away, too, then we can both be normal." Rae patted her horse's neck as the animal drank from the Belden River, which they'd reached in two days of leisurely riding. "The less attention we attract, the better."

"I have it contained... partly." Amarie kicked a pebble into the water, staring at the river's flow.

Rae studied the woman's distant gaze, glancing at the current.

What is she seeing right now that I'm not?

"Are you all right?"

Amarie stiffened. "I'm fine." Her voice barely carried over the roar of water.

A wide stone bridge spanned the river, high above them, providing shelter from the freezing rain. It pattered against the road above, the constant, dull rhythm of the downpour striking the bridge almost relaxing.

Rae had stopped at this river before, though not the same crossing. Rynalds had chosen a location further south, where Rae had left her crystal necklace for Damien to find. The cool surface buzzed with a hint of the power contained within. A token from her childhood cave. A gift from Damien.

I miss him.

She touched the pendant still around her neck, taking a deep breath.

Amarie met her gaze. "Where did you get that?"

Rae let go of it, smiling. "It's from a cave outside Eshlea Chasm. My father used to take me there as a child."

"Do you still see him?" Her tone softened, her gaze haunted.

"No." Rae shrugged. "I don't know where he is."

If I did, I could ask him about my mother.

Amarie nodded, glancing at the water again. The gentle ebb of the Key's power subsided, leaving a void in its wake that made it easier for Rae to breathe.

"Better?" Amarie walked to her horse, stroking the black beast's nose.

"Yes. Will you keep it locked down?" When the woman didn't answer, Rae sighed, rolling her shoulders. "I tried to give your horse a carrot this morning, it didn't go over well."

Come on, woman, open up a little.

Amarie smiled and, for the first time, it reached her eyes. "He's picky with people he doesn't now."

"What's his name?"

"Viento."

Rae approached the Friesian, admiring the shiny waves of his mane. "I don't think I've ever seen a prettier horse." She narrowed her eyes at the horse's bridle, a silver plate engraved with a depiction of the araleinya flower. "Exceptional tack, too. Did you get that made in Eralas?" The rare Art-laden bud bloomed once a millennium, native only to the auer homeland.

As quickly as Amarie's smile had appeared, it vanished. "It was made in Eralas, yes. It was a gift."

Tread carefully.

"From someone still in Eralas?"

"I don't know. Going to find out, I guess."

"Why the flower?" Rae cringed, biting her tongue as she

waited through a prolonged silence.

She's going to ditch me here for asking too many questions.

Amarie let out a long exhale. "He nicknamed me after the flower."

Rae's heart ached, reaching into her pocket where she kept one die. She'd left the partner in Damien's pocket after she'd stolen his pocket knife before leaving the sanctum.

How long have she and Kin been apart?

"I'm sorry, I shouldn't have asked."

The Berylian Key turned around, meeting her gaze. "It's fine. Not everyone has a happy ending."

Rae swallowed. "Maybe the end hasn't come yet."

Amarie scoffed and shook her head. "Talon and I won't be together again."

Talon? Who's Talon?

Rae paused, hiding her confusion with a frown and nod. "I understand that kind of finality. I loosed arrows at a lover once. Thought for sure he'd come to kill me."

The Key raised an eyebrow. "And? Had he?"

Chuckling, Rae shook her head. "No. I couldn't have been more wrong."

"I don't think I'm wrong on this."

"Do you want to be?"

Amarie bit her bottom lip. "There was someone else before Talon. His name is Kin. Do you think it's possible to love more than one person?"

Rae sat on a boulder and shrugged. "I don't see why not. Nothing says the heart can only have enough love for one. I don't think love is so finite. Even if you don't think you'll be together."

Amarie ran a hand over her hair and tightened her ponytail. "I doubt I'll see either of them again."

"But do you want to?"

Cringing, the Key looked away. "I wish I could see everyone I love again."

Rae hesitated, glancing at the crystal necklace resting against her sternum. She thumbed it again, thinking of Jarrod and Corin, too. Her new family. "Maybe—"

Hooves clattered on the bridge above and they both stiffened, listening through the patter of the rain. The horses slowed, a murmur of voices garbled by the rush of the river.

Rae gestured with her head to Amarie and they both withdrew from the bank to press against the stone of the bridge's barrel, taking the horses with them.

"This was the last place I felt it." A man's voice carried stronger than the others, and Rae imagined him leaning over the edge of the bridge.

Reapers.

Unlatching her bow, Rae silently drew an arrow from her quiver. The Art-crafted bow still waited within the rings on her left hand, but she dared not use it unless she had no other option.

"Get your ass down there, then. Go check."

"It's too fucking cold in this rain. You go, but they're probably long gone."

"I ain't going down there if they're gone already."

Rae rolled her eyes, looking back as Amarie mounted Viento. "We can wait them out," she whispered. "No need to rush it, and we should avoid the fight."

"Why? Fight sounds real good right now."

"They're probably Reapers, looking for you and your loose aura."

Amarie frowned. "Why would Reapers be in Olsa?"

"They venture out of Helgath sometimes. I've encountered them in this region before. Always looking for more Art practitioners to kidnap for the academies. Let's wait them out, I'd rather not fight Reapers in the rain again."

Amarie shrugged, and Viento pawed at the ground. "As you wish."

Chapter 10

One month later...

THE BANYAN TREES ON THE Eralasian coast near Maelei grew in a tight weave of cross-hatched roots, shaped by the auer. Two guards stood at either side of the doorway Kin had already passed through.

The escort from the council followed the Shade, disappearing into the dim light of the sacred Slumber chambers. The council had accepted Damien's request, much to his surprise, with little question.

Neither of the guards, their decorative armor shimmering in the sunlight, seemed interested in Damien as he stepped from the white sand beach onto the moss-coated stairs leading beneath the forest.

Rae walked down these steps before they took her memories.

He touched the wall, the buzz of the tree's ká a rumble of ancient tones in his mind. The chambers predated all the human kingdoms by thousands of years, and the sheer presence left the Rahn'ka dizzy.

Kin vanished down a tunnel ahead, a lime-colored glow emanating from motes resting within dimples of the sod walls.

Damien glanced back at the rolling clouds before he descended deeper into the never-ending hallways. Jogging to catch up, he passed another set of decorative guards, their faces ghostly in the green light.

One gave a subtle gesture down the right hall.

Locking down what remained of his senses to the plethora of voices in the Slumber chambers, Damien entered one of the circular rooms. The auer escort's hair, once white, glowed sea-green as she gestured to the stone table at the center of the room. It looked like a crypt, carvings decorating the surface and sides.

Kin stood beside the stone bed and turned to Damien. "This doesn't look foreboding at all." Bags darkened his eyes. The stubble on his chin seemed thicker in the dim light, his face worn like a man twenty years older.

Damien's lips twitched in a supportive smile. Looking at the Slumber platform, he could only imagine Rae laying there. A knot in his stomach tightened, leaving him nauseous.

"The process is painless." Another auer stepped from the shadows, her long robes whispering along the moss floor.

Kin looked at the newcomer and his escort. "Could we have a moment?"

The auer nodded together and exited.

Damien watched them before crossing to the stone table, eyeing the little neck rest at the end. As he ran his hand over it, Kin tensed in the edge of his vision.

"Are you sure this will help?"

"Yes." Damien turned to him. "You've suffered enough and deserve some rest in what you're fighting. When you wake in a year, all symptoms of withdrawal should be gone."

Kin nodded, rounding to the other side of the stone. He met Damien's eyes. "And the dagger? I hope you still understand why I asked for it."

Damien gritted his teeth.

Damn my conscience.

He reached to his belt, withdrawing the obsidian dagger he'd crafted. The silver runes along the blade glimmered as he passed it across the table. "I understand. Even if I still think it'd be better if you trusted me with it."

Kin gave him a crooked smirk. "Sorry. Not with this. Not with Amarie. I need to be there if this is going to happen."

Damien sighed as Kin slid the dagger into his belt. "At least I know it'll be safe down here with you. And I'll wake you as soon as I can."

Kin shook his head. "As long as Amarie is safe, keep me down here as long as you want. I have nothing left except her."

The man looked back to the stone table, his pale blue eyes resigned.

"So you trust me with her life, but not her death..." Damien quirked an eyebrow, then huffed. "Ready?"

"You're sure you can return my memories?"

Damien glanced towards the door, ensuring the auer weren't within earshot as he nodded. "Done it before," he whispered.

"Thank you." Kin extended his hand over the platform, a spiderweb of scars hiding his old tattoo on the inside of his forearm. The brand all Uriel's Shades shared, and the symbol of their rank and power.

Damien took his hand. "Don't thank me yet. Thank me when this is all over."

Kin smiled. "I will."

Damien went to the door to summon the auer back in as Kin hoisted himself onto the stone.

The auer in long robes crossed to him, her eyes black. She lowered Kin's head down onto the headrest and touched his temples as he closed his eyes. "Please, clear your mind. It will make the process quicker." She lifted a palm towards the ceiling as the roots and vines above wriggled. They twisted together, spinning downward in a point towards Kin's head, a bubble of green motes gathering at the tip.

The auer escort encouraged Damien towards the door, but he waved a hand at them and turned to watch.

Like ants crawling down a branch, the motes of power ebbed from the ceiling into the gathering orb of energy at the end of the dangling roots.

Kin's chest rose in a deep breath, his legs twitching and tense.

The auer standing near his head waited as the orb grew and, once it was the size of her fist, she removed her hand from beneath it.

The power dropped, colliding with Kin's forehead before spreading in a thin sheen of green energy down his entire body. He relaxed and, for the first time in months, the lines of pain on his face faded.

Above his head, thin wisps of power emerged from the roots on the ceiling, a slow drip feeding the aura covering the Shade.

"We should leave." The auer escort put a hand on Damien's arm. "The process of moving him to a more permanent resting chamber is delicate, and we should not remain to interrupt."

Damien watched Kin for another moment as his chest rose in a steady, sleep-filled breath, then turned with the escort to depart the Slumber chambers. The uneasy energy of the tunnels encouraged his quickened steps.

As he ascended the stairs, a silhouetted figure appeared at the top.

"Maith." Damien sighed, extending his hand to the tall, lean auer, meeting his amethyst eyes. "Good to see a friendly face."

Maithalik accepted his hand and squeezed before letting go. "I heard of your arrival and thought I would come meet you. I have news." Turning, he motioned for the Rahn'ka to follow.

"It's time I get back into the swing of things with politics." Damien fell in step beside the dark-skinned auer, bidding his escort farewell with a nod.

They returned it, and walked to the staircase wrapped around a tree trunk, leading to the bridged walkways of Maelei.

Damien smiled at Maith. "Have you been busy with your work here? Your Common is much better."

"Lots of paperwork. Meetings. Discussions and compromises. You know. Has a way of speeding the learning of a language. Jarrod and Corin are looking forward to including you once more. It was good to see you have tamed the wolf."

"How's Jarrod managing this whole thing from here? It'd drive me crazy."

"I said *tamed*, not subdued. He's not... enjoying it." Maith smirked. "Lots of recreational running from what I understand."

"Exercise always helped me, so I can't blame the man." Damien rubbed the back of his head. "As long as the barrier is holding strong, everything should be fine. I'll double check it when we get a chance. But I'm still leery about using my power anywhere near a city. Where have they been staying?"

"I have a carriage waiting to take us to them in Quel'Nian. Are you ready to go now?"

Am I?

Damien paused, but all his mind could focus on was the promises he'd made Kin, and where Rae might be. She was still on the mainland, trying to escort Amarie to safety. She'd sent Din to confirm they were headed towards Eralas and Amarie had agreed to hide her power again, but there was no telling who she might have already gotten the attention of.

I need to focus on what I can control.

"Politics." The word tasted sour as Damien said it, and he contemplated as he looked at Maith.

"Do I sense regret for your role?"

"Regret isn't the right word. I don't regret it. I'm just... tired." Damien stopped, looking at the stone path they followed towards the main road to Quel'Nian. The Eralasian forest surrounded them, rife with birdsong. "I know what is happening in Helgath is important, but it... feels so small compared to other things. Yet giant and overbearing at the same time."

Maith nodded. "You have many areas of focus. And when focus is spread too thin, nothing wins. How is your relationship with Raeynna?"

"Good." Damien spoke too quickly and frowned. He reached into his pocket, his thumb tracing the edge of the die she'd left behind after absconding with his pocket knife. Her habit of stealing from him resurfacing helped him believe what he said. "I think. It was rough, but then good. I haven't seen her in a month. And I already fucked up there, letting the Rahn'ka thing be more important than her. I won't do that again..."

"Perhaps when she arrives, you'll have a chance to focus on your relationship, even if it's only for a day without distractions." Maith approached a carriage equipped with two white horses and a driver. "As much as I have always hoped for happiness in your marriage, your relationship is also vital to the success of Jarrod's council."

Damien chuckled. "I suppose in-fighting between his personal and political strategist might have negative effects."

Maith laughed. "Mhmm. Though lucky for you, the auer have chosen an amicable chief vizier. The *news* I mentioned."

"Finally made up their minds, huh?" Damien walked towards the carriage, the driver pulling the door open for them to enter. "Who is it? Anyone I know?"

Maith climbed in first, taking a seat on the bench as Damien took the one across. The door shut, and the auer smiled. "Me."

Corin embraced Damien before he got two steps into the doorway of the luxurious homestead the council granted them for their stay. Large banyans and a single massive beech tree comprised the mansion, a sprawling single-story compound surrounded by decadent gardens.

They're probably showing off.

Damien patted his brother hard on the back, urging him to let go so he could suck in a deeper breath. "Missed you too."

Corin stepped back, slugging Damien in the shoulder. "About damn time."

Damien shoved him and met Jarrod's amber eyes with a sheepish smile. "Sorry it took me so long."

The proxiet smiled and pulled Damien into a hug, clapping him on the back before letting go. "Just glad to see you're safe. Now if we could only get that wife of yours to join us. Did all go well with your Shade friend?"

Claws scratched across the floor behind Jarrod as Neco bounded from another room, hurtling towards the Rahn'ka as Maith entered the home.

The auer sidestepped out of the way as the wolf tackled Damien backward.

All the air left Damien's chest as he hit the ground under the black blur, Neco's tongue lapping at his face. "Gods, Neco. It hasn't been *that* long." He shoved at the wolf's chest, protecting his face with an arm. Laughing, he felt lighter than he had in months.

The wolf whined, and Jarrod helped Damien to his feet.

Damien wiped Neco's saliva off his chin. "Kin is in Slumber, so we'll see how that progresses. But what Rae is dealing with is far more volatile. All I'm getting are stories of tavern brawls and reckless behavior. Not sure what happened to Amarie, since she hasn't told Rae much, but..."

"If anyone can guide her here, it's Rae." Jarrod scratched behind Neco's ears as the wolf sat beside him. "Tavern brawls in Helgath, huh? Maybe Rae is having fun."

"Oh, she's having the time of her life after how bored she was at the sanctum." Damien shook his head. "Makes me wonder why she was crazy enough to marry me, sometimes. But grateful." He straightened his shirt, tucking it in where Neco had displaced it. "We can talk about it later, though. You need to fill me in on what's going on at home."

Chapter 11

JARROD LOOKED FROM DAMIEN TO Corin before nodding at the far doorway that led to the banquet room they'd been using for their meetings. "Come. It'll be easier to show you everything." He motioned to one of the Martox guards stationed inside. "Would you let Vinoria know Damien has arrived?"

The woman nodded and disappeared down the hallway towards the east wing.

Pushing open the tall double doors, Jarrod led the way to the square table in the center of the room. Just like the rest of the auer structure, they had grown the large dining table out of the roots of the trees. They'd woven together and flattened into the surface, which held a giant map of Helgath, dotted with wooden figures representing different armies.

The far wall boasted gaudy Martox banners Jarrod had requested taken down, but their auer hosts had ignored him. Narrower tables along the left wall offered an abundance of food and pitchers of water and wine. To the right, political documents and ledgers of coin, troops, Hawks and rebels sat stacked on desks.

Neco loped to the far corner of the room, where a pile of cushions served as his bed, and curled up on them.

Damien whistled. "I've missed a lot." He approached the table, eyeing the figures on the map before picking up and studying the more intricate wolf that Corin had carved. "No sign Iedrus is going to be reasonable in all this?"

"He sent Corrupted after us in Rylorn. I think the time for *reasonable* has passed." Jarrod cringed at the memory of Keema's death. Images of Corin trying to hold her throat together as she bled out. He growled, pushing the thoughts away. "He has no inclination to hand over the throne peacefully, and I've received word from Sarth that the Hawks have observed mass amounts of the military gathering in Veralian."

Damien sighed, replacing the figure. "So that's where the last stand is going to be. Veralian."

"Looks like it." Corin pointed to the table. "Iedrus received the contracts of support weeks ago, and since then he's expedited gathering his forces. The rebels are grouping together, too, and some are joining the Hawks temporarily. Sarth has been invaluable with coordination."

Damien snorted. "Glad to be wrong about that one, then."

Vinoria entered the room, pulling her black hair, highlighted with grey strands, into a ponytail as she entered. "Apologies for the delay, did I miss anything?"

"Just catching Damien up." Jarrod nodded at his trade minister.

Vinoria met Damien's gaze with a frown. She'd been vocal about her disapproval of his absence. "Good."

"Walk me through it, Corin." Damien gestured with his chin to the map.

Corin nodded, approaching. He began pointing and explaining the attack strategies they'd agreed on before Damien's arrival.

Vinoria crossed to Jarrod, tucking loose strands of her hair behind her ears. She eyed Maith, who stood at the end of the table, hands behind his back. "What's Maithalik doing here?"

Jarrod chuckled, lowering his voice to match hers. "He's our appointed chief vizier."

Her frown deepened, accentuating the age lines on her face, and she shook her head. "I still don't like having an auer as part of your council. It should be a Helgathian. But... at least it's a familiar one." She stepped towards one of the side tables, lifting a goblet and filling it with wine. She sipped it as she joined Corin.

Damien chewed his lip, leaning from the table. "It's a solid plan, but Veralian is a fortress. And the civilians inside the city will become collateral in the battle if it comes to a full siege."

Corin frowned. "I know. That's the part we don't like. Whole point of taking the throne is to protect the people, not put them in more danger."

"Trying to come up with a solution." Jarrod rounded the table. "We can get troops inside through the tunnels, but it would be too slow without a place inside to gather."

"Troops aren't going to help if we can't get inside the castle itself. Iedrus is the root of it all, and he could hole up inside for months."

"The tunnels are under the castle, too, but they're narrow. And the castle will be full of soldiers and civilians."

"They'd hear an army coming."

"Need someone with an even temper and good aim then, so as not to take out the innocents inside. A troop is too unpredictable. Jumpy in those kinds of situations."

"Rae could do it, but what about when she runs out of arrows? Too many people."

Damien bit his lip, glancing at Vinoria before he muttered, "She won't run out anymore."

Jarrod focused on the Rahn'ka. "Say that again?"

Damien smiled slightly. "I crafted her a new bow. She won't run out. Regardless, she wouldn't be able to do it alone. This would require a small force. If it didn't sound crazy, I'd say we do it ourselves."

The room quieted and Maith sipped a glass of wine as he returned to the table. "Are we talking about assassinating King Iedrus within his own castle?"

Jarrod met the auer's gaze, swallowing. "Sure sounds like it to me." He stared at the map and the sketch representing the castle on the tallest hill of Helgath's capital. "It could work."

"Cut off the head of the snake. Killing him won't be necessary if we can make him back down. Seeing Jarrod right in front of him might encourage him to accept the defeat we already handed him on paper."

"Are you insinuating that Lord Martox should be a part of the group sent inside the castle?" Vinoria glared at Damien and pointed at the proxiet. "If he dies, this will all be for nothing."

Damien pursed his lips. "He won't die. I'll be with him."

Jarrod frowned. "If thousands of civilians die while obtaining the throne and we accept that, this is all for nothing already. The point is to change Helgath, not just take it over. If we're sneaking into Iedrus's castle, you're damn right I'm going."

"Arguably, you're more qualified for it than the rest of us." Corin smirked. "Being an Ashen Hawk and all."

"I still fail to see how putting Lord Martox at risk is worth it in this case. Loss of civilians is horrible, yes, but better than losing our proxiet."

"You'll lose neither." Jarrod smiled at Corin. "And my husband is right. I'm the Hawk in the room. If I have Corin, Damien and Rae with me, we won't fail."

Vinoria crossed her arms. "Well, I suppose if our proxiet is putting himself in danger, he may as well bring his council to be in jeopardy with him."

Jarrod laughed, but he found no humor in her words. "Maithalik and you will stay behind and keep up correspondence with the others while I'm unavailable."

"You're sure the tunnels will get us directly into the castle?" Damien straightened, looking at Jarrod.

The proxiet nodded. "I haven't taken them there myself, but Sarth sent a crew inside once or twice. We can debrief with them before going in."

"You mean the Hawks could have assassinated Iedrus a long time ago?" Corin's tone took on an air of teasing. "Though I admit I'm thrilled to participate... as an honorary Hawk by marriage." He paused, chewing his lip. "Gods, I never would have imagined saying that just two years ago."

Jarrod rolled his eyes. "In any other circumstances, Iedrus's death would have only meant the ascension of his son to the throne. Which wouldn't have changed anything." He smirked, rotating his wedding band. "And don't worry, *you* don't need to be an honorary Hawk to get access to the hot springs."

"Hot springs?" Vinoria raised an eyebrow.

"Nevermind." Jarrod shook his head. "There's a chance none of this will come to pass. Once Eralas's army has arrived outside of Veralian with our rebel Helgathian forces, Iedrus may concede."

"That'd be awful noble of him." Damien rolled his eyes. "But it's good to have a plan."

"Even if we don't all like it," Vinoria grumbled, downing the rest of her wine.

"It's a direction. We can re-evaluate as the deadline grows closer for Iedrus to pass over the throne. But overall, morale among those loyal to Martox remains high, even if Jarrod isn't actively present. Iedrus could see reason and give up when he realizes it's pointless." Corin slid the wolf figure to stand on top of Veralian's castle. "I'm just glad you're finally back with us, little brother."

Damien nodded. "Now we wait for Rae."

Chapter 12

Spring, 2612 R.T.

RAE LOOKED OVER HER SHOULDER, scanning the crowds in the Lazuli streets for anyone who might recognize her. They'd entered one of the narrower alleys, lined with shops. The scent of the tanner hung thick on the air, already warming in the first week of spring. Even secluded from the greatest crowds of the busy trade city, Rae felt too exposed and her stomach roiled.

Being here is beyond risky.

She walked next to Amarie, who had fortunately kept her power hidden since the close call with the Reapers. The woman had told her she wasn't adept in her Art, but her hiding aura was admirable.

I can't even sense it.

"You need to teach me how to do that." Rae gestured up and down Amarie. "It's impressive."

The auburn-haired woman smiled and shrugged. "Sure. It's not as difficult as you'd think." Her smile faded. "You seem uneasy being here, you haven't seen our shadow, have you?"

Rae ignored the glimmer of excitement in Amarie's eyes. "No. I just... have history here and I'm not keen to relive it."

Amarie nodded, expression sobering. "Is this where those posters are? The ones with your face on them?"

"It's likely." Rae wished she could tell Amarie the truth. Lying to her had been easier before they'd become friends. "But maybe it's been long enough that they've given up."

"Never known Helgath to give up."

Studying Amarie as they walked, Rae could see nothing but pain lining her features. None of it had faded in the month they'd been together.

She's still holding on to something if she's not allowing herself to heal.

Rae rolled her lips. "What if Talon is waiting for you in Eralas? For you to come back."

Amarie's gaze hardened as she stared ahead. "I doubt it. Talon left me. It wasn't an accident. If he wanted to find me, he could. At this point, it's easier if he doesn't."

It's Kin she still loves the most, even though he left her, too.

"Maybe you'll see Jett again?" Rae smiled, her tension easing when Amarie returned it. "Rebels have a way of making you forget your troubles."

"Gods, I hope not. I think I'll stay far away from Quar for a while."

The steamy finish after the brawl hadn't healed Amarie like Rae had hoped. The Key's behavior had continued to be reckless, despite hiding her power.

Rae stopped walking, motioning to the shop next to her. "You want to replace your gloves, right?"

That's the whole reason I even agreed to set foot in this city.

They'd been ruined during an incident with their campfire several nights prior.

Amarie nodded and put a hand on Rae's shoulder. "You don't have to worry about me, though I appreciate the thought. I have plans. And having you with me has helped, really."

The Mira'wyld nodded, watching her friend disappear inside the shop.

Why does Amarie having a plan sound ominous?

A middle-aged woman exited with a package in her arms. She turned towards the street, eyes passing over the Mira'wyld before widening. "Rae!"

Shit.

Rae looked at the shop door again, but Amarie was safely out of earshot inside. "Viola." She met Damien's mother's gaze. "I heard you and Gage relocated to Lazuli. How are you?"

Viola's greying blond hair bobbed around her shoulders as she used her free arm to pull Rae into a firm embrace. "Relieved to see you. And we both know you should call me Ma now." She grinned, brushing a strand of Rae's hair from her face.

Rae's chest tightened, unexpected heat sprouting behind her eyes. She hadn't seen Viola since marrying her son. "That will take some time to get used to."

Gods, why am I so emotional lately?

Viola pursed her lips. "Why are you in Lazuli? Jarrod and Corin left weeks ago. I assumed Damien and you would go directly to Eralas."

Rae nodded. "I'm on my way there to meet them. I'm escorting the woman who just entered the tanner's shop. But she doesn't know who I am, and she can't. I'm sorry to involve you in this, but you can't tell anyone you've seen me."

Viola narrowed her eyes, nodding slowly. "All right, sweetie, but how are you doing in all this?" She touched her arm, giving it a subtle squeeze. "You look tired."

What everyone loves to hear, even if it's true.

"It's been a long journey so far, and now we can't even take a ship from here. When did the docks close?"

"Just a few days ago. Lord Martox has been battling the local peace officers to reopen them, but the order came from Iedrus. Until Jarrod takes the throne, he's technically still within his right to make those orders."

Rae sighed, fidgeting with her shirt. "Can I ask you a personal question?"

"Of course." Viola's focus never wavered, somehow making Rae feel more comfortable in her presence.

Glancing at the door again, Rae lowered her voice. "What, um. What was it like, being pregnant? Like, how did you know?" She was too young to remember her mother's pregnancies and, even though Sarth was like a mother, the Ashen Hawks' leader never bore children.

The woman's grip tightened on Rae's arm, a smile springing to her lips, but she quickly controlled it. She brought in a deep breath, the wrinkles at the corners of her eyes more defined. "There are a few signs, and I suspect the obvious ones you're already familiar with since you're asking how it *felt*. There are subtle symptoms you can use to confirm, though. Sweetie..." She squeezed again. "Do you think you might be?"

Rae shook her head, nerves fluttering in her gut. "I don't know. I just... feel emotional all the time and..." She made a face. "Bloated and a little nauseous. And my breasts..." Clearing her throat, she huffed a breath. "Wow, I really shouldn't be sharing all this."

"I'm *your* mother now, too." Viola touched her hair, smoothing her hand over Rae's braid. "You can share anything with me."

"This is terrible timing." She ran her hands over her face. "Please don't say anything to anyone. I'm not even sure I am."

"Babies rarely have convenient timing. I became pregnant with Damien when things seemed desperately difficult with three other children to care for, along with a struggling homestead. Yet, he became the blessing all children are." Viola squeezed Rae's hand. "And I admit, rather selfishly, I'd love to be a grandmother."

Rae laughed, touching her abdomen. "I can't imagine—"

Amarie exited the tanner's shop, donning new gloves.

Viola released Rae's arm, taking her package in both hands again. "I won't keep you. But it was wonderful seeing you and hearing you're well. Please take care of yourself."

Rae smiled, nodding. "And you as well."

Amarie approached, but hung back until Viola took her leave. "Who was that?"

"Someone I haven't seen in a long time." Rae swallowed, her insides churning again.

"Trouble?"

Refocusing, Rae rolled her shoulders. "No. I did learn that the docks are closed over some political conflict, but hopefully we won't have any issues in Hoult. You still want to go there, right?"

Amarie sighed. "Yes. It's the closest port to Eralas, so it shouldn't be difficult to find a boat to cross the strait, even if the dock is closed." She put a hand on Rae's shoulder. "I'm sorry. I know you wanted to avoid running into anyone you know. Let's get going before it happens again?"

Rae nodded. "Sounds good to me."

Chapter 13

DAMIEN,

Maith is Jarrod's chief vizier? I didn't see that coming. Did you know the Key can kill any Art practitioner with a touch? I haven't seen her do it, but I believe her. Iedrus closed the docks in Lazuli - Also, I ran into your mother, did I mention I like her? I thought someone followed us when we left, but I haven't seen them since... We're getting closer to Hoult. A couple weeks now, at most, but Amarie isn't in a rush. She's been letting her hiding aura down at night. She's planning something, but I don't know what, and it's making me nervous. We've grown closer, but she's still erratic and won't tell me why she was in

Olsa. Don't send Din back to me. Every time Amarie sees him, she gets more on edge. I'll meet you in Ny'Thalus.
I love you,
Dice

Damien scratched Din's head, ruffling his grey feathers, and the hawk cooed from his position on the garden's fence. He disliked not sending the hawk back.

But we can't risk losing Amarie after all this work.

He tucked the note into his pocket, brushing against the six-sided die, and held out his arm to Din.

The hawk hopped on, talons digging into his navy tattoo.

"Ny'Thalus then. I wonder if the auer have a fancy house like this one there, too." Damien gave the creature another scratch and Din tilted his head. "Stay close, buddy. Maybe we'll use you for a message to Sarth if I can't send you back to Rae."

Weeks later...

The crash of distant waves did little to lull Damien's anxiety as he looked across the strait between Eralas and Helgath. The jagged shape of his homeland's coast was perfectly visible, the occasional coastal haze absent in the early morning sunshine.

The region was rife with hills, emerald in the spring. They broke into craggy grey cliffs towards the sea until gently curving to the beaches around Hoult.

Leaning on the thin balcony banister, he tried to sense if Rae was near Hoult's town square, oddly still for a morning in the fishing village. No smoke rose from the chimneys, and the small dock hosted a galleon instead of the usual fishing dinghies.

Something feels wrong.

Someone rapped on the open door behind him, and he'd been so focused on Hoult he hadn't heard them coming. Turning, he met Jarrod's amber eyes.

The proxiet quirked an eyebrow. "What's the saying about watching a pot of water boil?"

Damien snorted. "I'm just anxious. She wouldn't be over there still if it wasn't for me."

"Didn't you say it was her idea to go after Amarie?" Jarrod leaned on the banister, eyes trained on Hoult. "I can hear what everyone is saying nearby, but my sight isn't any better than it used to be. What's that ship doing at a fishing village?"

Damien turned back to the distant coast and shook his head. "I was wondering the same thing..."

Jarrod reached into the satchel slung over his shoulder and produced a telescopic spyglass, offering it to the Rahn'ka. "Snagged one of these from a merchant. Thought you might enjoy having a better view."

Taking the spyglass, Damien smirked. "Now I can pretend to be a pirate and a thief."

Laughing, Jarrod clutched his chest. "You wound me. I paid for that." He motioned inside. "They brought breakfast if you're hungry."

Extending the brass spyglass, Damien shook his head. "Maybe later." Lifting it, he turned back to the coast.

At the center of Hoult was an open square, remarkably empty. Surrounding it, the doorways of the local businesses were closed and quiet, their shutters drawn.

Where is everyone?

He surveyed the town while munching on the biscuit Jarrod had brought him despite his refusal.

Nothing changed. Everything stayed quiet, including the ship at the dock.

A flurry of motion passed through the square at the moment he'd lowered the glass to take up another biscuit.

"Shit." He struggled to reposition the glass to watch two riders enter the square from the south, stopping. The one riding the black horse dismounted, and they had an exchange before the other rider departed with both horses.

Rae?

"What's happening?" Jarrod nudged him, ruining the perfect position he'd gained to watch. "I see movement."

Damien batted at Jarrod. "Well, now I can't see, but two riders came into town. I think it's them. But... something's definitely wrong." He blinked, trying to see without the spyglass, but everything was too far away.

Lifting it back into place, he struggled to find the woman he suspected to be Amarie. Her dark auburn hair was pulled back into a ponytail, but he couldn't make out the features of her face.

Several of the doorways beside her swung open, armed figures emerging and approaching her. After a moment, she lowered her sword, and they all turned towards the dock.

Who are they? And where did Rae go?

"Some people are taking Amarie towards the ship, but Rae went off somewhere with the horses. I lost sight of her." Damien scoured the edge of the town but saw no sign of his wife before trying to find Amarie again. His breath caught. "Shit. They're dead. The people escorting Amarie." The details were impossible to decipher, but limp bodies with black pools beneath them lay strewn across the dock. His stomach dropped. "Fuck."

Amarie backed up from a man, her sword ready.

Details beyond his chestnut hair and tall frame blurred together.

Damien thrust the spyglass into Jarrod's chest as he rushed towards the door.

I have to get over there.

"Talk to me." Jarrod raced after him. "What's going on? Who killed them?"

"It's Uriel."

Jarrod grabbed Damien's arm before he reached the door and spun him around. "Like the all-powerful master of Shades? What do you think you're going to do?"

"Rae is in danger if she's anywhere near that creature. And Amarie is just standing there like she's going to face him." Damien twisted free of Jarrod's grip, glaring at him. "You can't stop me from going."

"Fuck. I'm going with you, then."

Damien growled, but there wasn't time to argue. They rushed together out the door of the accommodations the auer provided, and into the stone hallway leading towards the docks of Ny'Thalus.

Auer yelled as he and Jarrod shoved past them in the narrow walkways, boots pounding down the stairways to the long slanted road that passed through the middle of the city. They turned the corner as a wave of power struck Damien in the chest, leaving him breathless.

The auer around him gasped, their eyes all turning towards the coast of Helgath.

A flash of beryl pink, with bolts of indigo, erupted within a thick cloud of black hovering over Hoult. A breath later, a rumbling boom shook the coast. The birds in the giant beech tree sheltering Ny'Thalus like a giant umbrella squawked their displeasure as Damien hurried for the docks. His feet slowed, his mouth agape as the cloud of fury and color expanded. The ship at the dock listed sideways before capsizing, a rip current of the ocean tearing it apart as it drifted away from the roiling energy.

"Nymaera's breath." Jarrod stopped beside him, eyes wide.

A roar, something primordial and monstrous, split the air, echoed by murmurs of panic as auer hurried inland.

The bubble of power engulfing Hoult vanished, leaving behind a looming bank of blackness as the water rushed inward. The ocean submerged what remained of the town and filled the crater Amarie's power left behind.

Jarrod lifted the spyglass. "Amarie is down, she looks... wait. Rae is there. Rae has her. Fuck, Dame, look." He thrust the telescope into Damien's hand.

Damien forced his eyes away from the hovering shadow of Uriel's power, left hollow with the departure of the Berylian Key's overwhelming energy. "Where?" He lifted the glass, and Jarrod redirected it to let Damien focus on Rae and Amarie once more on their horses.

The women raced, the ground beneath their horses turning to ash in a pulsing wave.

"Dame..." Jarrod pushed the spyglass to the side and Damien's vision blurred.

He lowered the device and stepped back.

Lumbering over the mouth of the Hoult crater, a gigantic black beast opened its squat canine maw in a roar. Its head rose through the hovering shadows, onyx scales shimmering in the sunlight on its serpentine neck. Snapping at the air with its rows of teeth, Uriel tore at the grey stone the ground had hardened to, rising on four legs. His shadow tendrils roped together, forming the bulk of the creature and the whipping tail which brushed away the remaining clouds of darkness. With each step, more vines of shadow emerged, arching across the Helgathian coast.

"They're riding for the strait." Jarrod took a step, auer bumping into him as they fled.

Damien swallowed, heart echoing in his ears as he watched the monster chase the two tiny shapes of Rae and Amarie as their horses galloped towards the sea. His nails bit into his palm as he balled his fists and ran down the docks formed of Ny'Thalus's roots. He allowed his power to build within his muscles, feeding on his tension.

Rae hit the waves first, but didn't sink into the water, racing above the surface directly towards him with Amarie right behind. Ridges of pale blue ice ruptured across the waves, freezing in a flurry of snow beneath their horses' hooves.

Rae's power.

The shadow beast plowed ahead, his roar vibrating Eralas's docks.

Uriel's tendrils wriggled as they struck the sea, maintaining their position as if the creature ran on solid land.

Please ride faster.

"Dame..." Jarrod's tone lowered. "What do we do when it gets here?"

"You hide. I fight. This is the purpose of the Rahn'ka."

"Hide?" Jarrod frowned. "You can't be serious. You can't face that thing alone. The Berylian Key didn't even hurt it!"

"What in the *hells* is that?" Corin panted, leaning forward to catch his breath as he came to a stop beside Jarrod. "And why are we standing here?"

"Uriel. And your dumbass brother thinks he's going to fight it alone." Jarrod looked back at the beast charging over the water. "Rae better ride faster."

Damien gritted his teeth. "Come on, Dice."

The beast snapped, tail lashing as he gained on the women.

Directly behind Amarie, a shimmer of green flickered in the air like the surface of a soap bubble.

The sheen flashed as Uriel collided with it.

The black mass of his body flattened against the invisible barrier, a thunderous boom reverberating through the air and shaking the Eralasian coast. The birds in the trees and cliffs erupted from their roosts, and the screams of the auer within the city doubled.

"Get off the docks!" Jarrod grabbed Damien's arm and yanked.

The three of them ran to shore, turning around in time to see Rae's horse's hooves hit the wooden dock. The horses galloped, not slowing even when they met land.

The sky darkened, waves of ink erupting from Uriel's body as he slammed into the ward erected around the island. A green line, hovering ten feet above the ocean, pulsed with vibrant light, hardening against his attacks as he howled in rage.

Damien sprinted after Rae, watching Amarie slump and fall to the ground off the back of her racing horse.

"I'll get her." Jarrod hurried towards the fallen Berylian Key, Corin close behind him.

Uriel gnawed at the barrier, crying out again as he slammed into it. His shadows spread thicker, climbing up the curve of the shield, blacking out the sky.

Rae slowed her horse, leaping from its back before it came to a stop. She met Damien's eyes and ran towards him as he opened his arms. She crashed into him, wrapping her arms around his shoulders and burying her face in his neck.

Tightening his hold, Damien kissed her hair before squeezing her shaking body. Wetness touched his collarbone as she sobbed, and he stroked her hair. "I've got you. It's all right, Dice. I've got you."

Rae clutched his clothing, her breath quivering. "Don't let go." She flinched when Uriel pounded again on the barrier.

The cries of the surrounding people quieted, though the energy of panic remained as darkness engulfed the whole city. A child cried somewhere in the distance and the motes of light sprung to life in their usual evening routine. But this black encompassed everything, and even the wildlife fell silent.

Damien supported Rae's weight as he wrapped his arm around her waist and rested his head against the top of hers. He brushed his hand through her hair while he watched Jarrod lift Amarie from the ground and Corin wave over the help of one of the Martox guards who must have followed them out of their accommodations.

The Berylian Key was out cold, her skin ghostly pale in the artificial light of a lantern held by the guard. Her leg was twisted at an awkward angle, along with one of her arms. All her visible skin appeared covered in scraps and thin abrasions.

Her horse whinnied, pulling on his reins to back away from the Martox guard trying to control him. He bucked, snapping his head backward, and reared.

Rae drew back from Damien but didn't let go of him. "Viento. Her horse doesn't like strangers."

Damien kissed her hair and nodded.

We don't need extra attention right now.

He focused the power he'd readied, directing the invisible threads of his ká towards the distraught creature. Targeting his voice within Damien's mind wasn't as difficult as it once was, already familiar with the timbre of horses. And Viento was being loud about his displeasure and concern for his rider.

With a subtle manipulation, Damien touched Viento's ká with his, running it up the stallion's nose like a gentle stroke. Without truly speaking, he uttered reassurances and promises to the horse.

Viento's eyes widened, but his pounding hooves slowed as the guard seized his reins again. He huffed, pawing at the road, but let the guard guide him.

Damien left the bond between them in place, disguising it with a rapid barrier so a nearby auer might not notice.

Good boy.

Rae pulled away just enough to gaze at Amarie. "Is she alive?"

Damien nodded, able to sense Amarie's ká firmly in place. "Hurt, but alive. I don't think she would be without that trick you pulled with the ice, though."

Rae slumped into him, wiping tears from her face. "I've never been so tired." Turning her face into his neck again, she took a deep breath. "Gods, this feels good."

He smiled against her, calm washing through him. "You scared the shit out of me."

Rae whimpered into his neck.

Closing his eyes, he allowed himself a moment before opening them again to the chaos still evolving around them. "We need to take care of Amarie. We should return to Quel'Nian." He met Jarrod's eyes. "This... will complicate some things for us, I suspect."

Rae nodded against him, pulling away and kissing him before letting go. "What can I do?" She turned around as Jarrod approached, pulling her into another hug.

The proxiet met Damien's gaze. "The horses are being taken care of and I've sent for some carriages to take us to Quel'Nian. We need to get Amarie to the Menders' Guild." He released Rae, who had new trails of wetness on her cheeks.

Corin took her in before she could recover. "Glad you're safe, sis."

Chapter 14

THE CARRIAGE BOUNCED, JOSTLING RAE'S head where it rested on Damien's shoulder, but he lifted it back into place without waking her.

Corin squeezed Jarrod's hand, glancing at the proxiet while he stared out the carriage window.

The forest, invisible in the darkness, grew wild beyond the glow of the lanterns lining the road to Quel'Nian.

"Do you think it's like this across the entire island?" he whispered to Jarrod. "This dark?"

Jarrod shrugged and shook his head, keeping his voice low. "I don't know. Probably."

The carriage behind them carried Amarie with two auer, the women's horses secured to the back of it. Damien had kept Amarie's Friesian calm.

Corin sighed, leaning his head against Jarrod's. "You don't think that monster will turn back on Helgath, do you?"

After a pause, Jarrod huffed. "I doubt it. It wanted Amarie. Hoult is destroyed. Even though no one seemed to be there today, for whatever reason. But the residents have no homes to go back to. Iedrus is holed up in his castle with his army. He won't help them. And I'm stuck here, useless."

Jarrod and Corin had argued with the auer guards about taking a ship back to the mainland, but they'd made it clear the barrier was impenetrable. Not only by Uriel, but by ships or anything trying to pass either direction.

Corin shook his head while still against Jarrod. "We'll find different ways to be useful, then. This won't change anything."

"I wish I believed you." Jarrod kissed Corin's temple. "It's a nice thought."

"Have I ever told you that you're a pessimist?" Corin touched his chin, turning him for a light kiss.

The proxiet chuckled. "No. I thought I was being realistic."

"We'll see if that's true when we get more information about the barrier." Corin looked across at Damien, who had shut his eyes and leaned his head back. "Or about that Uriel thing."

"I already told you I don't know," Damien whispered. "Nothing I read suggested its power being this substantial. Either something's changed, or this is temporary because of the power fed into it."

"Fed into it?"

"The Berylian Key is an energy source. Amarie's assault on Uriel likely fed him her power, granting him greater use of his own Art. It's the only conclusion I can come to. He'll eventually run out of energy allowing him to cover the barrier. He'll have to withdraw because without her, there isn't enough to sustain him."

Corin glowered. "When?"

"I don't know. Amarie might know more, but she's out cold. And our other source of Uriel information is in Slumber. Besides, I thought you wanted me to put all this Rahn'ka stuff aside so we could focus on getting Jarrod crowned?"

Corin pursed his lips, rolling his eyes. "That was before a giant shadow beast came running across the *ocean* at us."

Damien touched Rae's head as she shifted in slumber again. "Shhh." The Rahn'ka closed his eyes, marking the end of the conversation and making his brother scowl.

Hypnotized by the beams of dim light rhythmically passing by the carriage window, Corin dozed off, leaning against Jarrod.

When the carriage lurched to a stop, he jumped, nearly forgetting where he was with the images of Uriel's gaping maw of teeth clouding his mind.

Jarrod touched his face. "Dreams?"

"Something like that." Corin sat up. "Why are we stopping?" He looked out the window, but saw no city lights.

Damien laid on his bench seat, Rae curled on top of him, his hand still in her hair while they slept. The movement of the carriage hardly affected them, but voices murmured outside.

Jarrod stiffened. "It's a woman. She sounds distressed, but I don't speak Aueric."

Corin furrowed his brow. "What does she think we can do?" He didn't wait for an answer before he turned the handle of the carriage door and exited.

I need to stretch my legs, anyway.

Emerging beneath the darkened sky, he shook the thoughts of Uriel from his head and faced the driver, speaking quickly in Aueric with a frantic woman. Her long hair matched the black of the sky, and she gestured wildly, her voice pitched in panic.

Of course, the two who speak the language are asleep.

"What's going on?" Corin asked the driver, who looked up.

The woman turned to him, worry in her ruby eyes. She rattled something off to him he didn't understand, gripping his shirt.

"I'll get Rae." Jarrod returned to the carriage door.

Corin touched the woman's wrists, meeting her eyes. "Take a deep breath. Whatever it is, we'll help you."

The woman rattled off more words, and he tried to remember anything he'd overheard while staying in the capital.

Rae approached next to Corin, rubbing her face as she asked the woman a question in Aueric.

After several exchanges, Rae looked at Corin and Jarrod. "Her daughter is missing. They were playing in the woods this morning during the attack and the girl got scared and ran off. She's been looking all day and hasn't found her."

"How far are we from Quel'Nian?" Jarrod asked Rae, who translated for the driver.

"We're halfway. About another day by carriage."

Corin touched the auer woman's arm, trying to provide what comfort he could. "We can help."

Jarrod nodded. "Damien could probably—"

"Nope." Damien yawned as he stepped out of the carriage. "I haven't met the child before, so I have no way of possibly finding her using my senses. You're better suited for it than me, Jare. With the bond you have."

Jarrod's jaw tightened, and Corin recognized his usual hesitation in interacting with Neco or the bond to the wolf. "Fine. You should leave us a carriage, continue on with Amarie."

Rae eyed him before nodding. She said more to the woman that Corin didn't understand before she and Damien entered the back carriage.

"See, a way to be useful." Corin smirked at Jarrod, bumping his shoulder.

Jarrod scowled at him, but a smile twitched his lips. "Finding pleasure in a lost child. This is a new low for you, Captain."

"That's totally not what I..." Corin sighed. "Lets just find her. Poor thing is probably terrified."

The proxiet looked at the mother and pointed into the forest. "Show us, please?"

Corin unfastened the latch that held a lantern beside the driver's seat as the other carriage pulled past them.

The woman nodded, heading into the woods and pausing to ensure they followed. With a flick of her wrist, she summoned a small sphere of light.

Corin grumbled to himself.

Everyone makes the Art look so simple.

Jarrod glanced at Corin as they maneuvered down a slope, stepping over a ravine as they made their way deeper into the forest.

How far did she come to seek help?

The woman finally stopped, kneeling next to a tree stump and motioning with her free hand at the grass around it. She kept talking, but he understood none of it.

Jarrod circled the stump, and Corin eyed a small bundle of picked wildflowers.

Leaving the spot, the woman walked outward, calling into the darkness. "Ineniya!"

Lifting the lantern to penetrate through the black, Corin squinted at the dense tree line. The pines in this part of the forest grew tall and wide, leaving space between them for thick brush and undergrowth. It looked more haunting than he'd ever considered, often finding peace in long walks when they'd stayed in Quel'Nian.

Looking up at the sky, he couldn't see beyond the glow his lantern provided, and a shiver passed down his spine. "Pick up anything yet?" He glanced at Jarrod, who still circled the stump.

The proxiet nodded, gaze wandering into the trees as he traced some invisible thread. "She went this way." He touched the woman's shoulder, motioning with his head in the direction that led further from the road.

Jarrod walked so far ahead of them, Corin could barely make him out at the edge of his lantern's light.

I wonder what he sees.

Chapter 15

"NOTHING?" THE ARCH JUDGMENT GLARED down at Rae from his position on the council platform. "You have nothing to say about the shadow you've cast over your homeland?"

The crystal ceiling high above glowed with Art-crafted light, casting eerie shadows on the nine council members and their high-backed chairs.

Rae clenched her jaw. "While I've enjoyed parts of my time here, this isn't my homeland." She lifted a hand before they could yell at her for arguing semantics. "Regardless, as much as I want to help you, I don't have much to offer. I don't know what the beast was or why it chased us. I deeply regret the disruption this has caused Eralas."

"Disruption?" Lo'thec stood from his seat, his perturbed face more defined. "Darkness blankets our sky. Our people and our island will die in this creature's shadow. Which you led to us!"

Taking a deep breath, Rae resisted rolling her eyes. "No one died. No one *will* die. The shadow is only temporary."

The council grew quiet and Lo'thec grunted as he sat down with the arch judgment's wave.

"A bold statement to make before this council when you claim to know nothing about the creature. It makes me doubt your knowledge of how long it will last." Elder Erdeaseq frowned as he stepped forward from his center seat.

Rae glanced at the circle of roots she stood within before looking at the council again. "With all due respect, elders, my understanding of the Art is what gives me confidence that this is temporary. I don't need to know what the beast is to know it isn't always that... *huge*. Otherwise, we'd all have seen it before. It expelled *mass* amounts of energy to assume the form it did and it can't be sustainable. It's only been a couple days. Give it time. Its power will drain and it'll be forced to retreat."

"And you have no knowledge of its origin? Where this creature came from?" Kreshiida, sitting beside Lo'thec, waved her hand through the air, already seeming bored with the conversation.

"It's a little absurd, isn't it, that the people of Pantracia who've arguably lived the longest are asking *me* about the origin of that thing? I should ask you. You, with all your texts and ancient knowledge, tell me." Rae pointed west. "What is *that*?"

"You dare—"

"Enough." The arch judgment's voice boomed through the hall. "The Mira'wyld makes a valid point, and this council has much to discuss if she cannot deliver further knowledge."

"Her logic for the creature's eventual departure is also sound." Paivesh spoke for the first time, rising from her seat beside the arch judgment. "We should invite our scholars to predict how long our people must endure this." She faced Rae, steepling her hands in front of her. "You may leave, Raeynna. But please remain within the city where we may call on you."

"If I may, I have questions." Rae rolled her lips together. She'd talked to Damien about what information to seek from the council before they'd arrived at the Sanctum of Law after leaving Jarrod and Corin beside the road. Her stomach churned, reminding her of what she needed to tell Damien.

As soon as we're alone.

Lo'thec and Kreshiida grumbled, but Paivesh opened her hand towards her with a smile. "Ask them."

"Once the shadow fiend's assault ends, how long will the barrier remain in place? I ask this within my station as political strategist to Lord Martox, as Helgath's future balances in a precarious place. Even more so with his absence."

"And the attack by the beast on their lands." Paivesh nodded, glancing at her fellow council members as if challenging them to question her. "A valid concern, and we owe Lord Martox all we can in these desperate times considering our alliance."

"Elder Ietylon? Will you answer for the council, please?"

The eldest of the council, hunched in his seat on the opposite side from Paivesh, twitched as if he might have been asleep through the entire conversation. "Old timelines should remain true. After the threat has passed, the barrier will remain in place for a month, to ensure the danger is truly gone."

We will get back to the mainland before Iedrus's deadline to hand over the throne. Good.

"I'd also like to know what happened to Amarie. She's my friend and her injuries were extensive."

"She is being cared for." The arch judgment urged Paivesh to take her seat again with a subtle nod. "Our menders are doing all they can, considering the extent of her injuries and her Art's resistance to healing. But she will come before us to answer to this council when she is well enough."

Rae straightened. "Have you already decided a fate for her?"

"Not yet." He glanced to either side of him, some council members with larger frowns than others. "We have not fully discussed it, as we have greater matters on our mind. Is there more, Raeynna? We must resume our conference to discuss how to help our people in this time of fear."

"Of course. That is all. Will someone please update me if Amarie's condition or status changes?"

Erdeaseq nodded, gesturing to the back doors, which the guards opened.

Chapter 16

MOST SCENTS HAD A COLOR. The girl's wove through the underbrush in trails of orange and yellow, left behind on the leaves. Since her disappearance had happened half a day prior, the scent around the tree stump started off weak. Jarrod could only pick up on the haze by delving completely into his wolf senses, leaving his chest tight and mouth dry.

Save for the fight in Rylorn, he'd avoided using the full extent of his abilities.

Too much at risk if I lose control again.

Neco traversed the terrain fifty yards away, out of sight. He'd sensed the moment Jarrod honed in on his senses, opening the bond between them. His excitement encouraged him to abandon the hunt he'd enjoyed, preying on the already petrified animals of a darkened forest. His presence provided Jarrod with an extra set of ears and eyes.

And an extra nose.

The girl had stopped at a stream for a short while, leaving her scent and tracks all over the bank. Each footprint glowed in his vision, disappearing into the water but reappearing on the other side.

They walked through the darkness, the lantern Corin carried emitting plenty of light for him to see by.

Ahead, something rustled, and he stopped to listen.

Neco halted, picking up the whimpers of a child.

Gotcha.

Jarrod stood straighter and jogged further ahead, leaving the other two behind.

"Whoa, slow down, Jarrod!" The brush grew thick through this section of the forest, and Corin and the child's mother had struggled to keep up while he maneuvered through the brush. The light of the lantern dimmed, lost behind the foliage.

Jarrod didn't slow, reaching a pine with a hollow base. "Ineniya?"

The girl scuffled within, bursting from the tree but pausing when she met the proxiet's gaze.

Smiling, he held a hand out and crouched. "I won't hurt you."

Ineniya hesitated before approaching him and letting him pick her up. Her tiny arms clutched tight around Jarrod's neck, her face wet with tears.

Relief filled his chest, and he made his way back to the others, instructing Neco to keep his distance.

When lantern light touched the young girl's cheeks, her mother gasped and rushed through the brush. Her orb of light vanished as she opened her arms for her daughter, and Jarrod passed her over.

Circling around the woman, Corin gave Jarrod a smile, something softer in his eyes as he watched the child embracing her mother.

The auer woman kissed her daughter's hair as she reached for Jarrod, touching his arm. She repeated the words for 'thank you' in Aueric over and over.

At least I know that phrase.

Jarrod touched her hand, nodding. "I'm just glad she's safe." Tuning into his senses again, he tried to determine where the road was. "Come." He looked at Corin. "Let's get back to the carriage."

Nodding, Corin pulled the underbrush aside, lifting the lantern to beckon the auer and her child through. He paused, looking at Jarrod. "Nice work. You make it look so easy."

When the brush grew less extreme and they wove quietly through the trees towards the road, his husband took his hand and squeezed. Letting out a long breath, Jarrod shook his head. "Just lucky the girl isn't hurt..." He narrowed his eyes at Corin. "What's with the look on your face?"

Even in the darkness, Jarrod saw color rise to Corin's cheeks. "Nothing." He pursed his lips, glancing at the wide eyes of the little girl watching Jarrod and him over her mother's shoulder. "Just... I think I want a daughter."

A what?

Jarrod cleared his throat. "I don't know if we'll get the choice."

Corin chewed his lower lip. "I know. But... I want one."

Chuckling, the proxiet let go of Corin's hand to wrap his arm around the man's shoulders. "All because we saved a little girl? Now you *want* one?"

Corin leaned against him, resting his head on Jarrod's shoulder while they walked. "Just look at her. She looks so perfect and beautiful. And when you were holding her..." He shook his head. "It can wait until we figure out all this king stuff, but I enjoy imagining us as fathers together."

Jarrod kissed the top of Corin's head. "I do, too."

Corin sighed, wrapping his arm around Jarrod's waist. "Need to talk to Damien more seriously about what he can do to help, I guess."

Anxiety knotted in his gut.

As long as she doesn't end up like me.

"You'll be a great da." Jarrod rubbed Corin's shoulder. "Still not sure how I feel about this plan being concocted without me. Tell me again, Damien is going to merge our souls into a new one, and Rae is going to carry it to term?"

"It wasn't really *concocted*. We briefly talked about it, and Damien just said it was *theoretically* possible. And Rae volunteered." Corin frowned against Jarrod's shoulder. "But I wouldn't want to unless he finds something in those old Rahn'ka books about it being done *correctly* before."

Jarrod laughed, but it didn't ease his tension. "What? Appalled at the idea of a wolf-child?"

"I'd love her, anyway." Corin nibbled on his shoulder. "But I'm not afraid of the wolf in you and you shouldn't be, either. It helped today, didn't it?"

"Sure, today it did." Jarrod sighed. "I don't know why I can't relax about it."

"I don't blame you for being nervous, all things considered. But now that Damien is actually *here*, maybe you can start accessing it a little more to help find that confidence again?"

The proxiet nodded. "I'll try."

They stepped onto the road, farther west than where they'd left the carriage, and started walking east.

The girl still hung draped over her mother's shoulder, fast asleep.

The woman's steps were uneven, and Jarrod let go of Corin to catch up to her.

I love tormenting my husband.

"I can take her…" Jarrod motioned to the sleeping girl. "You must be exhausted. And there's still awhile until the carriage." He pointed east.

The auer hesitated, bags under her eyes, but nodded her understanding. She passed her daughter back to Jarrod, careful not to wake her. The girl's head rested on his shoulder as they continued on their way.

The proxiet glanced at his husband with a smirk. "This helping?"

Corin rolled his eyes. "No." He fell into step beside Jarrod, touching his waist. "And you're a bastard because you know it." He smiled, touching the scar on Jarrod's chin as he leaned in to kiss his cheek over the slumbering girl.

"Messenger birds can't even get through the barrier?" Corin huffed as he leaned over the dining table, still covered in their planning maps.

Jarrod slid a glass of wine towards him as Damien dispersed full glasses to Jarrod's council, all together for the first time in over a year.

Maith shook his head. "They designed the barrier to keep not only everything out, but everything in." He offered a glass to Rae, who shook her head, waving one of her hands while keeping her arms crossed.

I don't think I've ever seen her turn down wine before.

"The council says it will remain in place for a month, and that's only after Ur... the shadows leave." Rae stepped closer to Damien, who rubbed his jaw.

"So we're completely cut off from Helgath." Vinoria took a long gulp of the glass given to her. "At such a critical time."

"Not only that, but the auer military is trapped here. All troops used to convince Oraphin returned. There's no auer support anywhere near Helgath." Corin sloshed the wine in his cup as he slid it back and forth on the tabletop without taking a drink. "At least the Hawks and rebels are still there."

"We have to trust Sarth will keep putting on pressure from her end. It's likely she's caught word that something happened here. For all we know, she's rounding up the rebels as we speak." Jarrod looked at his wine and wrinkled his nose. "Don't we have anything stronger?"

"All that assumes whatever the hells is attacking the island doesn't turn back on Helgath. Did you say it began over there?" Vinoria turned to Damien as Corin plucked a decanter of amber liquid from the back of one of the side tables.

"It won't turn back on Helgath. What it wants isn't there, it's here." Damien glanced at Rae, his brow furrowing as she waved off Corin's new offer of whisky.

Jarrod picked up the glass Corin slid in front of him, generously poured full, and took a long drink.

"How do you know that?" Vinoria narrowed her eyes at Damien. "More secrets? Like where you were for almost a year."

"He was with me." Jarrod turned to his trade minister. "These are not secrets from me, Vinoria, and that's all that you need to be concerned with. Drop it."

Vinoria huffed, but turned from the table to down the rest of her wine and refill it.

Maith watched, his purple eyes passing across the room. "Tensions are high. But now is not the time for this council to be doubting each other. I trust they would tell us what is necessary to know." He met the Rahn'ka's eyes, and Damien gave him a subtle nod.

I'm glad he's the one the auer assigned. Damien's voice filled Jarrod's mind, and he almost choked on his whisky. It'd been far too long since the two of them had used the bond with Neco to communicate.

Does that mean you like him now? Jarrod turned his gaze back to the table as Corin gave him a concerned glance.

I might have distrusted his intentions before, but it was the jealousy talking. He's a good fit for this council.

Vinoria's eyes darted between Damien and Jarrod, catching the slight smirk on the Rahn'ka's face with a frown.

"This will not affect Jarrod's ascension to the throne." Damien sighed. "It is a separate matter entirely. The only effect is how long it traps us here on the island. We have to trust our allies on the mainland. Sarth and Corin's second in command among the rebels."

Rae nodded, crossing her arms over her loose tan tunic. "Luckily, we should be able to return before the deadline to take the throne, assuming the shadow beast doesn't linger too long."

The blue haze around Rae had tints of green, an evolution since last seeing her in Serityme.

Why is her scent different?

"The greater concern is how many more Iedrus will rally to his cause while we're stuck here. I'm sure he'll come up with a way to spin Jarrod being trapped in Eralas into more propaganda. At least we got word to Sarth and Belladora about the battle plan before the barrier went up." Corin turned towards Jarrod. "How are you feeling?"

Jarrod downed the rest of his whisky and put the glass on the table. "Like a caged wolf." He growled the words aloud without thinking, and several gazes landed on him.

Neco lifted his head from the floor by his feet and whined.

Corin's hand closed on top of his with a reassuring weight. "The positive side is that we are most definitely safe from assassins here."

Jarrod waved a hand at the map. "And what of everyone else?"

"Everyone else won't matter if you're not safe." Vinoria returned to the table. She eyed Damien, then the maps. "Everyone who is fighting for House Martox is doing so by choice, and will continue to. Like you said, we trust in our allies to continue the fight without us. The foundation has already been laid."

"She's right. This will ultimately be a great test of the support you will have as king." Rae met Jarrod's eyes, worry within hers. "Everything is in place as best as we could, so we wait."

Jarrod waved a hand. "Then let's take a break. I'm sure a few of us need sleep and we all need to eat. Nothing will get done if we all lose our minds."

Speaking from experience.

"I'll return to the Sanctum of Law to remain abreast on the council's decisions." Maith set his empty glass on one of the side tables. He looked at Rae, putting a hand on her shoulder before whispering something to her in Aueric. She smiled, touching his arm before he crossed to the door.

Damien met Jarrod's eyes while Vinoria silently slipped out of the room. "Find the kid?"

"Aye, we found her." Jarrod eyed Corin. "Safe with her mother. You should take a break, too. Go for a walk, a nap, whatever."

Damien glanced at Rae with a relaxed smile, the first Jarrod had seen in a while. "I was hoping my wife might accompany me to the gardens next door. For some time together."

Rae nodded, a nervous expression appearing momentarily on her face.

Something is up with her.

Jarrod nudged her towards Damien. "I, being the only one who didn't sleep in the carriage, need a nap."

Corin put his hands on Jarrod's shoulders from behind, rubbing his thumbs into his aching muscles. "I could sleep more, too."

Chapter 17

RAE'S ENERGY JUMPED AGAINST Damien's as they passed hand in hand through the side gate of the Lenoneishé Gardens of Quel'Nian.

Even in the darkness, the gardens glowed with bioluminescent lights throughout the trees and canopies above. In some ways, the wonder of auer artisans was even more impressive without sunlight.

Multi-tiered fountains constructed of floating orbs of water and vines cascaded into the streams, crystal bridges spanning across them. The gentle ebb of power, ever present in the constructions of the gardens, felt at peace. Each ká around him was content with the beauty it displayed, not yet concerned about the lack of sunlight. They basked in the quiet of the extended night, allowing Damien to breathe and loosen the control on his barrier.

"Have you been here before?" Damien turned to Rae, tapping her knuckles with his fingers as they passed beneath an archway of two magnolia trees. Their branches wove together, budding with white blossoms, each glimmering like a small flame nestled inside.

Rae nodded. "Kynis brought me here once as part of a lesson. Seems like years ago now. Have you?"

"Not until recently, when the auer moved Jarrod to these accommodations within the city. They're definitely showing off by putting us in a home right next door to their largest garden." He tugged her down a narrow path that passed between two sculpted drakes shaped out of vines and budding leaves. The statues' wings spread wide, their growth merging with the canopy above.

Beyond, the pathway opened into a circular clearing, a hill of grass and wildflowers parsed with walking stones. Surrounding it were more draconi figures, ranging from the smaller of them without wings, to the largest figure of the garden. The dragon's massive head protruded into the clearing, his mane formed of grass. Spheres of water represented his eyes, watching over the hill. His body wrapped around the far edge, as if it protected the clearing like a clutch of eggs. A wing outstretched above, forming a trellis of vines with glowing motes trailing down their length.

Walking backward so he could take both her hands, Damien guided Rae onto the hill. "I thought of you when I found this section." He sat on the grass, encouraging her down with him. "It's also my favorite meditation spot because of that."

Rae smiled, bending her knees and draping her arms over them. "I'm tired of being away from you so often. Do you think that will change now?" She looked at him, two-tone eyes studying his face.

He watched her, taking one of her hands as he shuffled closer, his shins touching her feet. "I hope so. It's hard to know what's going to come. But at least we know we have the next month?" He smiled, but shook his head. "I don't like being apart, either. I'm just happy you're safe. When I saw Uriel..."

Rae huffed. "You must have thought you were about to witness my death. I didn't know if we'd make it."

"I don't know what I'd do if I lost you." Damien touched her cheek before beckoning her forward. "Come here. I want to hold you." He opened his arms as Rae lowered her knees, crawling into his lap and resting her head sideways against his collar.

She tilted her chin up to look at him. "I have to tell you something."

Running his hand over her hair, he kissed her forehead. "As long as it doesn't change this, right in this moment." He wrapped his arms around her tighter. "I missed this."

Rae hummed. "Maybe I should tell you tomorrow, then."

Damien groaned and shook his head with a smile. "Just tell me."

"You're gonna be a father."

Everything in Damien's chest numbed.

I'm gonna be a...

Damien pulled back enough to meet her eyes, studying her face as he touched her cheek. "You're not teasing me, are you?"

Rae took his hand and placed it on her abdomen. "See for yourself."

Focusing on his breathing to control his ká felt impossible with the way his heart pounded. Swallowing, he urged the voices around him out so he could focus his ká on Rae's, searching it. Immediately, he could sense the subtle change. Portions of her energy focused under his hand, where a new tangle formed.

"Is it a boy? I keep thinking it's a boy." Rae's voice permeated his thoughts, and she kissed his neck.

Damien's throat tightened, a rise of heat coming to his eyes as he tried to keep hold of his senses to further explore the new life budding within his wife. Drawing in a deep breath, he rubbed his hand against her abdomen and the surprise shifted into pure joy. "It's a boy." His voice cracked, and she kissed him.

When she pulled away, her eyes glistened with emotion. "We're going to have a son."

Damien smiled, unable to form more words before he kissed her again, harder than before. The elation of the news made him dizzy, and he tightened his hold around her. He pulled away, kissing her neck before he looked down where his hand touched her stomach. His senses ventured to check again, to make sure he wasn't jumping to conclusions and came back with the same answers.

A baby boy.

"Dice." He met her eyes, trying to find the words. "I've dreamt about this. It feels crazy to be so excited considering everything going on, but... a baby." He kissed her again.

Rae's smile spread into a grin when he broke the kiss, and she nodded. "And you're lucky, you missed the icky first part where my stomach randomly rejected many things I used to enjoy."

Damien frowned, considering suddenly where she'd been for the first part of her pregnancy. "When did you realize what was going on? I wish you'd told me sooner..."

"You wish I told you in a letter so you could fret and worry about me... about *us*, the entire time?" Rae tilted her head and quirked an eyebrow at him. "I had suspicions before we reached Lazuli..."

Damien sighed, shaking his head. He knew what she said was the truth, but it still left a hollow spot in him. "You're right." He curled his back so he could kiss her abdomen. "You know I'm going to be extra protective of you both now, right?"

"I expected as much." Rae smirked. "So I'm not in trouble then?"

Damien chuckled and shook his head. "No. I'm too excited to think about any of it too much." He took both her cheeks in his hands and kissed her again. "You're going to be a wonderful mama."

Rae laughed and wrapped her arms around his neck. "I love you."

"And I, you." Damien held her, unable to contain his excitement, and once again allowed himself to feel the tangle of energy that was his growing son.

"Your mother is rather excited," Rae mumbled.

He scoffed. "Of course she is. She's been harping about grandchildren for years. You told her when you ran into her in Lazuli?" He tried to imagine what his mother's face must have looked like.

"Well... I didn't *tell* her, technically. She figured it out after I asked her what being pregnant felt like. I guess that gave it away."

He laughed again, grateful for the distraction. Nuzzling against her neck, he kissed beneath her ear. "When do you want to tell Jarrod and Corin? They might notice something is up when I can't stop looking at you."

"Might be fun to mess with them a little." Rae shrugged. "But I don't think I can keep it a secret much longer. It's been hell trying to get you alone."

"It's going to make the next few months even more interesting, that's certain." Damien counted backwards, trying to determine where she might be in the pregnancy as the time came to take the throne. He pursed his lips and shook his head. "As much as messing with them sounds like fun, we need to tell them. It might affect a few things, but it'll all be worth it." Pressing his hand to her abdomen again, power pulsed between him and his son once more.

"Don't get any ideas, Lieutenant. I'll be just as involved, pregnant or not." Rae narrowed her eyes at him, but still smiled.

Involved, but she's not going into that castle with us.

Damien stroked Rae's hair. "Too late. Lots of ideas already going through my head, though very few have to do with politics at this exact moment."

"Politics can wait." Rae kissed his neck. "Tell me your ideas."

He hummed. "Well, the more immediate ones pertain to kissing and spoiling you as much as possible. Don't women crave certain things when they're pregnant? So I anticipate many trips into the city to find things for you."

Rae bit him. "It will be nice not to fetch my own cravings. Like those sweet buns from that bakery in Lazuli."

"Lazuli's sweet buns might be a bit too much of a trip right now."

His wife paused. "There's something else, though."

Of course there is, can't all be good.

Damien furrowed his brow, touching her cheek. "What is it?"

"Sindré told me some things, back at the sanctum, and they might be relevant now."

The Rahn'ka straightened. Anything the guardian spirits said certainly had the potential to be important, but also rife with hidden agendas. "You mean other than this confirming Sindré's original threat of infertility was a lie?" The lingering fear of having the choice of children stripped away had continued to haunt him, and he realized the news also lifted that burden. But a new fear settled.

How can I properly be a father and the Rahn'ka?

"Other than that." Rae removed Damien's hand from her face and kissed his knuckles. "It's also why they finally accepted my presence at the sanctum."

"It was rather surprising how helpful Sindré suddenly became. Especially considering your heritage. I wondered what changed…"

Rae twisted his wedding band. "They said I'm the hope for providing Pantracia with more Rahn'ka."

Damien's breath caught. "More? As in more than one?"

She nodded. "Our child will become a Rahn'ka when he gets older."

He felt dizzy at the thought, considering the learning process he'd gone through.

But it won't be like that because we can prepare him.

"So not only are we going to be raising our son, but potentially rebuilding an ancient culture?"

"No pressure, right?"

He laughed despite himself, pressing his forehead to hers. "Boy, am I glad Sindré taught you Rahn'ka. It'll help to have a partner in all this."

"And until then, we have our own secret language." Rae kissed him.

He savored the affection, drawing it out as he ran his hand over her stomach. "Not even named yet, and he's already got the weight of the guardians on his little shoulders."

"Do you have ideas for names?" Rae walked two fingers up his chest.

Damien smirked. "Give me time, I only just found out I'm going to be a father. I haven't fully thought it through yet. But something with meaning?"

Rae nodded, falling silent against him.

He caught her hand on his chest, bringing it up and kissing her fingers. "Do *you* have any ideas?"

She hesitated, watching his face. "I had one, in case it was a boy, but we don't need to decide anything right away."

So close, with his senses already heightened, Damien could feel the distant voice of Rae's ká and who she thought of. He smiled, turning her hand in his so he could kiss her palm. "I like that name."

Rae scowled. "Did you just read my thoughts?"

"Not entirely on purpose. It's just easy with you. I do it without realizing sometimes."

Color rose in her cheeks. "And you like it? You don't have to. We can think of others..."

"No. It has the kind of meaning I was hoping for. I like it. I think it's perfect." He traced a finger around her abdomen before pressing his palm against where his child rested within her womb. He leaned down, kissing above his hand. "I can't wait to meet you, Bellamy."

Chapter 18

CORIN RUBBED SLEEP FROM HIS eyes. "He was humming... in the hallway. Out loud." He crossed to one of the side tables in the meeting room, pouring a generous amount of sugar into a cup of coffee.

"Can't imagine why," Jarrod huffed in sarcasm. "We need rooms farther apart."

Neco whined in apparent agreement as Jarrod scratched his ears.

"We're not exactly quiet, either." Corin smirked over the rim of his cup, savoring the rich aroma. "But it's weird. Damien's supposed to be broody and on edge all the time. I'm going to ask him."

"Just let him have it. It's good to see him like this. Maybe it means his head is finally clear."

Corin shrugged, lifting a steaming mug of black coffee and offering it to Jarrod.

The proxiet took it, breathing deep. "Smells so much better than whatever dessert drink you've made yourself."

"Good thing I don't judge you for your poor taste. So bitter... like you," he teased as he took another slow sip.

Jarrod frowned, lowering the mug. "What'd I do to deserve that?"

Corin leaned forward and gave him a soft kiss. "Nothing lately. A more general observation. But you're getting better."

Scoffing, Jarrod wrapped an arm around his husband and pulled him closer. "You complain when I'm sappy, you complain when I'm not. Is there anything that pleases you?"

"Ever consider that I just like complaining?" Corin grinned, playfully thumbing Jarrod's chin.

The proxiet kissed him, warming his veins. "At least you like something."

"I do. And I'm so very tempted to abscond back to the bedroom with my very favorite thing. If the others don't show up soon..." He slid his mug onto a map on the table so he had both hands free to trace Jarrod's waist. "It's supposed to be everyone, right?"

"Vinoria is meeting with an elder this morning about future trade deals, but everyone else should be here." Jarrod glanced in the door's direction. "Looks like Maith is first."

Corin strained to listen for footsteps in the hallway.

I don't hear anything.

"Still getting used to those senses of yours. If I wasn't your husband, I'd call it creepy." Corin indulged in placing a kiss near Jarrod's ear.

A few moments later, the auer entered the room, dressed in his usual fine coat and fitted breeches. He'd styled his short, light-grey hair straight back, his amethyst eyes landing on them. "Good morning, and isn't it a pleasant one at that?" Maith crossed towards the far side of the room. "I've never been more grateful to see the sun. Yet, you two stand here in darkness." He sighed, opening the large shutters covering the windows, letting sunlight stream in. "Better, isn't it?"

Corin groaned, burying his face against Jarrod's shoulder. "I'm still getting used to the sun being back, honestly."

Jarrod angled his mouth near Corin's ear, lowering his voice. "The upside to these senses is that I get to hear your heart race when you get excited."

It evoked exactly what the proxiet probably wanted, and Corin shivered. He turned his mouth towards Jarrod's skin, moaning softly. "You're making me want to skip this meeting, my king."

Oblivious, Maith poured a cup of coffee at one of the side tables before adding a liberal amount of cream.

Jarrod kissed Corin's head, loosening his hold. "Later, my love. Damien and Rae have finally shown up."

With another complaint against Jarrod's neck, he forced himself away enough to place an insistent kiss on Jarrod's lips. "I'll hold you to that promise of later." He reached for his coffee again as the doors opened at the end of the room.

Damien and Rae entered, speaking strange words in hushed tones.

Jarrod narrowed his eyes. "What language is that?"

Damien smiled with a minute shrug. "Rahn'ka."

Corin crossed his arms at Rae's appearance. "And why are you wearing a dress?"

The knee-length blue fabric settled around her legs as she halted and shrugged. "It's more comfortable."

Maith even eyed her, frowning. "Is something going on?"

The room stilled.

Damien and Rae exchanged a look.

"Everything's great." Damien grinned, making Corin's frown deepen.

"Oh no, you've been keeping something secret. We've all noticed, little brother. You've been practically dancing everywhere you go. And we all know that's not *normal*."

Jarrod put down his mug and eased towards Rae, studying her.

Neco followed, trotting to the Mira'wyld and sniffing her.

"Can you tell?" Rae tilted her head at the proxiet, who eyed the wolf.

"What do you think, boy?" Jarrod's shoulders relaxed once Neco's tail wagged, and he pushed his nose against her stomach. "Are you...?"

"She is."

"She's what?" A bubble of worry formed before he reminded himself Damien had been happy. "What's going on?"

Damien wrapped an arm around Rae, nuzzling his face against her hair, kissing it.

Rae smiled at Corin, rolling her lips together. "Hope you're ready to be uncles."

The proxiet enveloped her in a hug, cutting off anything else she might have said.

Uncles?

Maith shook Damien's hand. "Congratulations, my friend."

Corin narrowed his eyes as the information sank in. He focused on Rae's abdomen as Jarrod stepped away, and realized he'd completely overlooked the growth there. Now that he knew the truth, it seemed ridiculous that he'd missed it. "Whoa." He crossed to her, unable to avert his gaze. "You're having a baby?"

"That would be the required step to you being an uncle." Damien rolled his eyes, and Rae smacked his chest.

Corin laughed, pulling Rae into a hug. "Gods, I'm so happy for you both."

Rae squeezed him. "Thank you. I couldn't wait to tell you guys." She released him, holding his shoulders. "He's about halfway along." Her hands ventured to her stomach, where she pressed her dress to show the bump. "I can still hardly believe it, sometimes."

"Halfway already?" Corin eyed Damien. "You mean you let her run all over Helgath while pregnant?"

"I had no idea! Besides, you're implying I have any control over her wanting to keep running around in dangerous situations." Damien glanced at Rae, then met Jarrod's eyes. "Maybe she'll listen if it's more than just me telling her, though."

Jarrod straightened. "You mean Iedrus's castle."

"I'm still going." Rae crossed her arms.

"Uh... no. You're not." Corin lifted his eyebrows as he put a hand on Rae's shoulder. "Not if you've got a little Damien in there. There's no way, sis. I'm sorry."

Jarrod nodded. "I agree. You can't be in there with us. If something happened to you..."

Rae glowered at them. "I'm not some invalid just because I'm pregnant. What if something happened to Damien? Does he have to stay behind too?" She paused. "I didn't think so. So why is it different for me?"

"It's not just if something happened to you, though. Think about it." Corin tightened his grip on her. "You just being there would put all of us in greater jeopardy because we're going to be focused on keeping you safe. It'd make it harder to focus on what we're actually there to do. It's not about whether you can protect yourself... we know you can do that... But we won't be able to keep our chauvinistic minds from wanting to protect you, anyway."

"So because you all have trouble focusing, I get punished? And it's *just like that*?" Rae's shoulders drooped. "And I'm so expendable that you can just replace me?"

Damien sighed. "We can't replace you. It'll just be—"

"Don't." Rae's gaze fell. "Why don't you keep this a boys' party too, then. I'd hate to distract you." She turned, shirking away from Damien's reach and exiting the room.

"That could have gone better." Jarrod closed his eyes. "She's headed outside."

Damien shook his head. "About the way I expected, honestly. She'll cool off, though."

"I'll go talk to her." Corin went to the side table, preparing a cup of the tea Rae preferred.

"Are you sure? I could." Jarrod crossed to Damien and clapped a hand on his shoulder. "A baby. No wonder you're so giddy."

"Not an ideal time, but I'm excited, regardless." He glanced back to the door Rae had gone through. "I better go check on her, too."

"Nah." Corin waved his hand. "Better not to overwhelm her. You two have work to do, and I'm awful with decisions with laws. Especially those regarding the Art." Corin had already grimaced at the docket of political plans required for the day. "Besides, she's my sister. I can talk to her."

Damien gave him a shallow smile. "Good luck. I hope you're able to get her to see it. I haven't been able to."

Corin retrieved his mug and exited, crossing the foyer to the front door.

Hopefully she hasn't gone far.

Rae sat on a stone bench with her back to the grand home, facing a wall of roses in their entry garden. Sunlight shone off her dark braided hair, loose around her shoulders to her mid-back.

Corin stepped loudly across the cobblestoned pathway, settling onto the bench beside her. Without a word, he extended the mug of steaming tea.

She took it, bringing it to her lips for a sip before lowering it. "You make my tea better than your brother."

"I also pay attention to a lot of things better than my brother." Corin's eyes betrayed him by wandering back to the bump at her stomach. "Though, I somehow still miss things that should be obvious. I knew there had to be something behind Damien's mood swing."

Rae leaned on his shoulder. "It's something else we learned last night, too. Amarie requested Slumber from the elders and they gave it to her. She's with Kin and doesn't even know it. I can't decide if it's romantic or heart-breaking."

Corin hummed. "And I suppose that makes some of his Rahn'ka stuff a little easier?"

She nodded against him. "For a while, anyway. We can focus on Helgath."

"And gods know Helgath needs it right now. But I know this Rahn'ka stuff is important to him, too. And you. I mean, when did you learn to speak it?"

"After you and Jarrod left. Sindré taught me."

"Huh. Didn't think that guardian spirit did anything but complain."

Rae touched her belly. "Sindré also told me other things. Like that I'm part alcan and my child will be a Rahn'ka."

Corin choked on his sip of coffee. He turned to look at her as best as he could from her position against him. "I thought Damien said there was only one Rahn'ka?"

Rae nodded again. "There can be more, but only through *traditional* methods of procreation." She smirked, but her shoulders slumped. "I didn't mean to snap at him about the castle. This may shock you, but my mood hasn't been the most stable."

"No," Corin scoffed. "Say it isn't so. You're clearly the most stable one around here."

Turning her face into his shoulder, she let out a laugh that sounded mixed with a sob. "I don't want to sit useless on the sidelines. I can help. I know everyone's worried about the baby, but what if something happened I could have prevented?"

Corin wrapped his arm around her. "We both know you won't be sitting idle. There will be another way for you to help that's not on the front lines. You know as well as the rest of us do that you shouldn't go into that castle. Can you imagine what a mess Damien would be? And that's even if you stayed perfectly safe the entire time."

Rae sighed, falling silent. The breeze picked up, blowing a strand of her loose hair over Corin's chest, and she tucked another out of her face.

Thinking about what Damien and Rae's baby would look like led Corin down another path of thoughts. The little auer girl slumbering in Jarrod's arms. His chest warmed.

Am I really going to ask her to carry a child for Jarrod and me?

"How is the pregnant thing going, by the way?"

Rae chuckled. "Well, better now, emotional turmoil notwithstanding. The beginning was worse, with the constant nausea and bloated feeling. My body seems so foreign to me with how much it's changing."

"But all in all, you don't hate it? Good. That's good."

Rae cradled her tea in her lap and tilted her head to look at him with narrowed eyes. "Why are you asking?"

Corin's cheeks heated. "Don't worry about it, I'm being selfish." He shrugged his shoulder, jostling her head playfully. "You're going to be a ma! That's what we should focus on right now."

"Corin..." Rae poked his ribs.

He frowned. "I've been... It's funny timing, really. You being pregnant and all, considering I wanted to ask..."

Rae sat up straight. "By the gods, you want to know if I hate it because you want me to carry your baby, too. Is that what you're trying to figure out? I haven't even pushed this one out and you're ready to plan the next."

"And that would be why I was *trying* not to bring it up." Corin sighed. "Besides, we still don't know if it's possible, so no reason to talk about it. Let's just be happy for this one."

To his surprise, Rae laughed. She leaned on him again, taking his hand and pressing it to her bump. "He likes the tea you made. Can you feel that?"

Corin held his breath while he tried to feel the baby's movement. A flutter bumped against his palm and his heart missed a beat. "Let's hope he's not as bullheaded as his father and uncle." He grinned as he rested his head against Rae's. "You're going to be such great parents to this little guy."

Rae put her hand on his. "You and Jarrod will make great parents, too. Don't worry, I don't hate being pregnant."

Corin sighed loudly before he could contain it.

"Excuse me."

Corin looked up to see an auer standing in the garden. A light purple dress swished around her ankles, tailored to her thin frame. Her emerald eyes matched the foliage of the rosebush, focused on Rae. In the bright morning light, her pupils were pinpoints.

Rae stood, facing the auer. "You're one of the menders? I've seen others in the guild wear that necklace."

Corin focused on the jewelry Rae mentioned, the solid silver-plated band resting high on the woman's collarbone. Etchings ran along its surface in a swirled pattern, like vines.

The auer nodded, the bottom of her ebon hair brushing her cheeks. "I am. I apologize for interrupting. Are you the Mira'wyld?" Her Common was flawless, unlike most of the auer Corin had interacted with.

"I am. Is Amarie all right? I heard she entered Slumber shortly after the sun returned."

"She is as well as she can be, all things considered." The auer took a step closer to them, lifting three fingers to her forehead before lowering them in an arc down. "Though, she is the reason for my visit. My name is Kalstacia. I do not know if I may have come up between you two during your travels together, but more likely my brother's name did. Talon?"

Rae's posture relaxed, and she returned the Aueric greeting. "Yes, she told me about Talon. Is he here?"

Kalstacia shook her head. "No, and I don't know where he is. Though I suspect if he hears of the events that led to the closure of Eralas's borders, he will return when they open."

Rae motioned to the home. "Would you like to come inside?"

Kalstacia lifted a hand with a polite smile. "I don't want to interrupt your day longer than necessary. I merely wanted to say thank you. For what you did for Amarie. Her mind has clearly been unstable and I fear what might have happened had you not been there."

Rae glanced at Corin. "Amarie is important, but she's also my friend. I'm glad she's finally found some peace."

"If it is not too much to ask... and you are still on the island when it occurs, I would appreciate it if you met my brother. It would be good for him to know the state of Amarie these past few months."

Corin lifted an eyebrow. "You want your brother to know she was mentally unstable?"

Kalstacia nodded. "I believe it will be important in some decisions he needs to make in his own life. He must face the consequences his choices had on the woman he loves."

"That's some sisterly love..." Corin chuckled.

Rae scowled at Corin. "You mind?" She looked at the auer. "If I get word of his arrival prior to our departure, I'd be happy to. Where would I find him?"

Kalstacia produced a piece of paper from a pocket on her dress and held it out to her. "Directions to my home. I suspect he will go there after he arrives. I will send word."

Rae took the paper and nodded, watching the woman leave before looking at Corin. "When you royally screwed up your relationship with Jarrod, didn't I tell you? That's what sisterly love is."

Corin pursed his lips. "Fair. So I guess this Talon fella screwed up?"

"Yep. He promised to meet her on the mainland and never showed. Left her and didn't even have the guts to tell her."

"What a dick."

Chapter 19

One month later...
Summer, 2612 R.T.

RAE SHOVED THE PIECE OF parchment with Kalstacia's address into the pocket of her altered breeches. They hugged her legs, looser at the midsection to accommodate the bump that hadn't stopped growing. She touched her abdomen.

How much bigger am I going to get?

She approached the home on horseback, admiring the twin pomegranate trees framing the entry walkway.

The barrier around Eralas dissipated a week prior, and they'd been loading the carriages with their supplies when word came of Talon's arrival on the island.

Jarrod and the rest of the council would be on their way to Ny'Thalus already, but she could catch up on horseback after talking to Talon.

Sliding off her horse, she looped the reins over a branch and stepped onto the property.

Talon and Kalstacia sat on their porch and the distraught expression on the man's face softened her instinct to dislike him. She ran a hand over her braided hair, tugging her ponytail to tighten it.

When the two auer's gazes met hers, she swallowed. "I was hoping I could speak with Talon a moment."

Talon straightened, green eyes narrowing as he wiped a tear from his face. His dark hair matched his sister's, pulled into a ponytail at the nape of his neck. "And you are?"

"I'm the Mira'wyld. Amarie knew me as Mira. I was with her..."

He stood, as tall as Jarrod, but not as broad-shouldered. "You were the one who built the bridge of ice. The reason Amarie escaped him."

Rae nodded. "I wish I could've prevented the whole thing. I didn't know what she was planning." She looked down, holding back what she wanted to say about Amarie being in danger because of him.

"Even if you'd known, I doubt there was anything you could've done to stop her."

Kalstacia stood and smoothed out her dress. "I'll put some tea on." She disappeared into the house.

"What did you want to talk about?" Talon leaned on the railing.

Rae approached, keeping her hands in her back pockets. Her loose tunic hid the growth of her stomach. "I heard about her decision to enter Slumber. I thought I might be able to provide you with some peace with the surely unsettling news."

"Peace? What peace can you possibly offer?" His tone was strained.

Rae forced a smile. "I've experienced Slumber myself."

Talon narrowed his eyes. "And? What comfort is that?"

"People talk of endless nightmares, but there aren't any. It's rather restful and calm. And I regained my memories."

"How?"

"While our people are capable, they aren't the only ones. I encourage you to remember that she considered Slumber a gift."

Talon motioned with his chin. "Would you like to come in for tea? I'd like to ask you for more details about your time together."

Rae climbed the stairs of their porch and nodded. "Of course."

Talon held the door open for her as they crossed into the front room of the two-story home. It was larger than most of the auer structures around, but still followed the traditional styles of building. The interior boasted the warm natural colors of the trees that formed it, narrow windows allowing the sun to brighten the space. The scent of fruit tree blossoms wafted inside.

"My name is Rae. Raeynna Lanoret." She returned the nod from Kalstacia. "I met Amarie in Jacoby. Despite everything, she agreed to help me, and we became friends."

Talon's frown deepened as he took a seat on a couch in front of an unlit fireplace. Tugging on his dark grey tunic, he stared at the bottom of it for a moment. "I'm sorry. The news of Amarie's choice is still fresh, and I'm struggling to comprehend any of this. But I'm glad she had someone with her through this. I'm glad she had you."

With a gesture from Kalstacia, Rae sat in a chair opposite Talon and took the offered mug of tea. "Honestly, I am, too. She was a mess, more so than I'd expect from losing her lover." She tilted her head. "I don't know everything that happened to her, but she was reckless. And, believe me, coming from *me*, that says a lot. Do you know what that shadow beast was?"

Talon's mouth flattened into a line. "A monster that I'm not sure you'd believe if you hadn't been chased by it yourself. I'm not sure how much I should share, because the knowledge itself is dangerous." With a grim smile, he accepted a mug of tea from his sister before she joined them.

If he is friends with Kin, maybe he knows. But which side is he on?

Rae held his gaze. "And do you follow that monster?"

Talon shook his head, resting his tea in his lap. "Never. But I know plenty about him through my friends..." He glanced at Kalstacia. "And our sister."

Rae furrowed her brow. "Your sister is involved with Uriel?"

Talon's chin lifted, and he met Rae's eyes. "You know its name, suggesting you know full well what the beast was. Why ask me, then?"

"I thought the council didn't know anything about what attacked the island." Kalstacia settled her cup onto a table next to where she sat with her brother.

Rolling her lips together, Rae shrugged. "Talon is right when he says the knowledge is dangerous, and I didn't want to burden you with it. The council knows nothing. Amarie summoned him, intentionally. She wanted to kill him."

"That much, I had guessed." Talon chewed his lower lip. "And I can probably guess how. I suppose she had her reasons. But it doesn't make any of this easier."

"Tell us more about Amarie." Kalstacia touched her brother's knee.

"She had her moments of happiness during our journey, but I'm not surprised she requested Slumber. Her choice doesn't plague me. I understand. She was in pain, and I don't mean physically. Between losing Kin and then you..." Rae swallowed. "I suspect she needed to rest. Heal in a different way. It's only temporary."

"Only if the council doesn't decide she's more convenient without memories," Talon grumbled.

Rae shook her head. "The council decided I was more convenient without my memories, too, yet... Here I am, me again."

"And how did that happen, exactly? You mentioned another way, but I've never heard of it. Though Slumber has many secrets to it apparently, if it doesn't hold the side effects our council likes to advertise." Talon toyed with the mug in his lap.

Rae smiled. "I can't tell you how because I wasn't the one who did it, but I can tell you that the same option will be made available for Amarie."

Kalstacia narrowed her eyes. "You're being cryptic, which suggests you have things to hide."

Rae straightened, lifting her chin.

"Speaking of, I am curious why you felt it necessary to use an alias while with Amarie."

Damn it.

Setting her mug down, Rae debated how much she could tell them. "My real name is well known in Helgath, and I didn't want to draw extra attention for obvious reasons."

Talon put a hand on his sister's. "She doesn't deserve us questioning her when she chose to come speak to me. Besides, perhaps Amarie is better without the memories. I wouldn't blame her for desiring that particular side effect. She's experienced plenty that anyone would want to forget." He met Rae's gaze. "Thank you. For coming."

Rae nodded. "Even with everything, she spoke highly of who you are as a person. She said something once that didn't make much sense to me. She said... *His family is still his family, blood or not.* Does that mean anything to you?"

Talon's body tightened, his gaze dropping. "I think so."

Andi's eyes widened as Rae ascended the gangplank, gaze trained on her abdomen. "Whoa. Tell me you've just been eating too many pastries."

Jarrod passed them, Neco on one side and Corin on the other. He squeezed the ship captain's shoulder as he passed, chuckling under his breath.

Damien took his wife's hand. "Well, she *did* eat a lot of pastries, but I don't think—"

Rae smacked him in the chest, scowling. "I had one pastry, thank you very much."

Andi glared at Damien, pursing her lips. "Lanoret couldn't keep it in his pants, I see, even with a *civil war* brewing and you two at the forefront." She huffed, putting a hand on her hip. "Timing could have been better."

The Mira'wyld shrugged. "Perhaps inconvenient, but we're happy." She stopped next to Andi and wiggled her eyebrows. "I'll let you feel him kick later."

Andi eyed her stomach again. "Nothing I ain't felt before." A hint of a smile crossed her lips. "But maybe later, when I get this ship out to sea."

Martox guards funneled onto the ship, carrying the crates full of their supplies. Jarrod and Corin remained on deck, instructing the guards into the cargo holds below.

Neco trotted up behind Andi and pressed his nose into her palm with a lick.

Idly, the captain turned her hand to scratch his ears. "With more of you, accommodations are getting a little tight on this rig. I figure *their majesties* can take my quarters, since I hardly sleep, anyway."

Across the deck, Jarrod looked in their direction and approached. "Let Rae and Damien have the nicer room. That way you two can still have your nightly routine, even if it involves less alcohol."

Andi turned her glower on Jarrod. "How did you even hear..." She rolled her eyes, whipping her long braided hair over her shoulder as she turned with her hands in the air. "I leave it to the royal council to determine where their royal asses sleep. I need to get to work." She left with a final glance at Rae's pregnant belly, shaking her head.

Damien laughed as he wrapped an arm around Rae's waist. "Think she hates me even more now?"

Rae smirked at him. "Considering the last time me and her spoke, you and I weren't in the best of places, I think she's actually kind of happy for us. Can't you tell?"

Damien squinted towards the helm where the captain had headed. "I'll take your word for it."

The rest of the preparations proceeded smoothly, with Keryn stepping in to help load the supplies more efficiently through use of a pulley and the wide trap door on the deck. The Herald's crew adapted to Neco's frantic insistence on reintroducing himself to everyone, and the Martox guards helped where they could.

The sails billowed in the sea winds as soon as they dropped into place, the gentle lull of the ocean crashing against the Heralds' hull bringing a sense of peace over everyone as they settled into their quarters for the late afternoon.

Damien helped Rae with her boots, while she sat back on the four-poster bed in Andi's quarters. He grunted while he pulled the second one off.

"You do realize I can still reach those myself, right?"

"I like doing things for you, and this is just one thing I can." He knelt and rubbed the bottom of her foot with both hands. "Generally, you don't complain."

Rae smiled and laid back on the bed. "Not complaining. We established early in our relationship that I enjoy foot rubs."

"You mean because you enjoyed one from a bounty hunter while I was sitting in a jail cell?"

"Precisely." She sat up on her elbows and smiled at her husband. "Don't worry, your hands are much better."

Damien chuckled, switching to her other foot. "I feel remarkably validated now. Thank you." Sunlight from the windows at the back of Andi's quarters made his hair golden as he shifted between her legs and leaned up to kiss her swollen belly. Running his hands over her tunic to accentuate the bump, pale blue light flickered on his fingertips.

"Are you trying to communicate with our little Rahn'ka baby?" Rae quirked an eyebrow.

"I do talk to grass, so this feels slightly less ridiculous." Damien looked up at her as Bellamy kicked against his palm. "I still can't believe the guardians didn't mention anything to me about being able to father more Rahn'ka. You'd think they'd be eager to have more."

Someone rapped on the door.

Rae sat up. "That's probably Andi. What are you going to do while we catch up?"

Damien rocked back onto his heels and stood. "Don't worry about me, I promise I'll stay out of trouble." He leaned, giving her a soft kiss. "I'll be back in a few hours." He crossed the room, opening the door wide for Andi, who nodded at him as she stepped inside.

"Sticking around for girls' night?" She eyed the Rahn'ka.

Damien lifted his hands. "Who am I to interrupt tradition? I'm out of your hair for a few hours, but hopefully you don't mind if I choose somewhere other than the *brig* to spend my time."

"Some days, I'm just looking for an excuse, Lanoret." Andi gave him a wry smile. "Don't fall overboard or anything."

Damien laughed. "Have fun, you two." He walked backward out of the room, pulling the door shut behind him.

Andi let out a long sigh as she crossed towards the two overstuffed armchairs she and Rae usually sat in. Her rapier tapped at her side before she unfastened the buckles and tossed it onto a wide table pushed against her bookshelves. Kneeling at the little table between the chairs, she opened a wooden cabinet on it. She withdrew a bottle of amber liquor and set it alongside two glasses on the tabletop.

Rae rose from the bed, picking up her own bottle from the floor before joining her friend and taking a seat. "I brought something from Quel'Nian. You're welcome to it, but I doubt you'll like it."

"Fancy auer booze?" Andi lifted an eyebrow.

"Not exactly." Rae pulled the cork off the top and poured one glass half-full. Bubbles clung to the sides of the glass and she put the bottle down. "They call it guaritho. It won't get you drunk, but it tastes good."

Andi eyed the glass and picked it up to sniff, wrinkling her nose. "Gods, what the hells is that?" She quickly put the glass back down. "No, thank you." She uncorked her bottle, the smell of whisky drifting from it before she poured her glass.

Rae laughed and took a sip of the sweetly sour drink. "I'll return to whisky once I'm only drinking for one again."

Andi settled into her chair, casting a wary glance at Rae's stomach. "Little monster's already telling you what you can't drink, huh?" She took a long gulp of her whisky, wincing as it hit the back of her throat.

"Apparently." Rae settled back in her chair, crossing her legs in front of her. "How has working for Jarrod been? I saw the flag."

Andi scowled. "Money's good. Boring as hell. Bastard convinced me to fly his fucking flag. Pride aside, I suppose it's good *honest* work." She scrunched her nose. "Getting stuck in port in the middle of spring, though..."

"At least he's paying you well."

"Got some solid repairs in, too. So, arguably, the Herald is in the best shape she's been in a long time."

Rae grinned. "Look at you, seeing the silver lining."

Andi laughed and shook her head. "I have complete confidence that a Martox and a pair of Lanorets onboard will see to her being restored to her battle-scarred self within days."

"I hope you're wrong. I've had enough excitement for now."

Andi lifted a finger as she swallowed. "I was in Oso'Pae, on the opposite side of the island, getting repairs when the shadow thing filled the sky. Jarrod was wonderfully vague when I sent word asking what the hells was going on. But I got enough to know it came at the same time you arrived on the island. Care to share?"

Rae shuddered. "The shadow beast chased me across the strait. I've never been so terrified." She set her glass down and filled Andi in on her journey with Amarie. Leaving nothing out, she spilled the details of Uriel and Kin, and how it related to the Rahn'ka imprisonment spell. She told Andi about Damien's power and Jarrod's bond with Neco, weight lifting off her chest with the revelation of each secret.

Andi poured the last bit of whisky from her bottle into her glass, frowning. "I need more." She leaned over to dig another from the cabinet, her eyes distant. "No wonder Damien was distracted last time I saw you. That's a lot to be carrying on those shoulders, no matter how muscled they are. And you..." She shook her head. "Dealing with all that, and now this..." She gestured at Rae's pregnant belly.

"Oh, and I should also mention, apparently..." Rae lifted her hands. "I'm part alcan."

Andi lifted an eyebrow, grunting. "Well, that accounts for you not drowning." She downed what remained in her glass before uncorking a new bottle. "I had wondered when I fished you out of the water after you sank that Helgathian ship. But I thought you were part auer."

"I am. A quarter auer, alcan, and half human. I can't believe my father never told me. I have no idea if it was him who had alcan blood or my mother."

"Alcans sleeping with humans is pretty rare, so I'd say you and I are some extreme cases. They like to stay under water even if they can live on land. Course, my father did little more than impregnate my mother before never coming back. At least you had your parents for a bit, even if your mother was a raving bitch."

Rae laughed. "True. Just, I wish he'd told me. I haven't seen him in so many years."

"Where is he now? Maybe after all this you could see him."

"I don't know. Wouldn't be too hard to find, I suppose. His name is rather... unique on the mainlands. Zeran Keenshaw'lian."

Glass clattered as Andi dropped the whisky mid-pour, sending liquor pooling across the table and then the floor as the bottle rolled off the table. "Shit." Andi leaned to grab it, nearly taking the chair with her.

Rae snatched the bottle off the floor and braced Andi's chair with her foot. "Are you all right?"

Andi met her eyes, but then quickly tore them away as she stood. Her steps were wobbly as she circled towards the back windows.

Standing, Rae put the bottle on the table and replaced the cork. "Andi?"

The captain pushed open one of the windows, the scent of the sea rising with a breeze as she leaned against the window frame. Her shoulders rose in a deep breath, but she shook her head. "Zeran." The name sounded strained. "Your father. His name is Zeran?"

"Yes." Rae stepped closer to the captain. "Do you know him?"

Andi rolled her shoulders and stood up. "I need to check the helm." She spun, her steps more sure than they should have been for the amount she'd drank. Snatching her rapier from the table as she walked past, she tore the door open.

"You're checking the helm *now*?" Rae followed the captain out of her quarters.

How does she know my parents?

Andi didn't stop, climbing the stairs along the side of the ship beside her quarter's doors. She staggered midway, but gripped the railing with determination and continued.

The sky had darkened with a summer storm, the sun peeking through as it descended to the horizon, painting fields of purple and orange. The decks shimmered with a thin sheen of water, as if it'd rained while they were inside talking.

"Andi!" Rae stepped onto the deck, mind whirling. "Why won't you talk to me?"

The captain paused, glancing back. "When were you born?"

Why is that relevant?

"Spring, 2588."

Andi turned before Rae could clearly see her face again and started back up the stairs.

The Mira'wyld followed to the bottom of the stairs. "Andi! What are you hiding?"

"What's going on?" Damien emerged from the other side of the ship. He looked up towards Andi, then to Rae. "Everything all right?"

"No, it's not all right." Rae glanced at him before climbing the stairs to the helm. Her heart pounded as Jarrod and Corin joined Damien on deck. She stopped, staring at her friend. "You can't keep running away from me. There aren't many places to go. You know my father? Did you know my mother was half alcan?"

Andi's boots thudded on the deck, and she jerked her head at the helmsman. "Go get some grub. I'll take the helm."

The red-headed crewman nodded, casting a confused look at Rae before he hustled down the stairs.

Andi glanced at Rae before she ran her hand lovingly over the ship's wheel. "I took command of the Herald in the year 2588."

"And?" Rae approached, rain starting up again.

"I earned it. Worked hard for it." Andi glanced at the sky, raindrops dappling her tanned cheeks. "Proved to the previous captain that not only a woman, but a pregnant one, could command. He'd doubted me, of course... but I was determined and I won her in the end." She stroked the polished wood again.

A pregnant one?

Rae swallowed, heat building in her face. "Why are you telling me this?"

"Because I chose the sea. I chose it over the chance at a family with a man I loved." Andi chewed her bottom lip. "I didn't keep her. I'd worked too hard and took command of this ship instead. Zeran wanted to raise her... It was better that way. I wasn't meant to be a mother."

"No. You can't be." Rae shook her head. "My parents raised me in Ashdale. My mother..." She gulped, her head spinning so fiercely she grabbed for the banister but found Damien's arm instead to steady her. "My mother wasn't my mother?"

"She raised you. She's your mother. Not me." Andi met her eyes, hers glassy. "I thought about my little girl a lot, but over time... I thought it better she never know. But now..."

"She was awful to me!" Rae sucked in a breath through clenched teeth and turned away, squeezing Damien's arm before returning her gaze to the woman she thought she knew.

"Your father hadn't met her yet when I left." Andi gritted her jaw, her knuckles whitening on the handles of the helm.

"But that wouldn't have mattered, anyway, would it? What would you have done with me, had Zeran not been there? Dropped me in the sea?" Bile rose in her throat and she tugged on her husband's arm. "I can't be here. Take me somewhere else, please."

"Rae." Andi stepped forward, one hand still on the ship's wheel. "That's not..."

Damien squeezed Rae's arm, touching her cheek. "Let's go back to the room. Whatever you need."

Rae glared at Andi. "Stop at the next port. I want off your *beloved* ship."

Andi stared at her for a moment before she faced the helm. With a single solid shove, she sent the wheel spinning, turning towards the dark shape of Helgath's coast. "As you wish."

Chapter 20

JARROD LOOKED SIDEWAYS AT CORIN. "I didn't see that one coming."

Rae and Damien descended the stairs into the captain's quarters, doors clicking closed.

Corin frowned. "What the hells just happened?" He watched the horizon as the ship made a sharp turn towards land.

"Looks like we're stopping in Edrikston." Jarrod eyed the drunk captain at the helm. "I should talk to her."

Corin's brow furrowed. "Rae looked pissed. What'd Andi do?"

"Andi is her real mother."

"Fuck."

Jarrod nodded. "Fuck, indeed." He glanced at his husband. "Mind checking on her while I see what's going on in Andi's head?"

"Good luck." Corin gave Jarrod a quick kiss on the cheek before he crossed towards the captain's quarters.

The proxiet climbed the stairs to the helm, pausing at the top to lean on the front railing. He kept his mouth shut, studying Andi.

"Don't tell me you didn't hear all that, what with your wolfish hearing and all. Rather you not insult my intelligence, your majesty."

Rae must have told her.

Jarrod frowned. "Are you pissed at me because I didn't tell you or is something else bothering you, *Captain*?"

Andi glowered at him before she turned her eyes back to the coastline. She pursed her lips and shook her head. "Go meet Nymaera."

"No need for hostility. We're friends, no?"

Andi didn't change her expression or focus, but her shoulders relaxed minutely. "What do you want, Jarrod?"

"To see if you're all right. You're drunk at the helm and just had a bit of a blowout with your... dare I say... daughter?"

Gods, that's a fucked up concept.

"Ain't my daughter. I wasn't there. And ain't nothing to crash into. I'm fine."

Jarrod hummed and stood from the banister, walking closer. "She'll come around. I can't possibly believe you're ready to let her leave at the next port."

"Her choice. I'm not about to tell her what she can and can't do." Her face sobered. "Ain't her mother."

"Look, I've known you even longer than I've known Rae. This could be a good thing, if you let it. If you both let it."

"I'm incredibly interested in how you figure that?" Andi glanced at him. "Rae's angry, and rightfully so. I left her. I chose a ship over my child. And that decision's haunted me for years, but I've coped with it. Can't change what I did now. Rae has to grapple with the truth, but I can't tell her how to do it."

"Would you change it, if you could?"

Andi bit her lip. "You mean, knowing now the woman my daughter was going to become? Would I still pick the ship over her?"

"I mean, before you knew it was Rae, did you regret the choice you made?"

"Every damn day. But it was always too late to change anything."

Jarrod smiled. "And now that you know it's Rae?"

"It's like tearing open old scars that I finally almost forgot about. But when she said her father's name..." Andi hastily wiped away the tear that fell from one eye. "Fuck. I shouldn't have even told her. Damn booze got me all blubbery."

Chuckling, Jarrod put a hand on the wheel and pulled Andi into a one-armed hug, resting his chin on the top of her hair. "You made the best choice you could at the time. Rae will come to understand that."

"I was never meant to be a mother." Andi, surprisingly, didn't pull away. Instead, she relaxed into Jarrod's hold. "But now all I can think about is holding that baby girl." Her shoulders trembled as she heaved in a breath.

"That baby girl is about to have a baby boy. Your grandson."

Andi smacked his chest. "Don't make me feel old." She sniffled.

Jarrod laughed. "I'm not telling you that you're old. I'm telling you that you have a family, whether or not you like it. They may not know it, but they need you."

"Too bad I didn't know it before I could sway her from a Lanoret." Andi chuckled, swiping her hand across her face again as she pushed from Jarrod. Her jaw flexed. "I ain't turning this boat away from Edrikston though, not until she tells me to."

Jarrod nodded. "I understand. But I think she might surprise you..." He narrowed his eyes at the horizon, plumes of smoke rising from the port town they were destined for.

The Helgathian coast dipped into rocky beaches and low cliffs near Edrikston. The green fields behind it, which Jarrod expected to be full of livestock, were empty. The smell of burning flesh caught on the sea breeze, and Jarrod wrinkled his nose.

Walking around Andi, he plucked the spyglass secured to the helm and lifted it to one eye. "Something's wrong." He offered the device to Andi. "Make port as quickly as you can. I need to talk to Damien."

Did Uriel attack another village?

Jarrod paused at the bottom of the stairs, meeting Andi's gaze as she lowered the spyglass. "Rae will come around. Try to be patient."

Andi scowled, but jerked her head towards the stairs. "Go do your king thing. I'll get us to shore."

The proxiet descended the rest of the stairs to the main deck, searching for Damien with his connection to Neco. *We have trouble. Where are you?*

Trying to make sure my wife doesn't jump overboard to swim to shore. Damien's tone sounded irritated, even in Jarrod's mind. *What else could possibly be going wrong? Andi kicking us all off?*

Jarrod clenched his jaw. *Edrikston looks like it's burning.*

Shit. Damien's presence disappeared from their usual connection, forcing Jarrod to wait near the center mast, sidestepping out of the way as one of the crew adjusted the sails for the course change. Shouts rang across the deck. The crew emerged from below and the ship's bell tolled twice.

The floorboards inside the captain's quarters behind Jarrod squeaked, prompting him to turn towards the sound. One door opened just enough for Damien to slip out before he closed it, his eyes already on the coastline.

"It doesn't look like Uriel's work." Jarrod nodded at the smoke-choked air over the small port town. "Can you tell what's going on?"

The Rahn'ka glanced at him, but walked past to the banister, leaning out even though his senses shouldn't have required line of sight. His shoulders rose with a deep breath as Jarrod walked beside him, studying his face for any reaction.

Closing his eyes, Damien's head tilted slightly in his focus. A frown twitched beneath his trimmed beard. "This wasn't Uriel. It's... something else. Death, but mostly not human." His eyes fluttered open, squinting to the fires dotting the beach.

They'd grown close enough to see a pair of men, cloths tied around their nose and mouth, heaving the limp body of a sheep onto the pile of charred carcasses with fire twisted limbs.

Corin walked to the banister, stopping next to Jarrod. "What's going on there?"

"They're burning their livestock." Unease fluttered in Jarrod's gut.

"Plague." Damien leaned back. "Think it's Cerquel's? Doesn't that go for the livestock first?"

Jarrod looked at the Rahn'ka. "Are you able to heal the plague?"

"Did you just say plague?" Keryn, Andi's first mate, halted behind them and Jarrod cringed as she hollered at the captain. "Turn her about! We can't make land here!" Before anyone could say anything, Keryn stomped towards Andi, her stern features turned ashen.

"Dame. Can you?"

Damien shook his head. "I... I think so? I've never tried. But in theory..."

"This isn't something we should play with theory on." Corin touched Jarrod's wrist. "It's too big of a risk, even if they need help."

"Let me go ashore." Maithalik's voice made Jarrod jump.

The proxiet spun to face the auer with narrowed eyes. "You walk with exceptional stealth."

Maith chuckled. "Why, thank you. I also breathe with immunity to the plague, and can play the role of the ship's ambassador."

The ship listed to the side as Keryn took the helm from Andi, and the crew shouted as the sails swelled in another sudden shift.

"So it's true, then, that auer are immune to Cerquel's plague?" Corin eyed Maith, who nodded, before he looked back to the shore and pursed his lips. "What's your decision, Jarrod?"

The proxiet huffed. "Maith will go."

Corin nodded and sprinted towards the helm. He shouted at Keryn, who glared, his voice lost in the whipping of ropes and linen in the wind. The two exchanged indistinct words, Keryn's face flushing with anger as she argued.

Andi dropped the eyeglass she stared at the shore through and spoke quickly to Keryn, who shook her head. Rolling her eyes, the captain stepped forward. "Drop anchor. Now!" Her voice rang out over the deck, drawing the attention of the crew.

"Belay that!" Keryn grabbed Andi's shoulder, whispering to her.

Jarrod focused to catch the exchange between them.

"Even stopping offshore, we're putting this entire ship at risk. You're willing to do that for Helgath?"

Andi glared at her, shaking her shoulder free. "I've never known you to let your fear stop you from doing what's necessary." She straightened, any sign of her drinking cleared from her sharp blue eyes. "Pull yourself together. And don't you dare defy an order I give on my ship again."

Keryn's eyes hardened. "Your sympathies are going to get the lot of us killed. Maybe not today, but it'll happen."

"Captain?" The bosun shouted from where he aided in hoisting a sail with several crew members, fighting against the pull of the wind.

"Drop the gods damned anchor!" Andi snapped, waving her hand at Keryn, who stormed down the stairs towards the hold below deck. The order repeated from the mouths of the bosun and crew around him. The ropes pulled the sails up towards the beams supporting them, and a loud splash sounded as the iron anchor dropped on the port side.

Andi stalked down the stairs, flipping her chestnut braid over her shoulder. Lingering anger echoed in her face, and she jutted a finger at Corin. "Hope you know what you're doing, your *majesty*." She glared at Jarrod before following her first mate below deck.

Corin turned to the bosun, with no other commanding officer on deck. He ran a hand through his golden hair with a perturbed sigh. "Get us a dinghy in the water."

"Sir." The man nodded, shoving his stained white sleeves up his tattooed arms as he commanded a pair of crew into action.

"We need to know what's going on, so gather whatever information you can get." Damien turned his attention to Maith as Corin rejoined them. "In these kinds of situations, it's supposed to be city militia taking care of the bodies, but those are farmers." He gestured towards the men on the beach who'd paused in their work to watch the galleon, their ash stained hands shielding their eyes.

Maith rowed to shore, alone in the dinghy. The two farmers who'd been fueling the fires greeted him at the beach, where he stepped onto the rocky shore.

"I'll let Rae know what's going on." Damien moved towards the steps to the captain's quarters. "Come get me when Maith gets back?"

Corin nodded, then turned his worried eyes on Jarrod. "We'll do what we can, but there might not be much."

Jarrod sighed and leaned against the railing, facing his husband. "I know. But I have to try."

A small smile crossed Corin's face, and he slipped his hand into Jarrod's. "You've changed so much since that meadow in Olsa. Though, in a way, you haven't changed at all. Just... accepted who you are and what you can do a bit more, I suppose."

The proxiet gave him a playful frown. "You like being right, don't you?"

"I mean, who doesn't?"

Jarrod laughed, touching Corin's chin. "I'm glad I listened to you... eventually."

Corin held his hand, and they stood in quiet together as they watched the shoreline, the fires consuming the town's livestock growing as more were added.

When the auer returned to his dinghy and dipped the oars into the water, Jarrod found his connection to Damien. *Maith is on his way back.*

Corin straightened, standing from where he leaned against the banister. "Let's hope for good news. I think we deserve some." He walked to help the crew hoisting the dinghy back up out of the water, bringing Maith with it.

With perfect grace, the auer hopped from the boat as it leveled with the deck of the ship, balancing on the top of the banister for a moment before he dropped without much sound. His amethyst eyes met Jarrod's as Damien joined them, a grim look on his face. "The conditions of the town are dismal, though not because of illness. It's affected only the livestock, and none of the humans appear to have contracted it. I suspect it to be contained within the animals, not Cerquel's as we feared."

Damien heaved a relieved sigh, and the crew around them started whispering and spreading the news. The palpable tension Jarrod had sensed growing across the ship eased.

Corin's features remained skeptical. "But why are farmers dealing with the bonfires?"

Maith scowled. "Because the city guards left. They took what remained in the town's food stores and abandoned them. The people are starving with no grain or livestock to sustain them. Iedrus has offered no aid, though the mayor says he sent word to the capital weeks ago."

Jarrod growled, looking at Corin. "Can you organize the rebels to send support and supplies to help these people?"

"We can, but not from here. Better to do it from Lazuli. Could send a hawk, but we can get there just as fast on the

Herald." Corin shook his head. "Iedrus is stockpiling and stealing from his own people to do it."

Damien's fist thudded on the banister. "Fucking Iedrus. These people won't last long without something now. I'll go find Andi. We can spare some of the ship's stores." He descended below deck, where Keryn and Andi had disappeared earlier.

Maith gave a nod to Jarrod. "I'll be in my quarters should you require further assistance."

Corin took Jarrod's hand, lifting it to kiss his knuckles with a sigh of relief. "This is something we can certainly handle. And Iedrus is only further proving he's too selfish to rule our country as anything but a tyrant."

"He's panicking, stealing from small towns." Jarrod chewed his lip before meeting Corin's gaze. "We've got him worried."

Jarrod sat at the desk in the guest quarters, jotting down everything he could think of that his father needed to know so they could send aid to Edrikston without further delays. After sharing the information with the rebels, they could check in on other villages likely abandoned by King Iedrus.

Morning sunlight shone through the porthole window, creating a spotlight on the wall behind him. He'd felt the ship thump against his family's private dock, but needed to finish getting his thoughts onto paper.

Breathing deeply, he frowned.

The scent of burning lingered in his nostrils, stuck there since Edrikston.

Neco whined, his tail thumping on the floor, and the wolf's complaint echoed in Jarrod's head. *I want to run.*

"I know, boy. Not long now." He patted the beast's head and started on the next piece of parchment.

Someone's coming. Neco's head spun towards the door, ears pricking to attention before his tongue lolled out the side of his maw. *Damien.*

A soft knock came before the Rahn'ka's voice. "Jare?"

I thought Damien would have already gone into the castle.

"Come in."

The door swung open, and Damien hesitated in the doorway. His face looked pale.

Jarrod's stomach twisted. "What's wrong?"

A waft of smoke touched his senses again, tainted with the acrid scent of scorched flesh and pines.

There were no pines in Edrikston.

Damien swallowed, shaking his head. "You... need to come see yourself. It's... the castle..."

Rising, Jarrod stalked towards the door as dread built in his chest. "What's wrong with the castle?" He walked past Damien, climbing the stairs to the deck where Corin stood waiting.

"Jarrod." Corin's pale complexion mirrored his brother's. Turning from the guard he'd been directing, he took Jarrod's hand. "This..."

Whatever his husband said after fell on deaf ears as Jarrod's gaze landed on the remnants of his home. His heart thundered as he stepped to the side of the ship, taking in the rubble marring the once lush hillside. Black and white brick formed heaps of destruction, the lake dark with ash. The walls surrounding the front drive had collapsed, revealing the onyx skeletons of the castle's trees.

Please, no.

Jarrod struggled to breathe, letting go of Corin's hand. He strode to the gangplank, sucking in shaky, shallow gasps. His surroundings blurred, scents clouding his vision in a whirlwind of chaos.

Father?

His heart wrenched as his boot hit the dock. Someone behind him spoke, but he couldn't hear the words. He jogged forward, away from the distant touch to his shoulder, speed increasing until he sprinted over the burned grass.

Figures moved over the rubble, lifting their gazes as he barreled towards the decimated foundation of his family's home. His guards, only some from the ship. They'd already disembarked and begun to comb through the destruction.

Why didn't someone get me sooner?

Misshapen and charred bodies lay in piles beside the lake, a pair of Martox guards carrying another to add.

One guard caught him by the shoulders, mouth moving, but Jarrod didn't understand.

"How long ago?" Jarrod shouted the question, barely able to hear his own voice.

The guard shook his head. "Three days."

The proxiet pushed the man away, running his hands over his hair as he climbed a pile of charred wood and stone to see over the crest. At the top, he took in the vastness of the devastation. Remnants of walls dappled the far side, but everything else lay in ruins. Heaps of stone, cracked and black, followed the outline of his home, marking the familiar hallways and rooms.

A gaping area housed a fallen chandelier, flashing Jarrod's memory back to the ballroom where he fought the wolf in his mind. But when these flames faded, they left the iron twisted and melted into corrupted versions of the elegant decorations.

His muscles shook and gave out, dropping him to his knees in the rubble. Tears burned his eyes as he lowered his gaze. The sun shone on a dirty piece of silver, and he picked up the shattered piece of a Martox crest. He dragged his thumb over the marred surface, clenching his jaw before dropping it.

In the distance, Neco's howl broke through the ringing in his ears.

Someone grabbed his shoulders before blocking his view of the ruins, and he met Corin's bloodshot eyes.

His husband squeezed. "Baby, I'm sorry." The words sounded impossibly far away, like they were trying to burrow through the ash and crumbled stone to reach him. Corin touched his face, smearing his tears.

The dam Jarrod struggled to hold in place broke and he choked on a sob.

Corin embraced him, pulling Jarrod's head against his chest and forcing him to close his eyes.

A yell tore from Jarrod's throat into Corin's shirt, his pulse mingling with his connection to the wolf as he grabbed handfuls of his husband's tunic. His hands shook, his grief and fury rising in another scream into Corin's chest.

His husband's hold tightened, a sob escaping him, too, as they collapsed into the ash together.

Chapter 21

DAMIEN WATCHED AS CORIN AND Jarrod collapsed together to the ground, the proxiet's screams rattling his ká. The voices clawed at his barrier, and he closed his eyes to ensure it held against the assault. He swallowed, his knees weak for more reasons than the horrendous husk of the Martox castle.

He spread his stance, leaning heavily on a crumbled wall that had once been the hallway of the staff's quarters. His head rang with screams beyond Jarrod's, a headache numbing the back of his skull.

Everyone's dead.

Rae wandered ahead of him, a hand over her face as she cried. One of the Martox guards approached her, but they talked too quietly for Damien to hear. She nodded, turning back to Damien as the guard returned to his duty.

Stumbling, Damien sat on the edge of a broken wall and looked up to meet Rae's bloodshot eyes. He ran his hands through his hair, trying to banish the pain through steady breaths. But his mind wouldn't quiet with its questions. "Everyone was here. Reznik, my parents..."

Rae stopped a foot away from Damien, arms crossed as she shook her head. "Your parents left Lazuli for Mirage a few weeks ago. They weren't here. But Reznik..." She choked on a sob and shook her head again. "They found his body."

Relief turned to guilt and Damien looked at Jarrod, who shook in Corin's arms. "I didn't think Iedrus would get this desperate. To blatantly attack like this..."

Rae wrapped her arms around Damien, burying her face in his neck as she trembled. "This wasn't supposed to happen."

He shook his head next to hers. The stone beneath his hand felt hot against his power as he pushed away from it. "With so much death here, I can feel all of it." He winced as the headache mounted.

Rae lifted her head from him and met his gaze with glassy eyes. "If you need to stay on the ship..."

Neco's howl rang out again over the air and Damien looked up to see Jarrod walking towards the guards still working to find potential survivors.

He gritted his teeth. "We need to be here. For Jarrod." He swallowed, taking a breath to funnel more of his ká into the barrier against the voices. "I can handle it."

Rae followed his gaze to the proxiet and pulled Damien with her.

Corin walked beside Jarrod, their hands still entwined as they stepped over the rubble. He glanced back at Rae and Damien, his cheeks wet.

One body lay on a sheet where the rubble had been cleared, covered by a Martox flag.

Corin grabbed Jarrod's arm. "Baby, you sure you want to see?"

Jarrod nodded, his eyes glazed over as he sank to the ground next to the flag. Pulling back the covering, his jaw flexed at the charred corpse beneath.

Nothing was recognizable if it'd once been Reznik, the flesh scorched an angry red and black.

Removing the draping further, he lifted the blackened hand still adorned with his father's ring. Tears streamed down his face, and he cringed. "Dame. Is it him?"

Damien pursed his lips as he stepped forward, a lump forming in his throat. He studied the charred face, trying to determine what he could. Nausea gripped his stomach. "I don't know," he whispered as he knelt.

The proxiet's shoulders shook, and his voice caught. "Can you check? Please?"

Damien's jaw tightened. Checking for remnants of Reznik's ká required parting his barrier to allow his power to flow. Though, the risk of doing so hung like a noose in his mind. Even a temporary break might offer an opportunity to the volatile ká still suffering around him.

Opening the way for those ghosts in Ashdale was almost three years ago. I have better control now.

Damien nodded to Jarrod, flexing his hand to ready his power. Summoning what strength he could from the stone beneath him, he allowed the barest break in his barrier to extend his ká towards the corpse.

The echoes of the lord's ká remained, tangled in confusion with those who'd also died in the castle's destruction, but it'd been too long for Damien to follow his spirit to the Inbetween.

Reznik's soul had already passed beyond into Nymaera's Afterlife.

His headache multiplied, and the Rahn'ka flinched, withdrawing his hand as the searing anger of the echoes lashed through his barrier. They tore at the pinpoint hole, seizing on the weakness of his emotions.

"It's him," Damien choked out. He groaned as he grabbed the back of his head, the world spinning.

"Shit." Rae's voice came next to him. "We need to get Damien away from here."

A chill wind stabbed through the layers of Damien's clothing, and he shivered. Fear gathered in his gut, the voices around him screaming.

"What's wrong?" Corin grabbed under his brother's arm, lifting him to his feet.

Damien's knees gave way, but his brother held him upright. He fought against the barrier, trying to seal the rift pulsing through the air.

No, no, no.

"Get him away!" Rae clutched his arm, pulling him with Corin.

Corin stepped forward, but grunted as the pair stumbled.

Damien hit the ground, sending up a cloud of ash. His back ached and he couldn't breathe, realizing Corin was on top of him.

"What the hells." Corin rolled off, getting to his feet only to be pushed back down again, hissing. An invisible force tore at his tunic.

"Dice," Damien gasped, squinting through the harsh sunlight. "We can't see them."

Beside him, Rae used her forearms to protect her face from an unseen attacker. "I got it." She took a deep breath and ducked to the side. Rolling onto her front, she hit the ground with both hands and a burst of her energy.

Ash and dust lifted into the air with a gust of wind, billowing around them and giving shape to the angry echoes of spirits.

Damien rolled onto his back. The commotion of Rae's burst of power pulled the voices away from his ká long enough for him to seize control. Growling, he snapped his barrier back into place, fighting through the lingering pain. The cluttered air flashed blue as he funneled his ká into his left arm, his tattoo glowing through his shirt. His clenched fist opened enough to accommodate his spear, extending to its full length with merely a thought.

Corin rolled out from underneath his attacker, an indistinct human shape that had pinned him to the ground. He kicked, but his legs passed right through the spirit, and it launched itself at him again. Narrowly missing the pounce, he clambered to his feet. "Why can't I hit it?"

"They're not fully here."

"But they can hit me... That seems hardly fair." He dove out of the way again.

The Rahn'ka markings etched along Damien's spear pulsed as he channeled more into it, shifting the vibration of the Art-crafted weapon to match their attackers' as he had in Ashdale.

Rae jumped to her feet next to Damien and summoned her recurve bow in a similar fashion, activating the tattoo on her forearm through the rings on her left hand. The blue bow shot out of her fist and she lifted it towards her husband. "Fix it so I can hit things."

Damien rolled his eyes. "Always so demanding." He widened his stance as he shifted his attention to his brother. Hefting his spear over his shoulder, he breathed power into his burning muscles and threw the weapon to Corin. It whistled through the air before it collided with the attacking spirit, tearing through the vague outline.

A cry rose like the howl of the wind. The ash swirled around the spear as it protruded from a collapsed stone wall.

Venturing past the spear, Damien's gaze landed on Jarrod.

The proxiet still knelt next to his father's body, eyes glazed over as a spirit gripped him by the neck, its mouth wide in wailing.

Neco snarled and leapt over Jarrod from behind, tackling the angry echo into the ash.

"Neco can hit them." Rae shook her bow in front of Damien's face. "But I still can't!"

"Hold your gods damned horses." Damien snatched the bow, pushing more energy into it before giving it back. It left his body numb, and he collapsed as the headache he thought he'd conquered raged forward like a bull.

A roar erupted, like a maelstrom sucking the air towards the rift between worlds. Shapes shimmered in the clouds of ash, their energies taking on a tinge of red and orange.

Damien struggled to his feet, squinting as pale blue light flooded his vision.

Sindré's voice reverberated in his head. *Our patience has reached its limit, Rahn'ka.*

His back straightened, the pit of his stomach dropping out. "What?"

Rae spun to him, narrowing her eyes. "I didn't say anything."

He shook his head, but the pressure in his skull tripled. Crying out, he doubled over.

Your ineptitude is unforgivable. You will come now.

"No, no, no. Not now. I can't go now." Damien braced himself on his knees, trying to stand upright.

Somewhere in the distance, Jarrod screamed and Neco howled.

Rae reached for Damien, a spirit charging at her from behind. Before she touched him, his surroundings blurred in streaks of blue and white light. His ears rang, pitching to where he thought his head might explode as he clawed at them.

Blinking, everything stopped.

Overwhelming anxiety tangled in his stomach as he straightened. He stood alone in a field of short grass, stretching in every direction as far as he could see.

Each blade glowed with the power of its ká, streams of shimmering blue energy coursing within veins. He looked at the horizon, where the grass met the starless black sky, fathomless above him.

Yondé shook their ruff as they lumbered forward, dominating Damien's vision before he turned from the bear to Sindré. The stag shook too, as if clearing themselves of whatever lingering energy they maintained from the other world.

"Where am I?"

It cannot be defined in such a way. Jalescé's voice made Damien face the draconi guardian. Their lizard maw opened, their tongue flicking with an interested hum. *You are where you were a moment ago, yet nowhere near.*

"No. Put me back." Damien's heart pounded. "This isn't the time for your games. I caused a rift and—"

Precisely why you are here. Sindré stomped a hoof, their voice echoing despite their mouth not moving. *You. And your failures.*

Damien shook his head and closed his eyes to focus his power, seeking whatever streams of ká he could find to follow them back to the others. He sought their energy, but found nothing.

Rae.

"You can't do this! I need to be there to protect them. My wife. My son!"

Yondé grunted. *If you had not failed in your focus, there would be nothing to protect them from. Their deaths would be on your hands, regardless.*

We are pleased with the conception of a new Rahn'ka, but his protection does not take precedence over your need for further learning. Sindré's large navy eyes narrowed. *Your failure to control what we have granted you is a far greater risk.*

"There's more in this world than your grand Rahn'ka plan." Damien spun, glaring at each guardian. "Did it ever occur to you that all the other Rahn'ka failed because they didn't see that? Because they didn't have what I've had through all of this?"

And what is that?

"Friends. Family. You isolated every single one of them with this power and then wonder why they all went crazy." Damien clenched his fists. "Put me back. Now. Or you'll learn just how obstinate I can be."

You forget a vital aspect to your power, Rahn'ka, and should watch your tongue. Yondé's growl echoed beneath their words. *We will put you back, but not as a Rahn'ka.*

"What?"

It's time for the power to go to another. Jalescé hissed. *Conveniently, one of your companions proves promising.* A serpentine smile spread across the guardian's face.

"What? You can't—"

We can. And are. We choose the Rahn'ka. Not you. Good luck, Damien.

Chapter 22

Corin jerked Damien's spear free from where it protruded, looking back at where his brother had stood moments before.

Where in the hells did he go?

His gaze fell to Rae and the shimmering figure advancing behind her. "Rae, watch out!"

The Mira'wyld spun and loosed an arrow into the figure. It disintegrated in a cascade of reflective fragments, like shards of a mirror.

Corin shuffled his grip on his brother's spear to find the balance point as he jumped over the rubble towards Jarrod.

The proxiet remained motionless, hands on his knees with his eyes closed.

Why is he just sitting there?

A spirit charged, its movement exposed by the ash in the air.

Corin slid to a stop beside his husband, swinging the pommel of the spear up at the spirit's head, approximating where its chin would be. Spinning the weapon, a slash of red light bubbled over the spirit before it broke away.

A blue arrow whizzed past Corin's ear, shattering a spirit directly behind the one he'd just downed.

Turning, he caught another shape before Neco plowed into it, tackling it to the ground, fangs flashing as it tore the spirit apart.

Taking the opening, Corin examined the surrounding ruins. The Martox guard who had led them to Reznik's body lay dead, his throat torn. Another sprawled beside him, his condition impossible to read other than his pale face and closed eyes. More looked to be running in from the docks, but a wave of spirits swooped to stop them, forcing the guards to try another route.

"What are these things?" Corin shouted at Rae, looking back to where his brother had been.

Rae hurried over the rubble, protecting a Martox guard as she backed towards Jarrod. "Spirits. Sort of. Echoes of spirits. It's the anger that's left behind. Damien caused a rift." She loosed another arrow before gesturing to the motionless Jarrod. "What's up with him? Jarrod!"

"No idea." Corin circled around his husband to intercept another spirit, Damien's spear coursing with power as it collided with the shape. "More Rahn'ka shit. Where did Damien go?" He turned over his shoulder in time to see Neco pull another spirit away from Rae, granting her the opportunity to bury an arrow in its head.

"No idea." Rae drew back her Art-laden bowstring, and another arrow materialized.

That's ridiculously badass.

They flanked Jarrod, their backs to the proxiet.

The runes on the spear in Corin's hands flashed, and the shaft radiated searing heat. Hissing, he dropped it as Rae did the same with her bow in the corner of his eye. The two weapons never hit the ground. The energy within them exploded like a snowball hitting a rock, seeping into the terrain.

Blue light erupted between him and Rae.

Damien appeared, landing on his knees in the soot. His eyes widened, wildly searching his surroundings as his tattoos blackened.

"So kind of you to join..."

"Jarrod." Damien crawled as he focused on the proxiet, scrambling to get in front of him. He grabbed the man's shoulders, shaking him. "Jarrod. Focus on that barrier I taught you, but expand it. Make it bigger."

"Ignore him and help us fight these. Where's my bow?" Rae flexed her fist repeatedly, but it didn't reappear. "Shit."

Neco lunged past her, shredding a spirit before the last one tackled Corin.

Corin punched at the spirit's side, but his fist passed through without resistance. Cursing, he kicked against the ground to back away, but the veiled attacker's claws raked across his forearm. The three slashes burned as he rolled onto his side.

Snarling, the wolf barreled into the spirit, slamming him off the soldier. They rolled over each other before Neco's fangs found a grip and tore the visage apart.

Damien clapped harder on Jarrod's arms. "Come on, man." He lifted a hand to slap the proxiet, but Jarrod caught his wrist.

The proxiet's eyes snapped open, and he growled, throwing Damien's hand away. "I was busy."

Corin stood, dusting his breeches off as voices rose behind him.

At least the guards are finally coming.

Turning to face them, he saw nothing but ruins. The ash and dust settled towards the ground. The guards in the distance looked to be recovering from a blow that'd put them all on their backs.

Another voice hummed in Corin's ear like a wasp, and he batted near his earlobe.

"Jarrod. Focus your barrier. Use the breathing techniques and imagine that wall. Use it to block the voices." Damien sounded frantic, his voice pitched in concern.

"What voices?" Jarrod's dark tone mixed with the others in Corin's head.

The buzz of the invisible bug doubled, and Corin winced as he grabbed his temple. Shaking his head, it rattled them further. "Do you hear that?" He turned towards Rae. "Are more spirits coming?"

Rae stared at him, tilting her head. "Damien! Whatever you're thinking is happening to Jarrod, I think it's happening to Corin."

Corin frowned. "What's happening to me?" The indecipherable whispers resounded with different pitches and languages he couldn't understand. He met his brother's eyes, squinting through the headache that came with it.

Damien hurried to his feet, pursing his lips. "Fuck. Corin. All right." He grabbed his brother's shoulders, but the grip felt distant, like Corin was floating several feet further back than his body. "Center your thoughts... You—"

Damien's voice drowned beneath the voices, and all Corin could tell was they were yelling. Screaming. He could feel the aggression and it made his heart pound. When he looked at Jarrod approaching, the sensation grew worse and he closed his eyes. An arm encircled his waist, and he opened his eyes to see Jarrod supporting him. "What's happening?"

"We need to get him out of the ruins."

"I think I want out of the ruins..." Corin swallowed to calm his nauseous stomach. He tried to remember what Damien had taught Jarrod when he'd learned to block out the wolf's spirit.

If he could do the same, perhaps it would stop whatever the voices were trying to say.

The walk from the castle's ruins blurred amid the pounding in Corin's head, made possible by the man holding him. Collapsing onto a crate offloaded from the Herald to provide supplies to the guards still searching for survivors, he leaned his head onto his knees. "Gods, my head."

"The headache will stop if you can get a barrier in place to protect your ká." Damien knelt beside him. "You're being overwhelmed and your senses don't know how to sort everything yet. Just breathe."

"*You* just breathe," Corin snapped, wincing.

"Dame, where did you go?" Jarrod's uncharacteristically soft voice mellowed Corin's anger. "Why are your tattoos black and why is my husband experiencing what you usually do?"

"The guardians aren't happy with me." Damien's voice soured. "They're the ones who pulled me away. And they decided I'm not doing a good enough job. They took my power."

Corin blinked, lifting his head to watch his brother's face. "You can't be serious."

Damien sighed. "Congratulations, big brother. You're the Rahn'ka now."

Chapter 23

RAE STOOD WITH THREE MARTOX guards, but she couldn't hear anything they were saying. She stared at Jarrod, still next to Corin near the docks.

I can't even help him.

"Is he adept at healing?"

Rae blinked at the guard who'd asked. "Who?"

He furrowed his brow and motioned to the grey-haired auer who'd busied himself with helping in the dire search for survivors.

"Oh. Maith. No. He can't heal much." Rae shook her head. "The Artisan on the Herald might be able to help with healing."

"Lygen? He returned to the wounded once he finished with Lord Martox's arm."

He must mean Corin.

Looking at the docks again, Rae narrowed her eyes when she didn't see Jarrod anymore, just the Lanoret brothers.

Where did he go?

Rae sighed. "If you need direction, come to one of us instead of Lord Martox." She looked back at Damien, who still knelt next to his brother, the new Rahn'ka. "Nevermind, just come to me."

The guards nodded, and one offered her Reznik's signet ring. "And what of Senior Lord Martox's body?"

Her throat tightened, and she took the gold ring. "Make a pyre separate from the rest. Don't light it yet."

As the guards walked away, they drew Rae's gaze to the remnants of the castle, her eyes lingering on the dark lake.

"My crew is just about finished offloading supplies, then they'll join in the search effort." Andi stepped beside Rae, her azure eyes on the charred castle. She shook her head, putting a hand idly on her hip beside her rapier hilt. "Saw Jarrod headed east along the beach, that wolf of his with him. Don't blame him for needing to get away from all this."

"At least he's not alone." Rae bowed her head, closing her burning eyes for a breath. "His father is dead. They found the body."

"Shit." Andi chewed her lip. "What can I do?"

Rae shook her head, swallowing the lump in her throat. "I don't know." She walked away, running a hand over her braided hair.

I can't deal with all of this right now.

"I'm here..." Andi shouted it from behind her without chasing. "If you'll forgive me. I'm here, now."

Pausing mid-step, Rae turned around. "For what? Drunken nights and the occasional voyage?"

"For whatever you need. I don't see I have much of a right to choose in this. But I don't want to lose what we've had before all this." Andi approached her, but paused a few steps away. "If drunken nights and transport are all you want, I'll respect that. But our friendship is not something I want to lose, and something I figure a mother should have with her daughter."

The lump returned to Rae's throat. "But you said that you're not my mother."

"You're my daughter, even if I didn't raise you. I thought perhaps you wouldn't want a mother who walked away. But like I said before... I'm here now. I don't have a fucking clue what I'm doing, but I'm willing to try to be a mom. For you. But you're the one who gets to decide, not me."

Despite herself, Rae laughed. "How am I supposed to make a choice like that right now? I can't fault you for trying to give me a better life. You didn't know. And now, with all this..."

Her voice caught in her throat, but she forced the words out, anyway. "I need you and you're here, but..." She took a deep breath, trying to steady herself. "I've lost enough. We've all lost enough. I'm just confused. I don't know how to feel."

Andi stepped forward again, squeezing Rae's shoulder. "Day at a time. We'll figure this out. Right now there are other things to focus on, like you said." She looked over Rae's shoulder towards the ruins. "We'll talk more later. Maybe over a drink just like we used to, even if all you bring is that sour shit."

Rae laughed again, and it lightened the weight on her chest. "It's not so bad once you get used to it."

Andi scrunched her nose, smirking. "All yours. But it's time I get my hands dirty in this search, too." She hesitated before pulling her into a firm hug.

Closing her eyes, Rae returned the embrace. She rested her head on Andi's shoulder. "I didn't think you were the hugging type."

"I'm not, so don't get any ideas." Andi tightened her embrace before she let go.

"Too late. Now I'm gonna hug you whenever I want." Rae tilted her head. "Is that a problem?"

Andi laughed and shook her head. "Maybe try to limit how much it happens in front of my crew. Reputation to maintain, you know." She touched the side of Rae's head briefly, running her fingers over her braid. Her smile grew before she cleared her throat and dropped her hand, tugging on the bottom of her corset tunic. Stepping around Rae, she started towards a group of her crew who were coiling rope near the edge of the ruins.

Rae watched her go, touching her braid where Andi had.

Guess we have that in common.

She rolled her lips together, feeling more grounded than she had in days.

"Everything all right?" Damien touched her wrist.

Rae turned her hand to hold Damien's. She looked down at his black tattoos and sighed. The one on her forearm had turned black, as well. "I think it will be. How's Corin?"

"As good as he can be. Still working on a rudimentary barrier, but he got annoyed by my hovering." Damien frowned, following her gaze to his dull tattoos.

"And how are you coping?"

"I don't think it's sunk in yet. I got used to the voices, so now it feels... too quiet? Lonely?"

Her lips twitched in a half-hearted smirk. "I guess I get to protect you from now on."

"I can still fight. Will need to carry a sword again, though." He glanced at his brother. "But this is not what we needed right now. Fucking guardians just don't get it."

Rae nodded, her mind returning to the fight against the spirit echoes. "After you disappeared, Corin and I fought the echoes. Neco did, too."

"What about Jarrod?"

"He sat there, exactly how you found him, the entire time. His eyes closed and everything. Have you ever seen him do that?"

"No, and I guess we can't ask him since he's disappeared."

"Andi said he went east with Neco." Rae's shoulders slumped and she produced Reznik's ring from her pocket. "I'm worried about him."

"He's got a good reason to be messed up right now, and I'm not sure there's anything we can do." Damien touched her pregnant belly, running his hand towards her waist. "I'm just glad you're safe. I was so afraid when the guardians took me, but I should have known you'd be all right."

"I'm fine, but you *did* miss all the action."

He laughed. "Of course. I'd assumed they'd give the power to Jarrod as soon as I got back."

"Why?"

"Jalescé liked him when they met. Said he was a candidate for the power then."

"Oh, right. I remember you telling me the story. Wonder why they chose your brother instead. Maybe because of the wolf bond. Think Corin can power my bow again?"

"Doubt it. It took me months of study under the guardians to figure out how to do it. And I'm a rotten teacher. If I can even get him to put up a barrier, I'll be pleasantly surprised."

Rae smirked. "Something tells me that Yondé once felt similarly about you. Do you think this change is permanent?"

Corin hadn't moved from his position on the crate. He held his head in his hands, shoulders tense.

"I don't know." Damien closed his eyes, lines forming on his brow. "I... hope not."

Chapter 24

JARROD LIFTED HIS MUZZLE AND sniffed the air.

My improved sense of smell still has nothing on Neco's.

He traversed the forest, paws making little sound on the pine-needle laden ground. Looking behind him, he eyed his human form sitting in the middle of his childhood hideout, eyes closed and chest rising in breath.

Thanks for the loaner, bud.

In the back of his mind, Neco grumbled his discomfort at taking the passenger seat in his own body, letting Jarrod's consciousness take the reins.

He raced for the trees, entering the shadows. His ears twitched.

The scurry of a mouse.

A chirping finch.

Ocean waves hitting the beach a mile away.

Picking up speed, he found solace in the escape of running.

As the fight with the spirits escalated, Jarrod had sought the connection with Neco after seeing him tear one apart with his teeth. At first, the intention had been merely to be aware and assist as he could, but after the wolf grew frustrated with Jarrod's questioning, he relinquished control in a way previously unknown to them both.

He'd ask Damien later why the wolf could destroy the spirits when steel couldn't.

But I guess he's not the Rahn'ka anymore.

A familiar scent hit his nose, and he slowed, padding towards the source with a low head.

Corin trod along the worn trail from the beach, making his way with purpose deeper into the woods.

Of course he knows where to find me.

He stood still, watching Corin disappear towards his hideout.

Can't run around as a wolf forever.

Neco huffed. *I wouldn't let you, anyway.*

Jarrod loped after his husband, ignoring the wolf's comment.

Corin turned, facing the underbrush Jarrod hid within, but still jumped as he emerged onto the path. "Gods, Neco. Make more noise. I haven't figured out how to pick your voice out of all this other stuff." He waved his hand around his head, flinching.

Jarrod tried to apologize, but could only make a whining noise.

Corin sighed, scratching behind the wolf's ears.

No wonder Neco likes that.

Jarrod leaned into it, pushing against his husband's legs.

Corin stumbled, adjusting to hold the wolf's weight. "Easy, bud. Where's Jarrod?"

Jarrod sat on his haunches and lifted a paw.

Corin shook his head. "Guess you haven't mastered Common yet, then." He chuckled and ruffled the fur on Jarrod's head. "Let's go. I'm sure he's in his old hideout." He started down the path again, walking in uneven steps like Damien.

Huffing, Jarrod plodded after him, trailing behind until they reached the little clearing. He looked at himself, sitting on the mossy rug by the firepit with his human eyes closed, and dreaded the need to return.

How will anything ever be all right after today?

Corin paused at the edge of the clearing, watching his husband's body for a time. He sighed as he finally took a step forward. "Jarrod?"

Jarrod tried to bark, but Neco overtook his control. *Out.*

Inhaling, the proxiet opened his eyes, glancing at the wolf across the clearing before his gaze trailed to Corin. "I'll step louder next time."

Corin's brow furrowed as he glanced at Neco. "What?"

"I startled you on the path."

"*Neco* startled me on the..." Corin's eyes darted between them. "What?"

Jarrod shrugged. "That was me, not Neco. I borrowed him."

Corin frowned and shook his head. He winced, putting a hand to his forehead. "I didn't know the bond could work like that."

Jarrod let out a deep breath as his husband sat in front of him. "I didn't either until today. Neco has to let me, though." He clenched his jaw. "Have you come to drag me back?"

"No." Corin touched his knee. "I came to check on you. You can stay here as long as you want."

Lowering his gaze, Jarrod twisted the signet ring on his right hand. "I don't know how to move forward," he whispered.

"One step at a time. And I'll be right beside you the whole way."

The image of his charred home assaulted his memory, clouding his nostrils with the scent of scorched flesh and the visage of his father's corpse.

The proxiet cringed and his eyes burned. "I did this. All those people died because of my choices. My father..." His voice cracked, and he made a fist, hitting the ground before lowering his voice. "How can he be gone? We were just here, only a few months ago, talking to him. If I'd stayed in Mirage as a Hawk, this never would've happened. I... I killed him."

Corin touched Jarrod's chin, running his thumb over the old scar. "This isn't your fault. If you'd stayed away, who would stand against a king who would do this to his own people?" Taking the proxiet's hand, their wedding bands pinched in his firm grip. "Your father would never blame you for this. He was happy to have you home and supported your decisions. If you leaving Mirage caused this, then it's my fault, not yours."

Jarrod's shoulders slumped. "He deserved better."

Corin's thumb grazed over Jarrod's skin. "I'm sorry, baby."

Lifting his gaze, he met Corin's. "Iedrus will meet Nymaera for this, even if he steps down."

"All this tells me he never will back down. He's insane and growing more desperate. Between Edrikston and this..." Corin pursed his lips and touched Jarrod's face. Running his hand up his cheek, he brushed it over the proxiet's hair. "We'll see this through, and one way or another, it's almost over."

"You're right." Taking Corin's hand, Jarrod lowered it and tilted his head. "How are the headaches?"

Focus on him, instead.

"Survivable. I'll be fine."

"Damien's methods not working?"

He sighed. "Not really. It's odd, hearing voices that you don't understand. Good thing I'm already good at selectively blocking out things I don't want to hear." He gave a small smile. "Though, some are persistent. I'll have to figure out the barrier, but it can wait."

But it's a decent distraction.

Jarrod nodded. "I have limited experience, but maybe you should let me try to help?"

"I won't complain." Corin pulled Jarrod's hands into his lap.

"Close your eyes. I'll find you the way me and Damien used to talk."

"You think it'll work like that?" Corin peeked through one open eye.

Quirking an eyebrow, the proxiet frowned. "Haven't exactly done this before with you, so I don't know. Close your damn eyes."

Chuckling as he rolled his shoulders, Corin shut his eyes. "All right, all right." A wince echoed across his features.

Jarrod welcomed the darkness behind his eyelids and sought the connection to Neco first. Finding the wolf, he traced the paths through the fabric to Corin's mind. The same way he would speak to Damien mentally, he sent his husband a message. *This, here, is your barrier. This is where you need to build.*

"That's weird."

"Shh."

Corin's voice found its way into Jarrod's mind. *But if I build here, won't it block you out? This could be handy.*

No. Once you learn to find me, you can pass through your barrier. Dame and I communicated in Eralas like this, and the auer were none the wiser.

Sneaky. Corin took a deep breath as his grip tightened. *Damien was remarkably unclear on exactly how to build a wall in my head.*

I had to learn how to keep the wolf in check and control the bond. Jarrod pushed on the haphazardly built barrier Damien must have helped Corin construct. *Do you feel that?*

Corin hissed. *Damn it, don't do that. I worked hard on that, and I don't even know how I did it.*

Sit here with me, without saying anything for a while. Focus on the spot where I pushed and imagine strengthening it.

Jarrod relaxed his body, mentally circling the barrier lit up in blue within Corin's mind. He kept his distance, watching the man's mind lay a shimmering brick onto the layer.

The soldier looked up, watching Jarrod for a moment before he spread mortar onto another brick and studied the uneven wall between them. *I feel like I should just start over.* He put the brick in place.

Don't think of it so literally. These aren't real bricks. Jarrod approached, passing through the barrier to stand with Corin.

It's the only way I can do it. None of this Art stuff makes sense. Corin eyed where Jarrod had passed through the wall, frowning.

It's energy, my love. Move the energy where you want it. The proxiet knelt at an unstable spot and corrected the wall's form with a simple move of his hand. *Bend it and shape it.*

Well, I like my energy in the shape of bricks. Corin put another in place.

There's nothing wrong with that, but you don't need to start over. Jarrod helped straighten another spot before rising, admiring the multitude of tethers sprawling away from Corin's mind. *You're connected to everything.*

Corin's gaze followed his, and he sighed. *Why the hell did those stupid guardians think this was a good idea?* He stepped to the wall, adding another brick. He paused and studied his empty hand before he wiggled his fingers and another brick appeared. When he placed it, he hovered his palm against the wall for a moment before a ripple of power flashed and several bricks fell into place.

Jarrod smiled. *There you go. Do that again.*

Corin repeated the movement and let out a sigh as he stepped back to examine the growing wall. *Getting there. That takes off some pressure.*

When you meditate, come here and build your wall. It's different from mine, but you're definitely on the right track. Now try it without me here. Jarrod retreated from Corin's mind, retracing his route through Neco back to himself. Opening his eyes, he studied the face of the man he loved and swallowed the lump in his throat.

Corin's chest rose with steady breaths, his hands twitching in Jarrod's. They remained like that for several minutes before Corin's warm brown eyes slowly opened. They looked clearer than before. *I think I'm getting the hang of it.* He spoke still in the proxiet's mind as he smiled, and lifted Jarrod's hand to his lips, kissing his knuckles. "Thank you."

Jarrod forced a smile. "I'm glad it helped." Weight returned to his chest, and he looked away, dreading the inevitable return to the estate.

Corin guided his attention back with a gentle pressure on his chin. "I'm here if there's anything I can do," he whispered. "I wish there was something. I'm so sorry, baby."

Breath ached as it filled his lungs. "Can we just stay here a little longer?"

"As long as you want."

Chapter 25

DAMIEN'S MUSCLES ACHED, HIS BODY demanding he take a break despite only performing a fraction of the work he normally could. Growling at himself, he made his way towards the open tent the guards had erected for the injured. He stopped by the barrels of water offloaded from the Herald and downed a mug before taking another to savor longer. His skin felt scorched, the extended exposure to the sun leaving him craving the tent's shade.

The whimpers of the injured escaped through the parted canvas doorway where Lygen worked, yet the air hung oddly silent.

No voices. No pressure on my head.

Damien grumbled, downing the rest of his water before he set the cup aside and walked back into the sunlight. The roar of the ocean waves hitting the beach still didn't help to dull his awareness of the quiet. Marching towards the surf, he pulled his sleeves down to cover the Rahn'ka tattoo that reminded him of his failure.

I wasn't enough.

There weren't many survivors of the attack on the estate, not this long after the collapse. They'd gotten lucky and found three who'd hidden in one of the castle's store cellars. One of the staff was severely injured, and probably wouldn't survive despite Lygen's efforts. All Damien could think about was how easily he could've healed her if he'd still had his power.

Damien unlaced his boots, taking them off to feel the hot sand between his toes. The grains bit into the soles of his feet, but that was all they did. He couldn't sense the lingering power each tiny piece held, or the way it flowed into the next. Or how the sea carried little swirls of energy with each pulse against the sand.

He stared at the horizon, his clenched fist tightening on his boots as the waves soaked the bottom of his breeches.

Rae appeared next to him, wiping blood from her hands. The last he'd seen, she'd been trying to help Lygen with the injured staff member while he went to look for more.

"Did you find her son?"

Damien strained to hear her over the tide and chewed his lip. His chest ached. "Yes." He'd worked with the Herald's crew to pull away the rubble from the place the woman had begged them to check for her child. He had lifted the boy's broken body from the ruins and carried him to the pyres. "He's with Nymaera."

Rae nodded. "Then he's with his mother, at least."

Damien slouched, staring at the waves rushing around his ankles. He swallowed the lump in his throat as he wrapped an arm around Rae and pulled her close, burying his face in her hair. He kissed it, trying to form words that felt so useless. "None of this should be happening."

Rae rested her head on his shoulder, her arms around him. "No, it shouldn't." She sighed, breath quavering. "Have you seen Jarrod return yet?"

"No. Corin insisted he knew where he was and took off." Damien loosened his grip, closing his eyes, the image of Reznik's charred body eliciting a wince. "I can't believe he's gone. That Iedrus did all this." He looked in the direction Jarrod had gone, watching the shattered ruins of the castle. "Reznik deserved better. And Jarrod..."

"I can't imagine how he feels right now." Rae's eyebrows upturned in the middle. "I'm glad he's not alone, though, wherever he went."

"Corin's stubborn. Headaches will stop him about as much as they stopped me." Looking back to his wife, he kissed her hair. "It's probably better they're not here right now. Jarrod doesn't need to see all this. And Corin... I couldn't keep my ká controlled, and it'll be worse for him with all the activity here." Damien sighed, twisting one of Rae's braids around his finger.

Rae nodded. "I agree. What they're already dealing with is more than enough."

"What about you?" He shifted to catch her eye.

"I told the guards to come to me if they need anything, and I think—"

"No, I mean, *how* are you?" His hands slid around her, caressing the top of her pregnant belly.

"Oh." Her shoulders relaxed and her tone softened. "I'm still breathing, so there's that. What about you? I know you said losing your power hadn't sunk in, yet, but..."

"Everything feels so different. I didn't realize how much I tapped into the Art subconsciously until now. Though, I think I could adjust if the timing wasn't so horrible. The deadline is coming fast, and Iedrus obviously isn't afraid to fight dirty to keep the throne. What he did here is a message, and I can't help thinking how exposed we are the longer we stay."

"I know." Rae touched her abdomen. "As soon as Jarrod and Corin get back, we should go. And... maybe your power being gone is temporary?"

Damien placed his hand over hers, wishing he could extend his ká to check on their child. "I used to hate it, but now... I want to be the Rahn'ka again. How am I going to protect you both otherwise? That boy I pulled out of the rubble..."

"We're all right. Bellamy is fine." Rae turned her hand to take his, repositioning it on her stomach. Movement flurried under his palm and she looked up at him. "See? Fine. He won't end up like that boy. No one could've prevented what happened here, not even a Rahn'ka. What's important is that Bell will have his da here for him, power or no power."

Damien nodded, wrapping his arms back around his wife. "At least this way I can learn what not to do while teaching Corin." He kissed Rae's forehead. "How are you so calm?"

Rae laughed without humor. "Between Jarrod's grief, Corin's new struggles with his power, your loss of your power... Someone has to keep their shit together."

Damien chuckled and kissed her again. "That's why you're stronger than all of us."

"Or maybe I'm just—"

"Lady Lanoret!"

Rae jumped and let go of Damien, meeting the gaze of a guard who'd approached. "I told you to call me Rae."

"Apologies, Lady... Rae. There is a group approaching and we're preparing what's left of our defenses."

"Shit." Damien splashed through the surf towards the shore. "I need a sword."

Rae followed him, picking up her boots from the top of the incline where the sand met grass. She pulled them on as the guard offered Damien his sword. "How many?"

"At least a dozen. Maybe more. They're maneuvering through the forest, so it was difficult for our scouts to tell."

"A dozen?" Rae looked at Damien. "That's all?"

Damien shrugged while buckling the sword at his side. "Summoner, maybe?"

"There's no practitioner with them, confirmed by Lord Martox's chief vizier."

Damien withdrew his sword, testing the weight in his palm. "Well, then let's go see who it is."

Rae glanced sideways at Damien before they set off with the guard towards the threat. Several Martox guards joined the escort to the northwestern side of the property.

The fire that'd destroyed the castle hadn't spread to the surrounding forest, leaving the pine trees thick enough to disguise those approaching. A field of dense grass, reaching to Damien's knees, extended in front of them for fifty yards before falling to the shadows of the woods.

"Spread out." Damien gestured to the remaining guards, who lifted crossbows aimed at the tree line. "Wait for my word to fire." They did as he commanded and, for a moment, he felt like a lieutenant again.

A single cloaked figure emerged from the tree line, pausing at the number of weapons pointed their direction. Their hooded face turned until it lined up with Rae's and with deliberately slow movements, they lowered the hood.

Damien sighed. "Stand down." He waved a hand at the guards, their armor clinking as they lowered the crossbows. "They're friends."

Rae's lips twitched in a smile and she hurried towards the leader of the Hawks as more thieves exited the woods. "Sarth." She met the woman for an embrace, and the red-haired thief held onto her while the other Hawks exposed their faces.

Braka met Damien's gaze and gave a solemn nod as he approached. "Good to see you're alive."

"Iedrus has been trying for a different outcome." Damien offered his hand to the large thief, and they exchanged grips before he turned to Sarth. "Not that I'm complaining, but what are you doing here?"

The Hawks merged with the Martox guards, the murmurs of voices carrying over the air as they made their way back to the center of the estate.

Sarth released Rae, eyes lingering on her belly before she looked at Damien with the most empathetic eyes he'd ever seen from her. "We left for Lazuli when we learned Iedrus was advancing, but they had too much of a head start. I heard about what happened here a couple days ago. Word hasn't spread about whether Jarrod's alive and I wanted to come help. Please tell me he lives, too."

"He's alive. We weren't here." Damien glanced at the ruins. "But that doesn't make the whole situation any better."

Sarth closed her eyes, nodding and looking at Rae again. "No, it doesn't. But look at you…" She reached for Rae's midsection but paused. "If I may?" At Rae's nod, Sarth touched her belly, creases appearing at the corners of her eyes as she smiled. "Gods, I was worried about you. And you're pregnant?"

Rae shrugged. "Apparently."

"Some good news amid the wicked." Sarth walked with Rae to Damien, an arm still around her shoulders. "Congratulations. A child is a blessing, even in trying times."

"Kind of expected you to punch me." Damien eyed Sarth, still waiting to see the shift in her body like she would.

Sarth quirked an eyebrow. "Now, why would I do that?"

"Tends to be a logical reaction when you blame someone for something." He shrugged with a smile and offered a hand out to her. "But this is a pleasant alternative. A good surprise with all the bad lately."

Accepting his hand, Sarth squeezed it with a knowing look. "I'm not as heartless as you believe. Leadership has certain requirements."

"So I am learning. And I only ever thought of you as a little cold." Damien's gaze fell to Sarth's crippled leg, crooked as she stood with all her weight on the good one.

He'd intended to heal it, knowing the power of the Rahn'ka would surpass the old attempts by healers, but now she'd have to wait for Corin to have the skill.

"Only when necessary." The leader of the Hawks turned to Rae. "I'd like you all to come home to Mirage. You'll be safe there. The barracks packed up weeks ago, pulling all the military from the city. Iedrus thinks he's blocking our supply carts, but he isn't getting them all. Plus..." She motioned to Damien. "Your parents have been sick with worry and I'm sure they would love to see you."

Rae touched Damien's wrist, and he slid his hand into hers.

"Thank you for keeping them safe. Mirage sounds like the safest place for all of us right now."

Sarth nodded and motioned to Rae. "If you don't mind, I'd like to steal your wife for a short while. We need to catch up."

"You are the master of thieves." Damien grinned as he kissed Rae on the cheek. "I'll see you back at the ship. It'll be the fastest way to Mirage."

As Rae walked away with Sarth's arm still around her shoulder, Damien's gaze wandered and landed on a figure standing alone in the rubble watching Rae.

Andi donned a wide-brimmed hat, looking like the traditional depictions of pirates. The navy feather twitched in the breeze, her posture straight with hands on her hips.

Walking towards her, Damien considered how odd it was that he could so casually approach the woman who now looked the part of a Helgathian war criminal with her boot on the ruins of a Dannet castle. But dirt and ash stained her hands from helping pull bodies from the destruction.

Not to mention she's my wife's mother. Who killed my uncle...

Damien stepped over a ruined wall, and Andi turned her head towards him, though her gaze remained on Sarth and Rae in the distance.

"It's been awhile, but Sarth looks like she's doing well." Andi sniffed, shifting her hips. "Unusual for her to be out of that hideout of hers, though."

"She was worried about Jarrod. Rumor puts us all here in the fire, so she came to check."

"You sure it wasn't for Rae and not Jarrod?" Andi gave a wry smile before she faced Damien, tipping her hat back to meet his eyes. "That king of ours back yet?"

"I have no idea where he is."

Andi lifted an eyebrow. "Then use that funny power of yours to find him. We're not going to find more survivors, and the pyres need to be lit so we can get back to sea. Even though no one has told me where we're going next. Isalica sounds nice and safe right about now."

Damien ignored her statement about his power.

She doesn't need to know everything, Rae's mother or not.

"We'll head to Mirage. Sarth wants us all back with the Ashen Hawks."

"Lord Lanoret?" Auster approached from the direction of the tents, dressed in the formal Martox guard silver and black attire.

"Still getting used to that..." Damien ran a hand through his hair, hoping he looked somewhat worthy of the title. He turned towards the captain of the Martox guard and nodded. "What is it?"

Auster stopped a few feet away and glanced at Andi. "I need you to come with me, sir."

"Is something wrong?" Damien's body tightened, responding to the tension in the guard's tone.

Andi smirked, patting his shoulder. "I'll prepare the Herald for departure, if you'll excuse me, *Lord*." She dipped her hat before starting for the docks.

Rolling his eyes, Damien focused on Auster, wishing he could feel the man's ká to gain a better sense of what was bothering the usually stoic guardsman.

Auster waited until Andi was out of earshot. "There is someone here who needs to speak with you. It's about your work with your wife."

Damien furrowed his brow. "My work with my wife? If you're referring to something with the throne, perhaps we should wait for Lord Martox to return. Even as his personal advisor, I'm not—"

"No, sir. This is regarding Uriel."

Damien's stomach dropped, and his breath froze in his chest. He tried to steal the surprise from his face, but could tell that he failed because Auster's mouth twitched in a smile. "How do you—"

"Please, sir. Just come with me."

"Saying names like that so casually makes me wonder if I should." Damien glanced at the beach where Rae and Sarth walked. He scanned the terrain, but saw no sign of Jarrod or Corin. Most of the guards and crew had retreated from the ruins towards the tents to rest while the sun approached the western horizon.

Auster nodded. "I understand your hesitation, but I give you my word that I have always been loyal to Lord Martox and his council. This matter is unrelated to my duties to the future crown, as I also serve another cause."

Damien consoled himself by remembering he had never sensed an ounce of the Art within Auster. He'd diligently checked all the Martox guards for possible allegiances to Uriel and found none.

Damien ground his jaw, pushing the doubt from his head. He knew the man to be honorable and had already put himself in danger to protect Jarrod on multiple occasions. "Lead the way."

"Thank you, sir." Auster strode across the ruined estate, leading Damien to a smaller tent separate from the others. He held open the canvas door flap, standing aside.

Damien ducked to enter, eyes landing on a man inside.

The stranger stood, offering Damien a hand unmarred by the ash that covered the guards' hands. "Damien Lanoret. It's a pleasure to meet you. My name is Deylan."

Damien took the offered hand and gripped it hard. "Wish I could say the same, but I hope you'll forgive my suspicion. It's interesting times." He tried to find comfort in the weight of his sword on his hip and studied Deylan's weapon at his side.

No extra senses makes me paranoid.

Auster dropped the canvas flap, leaving the two men alone.

Deylan ran a hand over his short-cropped chestnut hair, nodding. "The stunt your wife pulled on the strait was impressive to watch, were you there?"

Damien pursed his lips. "You don't have to tell me that my wife is impressive. That's something I've always known."

"There's no need for hostility. I'm a friend. Amarie is my sister and I'm in Rae's debt for what she did." Deylan motioned to a second chair in the tent. "Will you sit with me? I have something we need to discuss."

Damien stared at Deylan, seeking whatever similarities he could find between him and Amarie. He'd spent so little time with the Berylian Key, he hardly remembered what she looked like. Reading his ká would have been far simpler.

This is too tedious.

Sighing, Damien turned towards the offered chair and sat. He didn't see an advantage in Deylan lying about something so obscure, but it didn't stop him from withdrawing his sword so he could set it within reach. He eyed Deylan for a reaction, but the man gave him none as he sat in his own chair.

"Amarie is your sister, huh?"

"Half-sister, technically."

Damien huffed. "If you're asking about what happened at the strait, maybe you should—"

"I'm not. I know your wife is a Mira'wyld. She created the ice bridge to outrun Uriel after my *sister* foolishly powered the beast with all the energy of the Berylian Key." Deylan leaned back in his chair. "I also know you've been planning with Rae to imprison Uriel."

"And how do you know that?" Damien narrowed his eyes. "Any man who saw what happened to Eralas would think that idea absolute insanity."

"I'm part of a secret faction tasked to protect the Key. We have eyes and ears everywhere."

Damien snorted, gesturing with his head towards the door. "And Auster is one of yours, huh?"

Deylan nodded. "He believes in our cause, but his loyalty to the Martox family runs deep."

"And what exactly is your cause?"

"Usually we focus on the Berylian Key, but with her in Slumber, we are broadening our watch. I visited the site of Amarie's encounter with Uriel at Hoult, and I found something you might find useful." Deylan reached into his cloak, holding his other hand out as reassurance as he produced a thick canvas wrap tied with twine and offered it to Damien.

Damien eyed the package before he leaned forward and took it. "Broadening your watch... Which would be why you've been using Auster to spy on my wife and me?"

Deylan shrugged. "More or less. It started because we were interested in Rae, but it turns out you all have some interesting secrets, don't you?" He smiled, but shook his head. "Open it."

Damien twisted the package in his hand, running his fingers along the twine. He considered how much Deylan might know, or what the faction had overheard. He'd sought to keep the power of the Rahn'ka secret, but now it was possible an entire faction knew about him.

Another failure to keep the power safe. But I still have a duty to the Rahn'ka, even if I don't hold the power anymore.

He untied the package, unwrapping the canvas in his lap. In the center rested a handkerchief, stained crimson brown with blood with specs of grey ash. "What's this?"

Deylan held his gaze. "Uriel's blood. At least, we're pretty sure. It was found on Amarie's dagger at the crater in Hoult."

Damien stared at the stain and frowned. "And you're giving this to me?" He carefully refolded the canvas over it. "Why?"

"For all I know, even if it *is* his blood, it's useless to you. But with your plans forming, I wanted to provide this in case it could help. What you do with it is up to you."

Damien's mind whirled through the possibilities. "It will help." He tied the twine sloppier than it'd been presented, and held it carefully against his leg. "It may help narrow down who the host is."

"I'm sorry, the host?" Deylan tilted his head.

Damien couldn't help but smirk, realizing he had information this Deylan didn't.

Clearly the faction hasn't spied on everything.

"You know about Uriel, which I assume means you know about its Shades. But it sounds as if your faction doesn't really understand what *it* is." He tucked the small package in his pocket, holding Deylan's gaze. "The Berylian Key is just a piece of this whole thing. Uriel is far more complex, its power is ancient. It existed long before the Berylian Key took human shape."

Deylan leaned forward. "You're implying Uriel's power isn't tied to its body?"

"No. The power itself is a parasite. A consciousness without a body which requires a host to carry out its physical desires. But it's able to infect beyond the single being and extend its Art across Pantracia through its Shades. However, there is still a primary host who suffers its complete domination, and this..." He patted his pocket. "Will help us find him, and hopefully free him of Uriel."

Once Corin is ready for that kind of thing.

Letting out a low whistle, Deylan rubbed his temple. "That changes things. Thank you for sharing that information with me. I have another question for you, if you're amenable."

"We're even right now, considering what I just shared in exchange for the handkerchief." Damien watched the man's angular jaw flex. "But I suppose I can answer another question, assuming it doesn't directly have to do with my abilities. I hope you might understand my hesitancy to share personal information."

"I'd like to know where Kinronsilis is." Deylan shrugged. "Perhaps another time I will ask more about the Rahn'ka."

Damien chewed his lip.

Of course he knows already.

"I'm going to have to be more careful where and when I'm called Rahn'ka, I see." He shook his head and settled back into the chair. "I took Kin to Eralas."

"Shades can't go to Eralas."

"They can when the husband of the Mira'wyld and personal advisor to the future king of Helgath asks for it."

"Why Eralas? Has Kin abandoned Uriel?"

Damien debated briefly, then nodded. "Kin came to me seeking a way out of his servitude. I gave it. But the side effects are... extreme. Slumber became the only option to help him recover."

Deylan's eyes widened. "Kin is in Slumber? With Amarie? Gods, that's ironic."

Damien shrugged. "I had no idea Amarie would end up there as well. That part wasn't exactly planned. But honestly, it's for the best right now. I'm in no place to be actively working on our Uriel situation, and I need to keep both Amarie and Kin where I can find them later. When it's time. Ironic, but convenient."

Something in Deylan's tunic pocket hummed with metallic vibration, and the man withdrew a compass. His thumb hovered over the button to open it, but he didn't press it. "I'd like to know more about your plans, if you're willing to share, but now isn't the time. Perhaps you'll welcome my company in Veralian after your friend is crowned?"

"Assuming we all survive this. If you haven't noticed, some powerful people have been trying to kill us lately." Damien shook his head with a smirk. "But we'll see. I suspect it would also be good for me to understand more about this faction of yours. Especially if our captain of the guard is a member."

Deylan rolled his lips together. "Only for the greater good. Don't hold it against him." He stood, pocketing his device without opening it. "Until we meet again."

Chapter 26

FIRE HEATED CORIN'S FACE, DRYING his eyes and eliminating the need to hide his emotion.

Jarrod stood next to him, holding his hand. The proxiet's gaze trained on the center pyre, where his father's remains disintegrated. He wore Reznik's signet ring next to his own and had been surprisingly stoic when Rae gave it to him.

The Mira'wyld stood with Damien on Corin's other side, tears racing down her cheeks faster than the fire could dry them.

Neco leaned on Jarrod's side, body rigid.

Auster approached in the corner of Corin's vision, patiently tucking his hands behind his back. He met Corin's eyes, minutely twitching his head towards one tent where a Helgathian soldier stood in his city guard regalia.

The work never ends.

Corin squeezed Jarrod's hand, turning back to the pyres as the flames lost their fury. The surrounding voices pressed against the barrier, but none filtered through. Still, the fire looked different, as if he could sense streams of energy. And the ashes of the bodies were emptier than their flesh had been.

He leaned against his husband's shoulder. "I'll be back, baby."

"Where are you going?"

"Rebel business, you don't need to worry about it. I sent for some reports from the barracks in the city."

Jarrod's amber eyes met his with a pained look. "I'll come with you. I can't keep staring at this."

Biting his lip, he nodded and led Jarrod towards the armored guard past Auster.

Neco padded beside them, keeping close to the proxiet.

The young guard's eyes widened as he looked at Jarrod, and he hastily rose his fist to his chest in salute. "Lord Martox. My deepest condolences."

The proxiet's face hardened. "Thank you. At ease."

The soldier relaxed slightly, his gaze turning to Corin. "I have the reports you asked for, sir. But I need to return promptly. I'm being transferred to Veralian in the morning."

Corin frowned, accepting the leather-bound package of parchments. "Time to join the rebels in Pruna, then."

"Yessir. I'll be making my way tonight with four others. Transfers like this are happening across the entire regiment here." He gestured towards the papers Corin held. "But you'll be able to see yourself in the reports."

"Thank you." Corin tucked the papers under his arm to give the rebel a rough pat on the shoulder. "Be smart and be safe. We'll see you soon enough when we meet in Ember."

The rebel saluted again with a nod. He spun on his heels and hurried towards the city walls on foot. Above, the sky darkened and the first stars shimmered through the haze of smoke still rising from the pyres.

Jarrod tilted his head, but didn't turn around. "What is it, Auster?"

Corin looked behind them, his gaze landing on the leader of the Martox guard standing a ways back.

Auster narrowed his eyes before approaching, clearing his throat as Jarrod faced him. "In addition to the thirty family guards who were stationed with you, we have fifty-six survivors."

That's all? There were hundreds, maybe more.

Jarrod cringed but said nothing.

Auster took a deep breath. "I think we should obtain a second vessel and accompany you and your council to Mirage. It—"

"No." Jarrod shook his head.

Corin unfastened the tie on the parchments, leafing through the pages.

"Lord Martox, there are bound to be further attempts on your—"

Neco barked.

"No."

Corin glanced at Jarrod from the top of his vision while he looked over the numbers and reports. "The Martox guard is needed here. Iedrus has effectively moved every rebel out of Lazuli, and replaced them with soldiers not only loyal, but with questionable morals. They're making the lives of the civilians here a living nightmare through their policing techniques. The guard can help protect them from the more *zealous* peace officers."

Auster looked from Corin to Jarrod, shifting his feet. "What about protecting Lord Martox?"

Jarrod's jaw flexed, and anger seeped into his tone. "What *about* protecting Lord Martox?" His gaze flickered to the pyres.

Corin put his hand quickly on Jarrod's shoulder, nearly dropping the papers.

The proxiet glared at Auster. "If all of them failed to protect my father, I cannot see how another fifty can protect me. Protect the people and, this time, I hope they do their damn job."

Auster flinched, but nodded.

Corin gritted his jaw. "The people are the reason we're even fighting for the throne. They need to be the priority. Besides, we all know this council is more capable than most at protecting itself. We'll take ten guards with us. I trust you can decide who the best candidates are, Auster. The rest will remain in Lazuli." He turned to check Jarrod's face for agreement, swallowing at the anger in his eyes.

Jarrod nodded once, and Auster took his cue to depart.

Corin stepped towards the nearby tent. He shouldered the flap aside, holding it open for his husband and the wolf to enter.

They had arranged the tent with supplies brought from the city, including several chairs and a large table. The air inside was free of the acrid smoke of the pyres, and Corin crossed through the darkness to the lantern on the table.

He considered attempting to use the power of the Rahn'ka, like Damien did, but opening his barrier felt impossible. He settled for the flint and steel starter set beside it. Spreading out the papers from the package the rebel brought, he considered them each, but his mind returned to Jarrod.

Looking at the proxiet, Corin could see the weariness in his stature as he stared at Neco.

I wish I could do more, somehow. Losing his father like this...

Corin paused, straightening away from the table. "We'll figure out a way through this, my love."

Glassy eyes met his, and Jarrod nodded. "I don't think I'll ever be able to forget this..." He waved a hand in front of his face. "Smell."

The pit of Corin's stomach knotted as he approached Jarrod. Touching the side of his head, he embraced his waist. "I'm sorry." He pulled Jarrod closer, encouraging his head onto his shoulder.

Jarrod turned his face into Corin's neck, wrapping his arms around him and breathing deep. "I don't know what I'd do if I didn't have you."

"You'll never have to find out." Corin held him firmly, kissing his temple.

They didn't move, and Corin listened to Jarrod's steady breathing as they held each other.

Eventually, Jarrod relaxed his hold and pulled away enough to kiss Corin before letting go. He cringed. "How long do you think you'll need to send orders and start redirecting supplies from Veralian?"

"Not long. I can write the command and give it to the guards remaining behind. I'll send word ahead to Ember, too. The rebels there are in the best position to help, and they'll be preparing for our armies and the assault on Veralian." Corin eyed the papers again, his mind whirling back to business. He leaned across the table, uncorking the inkwell.

Jarrod nodded. "I'll meet you on the Herald, then. I doubt you'll get anything done while providing solace for my nose."

Corin smiled. "You can always come hold me from behind." He shook his head. "I won't take long, and then I can provide any form of solace you'd like."

Lifting a hand, Jarrod touched the scar on his chin. "See you soon, then." He pushed the tent flap aside and Neco trotted out. The proxiet followed, leaving Corin alone with his paperwork.

Chapter 27

"I CAN SEE THE RESEMBLANCE now that you two are next to each other." Sarth tilted her head, glancing at Rae before her gaze settled on Andi. "If I'd known..."

Andi scoffed. "How could any of us have known? The gods clearly have a sense of humor." She passed a filled glass of whisky to Sarth, wrinkling her nose at Rae's fermented drink. "Besides, it seems it all worked out. This changes nothing between us, Sarth."

Rae made a face. "How can it change nothing? You're both about to be grandparents, more or less, to my child."

Sarth smiled, touching Rae's hand. "Andi and I have worked together a long time. You know that. If anything, I'm glad you have someone else, too."

If you can call finding out your mother is a privateering captain 'having' someone else.

The Herald swayed with the swell of the sea, a monstrous creak echoing through the wood as the wind picked up in her sails. They'd departed Lazuli the night before, and had agreed to early afternoon drinks. Damien had insisted on giving Rae her usual time with Andi, and they had invited Sarth to join. They had dragged a third, less overstuffed chair into position with the other two.

Sarth returned Rae's frown. "Sika. This will work out."

Rae looked at Andi. "Will you come to Mirage?"

"I haven't been out of sight of the sea in fifty years and don't know if this is the occasion to change it." She eyed Rae over the rim of her glass. "I don't—"

"No, of course not. Why would the birth of your only grandchild be important?"

"Hey, I don't see you popping this early. We've got time. I figure being pregnant, I should spare you the land journey and get you to Ember in more luxury. I'll see you before that rugrat makes his appearance."

Rae clenched her jaw. "So you want me to leave Damien, Jarrod, and Corin to sail with you around Helgath so you can drop me off alone at a closer port?"

"Whoa, whoa." Sarth lifted her hands. "We're supposed to be enjoying, how did this turn into an argument?"

"Got me." Andi huffed, collapsing further back into her chair. She downed what remained of her glass, roughly placing it onto the side table.

Rae stared at the sour drink she couldn't stomach drinking more of, the mirror surface reflecting the bright windows. "I can't go by ship when everyone else is going by land. I need to be with them, especially with the power shift between Damien and Corin. They need me."

"Well, then, that's your choice. Not that I understand any of that shit going on with those boys. But I can't just leave my ship. I've got responsibilities."

"Yeah, I guess it's a terrible idea to dump that responsibility on someone else." Rae lifted her gaze, her shoulders weighing heavy.

Andi pursed her lips as she stood from the chair. "This was a bad idea. I'll spare you my presence." She snatched one of the bottles and made her way to the door of her usual quarters. "We'll catch up later, Sarra." She disappeared, the door slamming shut behind her.

Sarth sighed, placing a hand on Rae's knee and leaning forward. "I thought you said things were getting better between you two?"

"They were. I thought they were, anyway..." Rae put her glass down. "Why did she call you Sarra?"

Sarth smirked, sipping her whisky as she leaned back. "It's my name. Though I haven't gone by Sarranthia in many, many years."

"How do I not know that, but Andi does?"

"We were... closer, once."

Rae sat up straighter. "You and Andi were a thing?"

"It was a different life. And we wanted different things." Sarth cleared her throat and eyed Rae as she refilled her drink. "So why are you upset with her now when things were improving?"

Rae's shoulders slumped. "She talks about this ship as if *it's* her child. How can she throw me away and yet refuse to even leave her ship temporarily? She's more determined to be there for this floating driftwood than her own daughter. *And* grandson."

Sarth squeezed her knee. "Give her time. This is all new and shocking for her, too."

"Whose side are you on?"

"I'm not on a side, Sika. I'm trying to give you some perspective. And, in a bit, I'll try to give Andi some perspective, too. Everyone just needs a little time."

"Why couldn't it have been you?" Rae felt like a child looking at her mother as she took in Sarth's knowing smile.

"It *is* me, too. Blood doesn't decide everything. Don't give up on Andi."

"You and her worked all these years, criminal allies, as former lovers?" Rae quirked an eyebrow.

Sarth laughed. "We're still friends. Powerful women need to stick together. Besides, in the eyes of the gods, she's technically my wife."

Rae gaped. "I'm sorry. Your *what*?"

"It's not a big deal."

"Gods, when will it end?" Rae closed her eyes and leaned her head back on the chair, looking at the ceiling.

Sarth cleared her throat.

Rae groaned. "Fine. I'll keep trying, I promise."

The ship listed so sharply to the side that Rae's glass slid off the table and smashed on the floor.

Gripping the armrests of her chair, Rae scowled. "She pissed and taking me to shore or something?"

Sarth snatched her cane before it fell, voices rising above them with the toll of the bell. "Don't think so, kid."

Rae stood as the ship leveled out, making her way with Sarth to the deck.

Keryn shouted as the crew scrambled with ropes across the beams above.

Three galleons in the distance blocked their route west, though they seemed innocent with white sails and no flag adorning the mast. But Keryn glared in their direction before she spun back the way they'd come. Rae followed her stare, spotting another ship behind them.

Damien crossed the deck towards her, arriving from the stairs to the helm.

She took his hand. "What's going on?"

"Iedrus. At least it seems safe to assume, considering the positions they're taking. Andi said she saw this formation during the wars." His jaw tensed as he touched her arm.

"They've got us surrounded." A chill ran down Rae's spine. "Is Corin able to fight, yet? With the power?"

"He can barely get through a day without a headache."

"Shit." Rae touched her abdomen and looked at the captain's helm.

Andi stood with Jarrod and Corin, talking too quietly for Rae to hear. Neco sat at Jarrod's side, ears pricked west.

"You up to using your power?" Damien placed his hand on hers, pressing against her stomach.

"Of course." Rae focused on him. "What do you have in mind?"

"Fog. Andi said if a fog bank rolled in, we could sneak past without them ever seeing us."

"I can do that." She kissed his cheek before climbing the stairs to the helm to get a better view. With each step, she let her Art into her veins, careful not to draw too much power to exhaust herself. Subconsciously, she crafted a bubble around Bellamy in her womb, protecting him from the draw of energy. Crossing to the banister, she gripped the smooth wood and sucked in a deep breath.

Clouds of mist swirled around the ship with her exhale, spreading across the ocean like the sea itself boiled. The air thickened, masking their view of the Helgathian ships and, soon after, the sky.

Rae turned to Andi, swallowing. "Does that work?"

"You'd make a damn fine addition to my crew."

Jarrod held out her bow to her, her quiver on his shoulder.

Rae huffed and took the weapon, slinging the quiver over her shoulder. "I guess sea battles are in my blood." She paused, considering the problematic circumstances. "What I said in there wasn't fair, and I'm sorry."

Andi stared blankly at the rising fog, her jaw twitching. "Though partially deserved. I'm sorry, too."

As the fog thickened, taking on a life of its own, Rae listened to the waves. "How do you navigate through this? Want me to clear a path?"

"No, leave it. Gives us better chances." She drew a compass out of her pocket and stepped to the helm, spinning it. She looked at Keryn as she reached the deck. "Run us silent, not a peep across this ship."

Keryn nodded and disappeared into a wisp of fog swelling over the Herald's decks.

Corin stepped to the banister, peering into the grey void. "So now we just hope we don't turn the same way they do?"

"You got it, Lanoret. So if you're the praying type, now's the time." Andi held the ship's wheel steady for a moment before spinning it back the opposite way again. "And keep quiet. We don't know what spells Helgath might use to find us. So we run as silently as possible."

The chime of the bell ceased, and the shouts between crew faded into eerie quiet.

Damien's hand slipped around Rae's waist as he approached from behind. "Nice work, Dice," he whispered.

Dread gurgled in Rae's stomach, and she kept her voice low. "It's not over yet."

No noise disrupted the creak of wood and the splash of waves as the Herald continued on in stealth.

Rae held her breath, eyes trained on the impenetrable fog as Damien held her.

I have a bad feeling about this.

Tension hung as thick as the fog, no one daring to move more than necessary.

A screech cut through the silence and Rae jumped, calming when a seagull soared through the fog over them and disappeared.

Relaxing her shoulders, she leaned back against her husband, Damien's arms squeezing her a little tighter.

We'll make it through.

A boom ruptured the air, and the ship shook like a great earthquake struck beneath their feet. In a thunderous roar, wood fractured and split. The fog rolled away from the impact, displaced by the collision of another ship's bow into the port side of the Herald. Splinters flew from the shattered banister, voices rising from both ships. A bell on the Helgathian galleon rang with fury.

"Shit." Rae gripped the banister as the ship leaned. "Still want the fog?" She shouted over the noise, losing track of Jarrod and Corin in the commotion.

"Yes. It'll make it harder for the other ships to broadside us. This one got lucky." Andi grabbed one of her crew and shoved him towards the helm. "Gotta get her off us."

"Lucky is the wrong word." Rae breathed in her power, feeling the swell of the ocean beneath them. Its energy mingled with hers, and she clenched her hand into a fist.

The water burst between the ships, jerking the attacking ship free from the Herald. Waves rose, sloshing onto the deck.

Rae faced the Helgathian vessel, thrusting her hand forward as a wave overtook the side of their enemy's ship, crashing into the masts.

The galleon leaned, her crew yelling as people tumbled down the deck into the far railing. The main mast cracked, sending their sails cascading into the tumultuous mix of fog and water.

Cheers rose from the Herald's crew, and Andi paused at the top of the stairs, her rapier half-drawn. "That works." She turned back to Rae, giving her a sharp smile. The elation disappeared as Andi's eyes widened, and she grabbed the banister. "Brace yourselves!"

Damien pulled Rae against him before she had time to react, shielding her from the eruption of wood as another ship collided with the Herald. The blow turned to groans of protesting hulls grinding as the Helgathian galleon slid along the side of the Herald, grappling hooks and rope locking the two vessels together.

Soldiers piled off the attacking ship before Rae could summon enough energy to dislodge it.

Swords clashed and chaos ensued.

Rae pulled her bow from her shoulder, freeing herself from Damien's protective hold to send several arrows blindly into the fog. She turned to her husband, eyeing the blood staining his shirt. Panic rose in her chest. "You're hurt."

Damien winced, straightening as he reached for the sword at his side. "I'll be fine." A large splinter of wood protruded from his lower back. Smaller specks peppered his shirt, proving just how much he'd shielded her from.

"Shit." Andi glanced at them as she withdrew her rapier.

An orange-red light flickered through the fog, the Art-fueled shield snapping into existence and sending the fog swirling at its edge.

"There's no avoiding this now. The fog's not helping anymore."

Rae lowered her bow and closed her eyes to focus on removing the fog, clearing the air. When she opened her eyes, they locked on an archer who aimed his crossbow straight at her. She gasped as Damien shoved her out of the way, the bolt whizzing past them.

Rae lifted her bow again and loosed an arrow back at the archer, but it shattered on the shield. "Not fair." Her muscles quivered, and she strived to find her connection to the ocean again, but it was buried beneath fatigue.

On the lower deck, several Hawks and Sarth fought the onslaught of soldiers. Her cane had disappeared, and she held a pair of wicked knives. Her uneven stance put most of her weight on her good leg.

Jarrod stood nearby, Neco tackling soldiers into a prone position. Pinned down by Corin, one struggled before the master of war ripped a pendant from the man's neck, tossing it to Jarrod. A Hawk finished the job of slitting the soldier's throat while Corin hurried to another body to retrieve the metal charm that'd allow safe passage through the barrier.

"Down!" Damien pulled Rae again as another volley of arrows flew at them, squishing her uncomfortably against the banister of the stairs. His sword in hand, he peeked up over the edge before turning back to Rae. "They're targeting you. We need to get you below deck."

"Like hells. I just need a few minutes, and then I'll be useful again. I can't pull energy from my surroundings like you can. Like you *could*." Rae shook her head. "I'm not going anywhere."

Damien frowned. "A few minutes of being shot at. Sounds like a great plan." He pushed away from her, moving towards the stair to block where a Helgathian soldier and one of the Herald's crew fought. He didn't engage like Rae expected, standing like a watchdog between her and the possible fight.

The fog had fallen into a thin blanket above the waves, twisting with the choppy sea.

"I need to see what's happening." Rae pulled on Damien's wrist to help herself stand. "I'm not hiding."

Damien growled, pushing her back down. "Don't be reckless. This ship has been in wars and can handle itself. I'm only worried about protecting you and our son."

Rae scowled at him. "There are three Helgathian ships surrounding us. The Herald won't hold out against that many."

"Legends and stories suggest otherwise."

A cry echoed from the base of the stairs as the invading soldier bested the crew he fought and started up the stairs only to receive Damien's boot to his face. He stumbled back, and couldn't recover before Damien thrust his sword into the break of his armor near his side.

He shoved the body down the stairs, where it tumbled to the deck. "You don't need to push yourself unnecessarily."

Rae covered her head as wood splintered somewhere behind her. Glancing back at the hole in the half-wall beside her, she stood. "Are you joking? We're all going to die if I don't..." Her gaze narrowed on a man crouched behind the bow banister of the Herald.

The archer.

His crossbow balanced on the railing, and Rae gasped as their eyes met.

Damien spun, throwing himself towards her as Sarth appeared behind the threat and locked an arm around his throat.

The archer stood, trying to pry the leader of the Hawk's arm off as he dropped his weapon.

Rae lifted her bow, finding the struggle unfolding between the two in her sights.

Hold still, damn it.

She loosed an arrow, but the man dropped in time for it to sail over his head.

Another soldier raced to his comrade's defense, his sword glinting.

Sarth, without letting go of her target, kicked up both her legs, the good one catching the edge of the blade. It soared from the soldier's grip, and he charged unarmed. He seized Sarth's middle to pull her off.

Rae steadied her bow and fired another arrow, which sank into the newcomer's leg.

The archer lifted a boot to the banister and withdrew a blade. He plunged it behind him, and Sarth's face twisted in pain, but she didn't let go.

"No!" Rae shot another arrow, but it only grazed the archer's shoulder in her haste. She pushed Damien out of the way and ran down the stairs as the archer stabbed backwards at Sarth again.

Rae lost sight of them while running across the slick main deck, taking the stairs to the raised bow deck two at a time.

Andi stood over the archer, her rapier dripping with blood as she kicked the soldier's body away from Sarth. She looked at Rae before cursing and picking up the crossbow from where it'd fallen.

"Sarth!" Rae collapsed to her knees next to the Hawks' leader, blood pooling over the planks. She dropped her bow, pressing her hands to the devastating wounds.

Blood oozed from Sarth's mouth, choking her attempt at words.

Heat built behind Rae's eyes, tears springing as blood coated her hands. "Please don't die."

Wood groaned, the Herald's sails filling with wind as the Helgathian ship beside them listed sideways. The Herald broke free of the bindings and pulled away as Jarrod, Corin and Neco bounded over the banister back onto Andi's ship.

Andi stomped to the edge of the deck, looking below. "Where's Lygen? Get him up here, now!"

Sarth grasped Rae's hand, wheezing in a breath and trying again to speak.

"It's all right. You don't need to talk." Rae touched Sarth's face before looking at Damien and letting out a sob. "You can't heal her."

Damien shook his head slowly.

Rae cried out and pressed harder to the wounds, where the bleeding slowed. "No, no, no. Stay with me." She looked at Sarth's face, watching the woman's eyes glaze over and her heart lurched. "Please."

When Lygen didn't come, Andi shoved the crossbow into Damien's hands and sprinted down the stairs, her boots hammering.

Damien stepped closer, but paused as he looked towards their attackers. "The other ships are closing in." He touched Rae's shoulder, his grip firm.

Rae shook Sarth. "Wake up. Look at me." When she got no response, she looked at her hands.

Blood no longer flowed.

Lifting her palms, she clenched her jaw as new tears raced down her cheeks, her bloody hands shaking.

"Dice." Damien's voice sounded far away and far too calm. "I'm sorry."

"She's dead." Rae gasped a breath, blinking rapidly. "Damien, she's dead."

His grip tightened. "We can't stay here. There's still more fighting coming."

"I can't do this without her."

The crossbow clattered against the deck as Damien dropped to his knees. He touched her cheek, brushing his thumb along her tears. "Yes, you can. And she'd want you to. There are still Hawks in danger on this ship."

Rae held his gaze, searching for strength in his warm hazel eyes. "What am I supposed to do?"

"Stand up." He took her hands. "Start there. Then we fight."

"You wanted me to hide." Rae looked at Sarth again, trying to comprehend what had changed.

Damien glanced down the stairs towards the deck where the crew were in a flurry to fortify the Herald. Crimson streams covered the deck, debris damming it into pools.

Rae stood, letting go of Damien as she took in the sight.

The sails of the lead Helgathian ship billowed, the side of its hull scarred from where it'd broadsided the Herald. Its bow dipped over an ocean swell, a grappling hook loaded in the front ballista shining through the spray. With a snap, it unleashed, piercing the air before smashing into the aft hull. The Herald shook, wood cracking, and the ship lurched as the chain connecting the two ships grew taut.

Debris cluttered the ocean's surface, three ships still threateningly close behind. Crew rushed into the captain's quarters, where the grappling hook held, while others worked to patch damaged sails.

Rae took a step to the banister, shaking her head. "There are too many."

From behind her, Damien returned to her peripheral vision and shook his head. "Not for you. This ship needs you."

Swallowing, Rae took a deep breath and clenched her fists. "For Sarth," she whispered. Reaching into the pools of her soul, she found the warmth of her power pulsing in excitement. The web of energies shifted around her with the waves, the fabric of Pantracia ready to be crafted by her Art. Sucking in a breath, she focused the first pull of power away from her son and the fire he already held within him.

I can't pull from him, not even for this.

Reinforcing the cocoon sheltering the child, her power washed around him, wicking up through her muscles to her hands. Finding icy water, invisible tethers dove towards the depths and she pulled. Sinuous vines of black water answered her call, emerging from beneath the surface like a great sea monster. Erupting from the white-capped gap between ships, they wrapped around the chain tethering the grappling hook to the ballista. The water crackled with bits of ice, cinching tight. Her hand outstretched to grasp the weaves of energy, and she yanked.

The giant weapon tore from the Helgathian ship's bow in a shatter of wood, crashing into the ocean as the chain snapped and vanished into the sea.

Redirecting what she already controlled, Rae twisted her hand and the tendrils of water splashed back into the depths. They swirled, and she coaxed the wind to join. A gust stung her face, flinging her braids to the side as she focused on the Helgathian ships. Her skin heated, tingling with energy as she funneled the air behind the Herald.

Still spinning her hand to keep the energy focused, the ocean churned. Her body ached from the push, but with a final check on Bellamy, she pushed what remained within her veins into the wind and sea.

A cyclone of water and debris rose from the surface. It stretched towards the cloudless sky, coalescing to block the Helgathian ships from view. The Herald lurched, the force pulling on the sails. The crew shouted, and Andi rushed to the helm, fighting against the wheel to keep the ship moving straight.

The waterspout collided with the first Helgathian ship with a boom, disintegrating it to splinters as it spun around the base of the cyclone. The sound of impacting wood escalated as it slammed into the second ship, leaving only debris in its wake.

Rae's muscles shook, her veins ablaze as her hair whipped behind her.

The third ship crumbled as Rae's final bit of energy left her. The wind ceased, the Herald's mast groaning as the pressure stopped. Crashing back to the sea in a downpour, a thin mist of seawater refracting into a rainbow among the destruction.

She sucked in a shaky breath and collapsed, but Damien caught her before she hit the deck. His face blurred. Only the bright blue of the sky pierced through the bubble of tears in her vision. Warm trickles fell over her temples, even as the icy mist engulfed the Herald.

Damien set her down and stroked her hair as Jarrod appeared next to her. Their mouths moved, but Rae couldn't hear anything above the ringing in her ears. Corin joined them, exchanging words with Damien she strained to hear. Still unsuccessful, she moved her hand over her belly, resting her palm on the side.

A flutter echoed inside, and her heart squeezed.

Someone took her hand, and she looked up, meeting her husband's gaze as he lifted her from the deck. She wrapped her arms feebly around his neck, burying her face against his collar and closing her eyes.

Chapter 28

JARROD STARED AT RAE IN DAMIEN'S arms, pride and sorrow mixing in his gut.

"Will she be all right?" Corin held open the door to the ship's guest quarters for Damien. The captain's quarters Rae might normally recover in had a gaping hole and a hook the size of a man in it.

"She needs rest, then she'll be her old self again." Damien crossed to the bed, laying his wife down before pulling a blanket over her. His hand on her swollen belly, he leaned over and kissed her forehead.

Jarrod touched Rae's bloody hand, but she didn't stir.

Sarth's blood.

He let go and shook his head, pacing away before turning again. His gaze landed on Damien's back, covered in dots of crimson. "Is that your blood?" He approached, moving his advisor's shirt out of the way to get a better look.

Damien batted at his hand with a hiss, but then stopped when Jarrod found the large wound on his left side.

"Gods, Dame. This doesn't look great."

"I'd imagine being stabbed by a flying hunk of wood rarely does." Damien tried to pull his shirt down, but Jarrod flicked his hands away.

"Can you talk Corin through healing you?"

"I'm fine."

"Stop being a proud dumb ass and talk me through it." Corin rubbed his temple, the familiar twinge of a headache wrinkling his forehead. "I need to learn, don't I?"

The scrapes and minor cuts on Jarrod's body stung, but they didn't compare to Damien's. Or what many of the Herald's crew suffered. He looked at Corin, noting the thin slash under his jaw and bruised knuckles.

"There's nothing anyone can do for Rae right now, so you may as well let Corin try. It's better he practices when things aren't life and death, anyway." Jarrod looked at the door and his chest weighed heavier. "While you do that, I'll attend to Sarth. Someone needs to clean up her... body."

She was a better mother to all of us than the ones we started with.

Damien lowered his head, sighing before he stripped off his shirt and sat backwards in the single wooden chair in the room.

He looked up and met his friend's eyes. "I'm sorry, Jare."

The proxiet nodded, swallowing through the tightness in his throat. He clapped a hand on Damien's bare shoulder, unable to respond.

Corin gripped his arm. "If there's anything we can do, come get us?"

Jarrod kissed Corin's forehead before moving towards the door. "Will do." He exited, shutting the door behind him with a sigh.

Too much death.

The proxiet climbed the stairs onto the deck, boots squelching in the muck. Everything had a brown haze around them, shimmering with the metallic scent of blood. He wrinkled his nose.

Wish I could take a break from the smell.

Neco trotted over from the aft, even his tail matted with blood.

"You need a bath."

Neco barked, and Jarrod looked at himself.

I guess I do, too.

Bracing himself, he climbed the stairs to the raised bow deck. Neco whined beside him as he gazed at Sarth.

Andi sat beside her, using a damp cloth to remove the blood from the woman's skin. She glanced up at him, but then returned to her task, chewing her bottom lip in the silence.

His gut twisted, and he knelt next to her, grateful Andi had already closed Sarth's blank eyes. He held out a hand, and the captain gave him one of the clean damp cloths next to her. Lifting Sarth's hand, he wiped the blood off her skin. "I thought she'd outlive us all. I've never met someone so resilient."

Andi brushed a strand of Sarth's red hair from her forehead, her eyes dark. "At least she went out in a fight. She missed the missions, and I know she feared she'd die quietly. This is exactly how she'd want to go."

"Protecting Rae."

"I couldn't get up here in time." Andi sat back, her body rigid as she stared at Sarth. An echo of a tear hovered in the corner of her eye but wouldn't fall.

"It's not your fault." Jarrod turned the guild master's hand over to stroke the blood off her palm. "Sarth was a force of her own."

Andi smiled, but it seemed distant as she touched Sarth's jaw. "I certainly can agree with that. Nothing could cause her to waver in what she believed needed to be done. Even when it was crazy." A dry laugh passed through her lips as she shook her head. "Kind of like Rae."

Jarrod furrowed his brow. "Rae is a lot like Sarth, but she's a lot like *you*, too. Sarth loved her Hawks, but I think Rae was always her favorite. Maybe because she reminded her of you, in a way."

Andi snorted. "You're too observant for your own good."

"I see things." Jarrod quirked an eyebrow at her. "And I'm sorry for your loss, too."

Andi sucked in a deep breath, straightening as she stared at Sarth's face. "It feels like all we do now is burn bodies. But I suppose it's not over yet." She pursed her lips, meeting Jarrod's eyes again. "You better not let one be you. Or Rae, because I still need time to fix that whole situation."

Jarrod nodded. "I'd say that I'd protect her, but I think Rae might just protect us all. She needs you, though, whether or not she shows it. Especially since she won't have Sarth anymore."

"Maybe. Either that or I'll fuck it up more. Seems like even chances either way, but I'm not usually a betting woman." Andi looked over her shoulder towards the rest of the ship.

Several crew still worked within the rigging above, patching the tears in the sails. Others sorted through debris, scrubbing to clean the decks. On the starboard side, in the least damaged section near the aft stairs, the bodies of their allies were being reverentially laid out.

"Sometimes those who need you the most show it in the worst ways." Jarrod quoted something Sarth once said to him, and he spied recognition in Andi's smile. "Rae will come around. After she sleeps it off. Even seeing it, I still can't believe what she's capable of, but you're not allowed to recruit her. She already has a job."

"I doubt she'd want to stay with me. But I hope she knows that I'll never be able to leave the ocean. I don't belong on land. And just like a life on the sea wasn't what I wanted for her, it isn't one I want for my grandson. Even if it is safer than this war y'all are fighting."

Jarrod placed Sarth's hand on her stomach. "The war will soon be over. No one expects you to give up the sea, but perhaps you could accompany us to Mirage? Sarth would've wanted you there for her funeral and your ship will take time undergoing repairs."

"Take me from the sea to the desert? You ain't making the transition easy on me, are you, Martox?" Andi shook her head.

"Temporary transition." Jarrod smirked. "Then you can return here to a fully functional Herald."

Andi ran her hand over Sarth's red hair, fixing the position of it as it trailed over her shoulder. She repeated the gesture, tracing one of the grey streaks. The captain's jaw twitched as she sniffed, touching Sarth's paled cheek. "Temporary. For Sarth, and Rae too."

"You ready?" Corin brushed his hand over Jarrod's shoulder, flicking away some speck of dust he'd already gotten twice.

"Do I have a choice?" Jarrod sucked in a deep breath and held it, trying to block out the roar of voices coming from the great hall.

Corin gave him a half smile, touching the side of his face. "We could make a break for it and be in Olsa by sundown?"

Jarrod smirked and shook his head. "Those are some fast horses you imagine us having."

Someone inside the great hall shouted something about Sarth, and his heart weighed heavier. Her funeral had ended only hours before, the stench of the pyre still hot in his nose.

"It feels wrong to be jumping back into business when Sarth has barely been laid to rest. I know the Hawks need direction, but do you think they'll accept Rae as their leader? When Silas suggested she take the lead... You know, I thought he might want it, being Sarth's brother and all."

Corin smirked. "I'd hate to go against that man in a card game. "

"He's a hard one to read, and he doesn't talk much." Jarrod started to turn, but Corin tightened his hold on his shoulder.

"Which means the Hawks will listen when he does, right?"

"*If* he does."

"I have faith he will if it becomes necessary. He obviously cares about the Hawks, and I doubt he'd recommend Rae if he didn't think she could do it. Present situations..." Corin rounded his hand around his belly. "...Aside."

Jarrod pursed his lips. "Don't let her catch you doing that."

Corin grinned. "Why? Not like I can't outrun her right now."

The proxiet choked on a laugh as he looked up, spotting Rae in the hallway frowning.

She held a few thin books and whipped one at Corin's back. It thumped into him as she readied another. "Don't need to outrun you, Lanoret."

Corin spun, catching the second book she threw at him. "No fair sneaking up. These fancy Rahn'ka powers don't work here in the headquarters."

Rae scowled and pointed at the first projectile she'd thrown. "Pick that up. I need these ledgers."

He laughed as he stooped and picked up the book, thumping their spines into his palm. "How do you know I won't just throw them back at you?"

The Mira'wyld approached and tilted her head. "Because you'd never want to accidentally hurt your nephew." She held out her hand, quirking an eyebrow.

Corin offered the books to her, and as Rae went to take them, he quickly swung them out and thwapped them against her backside before offering them in front of her again.

Gods, he's got a death wish.

Rae frowned to cover a smile and spoke quickly, words pointed. "And because you want me to go through this process again, yes?"

"At least I almost got a smile." He relinquished the books to her with an exaggerated sigh. "How's the crowd looking? They're noisy enough."

Her expression sobered, and she shrugged. "They're grieving. Angry. Not the easiest bunch, but as ready as they'll ever be."

Jarrod huffed. "I guess that's my cue. Better not keep them waiting much longer, or we can add impatient to that list."

Corin opened the main door leading to the front of the great hall and Jarrod followed, Rae behind him. She passed the ledgers off to another Hawk as she entered before walking to stand next to Silas.

Sarth's brother looked grim, his stormy green eyes sunken. The loose locks of his shaggy red hair bobbed as he nodded to Rae and exchanged a hard look with Jarrod.

"This isn't what Sarth would have wanted!"

"Where else is there for the Hawks to go?"

"Our leader is dead, we should elect a new one."

"This isn't a democracy. Did Sarth choose a successor?"

Jarrod wanted to rub his temples, but resisted the urge. He ran a hand over his black hair, looking out over the faces of all the Ashen Hawks as he took his place at the front.

Neco sauntered over from Damien and sat next to Jarrod, ears pricked.

The guild's great hall was filled to the brim, stuffed with all the Hawks called home with the brink of war. Jarrod couldn't recall ever seeing so many in one place. Hundreds. Most were silent, their faces grim, while the louder, more questioning individuals had made their way to the front.

Several Hawks stood at Jarrod's side with Rae, though slightly behind him. The seven higher ranking members had joined them in discussions for who would lead the criminal guild with Sarth's demise.

"Just because you're a proxiet doesn't make you our leader!"

Jarrod cleared his throat. "I have no intention of taking Sarth's place. Her most trusted Hawks have agreed on the future for this guild. Sika will lead you from a new position within my royal council. You will continue to operate within the new laws I will pass as king, becoming a part of Helgath's most elite."

"You want us to be soldiers?" Nyphis spoke up, his tone incredulous. His crooked nose lifted in defiance. "We are criminals!"

"But we don't have to be. We could be more."

"Are we leaving Mirage?"

"We can't leave. Where would we go?"

"Sarth died because she got involved in your politics."

"We're better off staying thieves and working against the crown."

Jarrod cringed and spun his wedding band with his thumb.

"This is a shit show." Even though Andi whispered to Corin and Damien from their position in the corner, Jarrod heard it clearly. "He needs to make examples of the ones questioning."

"Shh." Damien sounded annoyed. "You can't blame them for wanting answers."

Jarrod glared over his shoulder at them, and Corin smacked his brother in the chest.

Rae straightened from her position and approached the front. "Let me try."

Sighing, Jarrod stepped aside.

The Mira'wyld waited for the hall to quiet, eyes gradually landing on her. "This guild, and all of you, are Sarth's legacy. She always wanted more for us. She always fought for us, and she died protecting me. Some of you have questioned my commitment because I'll soon be a mother. Sarth was strong because she didn't have a family to distract her, right?"

Nods rippled through the crowd and Rae smiled. "Except that's not true. Sarth may not have bore children, but she had a family. She saw all of us as hers. All of us orphans and misfits and outcasts. She took us in. She took *me* in, becoming the closest person to a mother I ever had."

Jarrod glanced at Andi, who'd lowered her gaze, digging the toe of her boot against a crack in the floor.

Rae cleared her throat. "I know you all question what she would've done, but you don't need to. She chose this route for the Hawks long before perishing and long before even Lykan defied Iedrus. It's *our* job to see it through, and I've stepped down from my role as political strategist to make sure it happens. The only way to honor Sarth is to defeat Iedrus and claim the country as our own. The only way we can accomplish this is to continue our alliance with House Martox. Stand with the rebels. Fight alongside them and when it's all over, the Ashen Hawks will be reborn into something Sarth dreamt of."

"How do you know what Sarth wished for us?" A voice shouted over the silence. "Without her here to confirm, you could tell us whatever suits you best."

"Except she isn't." Silas stepped from behind them, joining Rae, and Jarrod let out a breath. Grey streaked his hair and beard, grief showing in the lines near his eyes. He stood almost a foot taller than Rae.

I've never seen him address a crowd of Hawks like this before.

"My sister was exceptional. She wanted the best for us and for you." Silas's tone quieted even Nyphis. "She wanted to see Iedrus fall for what that tyrant has done to this family. *Her* family. And I'll be damned if we fail her now. Sika is right. Lykan is right. You all know her as Sarth, but I knew her as Sarra. As Sarranthia Highborne. The ambitious thief who made this guild what it is today." He gestured to Jarrod. "This is how we honor her. *This* is how we make sure her legacy lasts forever. I stand with Sika and support her as this guild's new leader."

The hall grew quiet, everyone staring at Silas before their gazes shifted back to Jarrod when the older thief stepped back.

He rarely speaks, but when he does...

Jarrod's chest swelled with pride as he advanced to address the Hawks again. "I may be a proxiet, but I was one of you long before I ever sought the crown. I am doing this for you. For the people of Helgath. For my father and for Sarth. But I *cannot* do it alone. We are strongest as a united force and, together, we can give that bastard Iedrus what he deserves."

Scattered shouts of support burst from the crowd and hope surfaced in Jarrod's mind.

"Together, we can take Veralian. Together, we can change the course of Helgath's future and rid this country of tyranny. Make the corrupt fear the Ashen Hawks. Nothing can get better if *nothing ever changes...* Nothing will get better if we don't fight for it!"

Cheers erupted, Hawks stomping their feet and clanking their weapons together.

"We must make our own history!" Jarrod clapped his fist to his chest and thunder rumbled through the hall as everyone followed suit. "Rise with me!"

Chapter 29

"I'M NOT YOUR SERVING BOY," Damien grumbled, roughly tossing a damp cloth at Andi while handing the other to Rae.

"And yet, you play the role so well." Andi waved her fan, the current from it blowing the loose strands of her braid from her face. She frowned. "Gods, why is it so damn hot?" She draped the wet cloth around the back of her neck.

"At least you don't have a little furnace cooking you from the inside out, too." Rae shifted position in her chaise with a groan. "I can't believe I have another two and a half months left of this."

"It's miserable," Andi confirmed, speeding up the pulse of her fan. "Come on, Lanoret, where's my whisky?"

"Alcohol is going to make you hotter."

"But it'll also help me care less." Andi glowered, lifting her cup and wiggling it back and forth in front of her. "Please?" The politeness sounded painful for her to say.

Rae laughed. "At least she's using manners now?" She offered Damien a sheepish smile. "I could actually really use more water..."

The overhang wafted in the heated breeze, the fabric casting a pink sheen of shade over the women.

They would leave Mirage in a few days, and he couldn't wait for a break from the desert.

If I had my power, I could cool all our ká to a more comfortable temperature.

With no indication that the guardians might change their mind and restore his status as the Rahn'ka, Damien struggled to cope that the shift might not be temporary. Especially when Corin had finally started to understand the power and used it.

Damien took the pitcher from the table beside Rae, leaning to kiss the top of her head. "I'll go get some more. You all right with Captain Whiny still being here to disrupt your rest?"

Andi kicked the footrest, and it collided with the back of Damien's knees.

He grinned, kicking it back at her.

"She's distracting me from the heat. Can you bring extra water so I can make ice? Oh, and maybe a bread roll or some fruit. I'm hungry."

"You *just* ate lunch."

Rae stuck out her bottom lip in a pout. "The baby ate it all and wants more."

How she ate as much as she did baffled him. As much as her belly was growing, the rest of her hadn't changed much. Though, her cleavage distracted him even more than usual in recent days. His eyes deceived him by wandering to admire.

Rae touched the top of her chest and tilted her head with an innocent smile. "Please, my love?"

"Anything you want, Dice." He lifted her hand to kiss her fingertips before he turned towards the door.

"She also wants whisky!" Andi called after him, and Rae's laughter echoed with it.

Sighing, Damien shook his head as he crossed into the stifling hallways of the guild headquarters. Several Hawks passed him, giving a nod of acknowledgment as they went about their business of preparing for their departure.

Entering the kitchens, Damien went to the cold stores first, pausing when he found Corin already there.

"Couldn't wait for dinner again?"

Corin turned, a roll hanging out of his mouth. He grunted, biting down and taking it away from his face. "I'm starving. Always am, now. And those stupid meditation exercises you make me do make it worse." He took another large bite as he turned back to the food storage and pushed aside the hunk of dried meat he would normally go for first. Instead, he pulled out a bowl of grapes. He plucked off several and shoved them into his mouth with the half-chewed roll.

"Gods, man. The food's not going anywhere. Slow down."

Neco loped into the room and sat next to Damien, whining at the dried meat.

Corin glanced at Neco, scowling. "I gave you some last time. Go work for your food. I earned this."

"Corin!" Jarrod walked through the doorway next, his eyes landing on Damien. "Oh, hey, Dame. How's slavery treating you?"

Damien scoffed. "I'm not her slave. I'm choosing to spoil her. It's different."

"I didn't mean Rae." Jarrod smirked, looking more alive than he had since Reznik's death. "But how is our baby mama doing? I haven't seen her today."

"She's lounging out on the south patio with Andi. It's their new favorite spot. She's just hungry... again."

"She's not the only one." Jarrod made a face as Corin stuffed more food in his mouth. "Did you tell him yet?"

Damien furrowed his brow. "Tell me what?"

Corin shrugged, picking up a leftover hock of ham and tossing it to Neco.

The wolf snapped it from the air, turning to take it from the kitchen as Jarrod glared at Corin.

Damien's brother shrugged. "He wouldn't shut up."

"You're going to make him fat and lazy." Jarrod crossed his arms.

Damien sighed. "Tell me what?"

Jarrod reached for Corin's belt and withdrew his sword. The metal gleamed with a blue-white glow, and he offered the hilt to Damien. "He did *something* to his blade."

Damien took the sword, eyeing the Rahn'ka symbols shimmering along the steel. He ran his finger over them, imagining what the hum of power would feel like. His stomach knotted, but he swallowed the grief of not being able to fully admire Corin's work. Twisting to examine the other side, he looked at his brother.

Corin looked wary, like he had when they were boys waiting for their father's approval. It felt odd to consider himself in that role, but Damien smirked as he held the sword back to his brother. "You did it."

"Not quite summoning a spear from tattoos..." Corin looked down at it before returning the blade to its sheath.

"But still progress. It's good. I'm proud of you, big brother." Damien clapped Corin on the shoulder, and the soldier smiled.

"Tattoos next, then?"

"In time. I didn't manage that until I'd had the power for several months. You're ahead already, but we have other things to focus on."

"Every time I see Rae, she asks where her bow is."

Damien laughed. "She can wait. Besides, we all know she won't be going into that battle. She won't need it."

"But does *she* know that?" Jarrod leaned against the wall.

"I'm working up to it." He eyed the proxiet.

"At least your parents are more agreeable with staying out of trouble." Jarrod spoke in an even tone, but a muscle in his jaw flexed.

"Da knows better than to fight Ma, that's the truth of it." Corin plucked several more grapes while he looked at Jarrod. He and Damien had agreed to not talk about their parents around Jarrod, to avoid dredging up memories.

Reznik's pyre still burned in Damien's mind when he closed his eyes, and he could only assume it did in Jarrod's, too.

"They'll be safe here. Iedrus doesn't even have a presence in Mirage anymore. And enough Hawks are staying behind to maintain security." Damien stole some grapes from the bowl in Corin's arms, popping one into his mouth despite his brother's possessive glare. He looked at Jarrod's distant gaze and cleared his throat. "How are preparations for the battle going?"

The proxiet blinked and rolled his shoulders. "Well enough. We're on schedule to leave in two days for Ember, though a crew of a hundred left this morning to get started early."

"If it's a hundred, I don't think you can call that a crew." Corin smirked through another bite of his dinner roll.

Jarrod chuckled. "Considering the next two groups to leave are triple that in size, I'm not sure what else to call them. But everyone is doing their part. We're on track to be in Ember by the deadline. Assuming you and that wife of yours are ready to go by then? I can't imagine she's enjoying this heat."

"Both her and Andi are eager to get out of Mirage. We'll be ready."

"Is Andi coming with us?" Jarrod crossed his arms, eyeing Corin even though he'd directed his question at Damien.

Corin's gaze wandered down Jarrod while he shoveled more grapes into his face.

Damien rolled his eyes. "I swear, all your brain can think about is sex and food."

Corin glowered, swallowing. "I think about other things. Don't project your problems onto me."

Damien took the bowl of grapes from his brother, cradling them under one arm. "The girls will like these. Thanks for spotting them for me."

Corin reached for more, but Damien smacked his hand down.

Jarrod tilted his head. "You going to answer my question? What about Andi?"

Damien pursed his lips. "A conversation I'm glad I wasn't present for. Andi's going back to her ship. Word is the Herald's repaired, and she intends to sail west. Away from Helgath."

"I can't say I'm surprised. I wouldn't wanna be near this shit show either." Jarrod's lips twitched.

"She tried to convince Rae to stay with her, even agreed to head to Galestrom to keep her close to us. Rae said no, of course. Though I wish she'd have thought about it more. But I guess she can't, seeing as she's running a part of this shit show now."

I still can't believe my wife is the leader of the Ashen Hawks.

"Think of the benefits!" Corin grinned, patting Damien on the shoulder. "Being so close to the leader of the Hawks means you definitely have lifetime access to the hot springs."

"If we weren't moving them all to Veralian, you mean." Damien pursed his lips. "Still need to find a new political strategist."

Jarrod huffed. "The Mirage headquarters will always be here. And lucky for me, I have a great personal advisor to aid in finding a new political strategist. But why would you want Rae to go with Andi? You'd be all right missing the birth of your child?"

"If it means they're safe, then yes."

"They are safe. That won't change."

"Unless something happens. Unless we've underestimated Iedrus. Then everything can go wrong."

Corin shook his head. "It's the other way around. Iedrus has underestimated us. He's going to get a rude awakening when we walk into his castle halls from the tunnels."

A humorless smile crossed Jarrod's face.

Damien sighed, shaking his head. "We need to be logical

about it, though. Smart. We can't get sloppy because we're so close to it all being over." He studied Jarrod. "Without an experienced Rahn'ka to back you, we need to be more cautious."

The proxiet rolled his shoulders again. "Don't you need to get those to Rae?" He nodded at the grapes with a smirk. "Maybe some water, too? A foot rub? She told me about this guy once, who gave the best foot rubs..."

Damien growled. "Oh, come on, she told you about him, too?"

Jarrod's amber eyes danced. "No. But now I want to know who *you're* talking about."

Laughing, Damien walked towards the door, stopping to fill the pitcher he brought with fresh water. He turned and gestured with his head towards the liquor shelf at the back of the room. "One of you grab me a bottle of whisky?"

Jarrod straightened and plucked one from the top shelf, dust covering its cork. "One of the better whiskys we have. Tell Andi to savor it."

"Maybe it'll last to tomorrow if I tell her that." Damien tucked it under his arm. "Any advice on convincing Rae she can't be in Veralian?"

"Keep her arrows out of reach?" Jarrod smiled. "Or just put them on the floor. She can't even reach her boots anymore."

Damien smirked. "Then she'd pick them up with her toes and still stab me. She's coming to you next if I can't convince her. You'll have to use your kingly powers."

Jarrod looked at Corin. "When do I get those, again? They sound handy."

Corin chomped down on more bread, talking with his mouth partially full. "If all goes well, three more weeks."

Rae sat with a sigh on their bed, kicking her boots off.

"The guild master's room doesn't have all those stairs leading to it." Damien picked up her discarded boots, putting them together under the edge of the bed. He looked at her while he knelt and peeled off her socks. "Sarth wouldn't want you still up here in your old room."

Shrugging, Rae shook her head, a shadowed look in her gaze. "I'm not ready to be in her room yet. It's only a couple more days, anyway."

He nodded, shuffling forward between her legs, and ran his hands over her pregnant belly. Kissing her tunic, he felt Bellamy twist inside beneath his hands. He imagined what it would be like to hold the boy after he was born, the excitement building.

But that'll only happen if they're both safe through the battle.

"What's on your mind?" Rae tilted her head, her eyes narrowing on him.

Damien chewed his lower lip, leaving his hand where he could feel the baby's kicks. "Thinking about how to keep you both safe, with everything coming."

"I had a thought about that, too."

He took her hand, kissing the back of it while he met her eyes. "Please tell me it doesn't include entering the castle."

"Well..." She sighed. "I'm coming to Veralian, but I don't think it's wise for me to enter the castle. I didn't know what being pregnant would feel like, and I imagine it's only going to get worse as I *keep getting bigger*." She enunciated each word with an exasperated tone. "But I need to run the Hawks, so I'm thinking the tunnels might be the best place for me to stay."

Damien smiled in relief. "You sure I can't convince you to stay in Ember?"

Rae scoffed. "You're lucky to get this much from me and you know it. But it comes with a condition."

He squeezed her hand. "And what's that?"

"Nothing can happen to any of you. If it did, while I hid uselessly in the tunnels, I'd never forgive myself. I don't want to attend any more funerals."

He nodded, kissing her hand more fiercely. "I'll do everything in my power to keep us all alive, I promise. I have plenty of incentive." Bellamy kicked against his hand again. "I want us to have this family. That's what I'm fighting for."

Rae nodded, putting her hand over his. "We need you."

Chapter 30

Three weeks later...

A SEA OF TENTS. PILLARS of smoke rose from the campfires, and Martox banners hung from tall beams.

Corin hadn't compiled an official headcount after the auer arrived several days prior. Their accommodations contrasted the Hawks' and rebels', and took up even more space in the barrens outside Ember. The wind rustled through the elegantly formed auer tents, grown of the shrubbery strewn across the shallow hills. Sagebrush and creosote wove together to form posts, thin layers of fabric draped between. Each of their domed roofs supported the Martox flag, the silver embellishments shimmering in the sunlight.

Thousands of soldiers. All there for Jarrod.

A lot of bloodshed if this goes wrong.

Uneasy energy emanated from Corin's surroundings, pushing against his barrier. Whispers of excitement and anxiety slipped through, and his fist clenched the binding of reports tucked against his side.

He stepped over the ground, once lush with wild grass, towards the large tent near the center of the encampment where Jarrod and Damien mulled over maps of the tunnels.

He paused at movement on the northern horizon, where a trio of riders kicked up dirt as they approached the Martox battalions.

The north guard post stopped the riders, who remained on their horses through an exchange. One dismounted as an auer stepped forward, inspecting them. After a moment, and with a nod from the inspecting auer, a pair of guards escorted the one rider into the encampment, leading him down the path designed to limit his visibility of the rest of the army.

A messenger from Iedrus. Lovely.

Corin pursed his lips, walking to the front of the command tent and intercepting the escorted messenger before they could step inside. The knowledge of what Jarrod and Damien worked on had been controlled and kept even from their own soldiers, and this one didn't need to walk in and have questions if he saw the maps.

"War Master, sir." The rebel soldier slapped a fist to her chest. "A messenger for King Martox's council." She eyed the young man beside her, as if she didn't trust the auer's inspection. Their allies were far better at identifying practitioners, but it didn't negate the need for caution.

Hearing her use Jarrod's official title sent a shiver down Corin's spine. The troops had taken to calling him king with the pass of Iedrus's deadline to give up the throne, even if the old tyrant refused to budge.

Corin examined the young messenger, who avoided meeting his eyes. He wondered if he'd volunteered for the job, or been told he had to ride into the heart of the enemy. The boy clutched a scroll in his right hand, sealed with Iedrus's insignia.

"Give me a moment, I will summon you inside when the king is ready. Then we will hear what Iedrus has to say." Corin spoke loudly, so those inside would hear. He shifted his attention to the rebels. "Stay alert."

The rebels saluted again as Corin turned from the messenger. Even if he looked young, he could still be an assassin sent to make an attempt on any of Jarrod's council. He didn't turn his back fully until the flap of the command tent fell into place behind him.

Inside, three massive posts supported the center of the tent, before it swooped out towards the edges twenty feet out. A large table dominated the right side of the open space.

Jarrod looked up from his position next to the table, dressed in formal Martox attire buttoned halfway up his neck.

As he watched Corin, Damien and Maith draped a thick canvas sheet over the table to hide the maps and documents.

"Initial thoughts on the messenger?"

"He's a kid." Corin glanced at Rae, who sat in a chair near the outside wall of the tent, a damp cloth wrapped around her neck to help keep her cool. Her presence in the war tent seemed out of place with her swollen belly, but Corin knew better than to challenge her.

Pregnant or not, she'd probably still kick my ass.

Neco laid at her feet, head lifted from his paws and tongue lolled to the side. He met Corin's gaze and whined, unhappy with the heat.

Damien frowned, glancing at Rae too. "Don't know why Iedrus is even bothering. We all know he intends to fight."

The information the rebels and Ashen Hawks had compiled through their reconnaissance throughout the region confirmed that Iedrus would hole up inside his castle and prepare his army for battle. Edrikston wasn't the only Helgathian town plundered by their supposed king for supplies to feed his armies.

"Bring him in," Jarrod shouted towards the doorway and took a drink from a bronze goblet. Lowering it to the table, he poured more water into it. "Perhaps he came for the refreshments." He refilled the goblet his husband typically used, and Corin stepped forward to accept it.

Cold water in the heat of summer wasn't unheard of, but definitely not the norm. Luckily, their resident Mira'wyld had decided ice was a necessity.

The drink cooled Corin's throat as he tossed the leather-bound collection of troop assignments and numbers on the end of the table farthest from the door.

The tent flap opened, and the rebel soldiers from the post escorted the messenger inside.

They stopped near the entrance, one with their hand on the shoulder of the messenger to stop him, too. Bowing their heads, their fists thudded against their chests in a salute to Jarrod as they spoke in unison. "We rise as one."

The messenger shifted his boots, avoiding looking at anything other than the dirt at his toes. He almost did the salute himself, but then paused, turning it into a half-hearted pat against his chest. "Sir, I bring word from King Iedrus, he requests you send your response with me." He lifted the scroll, offering it to Jarrod without taking a step forward.

Poor kid looks totally lost.

Neco stood from next to Rae and loped over to Jarrod, growling.

The messenger's eyes shot to the wolf, and he stepped back, but the rebel beside him held his shoulder, keeping him in place.

Kid's not dangerous. Corin directed his thoughts through the flow of his power, using Neco to bounce the message to

Jarrod. Corin saw his jaw twitch in reaction. *He's terrified, probably forced to serve by the look of it.*

Jarrod touched the wolf's head, and he quieted. The king lifted his chin, seeming taller as he studied the boy. "My war master will take that from you."

Corin advanced, the messenger's eyes locked on the wolf. Stepping to block the young man's view, Corin held out his hand. "What's your name?"

The boy stammered, his eyes flitting to Corin's face before they dropped to stare at the Martox insignia clasped at the left side of Corin's collar. "Jasper, sir. Private Pol Jasper." He slapped the scroll into Corin's hand.

"Jasper." Jarrod paced around the table, but the wolf didn't follow. "Might we offer you a drink?"

Without waiting for the messenger to answer, Maith retrieved another goblet and filled it. He paused near Rae, and the Mira'wyld waved a hand to create shards of ice within the liquid before he offered it to the private. "Must be hot under all that armor." The auer smiled, not a bead of sweat on his brow.

Jasper hesitated, looking at the goblet before looking up at Maith. "Thank you, sir." He took the water as Corin turned from him and broke the seal on the scroll.

"Can you tell us about the conditions in the city, Private?" Corin eyed him as the kid nearly choked on his drink. "How the people are managing under Iedrus's armies crowding the streets."

"Sir, I..." Jasper stared at the water in his cup. "I can't, sir."

Corin shrugged, unfurling the scroll. "No harm in asking. I understand the need to cling to your belief of loyalty."

Damien chuckled as he leaned against the table, crossing his arms. "Leave the kid alone, Corin. He doesn't know any better. Not yet."

Jarrod nodded at the parchment. "Read it out loud."

Corin skimmed the scroll and looked at Jarrod. "You sure?"

His king nodded once.

Clearing his throat, Corin read from the letter. The sloppy cursive forced him to squint to make out the loose loops of Iedrus's handwriting. "Usurper. You are difficult to kill, I'll give you that. You and your self-righteous cult. You unrightfully claim the throne to be yours using foreign power and criminals. The throne will forever belong to House Iedrus, not a boy who ran from his responsibilities and upon returning, caused his father's death." He glanced at Jarrod, seeing the hardness in his eyes.

Now isn't the time for comfort.

"My attempts against you have been mere child's play, but now my gloves are coming off. Let me tell you who isn't difficult to kill. The civilians inside Veralian. The poor, innocent women and children you so foolishly seek to protect. Advance on our walls, and their deaths will be on your conscience. Disperse your armies within the week. Go home to the ruins of your castle, and my mercy will leave you in peace to die there. I expect word of your surrender and acceptance of these terms, or I will begin the purge of this city tonight. The *rightful* king, Leorithin Iedrus."

Damien whispered a curse Corin couldn't make out.

Jarrod's amber eyes drifted to the messenger. "What a wonderful king, indeed." His voice dripped with sarcasm, and he rounded the table to return to Neco.

"You're lying." The private's face reddened as he glared at Corin. "King Iedrus would never threaten his own people."

Corin strode towards Jasper, and the private shirked away as if expecting an attack. He thrust the scroll forward in an offer. "Read it yourself, then. See the truth of what kind of king Iedrus is. I could see it in your eyes when I asked the question. You know the soldiers in the streets of Veralian wouldn't hesitate on this order. In fact, I suspect the people already suffer at their hands."

Jasper cautiously took the scroll, doubt and fear warring in his light eyes.

"Take him outside and wait." Jarrod motioned to the rebels, and they guided Private Jasper outside, letting the canvas flaps fall back into place. "I should have seen this coming."

Maith touched the tent, sending a ripple of purple light over the material to seal the air with his Art. Their voices wouldn't escape to any looming ears. He gave a nod to the group and Damien spoke first.

"It accelerates the timetable." He crossed his arms. "We're going to have to make our move soon. He's paranoid. Even if you surrender, he'll murder the civilians."

Jarrod nodded. "We can make it look like we're packing up the camp, but we need to go in tonight." He looked at Rae. "Are the Hawks ready?"

The Mira'wyld smirked. "They might just leap for joy. Sitting here, twiddling thumbs, isn't exactly how we like to spend our days. I have already assigned teams, each with two auer to locate the summoners within Veralian. We'll use the tunnels to enter different parts of the city, and yes, Damien, I will stay in the tunnels."

Jarrod glanced between the Lanoret brothers. "Are you both ready to move tonight?"

Damien hesitated as he met his brother's eyes. "We have to be. You just have to keep your mind clear and remain in control, or you'll be a beacon to any practitioner near the castle."

"I've got it," Corin growled. Despite himself, he did a mental check of the fortified brick wall holding the power of the Rahn'ka inside him.

Neco barked.

"Aye, boy. You're coming, too."

"I'd like to accompany you." Maith faced the group, and all eyes turned to him.

"What? Why? You're a scholar." Rae sat forward in her chair.

"I've been reading up on House Iedrus's tactics for war, and many texts speak of trap wards within the castle meant as a last line of defense. Undetectable by most. But I could detect them. Disarm them. Though, only if I am with you."

Jarrod gestured to Corin. "What do you think?"

"I sure as hells couldn't do anything about wards." Corin pursed his lips, knowing that if Damien still had the power, he might have managed it. It meant they'd have to keep an eye on Maith if the auer couldn't protect himself. "Please tell me you know how to use a sword."

"I underwent the necessary training for the traditional thirty years. I suspect I'm adequately able against humans."

"Thirty years?" Rae gaped at him. "You said you only took the initiation training!"

Maith shrugged. "That *is* the minimum required length. To join the military, it takes at least a hundred years, then continued training during service."

"So you've had sword training longer than we've all been alive." Damien rolled his eyes.

"This is why no one wants to pick a war with the auer." Corin huffed. "And why we're oh-so-grateful you're on our side."

"In this case, I think you'd be an excellent addition to our crew tonight." Jarrod looked from Maith to Corin. "Agreed?"

"Agreed. Maybe we should take some more auer, too." Corin smirked. "Too bad we're keeping the circle of trust small."

"We don't need the auer learning about you being Rahn'ka." Damien pursed his lips. "Too much of a chance you'll lose control in there somewhere."

Corin grumbled, "So little faith in me, brother?"

"I know what it's like to keep that power hidden in battle. It's not something you're ready for. Trust me."

Jarrod took a piece of blank parchment from under the canvas sheet and Maith provided him with a quill to write his response to Iedrus. His jaw flexed as he wrote, signed, and sealed the document with his crest. "Let the troops know we're moving the camp. It'll look genuine, and if we have any leaks in our ranks, they can't tell Iedrus the truth." He handed Corin the response scroll. "While we wait for dark, we should all get a little sleep. It's been a long day and the night will be even longer. Rae, instruct your crew to do the same."

Rae made a face at him, a smile twitching her lips. "Yessir, Mister King, sir."

Corin snorted at Jarrod's frown. He leaned to give his husband a quick kiss on the cheek. "It'll all be over soon." His hand tightened on the scroll before he moved to the flap of the tent. Maith's sound barrier flickered out as Corin broke through.

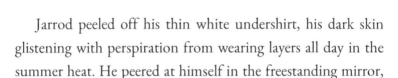

Jarrod peeled off his thin white undershirt, his dark skin glistening with perspiration from wearing layers all day in the summer heat. He peered at himself in the freestanding mirror, his eyes weary. Touching the marquise scar on his ribs, he let out a slow breath.

Corin slipped off the decorated four poster bed, his loose silk sleep pants brushing against the lush rugs strewn across the ground. Approaching his husband, he wrapped his hand around Jarrod's waist, entwining their fingers.

The tent crafted to sleep Jarrod and Corin hardly resembled a tent from the inside, if not for the thick canvas walls. Furniture crafted by the auer decorated the space, providing a large bed, desk and armoire. Candles illuminated from multiple sources, daylight unable to penetrate inside.

At least I can get a little alone time with my husband.

Corin kissed Jarrod's shoulder, savoring the salty taste of his skin. "You all right?" he whispered.

"The fate of Helgath and all those civilians inside Veralian is resting on my shoulders." Jarrod closed his eyes. "I can't fail them, when I've already failed others enough."

Pressing their skin together, Corin held Jarrod close. "It's not all on your shoulders. That's too much for one person. You haven't failed anyone, my king."

"I failed Sarth." Jarrod turned around in Corin's embrace. "I failed my father. Is this anything like what you imagined, when you suggested it the first time we arrived in Lazuli?"

Corin touched his hard jaw, meeting his amber eyes. "Those deaths were not your fault. Nor will any of those that may happen tonight. That blood is on Iedrus's hands, not yours." He lifted Jarrod's hand to his lips, kissing his palm. "Neither of us could have imagined this."

Jarrod wrapped his arms around Corin, slowly kissing him. "No regrets?"

"Of course not." Corin rested his forehead against Jarrod's, tracing a line down his chest. "I'll always be at your side. In whatever form you need me."

"Everyone else can focus on me. What about you? What do you need?" Jarrod tilted his head, touching his chin.

"Me?" Corin half-smiled. "I'll settle for some time to kiss and cuddle my husband before we go to finish this rebellion."

"Soon, you won't be able to call it a rebellion."

"Which I look forward to." Corin kissed Jarrod, letting it linger and continue into another. "Then we both can finally have some time to rest."

"I know I said we should sleep, but I doubt I can." Jarrod tugged Corin towards their bed. "What do you think?"

Corin hummed, pushing Jarrod onto the bed so he could crawl on top of him. "I never had much intention to sleep." He traced the curve of Jarrod's bicep. "Glad to hear you might feel the same." Nuzzling close, Corin trailed kisses along Jarrod's neck towards his collar.

Jarrod's chest rumbled, each of his boots falling to the floor with a thump. "You have my full attention."

Corin grinned through the kisses, running his hands down to unfasten the buttons on the front of Jarrod's pants. "I can tell." He leaned up, placing a rough kiss on Jarrod's mouth as he slid his hand down the front of his husband's loosened breeches.

Jarrod's spine straightened, a moan echoing within the deepening kiss. "This is much better than sleep, anyway."

Corin woke with a start when Jarrod sat up, jarring his head off his chest. He groaned. "What is it?"

"It's that messenger. He's being escorted to our tent right now." Jarrod slid out of bed, pulling his breeches on. "Why would he come back?"

Corin rubbed his eyes, trying to wake his muscles with a stretch as he hopped from the bed. His body yearned for Jarrod's again, but he hurried to the pull on his clothes. "The kid?"

"Aye, the kid." Jarrod pulled a black shirt over his head, followed by his knife-lined vest, trading his royal appearance for the one Corin fell in love with.

A commotion evolved outside their tent's entrance. An exchange between the Martox guards and the rebel escorting the returned messenger.

A headache twinged at the front of Corin's skull, the waves of anxiety outside the tent pressing hard against his barrier. He swallowed, focusing his will to harden it further.

Gods, I wish the guardians would give it back to Damien. Being chosen sucks.

Corin tugged on his undershirt, hurriedly grabbing his light armor, similar to what he'd worn as a Helgathian scout, though constructed of some special black alloy the auer had developed. A gift given with the arrival of the auer armies to symbolize their loyalty to his command through the coming battle.

Jarrod buckled a sword to his belt and rounded the bed. He touched Corin's jaw, lifting his chin to catch his gaze. "Something tells me our time to rest is over for now, so before things fall into chaos... I love you."

Corin's chest tightened, and he paused in buckling his chest piece. He closed the distance between them, kissing Jarrod hard. "And I love you. We'll make it through this." He returned to securing the various latches, fingers struggling with the unfamiliar. He slid the sword at his side partially from its scabbard, and the pale blue runes of the Rahn'ka flickered, casting shadows across the room.

Someone shouted outside their tent. "I need to talk to King Martox!"

Jarrod's bright eyes met Corin's as he started towards the entrance flap. "Did he just call me king?"

"I guess we won him over." Corin followed close behind, double checking the armor.

"Or that's what he wants us to think." Jarrod pushed the heavy flap aside, torchlight landing on his face as he and Corin exited into the fresh night air.

A mixed group of Martox guards, Hawks, and rebels stood in the bonfire area outside, surrounding Private Jasper.

The young soldier's eyes widened when they landed on Jarrod, and he dropped to a knee so fast that the nearest guard drew his sword.

Corin raised a hand, shaking his head at the guard. He gestured, and it was all it took for the crowd to take a collective step back from young Jasper.

The private shook, his head bowed low.

Jarrod entered the ring of guards and knelt a few feet in front of the messenger. "What is it you need to tell me?" His gentle tone reminded Corin of Reznik's voice.

"The king..." Jasper gulped, lifting his chin to look at Jarrod, but then hastily lowering it again. "Iedrus. He... he's not waiting like he said. They're coming. Now."

"What?" Corin stepped forward, wincing against the new pulse of his headache. "What do you mean they're coming now?"

"Is Iedrus killing the civilians?" Jarrod dipped his head to catch the boy's gaze.

Damien and Rae emerged at the edge of the crowd, and Corin met his brother's eyes.

Neco trotted over to Jarrod, sitting next to him and licking his elbow.

Jasper jumped as he saw the wolf, starting to back away, but Jarrod leaned forward and caught his shoulder.

"Focus, Private. What is happening?"

"The armies are marching from the city. They're attacking now. But he sent the Artisans ahead. I don't know why." He shook his head, staring at Jarrod's chest. "I ran here as fast as I could, to warn you. You need to disperse your troops faster."

"Artisans." Corin grimaced, shaking his head. "Summoners." He didn't wait for Jarrod before he beckoned one rebel to him. "Tell the line to prepare for Corrupted. And send word to the auer that we'll need their troops to assist."

She nodded, wide-eyed. "Yes, sir." She spun, sprinting towards the Veralian side of the camp.

The capital city glowed on the northern horizon, black spires blotting out the stars.

Jasper's brow furrowed. "You aren't retreating?"

Jarrod stood and offered the private his hand. "And leave this country to the mercy of a tyrant?" Once the boy overcame his hesitation and gripped Jarrod's hand, the king hauled him to his feet. "You'll stay here under our protection. Iedrus would kill you for warning us."

The Martox guards led him away, and Corin looked at Rae. "Can you have the Hawks ready to go as soon as possible?"

Rae nodded. "They're restless, anyway. How much time do you think we have until the Corrupted reach us?"

"Not long." Jarrod shook his head. "They move fucking fast and it would've taken Jasper awhile to get here on foot."

"We need to get to the tunnels." Rae looked at Corin. "Everyone here is briefed on how to kill Corrupted, but the only way to end this is to stop the source." She turned, hurrying off between tents to round up her crew.

Damien shifted, watching her go. "I'm going to stick with Rae for now. We'll meet at the east post with the Hawks." He didn't wait for Jarrod or Corin to respond before he jogged after his wife.

Maith sauntered into the area from behind Corin, not a hair out of place or a wrinkle on his dark clothing. "Looks like we're moving up the timetable again?" The sword hanging at his side donned a crystal-cut silver pommel, glittering in the dim light.

"No second thoughts about accompanying the crazy humans, then?" Corin smirked, obsessively checking his armor again.

The chief vizier laughed, pausing when an auer commander approached and spoke to him in rapid Aueric. He responded with pointed words, and she took off to relay the orders. "Not at all. Though we've spotted movement on the southern ridge. Looks like Iedrus planned to attack from behind first, like we expected. The soldiers are ready."

Corin looked at Jarrod, who scratched Neco behind the ears. The wolf's head already faced the south, his hackles raised. "They will attack from the north after the Corrupted have done some damage." He turned to one of the officers. "Make sure the troops at the north line hold their posts."

The officer nodded and ran north.

Maith crossed his arms. "Would you like to stay and assist or head for the tunnels now?"

"It'll be good for the soldiers to see the king before we leave. It'll raise morale."

"I agree. And if Iedrus's troops see me, all the better. Lowers suspicion of what we're going to do. Where's a—"

Maith offered him the reins of a dapple grey that reminded Corin of Titian, the horse Jarrod bought from the Lanoret ranch when they were kids. The Martox guard who Maith had taken the reins from offered another set to Corin, belonging to a black Friesian warhorse.

Rather fitting, if you ask me.

Jarrod swung himself onto the horse, watching Corin do the same. "We'll go address them from the center and then head north back through the encampment to meet Damien and Rae." He motioned to Maith. "And you, too. Gather what you need."

The king wheeled his horse around, and Corin kept pace behind him as they maneuvered through the camp at a canter. There was very little chaos for the amount of movement rippling through the whole of the camp. The soldiers moved efficiently to the weapons tents, marching to take up their positions on each line. Corin had worked with Belladora to ensure they had a plan for whatever Iedrus might attempt, including this. And the rebels fell into position with a spattering of Hawks willing to operate on the battlefield.

Neco ran beside Jarrod's horse, a black blur in the darkness.

When they reached the formation of soldiers, rebels and Hawks coming together, Corin gaped at the magnitude of their troops. He'd assigned the numbers himself, but it was different to see it. Even as a captain, he'd only ever commanded a troop of seventy, but lining the hill before it dipped down into the southern valley were hundreds. They'd constructed bonfires along the edge of the camp, soldiers taking up positions between and just in front of them.

Darkness shrouded the valley beyond, and Corin eyed the shifting shadows. They had built more pyres in the valley, but their archers had yet to light them.

Hooves pounded behind Corin, and he looked back, meeting Auster's gaze as the leader of the Martox guard followed him with a few more guards, all on matching black horses.

Jarrod slowed to work his way through the lines of defense, the soldiers parting to let the horses pass. He looked far from the king who'd addressed them last, no longer in his formal attire, but somehow still regal on the light grey horse that stood out from the others.

As he passed each row of troops, they clapped their fists to their chests.

Corin rode next to Jarrod into the open area between bonfires, Auster and the other guards forming a line behind them as they turned to face their army. Neco stood next to Jarrod's horse, blending into the shadows. The ominous valley behind them made Corin's back rigid, and he glanced at Jarrod, who nodded.

Corin swallowed, trying to calm the rising swarm buzzing in his stomach. The headache thudded against the back of his skull, so many voices assaulting the barrier. He could feel something in the valley, a twisting corruption slinking through the darkness and sending the wildlife into a frenzy.

The master of war squared his shoulders, looking at the men and women who stood before them, ready to die for their king.

For Jarrod.

To save their country.

Corin sucked in a deep breath and addressed the soldiers. "There are no words to describe the evil you all bravely face. They will attack hard, and they will attack fast, but we will hold this line." He squeezed his calves, urging his horse into a canter along the line of rebels and bonfires, raising his voice to conquer the sound of hooves. "These Corrupted will not sway us, they will not stop us from standing here before our capital demanding justice. And we *will* have justice this night!"

The soldiers stomped a boot in unison, shouting a short, throaty roar.

Corin steered his horse back towards the center to rejoin Jarrod. "Justice for our king!"

The soldiers shouted again, louder.

As he came to a stop beside his husband, the king walked his horse forward a step. "We all deserve justice for the wrongdoings of House Iedrus. Iedrus has punished you. He has corrupted this country far worse than any Art could accomplish and he does it without remorse. This night, it will end." Jarrod's voice carried over the silent night air, deep in timbre. "This night, the people will win. We will not fail. Together, we rise!"

The army chanted back at him. "We rise as one!"

Jarrod clapped his fist to his chest. "Together, we rise!"

"We rise as one!"

"Light the pyres!" Corin shouted the order and the archer's arrows burst into flame. "Loose!"

The arrows soared over their heads, streaking the sky with orange like fireworks at the Xaxos solstice festival before landing in the piles of wood far into the valley. The bonfires, doused with oil, erupted into blazing pillars of flame.

The dark creatures creeping around them shirked back, letting out hisses and unnatural growls as they tried to find the shadows between pyres again. Each amalgamation differed from the one beside it, their animal forms grotesquely twisted by the Art of the summoner who brought them forth. Scaled and furry hulks lumbered through the orange blazes of light, their feet speeding across the valley floor.

"Archers draw!" Corin watched as their line shifted, those with longbows drawing back their nocked arrow.

Jarrod drew his sword, prompting the army to follow suit.

"Loose!"

Something screeched overhead, choking when an arrow met its mark. The hawk-like Corrupted thudded to the ground in front of the soldiers, shrieking and pawing at the dirt with clawed paws.

One fighter stepped forward and slammed their sword down, decapitating the beast.

Cheers escalated from the group, the rows of soldiers shifting in anticipation.

Corin eyed the fallen beast and growled. "Don't think the next will go down as easy! Front line, ready!" He wheeled his horse around, gesturing with his head to Jarrod towards an opening in the line back towards the camp. "Auster, take command."

The captain of the Martox guard gave a grave nod. "Yes, sir."

Corin's horse shook, shifting restlessly as a Corrupted howled close behind. The stench of the flying thing struck Corin's nostrils as he tried to calm his mount

"Gods, I hate this smell." Jarrod kept his voice low. "We need to meet the others."

Before Corin could respond, Jarrod's horse screamed and reared, a Corrupted clinging to its rump with long, serrated claws. Its serpentine head writhed, forked tongue lashing at the horse's flesh, rust-colored fur shaped like spikes on its spine.

The king kept his seat, swinging backwards with his sword and clipping the deformed beast to send it to the ground. He dismounted as Neco pinned the Corrupted and slammed his sword at the thing's armored neck. On the third attempt, the head severed.

The grey horse panted, and Jarrod slapped his rump, avoiding the jagged slashes, to send him back into the camp riderless.

One of the Martox guards dismounted and shoved the reins of his black horse into Jarrod's palm. "Your highness, it's time to go."

Corin circled behind Jarrod and Neco, looking at the valley now crawling with Corrupted. He spun his Rahn'ka-etched blade, a flash of blue light easing the pain in his mind.

Battle rose around them, hells' creatures hurtling at the front line.

Corin looked at Jarrod as he settled into the saddle, their eyes meeting. "Let's hope the Hawks can find and take care of the summoners in the city, like we planned. Otherwise, we might be in trouble."

Chapter 31

"REMMY, WHAT ARE YOU DOING here?" Damien glared at the young soldier who'd decided last minute to join Rae's crew instead of the front line.

"I'm sorry, but I can't leave her, sir." Remmy shook his head.

"Leave who?"

Rae rolled her eyes at her husband's ignorance.

Remmy reached to his side and took Meeka's hand.

The woman who'd lost her twin smiled with genuine emotion, and she rubbed her flat stomach. "He's a little protective, since we have a little one coming." She gestured to Rae. "I mean, I'm obviously not *there*, yet, but it's all the same, isn't it?"

Shit.

Rae coughed. "You're pregnant? You shouldn't even be here."

"*You're* here." Meeka poked Rae's belly. "And a *lot* more pregnant than me, boss."

Groaning, Rae squeezed Damien's arm. "Fine. But damn it, you'd better keep out of trouble. Remmy, you can stay, just stick with Meeka."

Swords clashed at the front lines on the south side of the encampment, sending a shudder down Rae's spine as she watched from the west post. The troops on the north end seemed unfazed, holding their ground and waiting for the inevitable advance of Iedrus's soldiers from Veralian.

"We need to move into position. Jarrod and Corin know where to go. Where's Maith?" Damien fiddled with the buckle of his sword.

He'll be fine, even without his power.

Rae motioned with her chin. "He went ahead to make sure the way to the tunnel entrance is clear. He's got five Hawks with him but won't enter without us."

A screech reverberated through the air, rattling her teeth. Shouts rose from the center of the camp, the moonlight blotted out by a massive creature above. Its membrane wings drummed in the air. Its beady eyes reflected the orange of the bonfires, wicked avian claws flexing as it dove. Arrows stuck out of its scaled flanks, but its form disappeared from her view as it met the ground between tents.

Screams of pain mingled with another screech, and its wings beat to take it skyward again. It lifted a pair of soldiers in its talons, flinging them into a bonfire and sending ash and embers into the sky.

"We need to go." Damien tugged Rae's arm. "There's only one way to stop this."

"We need to wait for Jarrod and Corin!" She resisted his pull, turning to the sound of hooves.

The two riders galloped on black warhorses towards them, and Rae sighed with relief. Jarrod and Corin came to a stop as Rae mounted her dark bay. The other thieves and auer followed suit, with Damien on his horse next to her.

Without needing to speak, they all rushed towards the forest, weaving between trees in the shadows towards the tunnels' hidden entrance. The sounds of battle behind them faded, the occasional burst of fire lighting the sky.

Rae's belly ached with each stride of her horse.

Don't even think about it, little one.

Their horses eased to a walk as they approached the tunnels, and Rae swung to the ground with a grunt. She clutched her stomach, cringing as she faced away from the others.

Damien's hand closed on her shoulder, and he stepped in front of her to force her gaze up. His brow knitted, lips pressed in a thin line. "What's wrong?"

Rae shook her head. "It's nothing. Riding can be uncomfortable and cause a little pain, is all." She straightened, the tightness in her abdomen subsiding. "The midwife in Mirage warned me this could start happening, but it doesn't mean anything."

Damien frowned, and didn't move away while the others dismounted, a pair of Hawks taking the leads of the horses to hide them in the woods.

Maith emerged from the mouth of the cave, a Hawk on either side of him with their black hoods in place. "There's no sign that Iedrus has discovered this entrance. We should be safe."

Corin approached the cave, his eyes narrowed.

Jarrod put a hand on his husband's upper arm. "You all right?"

The master of war nodded before facing Rae and Damien. His eyes lingered on her and she gave a subtle shake of her head to deter him from voicing his concern. "Ready?"

Rae nodded, taking a deep breath and stepping with the others into the cave.

"Excuse me." A short hawk in a deep maroon cloak pushed past Damien, making him step closer to Rae. A grey-blond curl popped out from the edge of the hood, and Lucca gave Rae a bright smile. She continued on with the first group of Hawks, towards a rock wall at the back of the cave that pushed inward before sliding to the side.

Another Hawk paused next to Rae, and Silas tilted his chin enough for her to see his face. "Sarth would be proud." He strode ahead without waiting for a response, but Rae's eyes burned.

Damn pregnancy emotions.

Rae entered the tunnels beside Damien, and the humid, stale air hit her lungs like a wall. She wrinkled her nose, unable to remember the last time she'd set foot in the Hawks' paths beneath Veralian.

Meeka shot up next to her, Remmy in tow. She held a torch, lighting the way as she guided the second group, including Rae and the others, to the center hub that connected the main paths. As they approached, the oil sconces embedded in the tunnel walls allowed Meeka to abandon the torch.

The large crew of Ashen Hawks, sent weeks ahead, had set up tables and chairs in the circular area beneath the city's main square. A huge sun dominated the floor, its rays stretching into the different paths branching out.

Damien hovered close to Rae as she approached the table, eyeing the maps they'd worked on for weeks to coordinate what all was about to happen. He touched her hand, tangling his fingers with hers.

Lucca and Silas's crew vanished down the northern tunnel towards the barracks district of the city, while Meeka looked at Rae for her orders.

Rae looked up at the rest of the Hawks waiting for her command.

Sarth made this look so easy.

"Meeka, take your group here." Rae pointed to the first marker on the map. "Jeni, go here. Fan out and hopefully our auer friends can help find the summoners." She met the jeweled eyes of the auer who'd volunteered to join the Hawks, to use the Art to seek those practicing it within the city walls. She switched to Aueric. "Thank you for your assistance in this matter, friends."

Each lifted three fingers to their foreheads, lowering them in a respectful gesture before turning to their respective Hawk crew leader.

Rae pointed to the markers on the maps again. "Murray and Bates, here. Luo and Veck, here. Karim and Luis, here." She circled the entire city, one district at a time. "Send someone to check in each time you find and destroy a summoner."

Once each group received their marker, they disappeared into the tunnels, making room for the next leader to get their orders.

Six Hawks would stay behind with her, including Braka.

After Rae had dispersed the last group, she looked at Damien. "Even if Iedrus doesn't keep summoners in his castle, the place won't be without its defenses. Please be safe."

Damien stood close to her side, and he squeezed her hand. "What could go wrong? We have Maith." He smiled as he kissed her temple. "Promise me you won't leave the tunnels."

"Not unless I have no other choice." Rae looked back and forth between his eyes. "Come back to me, Lieutenant."

"He'll be fine." Jarrod patted Rae's shoulder, and Neco nosed her hand. "As soon as it's over, you'll hear the city's horn ordering the troops to surrender."

As Jarrod stepped back, Corin gave Rae a rough kiss on her hair. "Love you, sis." He pinched her cheek, and she frowned as he walked with Jarrod towards the tunnel that'd take them to the castle.

Neco's claws tapped on the stone as he disappeared after them.

Damien touched her side, pulling her close and kissing her. His hand pressed firmly against her stomach, then her cheek. "I'll see you soon."

Rae nodded, dropping one of her dice into his pocket without taking anything. "Soon."

Damien watched her eyes for a moment, then his grip loosened. He stepped back, but didn't turn as he slipped his hand into his pocket. She smiled as he pulled the die out, holding it between two fingers. He kissed it before pocketing it again and turning to vanish with Corin and Jarrod.

Rae swallowed, staring into the flickering sconce light.

Nymaera, please don't take them.

Chapter 32

"I NEVER KNEW HOW MANY awful smells I was spared before." Jarrod wrinkled his nose, the tunnels' air heavy with the stench of mold and rat urine. "You three should be grateful for your inferior noses."

Neco sneezed, agreeing with the sentiment as he trotted ahead of Maith into the darkness.

"I think I'd be willing to endure some bad smells to have the other advantages Neco gives you." Damien brought up the back of the group, his voice echoing against the stone walls.

"You mean like the extra strength, endurance, improved night vision, and incredible hearing?" Jarrod smirked. "Though the hearing has its downfalls, too, the rest I suppose has come in handy." He looked sideways at Corin. "My husband doesn't complain."

Corin furrowed his brow to hide a smile. "Can we focus, please? I don't need more distractions like thinking about where I'd rather be *with my husband* right now." He brushed his hand against Jarrod's.

Maith touched the wall of the tunnel, pausing.

Jarrod halted beside him. "What is it?"

"Nothing. The energy here is so... different from most I've felt since arriving on the mainland. It's undisturbed, save for the Charcoal Doves."

Damien snorted.

Jarrod frowned. "Ashen Hawks."

"Yes, them."

Rolling his eyes, Jarrod motioned the way they were going. "Can we continue, or...?"

"Of course."

When they reached the trapdoor beneath the castle sewers, Jarrod sighed. "Something tells me the smells are going to get worse."

"And this is the last time we'll be able to speak out loud, at least until we run into trouble." Damien eyed his brother.

Corin scowled during their silent conversation. "I've got it locked down," he grumbled as he waved a hand at his brother. "I might not be able to maintain it if you keep pestering me."

"Silence it is." Jarrod gave Damien a look and tugged on the overhead hatch door. It swung open, adding a new green haze to the air and making his stomach roil.

Neco whined, looking up at the opening.

Gonna need this, bud. Jarrod took the pack from Maith at the auer's offering and unbuckled the top. He retrieved the harness that had been fashioned for the big wolf.

Groaning as Jarrod put each of his paws through, Neco shook his body. *I don't like it. It pulls my fur.*

I know. Just for now. Jarrod cinched the buckles at Neco's chest and behind his shoulders. He laced rope through the hardware. *We'll pull you up.*

Neco lowered his head and whined again, laying down with a huff.

Maith pulled himself through first with little effort, reaching down for the rope Jarrod passed up.

Damien stayed behind as Jarrod and Corin climbed into the sewers above and used the rope to haul Neco up to join them. The wolf refused to help, hanging limply even as Damien hoisted his weight up.

When the former Rahn'ka joined them, they shut the hatch door, and darkness engulfed them.

A dim ball of light appeared with Maith's snap of his fingers, revealing Damien's struggle with Neco to remove his harness.

Dripping echoed from several sources, the noise ricocheting in Jarrod's head.

Corin shivered beside him, rubbing his temple with a wince.

Jarrod touched Corin's face, tilting his head to catch his gaze. *You all right?*

Corin shuddered again, but nodded. *Just building pressure.*

Tell me if it becomes too much, I can try to help.

Squeezing Jarrod's hand, Corin gave him a smile. *Let's get through this. That is what will help me. I can stay in control long enough to take down Iedrus.*

Jarrod kissed Corin's knuckles and motioned with his head down the sewer tunnel. Nothing disturbed the quiet air except their soft steps and Neco's claws tapping on the damp stone floor.

Streams of water ran on either side of the sewers, rats chittering as they scurried away from the light.

Jarrod led them through several turns, up a slant, and stopped when they reached a dead end. He felt along the wall, looking for the entrance all the Hawks' maps suggested existed. Finding a wooden latch, he flicked it to the side and pushed on the half-size door.

Maith snuffed out his light with a flick of his wrist, plunging them back into darkness.

Jarrod blinked, trying to get his eyes to adjust, but too little light penetrated this deep into the sewers. Keeping his hand on the door's latch, he leaned blindly against it.

It resisted the movement, and something scuffed along the stone floor on the other side. Pausing to listen, Jarrod pushed again until Maith squeezed his arm and slipped through first.

Jarrod waited with the others in the darkness, heart pounding in his ears. He ground his teeth, willing it to slow with no success.

Dim light brightened the opening, and Maith's face appeared, a new orb of light floating above his palm. He nodded, motioning for them to join him.

Even Neco had to squeeze through the narrow opening, the door weighted in place by a giant bag of flour.

We're in the pantry.

Jarrod stood once inside, looking around the cellar. The crates stacked in the corners brimmed with grain, while the shelves overflowed with dried meats, cheeses, and jars of other cooking ingredients.

Anger bubbled in Jarrod's gut, and he shook his head.

While his people starve.

Corin walked to the stairs, withdrawing his blade while he started up them. Pausing at the sealed door, he listened, his grip flexing on his imbued weapon. He touched the doorknob, pushing the door open a crack. A thin stream of orange light shone across his face, growing wider with each slow movement of the door.

Smells like bread. Neco's thought matched Jarrod's, and he took a step forward.

Corin, stop.

Jarrod's instruction came too late, and a woman gasped on the other side of the door.

They all froze for a moment, wide-eyed, before Corin pushed the door open the rest of the way without further hesitation, Jarrod close behind him.

Within the castle kitchens, a young woman stood at one of the long preparation tables kneading a ball of dough next to several more. She held still, like a frightened doe, as Corin lifted his finger to his lips.

As Jarrod stepped from behind Corin, her eyes widened even more. "You're... You're Jarrod Martox." Her face paled in the orange firelight from the nearby hearth and ovens. Her gaze flickered to the knife block across the room.

Jarrod listened, trying to assess the other rooms of the kitchen, connected through open archways, but heard no sign of another. "Aye. I am. And you are?"

"Corise," she squeaked. She looked down at her hands and frowned, brushing them off on her dirty apron. The clay beads on her bracelet tapped together, drawing Jarrod's gaze.

Runes decorated the different beads, and Jarrod recognized the purpose behind the jewelry. Most staff wore them in the more distinguished Helgathian households, granting them access beyond wards that'd otherwise prohibit unwelcome visitors. The same wards Maith had come to help with.

"You alone, Corise?" Corin had crossed to the other side of the room, allowing Damien to slip around the edge of the kitchen towards her only exit.

Confusion and fear clouded her light eyes, but she nodded before suddenly shaking her head. "Please, don't hurt me. I'm just... doing my job."

"We're not going to hurt you." Jarrod lifted his hands as Maith and Neco entered behind him, shirking along the back wall away from the cook.

"Have you come to kill Iedrus?"

Corise's question rattled through Jarrod, and he paused, lowering his hands while he considered his answer.

"I won't stop you. I won't tell anyone you're here."

"I think you know we can't take your word for it." Corin met Jarrod's gaze before motioning with his chin towards the pantry door behind him.

"Still won't hurt you." The king shook his head.

"I know." Corise's eyes softened. "I've heard about you. What you've done..."

"Only the good things, I hope." Maith leaned against the far wall, arms crossed.

"What you did for Edrikston." Corise's shoulders relaxed, and she lifted a cloth to drape over her balls of dough. "My sister lives there. She told me how House Martox kept them from starving."

Jarrod's heart twisted as he remembered the events that followed his stop in Edrikston. "I did what any good leader would do."

Corise looked at Corin and then glanced behind her at

Damien. "I won't run. And I know you can't trust me, not with something this important." She sighed and walked away from the preparation table towards the pantry. "You're lucky I'd just gotten back from the pantry with a bag of flour and forgot to lock it." She offered Jarrod a sheepish smile and pulled a small bronze key from her apron.

Jarrod accepted it, closing his other hand on top of hers. "We'll let you out when we're finished here." He squeezed her hand, looping his fingers around her bracelet to remove it as he let go. Tucking the beads into his palm, he nodded at her. "Thank you for cooperating."

Corise bowed her head. "I merely loyally serve my king, my lord." Tugging the pantry door open, she slipped inside.

Corin gave a little huff. "Well, that was easy."

"Don't get too comfortable. That was lucky." Damien crossed the room as Jarrod locked the pantry door.

Meeting Corin's gaze, Jarrod held up the beaded jewelry. "Should help."

Corin smirked, looking past the bracelet at Jarrod. "Can't help those sticky fingers, huh?"

Jarrod joined him at the doorway to the dining hall, and Corin touched the scar on Jarrod's chin. He tossed the beads to Maith, who caught them and slid the jewelry onto his own wrist.

They continued through the main floor of the castle, entering the hallway and avoiding the west court to reach the stairwell that led to the second floor. Maith tested the beads at the ward present and smiled when he passed beyond the archway without anything noticeable happening.

The auer tossed the beads to Corin, and one by one they passed beneath the archway. Jarrod caught the beads last and stalked through with his hand on Neco's ruff.

From there, they maneuvered through the maze of hallways towards the grand tower where Iedrus housed his family and highest ranking staff. The closer they got, the more soldiers lined the hallways, making their route more convoluted. They had to repeat the strategy of tossing the beaded bracelet between them several times.

As they crossed an upper-floor hallway, the rattle of armor and boots thudding on the polished tile floor signaled an unexpected patrol.

Jarrod froze, evaluating the surrounding rooms, and hurried towards a quiet door that smelled of parchment and leather bindings. He opened the unlocked door, ushering their entire group inside as the shine of the patrol's armor rounded the corner ahead. Holding his breath, he closed the latch on the door as silently as possible and crouched beside Corin.

If this doesn't earn me official membership to the Hawks, I don't know what will. Corin's voice teased in Jarrod's mind.

Jarrod glanced at his husband, whose face twisted in discomfort in the moonlight cascading through the small study.

Closing his eyes, Corin's jaw tightened. *I can tell we're coming up on more powerful wards. And more guards. We can't keep avoiding them.*

Might be time to fight, then. Jarrod drew his sword, keeping a gloved hand on the sheath's opening to silence the sound.

Maith withdrew his weapon as well, the blade half the thickness of a traditional Helgathian sword, but Jarrod didn't doubt its effectiveness.

They sat in silence, waiting for the footsteps of the patrol to pass the doorway.

Damien stood first after they were gone, gesturing to Maith as they crept back into the hallway. As they rounded the corner, Maith stopped mid-stride, prompting all to do the same.

Maith touched the bracelet, eyeing a nondescript archway ahead and shook his head.

At least the bracelet got us this far.

Jarrod hesitated. They'd discussed what would happen if Maith nullified a ward. This far into the castle, it would likely be written off as faulty if the disabling alerted anyone.

Taking a deep breath through his nose, Jarrod nodded at the auer.

Maith propped his sword against the archway and touched the stone.

As he worked, Damien skirted along the wall to keep watch of their backs.

Distant voices touched Jarrod's ears, and he closed his eyes to listen, hearing Corin's sword being drawn from his belt. Still unable to pick up the voices, he funneled his consciousness into Neco to borrow the wolf's ears.

"We've won. I bet Martox is dead already."

"If not yet, soon. You see the horizon? Glad I'm in here and not on that field."

"I don't know, I'd have liked to show the rebels how a soldier of Helgath is supposed to fight."

"You'll still get that chance. Iedrus promised he'd capture some alive for sport later."

The other soldier chuckled, his armor clanking as he leaned against something. "Good, put them to some use then. Been a little lacking in entertainment around here since we all gathered. I miss the executions and raids."

Jarrod disconnected from Neco's senses, opening his eyes to find Corin staring at him. *Two guards are manning the grand tower entrance. Two very loyal guards. We'll have to take them out.*

Corin's body tightened, and he nodded. *Strike fast, then.*

Backing away from the archway, Maith lowered his hands and picked up his sword with a tilt of his chin.

With Jarrod's nod to the group, they all continued through the archway and down the hall. They moved slow enough to silence their footsteps, pressed as close as they could get to the paneled walls, and neared the corner in front of the stairs.

Corin flattened against the wall opposite Jarrod, and they stopped. The runes on his sword flickered as he channeled power into them.

Neco hung back with Damien and Maith.

Jarrod looked at Damien and drew his finger across his throat, and Damien nodded. He paused in the doorway they'd come from, looking down the lush hallway that led to the stairwell they needed. On either side of the maroon rug were finely carved tables with decorative statues and vases. Far gaudier than any of the decor House Martox had kept in their castle.

A pang of grief struck Jarrod's gut, and he cringed.

This is for you, Da.

Damien nudged one of the gold-leafed vases with his sword towards the edge of the table. It teetered off and exploded against the uncovered portion of the tiled floor. He leaned against the wall beside the table, not bothering to hide, and watched for the guards.

"What was that?" One guard drew his sword and shuffled forward. "Damned clumsy servants?"

Both guards rounded the corner and stopped when they saw Damien standing next to the table with a big valley wolf at his side.

"Sorry fellas, my wolf friend is kinda clumsy. He'll pay for it, I swear." Damien lifted one hand, his other maintaining his sword.

Neco huffed.

"What the…"

"You're Damien Lanoret!"

Jarrod made eye contact with Corin as the guards walked past them without pause.

Now.

"How in the hells—"

Jarrod and Corin leapt from their spots, clamping arms around the guards' necks. The king used his free hand to twist the sword out of the guard's grip while Corin buried his blade into the other.

"Move them, now." Maith strode towards them. "The patrol is coming back." He waved a hand, reconstructing the broken vase on its pedestal.

"Shit." Corin dragged the body of his soldier.

Jarrod jerked his arm to the side, the crunch of bone making him shudder. "Hurry."

The guard in his arms fell limp.

Damien shuffled around them to open the door of a small storeroom, and Jarrod threw his body in. Corin tossed next, his sword sliding out from the pierced armor like coming from a sheath. The spelled blade had cut clean through the steel plates of the soldier's carapaced chest piece.

Damien tugged the door closed.

Rushing forward, Jarrod led the way to the grandiose curved staircase, but Neco bounded past, a low growl in his chest.

The wolf barreled straight into a pair of guards standing at the top of the stairs. The one he tackled had no time to react, flattened onto the floor with fangs sinking into his neck.

The other guard drew his sword with a shout, and it reverberated down the wide hallway and stairs. He lunged at Neco with his blade, but Jarrod grabbed him by the collar and heaved him down the stairs.

Damien let out an unintelligible curse as he threw himself against the banister to avoid the man, Corin diving in the opposite direction.

Maith sidestepped, lifting his hands as the guard clamored down the stairs, landing with a crash at the bottom.

"Well..." Damien huffed for breath as they reached the top of the stairs. "Pretty sure the other guards heard that."

The sound of more armor clattering echoed back up the stairs from the patrol they'd narrowly avoided. Another pair emerged ahead within the hallway decorated similarly to the one below, with the addition of long banners of maroon fabric draped between ceiling joists.

"I guess the time for stealth is..." Jarrod narrowed his eyes as Maith sprinted up the stairs two at a time towards the approaching guards.

The auer spun his nimble sword, boots making no sound as he lunged. When one of the guards raised his weapon in defense, Maith twisted backwards and tossed his sword to his other hand to land a diagonal downward strike to the man's shoulder. It sank deep into his collar, but the auer didn't pause before withdrawing the blade and dancing it over to meet the other guard.

Gods, do all auer sword fight like that?

The two fell to the thick carpet, blood darkening the maroon beneath them.

"Show off," Corin grumbled as he spun to face the patrol coming up from below.

They met Damien first, who caught the first soldier's blow on his sword, forcing it up to kick him in the chest. He tumbled backwards, yelping. The third patroller caught him, while the other charged at Corin, but his sword was ready and the sound of steel against steel rang through the halls.

Jarrod turned from the stairs at the sound of armored boots running. Focusing, he counted. *Three more.* He relayed the message to Neco, who snarled.

"We need to push through to the next floor!" Maith stooped to pick up one of the swords from the defeated guards, testing its weight in his left hand with a spin.

Take them for a run, bud. Jarrod nodded at Neco and the wolf took off. He rounded a corner, his growl rising in his chest loud enough for Jarrod to hear. The guards cursed, armor banging together as Jarrod imagined Neco barreling through them in the opposite direction of the next set of stairs.

The guards took the bait and chased the wolf, leaving the next portion of their path clear.

Jarrod looked down the stairs again as Corin shoved the last patrol guard's body down the stairs. The brothers huffed as they climbed back to the top, and looked at Jarrod.

"Neco's distracting some that way." Jarrod gestured in the direction they'd gone.

"We can go this way." Damien motioned with his chin to the left. "Staff passage around the meeting halls. Long way, but it'll get us to the stairs for Iedrus's private chambers."

"Lead the way. I'll keep track of our furry friend." Jarrod felt for Neco's location, finding the wolf had gathered more guards on his run through the middle floor of the tower. He led them like a line of ducklings scurrying through the halls.

Damien pushed through a narrow doorway, partially hidden by a lavish tapestry. The passageway, meant to hide the staff as they traveled from room to room, boasted plain stone walls and floors.

Corin paused at the door, holding it open for Jarrod as he glanced down the hall. Blood speckled his dark armor, but none of it was his.

The hallways ran the entire distance of the outside of the tower, but Damien turned sharply down a hall that would take them towards the center. A distant bell chimed, the alarm they'd all known would come.

Only way now is to fight.

Damien paused at a door, looking back at Jarrod. "Pretty sure this is the one. We ready? It'll be another run up the stairs which will have more guards."

Jarrod connected with Neco before nodding. "Our furry companion is coming back to meet us. He's going to try to lose the guards on the way. Let's go. Leave the door open."

Damien nodded and looked at Maith. "I'll take care of the door. After you." With a nod from the auer, he tugged the door open to stay out of the way so Maith could charge through, a sword in each hand.

Jarrod and Corin followed Maith, rushing up the stairs with long strides to keep up.

Maith had already downed one of the guards by the time Jarrod got in sight of the top, spinning around an attacking blade to bury his in another's chest.

Jarrod looked at his husband, heart pounding. "It's not just me taken aback by him, right?"

"One hell of a scholar." Corin smirked. "No wonder no one picks wars with the auer if their librarians fight like this. Glad they're on our side."

The stairs had led to an enormous room, elaborate banisters at the center. Lush carpets spanned the thirty foot distance to more hallways leading out either side.

The wall in front of them stood two stories tall, a mural painted on it. It depicted the lands of Helgath rolling behind valiant generals and soldiers. At the center of it all, god-like, Iedrus's stern likeness. His deep-set eyes bored into the viewer, a gaudy gold crown adorning his bald head.

Maith wheeled on another guard, deflecting the attack with one sword while jabbing the other into an opening in the guard's armor. "Talk later, fight now," he grumbled in their direction, motioning towards the right hallway where a group of six soldiers ran into the open foyer to join those already present.

Iedrus kept more soldiers in here than we expected.

"To the hallways!" Corin pushed Jarrod towards the open doorway.

Maith cut a path just as Damien reached the room, and they rushed through, forcing the soldiers to pursue them into the tighter fighting quarters.

Large windows in the hallway overlooked the city, pillars of smoke on the southern horizon like smoke beasts reaching for the starry sky.

Jarrod's shoulder lurched forward with searing pain and he stumbled, bracing himself against the outer wall as he eyed the bolt protruding from his flesh. "Damn it."

Corin caught his hand before he could pull the bolt out. He lifted his sword, holding the bolt still against Jarrod's flesh, and hacked off the back of the exposed wooden shaft.

Jarrod growled, his vision flashing with bright colors. Before he could advance, his eyes landed on the crossbow aimed at Corin. He grabbed his husband's shoulders and yanked him to the side, the bolt whizzing past where his head had been. It shattered a window, sending glass scattering over the floor.

Sounds and smells rushed in from the outside, smoke and screams.

Jarrod dared a glance at the city, realizing the flames rose from the southern district.

Maith cried out as a club slammed into his wrist, sending his pilfered Helgathian sword skittering across the floor. He'd faced three, and one found the necessary opening.

A boot collided with Maith's chest and the auer sprawled backwards, scrambling to rise to his feet.

The same guard kicked his ribs, and when Damien tried to intervene, two others attacked, pushing him against the windowed wall.

We need to get out of this hallway.

Jarrod looked behind him for an exit, but found another group of guards approaching from the far side, this one led by a decorated officer.

Light from the wall sconces glittered off his perfectly polished armor, which had likely never seen a day of actual battle. At his left shoulder, his golden insignia secured his cloak. Four stars identified him as a general of Iedrus's military.

"Hold." The general lifted his hand, and the guards stiffened.

"Fenner," Damien whispered. He kicked off a guard and, this time, the man didn't attack again. "You've got to be shitting me."

The guards took up positions around them, their swords ready.

Maith rose to his feet, still gripping his slender sword with a bloody hand.

The general glared at each of them, sucking on his teeth. He paused on Damien, his eyes narrowing. "Damien Lanoret. I'd hoped I'd get to see you again before you died with this silly rebellion, fighting for a usurper foolish enough to break into King Iedrus's castle himself."

Jarrod growled, warm blood dripping down his left arm to fall from his fingers. "Men like *you* are precisely why I'm here. Because when Iedrus falls, men won't be promoted for killing innocent people anymore."

The Rahn'ka had told Jarrod of the events leading to his desertion of the Helgathian military, when General Fenner was only a colonel. Damien's battalion had been tasked with capturing a fugitive and had narrowed down the location to a small village. Fenner ordered Damien to burn it down with the locals trapped inside their homes after they didn't cooperate with the military's search. Damien had refused, disobeying orders, but Fenner saw to the destruction and death, anyway.

"Insubordination, cowardice, those are the traits you'll find in this sorry excuse for a man." Fenner gestured at Damien and spat on the floor. "Your spineless attitude disgusts me."

Where's Neco?

Damien pushed away from the wall, stepping closer to Fenner, his eyes fiery. "You've *murdered* countless innocent people in the name of this *king*." He gestured at the windows. "And it's still happening. The real traitors to our country are Iedrus and all who serve him."

Jarrod grasped Corin's shoulder for balance and closed his eyes, seeking his connection to the wolf. He found Neco, still on the lower floor.

"Your daftness astounds me. I can't..."

The voices vanished as Jarrod merged his consciousness with Neco's, requesting control of the wolf. Neco conceded, and with a snap, Jarrod looked through the wolf's eyes.

He pricked his ears behind him, not hearing anyone chasing him anymore. *Where are the guards, boy?*

I ate them.

Neco...

Fine. I found a room of stuffed dead animals, and I pretended to be one. They couldn't find me and gave up.

Creative. But we need you, now.

Jarrod ran with Neco's body to the door, still ajar, and bounded up the stairs. Fenner and Damien's voices touched his ears again as he raced towards the hallway they were trapped in.

Eyes locking on the guard with the crossbow, he lunged through the ranks. They toppled sideways from his bulk, and Neco's teeth sank into flesh and chaos erupted again.

Letting go of the connection, Jarrod spun around to attack Fenner just in time to see the general surge towards Damien.

Fenner's face purpled as he grabbed Damien by the collar and shoved him towards the windowed wall.

Damien caught him, kicking out at Fenner's ankles, and they spun together into a window. It shattered, spraying shards of glass as the pair tumbled over the sill.

"No!" Jarrod raced for the window, heart leaping into his throat.

Damien let out a short shout of surprise as he and the general vanished from view, falling through open air.

Chapter 33

WIND RUSHED, BLOCKING OUT ALL SOUND.

Damien's stomach whirled, left somewhere in the air above him.

Time slowed.

He kicked Fenner, pushing the general and forcing them both to spin in the air, granting Damien a view of the ground rushing towards them.

I'm sorry, Rae.

He closed his eyes, willing himself not to fear what came next. He struggled to suck in a calming breath, imagining the journey his ká would embark on to the Afterlife.

His muscles tightened, prepared to strike the ground, and the roar of the wind stopped.

All sound vanished, as if sucked out of existence, but the pain never came.

Damien furrowed his brow, refusing to open his eyes and see the ground at the last moment before his body broke against it. He counted.

...fifteen, sixteen...

Open your stupid human eyes.

Damien's eyes snapped open, and they focused on Sindré's navy gaze.

The guardian hovered in their humanesque form, arms crossed, glowering from beneath the crown of antlers.

So eager to damage your vessel. Jalescé's hiss rattled in laughter. *You ignored my warning.* They shook a finger, donned with a wickedly long nail. Their bearded face appeared youthful, the hair braided with beads and feathers.

"Am I dead?" Damien looked the other way, but time had frozen him inches above the ground, an unconscious Fenner moments from his own death.

You think we would let you die? Sindré rolled their eyes.

As stubborn and frustrating as you are, you are still the best Rahn'ka we've encountered since the world broke apart. Yondé's bare chest swelled with an annoyed breath. *But your near death cuts this lesson short.*

"Lesson?" Damien grumbled. "Seriously?"

It will become clear in time why this was necessary. Sindré waved a hand, and Damien's arm tingled.

The Rahn'ka clawed at his sleeve, the tattoos glowing through the material. The swarm of pins on his skin passed into his chest, and his mind surged with the sudden return of awareness. Even in the stillness of time, the slow rise of voices pushed against his senses, requiring the instant erection of his barrier. He took a breath, feeling more alive than he had in months, the tide of power reacting to his soul.

Emotion threatened his eyes at the relief it brought, but he swallowed to control it. "Thank you, guardians." He looked between each of them. "I know I may not understand your reasoning for all you do, but thank you for trusting me with the power again."

Don't disappoint us. The hint of a smile crossed Sindré's thin lips.

As time gradually resumed, Damien twisted in the air. With another steady breath, he channeled his Art into his legs and the air. His surroundings lurched into motion again, and he landed on the stone path of the courtyard, kneeling. The slab of rock split down the center, cracks radiating out from where his knee hit with flashing pale blue light. His left hand steadied the landing, arm shining beneath his sleeve.

Fenner lay dead a few feet away, blood splattered around him.

Damien shielded his face from the falling glass and looked up, finding the broken window close to one hundred feet up. Stepping forward, the glass crunched beneath his boots and he sought the energies of the courtyard. He welcomed the voices into his ká, grateful to feel them mingling with his own again. He greeted each one in a flurry of relief, accepting the energy they offered to empower his own.

Now isn't a time to be bashful about accepting help.

With a deep breath, the voices surged, and he soaked up all he could as he crossed to the wall. Placing his hand on the stone, he felt every weave within it. Those from the original quarry where the bricks had been hewed, to the grains of clay within the mortar and the new patterns they made together.

With a flicker of his Art and an ushering of his ká, the stone gave into him, and ripples of pale blue light encouraged protrusions to emerge. He grabbed the first handhold, pulling himself off the ground. Drawing more energy into his tightening muscles, he climbed. The edges of his vision blurred with the light of the Rahn'ka, and he didn't need to look to know where to grip.

His lungs burned with the smoke from the fires consuming the southern region of the city, but he continued at a pace impossible without the energies pulsing through him.

The wind roared in his ears the higher he got until his hands closed on the sill of one of the windows where he could still sense his friends. With a grunt, he swung himself up, slamming his boots into the unbroken window as runed shields of light boiled around his body.

His head buzzed, a distant pounding from the rapid channeling of power, but he found his feet as the tattoos on his arm pulsed brighter. From his fist, the shaft of his spear erupted, the light refracting off Iedrus's soldiers' armor.

For a moment, the fighting in the hallway paused, all eyes locked on him.

A smile twitched Jarrod's lips.

The soldiers blinked, and two charged at Damien.

Clenching his free hand, Damien focused on connecting his power to every ká in the room. It took longer than he'd have liked, but when the two attackers lifted their swords, they froze, wide-eyed. Lifting his hand, the thin ropes of power flickered in the air like an illusion, connecting Damien's ká to all the soldiers in the hall.

They stood rigid, like an invisible grip closed around their throats.

With a tug, Damien separated their ká from their bodies.

Every guard collapsed in a cacophonous explosion of metal crashing. Wisps of blue flickered around their heads before they floated downward.

Corin sighed, collapsing against the stone wall, grinning. "About fucking time." The runes on his sword were dull, like Damien's tattoos had been.

Maith sheathed his sword, blood dripping from his hand.

"Gods, it's good to see you." Jarrod looked at the bolt still protruding from his shoulder. "I hate to put you to work immediately, but..."

Damien grinned as he walked towards Jarrod, stepping over the fallen guard. He leaned his spear against the wall before putting both hands over the bolt. With a jerk, and no warning, he removed the projectile. Jarrod's blood gushed against his fingertips before his ká began the healing process.

Groaning, the king cringed. "Nymaera's breath. Did you miss hurting me or something?"

"I didn't think you needed the coddling." Damien pressed his fingers a little harder against the closing wound. "Did you want a hug, too?"

Jarrod looked at Corin. "Your brother is trying to kill me."

Corin clapped Damien hard on the back. "I'm just fucking glad he's alive. Damn guardians finally got their heads on straight." As soon as Damien took his hand away from Jarrod, Corin pulled him into a rough hug while the king inspected his wound.

Neco pressed his wet nose into Damien's palm, licking. *You're alive. That is good.*

"Thanks buddy." Damien gave the wolf a quick scratch under the chin before he pushed firmly away from Corin. "We'll have time to talk about it later." Looking at Maith, he stepped forward and gingerly lifted the auer's broken wrist. The beginning of a headache threatened, but he pushed it down as he aligned the man's bone and pushed power into him.

Maith cursed loudly in Aueric.

"Hold on to some of that energy. We're not done fighting yet, I bet." Jarrod stepped over the dead bodies, picking up the crossbow and moving down the hallway. "You think they're smart enough to evacuate Iedrus?"

"That smug asshole? No way." Corin walked back to his brother, holding up his sword. "If it's not too much, I kind of liked being able to cut through just about anything."

Damien rolled his eyes and snatched Corin's sword. Most of the work lay in the runes, so it didn't take much energy to reactivate them. His brother beamed as Damien handed it back. "You won't be able to deactivate them until I can build you a trigger later, so... be careful where you wave that thing."

"We should get moving. Iedrus knows we're coming by now." Jarrod motioned with his chin. "His personal chambers are this way."

Damien snatched his spear from the wall and hurried to follow, tensing his muscles as they moved just to feel the way his ká flexed with them.

Gods, I missed this.

Most of the guards from the floor must have converged on the men in the hallway, because no more stood between them and the final stairway that went into Iedrus's private chambers.

Can you check the rest of the floor, boy? Damien glanced at

Neco, who snorted in dislike. *We need to know if they evacuated him, and you're the only one for the job.*

Flattery. Neco swung his head in his own version of an eye roll. *Save that for cats.* He loped off anyway, tail swishing behind him.

"He's gotten even smarter in the last two months." Damien looked at Jarrod as they started up the stairs, finally pacing themselves instead of running.

"Tell me about it. He pretended to be a taxidermied animal to escape the guards earlier."

"That wolf is going to be the one ruling Helgath. Jarrod's just a figurehead." Corin smirked, bringing up the back of the group.

Jarrod huffed. "Pretty much."

"You able to do that..." Corin wiggled his fingers at the air, looking at Damien. "...Ká-y thing again up here if there are more guards? Rip their souls out?"

Damien frowned. "You were the fucking Rahn'ka for two months and you're still making fun of it?"

Corin shrugged.

"No. That took a lot of energy. I need to be more conservative in case we run into real trouble." Damien couldn't help but believe they hadn't yet encountered the hardest part of dethroning Iedrus.

Jarrod met Damien's gaze. "Whatever you do, Iedrus is mine."

Chapter 34

"WE'RE BACK, BOSS."

Rae looked up from the maps on the table and met Meeka's gaze.

Remmy held her hand, standing beside her as they approached with their team of Hawks and auer.

"Downed another summoner." Meeka grinned. "Killed its Corrupted pet-thing, too. Ugly shitters."

Rae smirked. "Good. The two teams before you came back and reported they found no more summoners in their district, so we might be close to getting them all. I need you to reroute your efforts to focus on the military officers. Hopefully, this will all be over soon."

Braka put a piece of dried meat in his mouth. "You smell like smoke."

"South Veralian is completely ablaze. It looks like Iedrus is trying to force King Martox into backing down by blocking the armies from entering that side of the city." Remmy rolled his shoulders. "Should we divide our efforts between searching for summoners and rescuing civilians? The tunnels are a good way to get people out of danger."

Rae sighed and nodded. "When you can help civilians, do it, but don't bring them down here. We can't risk any of Iedrus's guards following them. Take them to the northern part of Veralian. Lucca and Silas report that it's less volatile in that district."

Remmy frowned, but nodded. "Yes, ma'am."

A shudder ran down Rae's back. "Don't call me ma'am."

Meeka smirked and tugged on Remmy's hand. "She prefers boss."

Rae laughed. "You call me boss like you call everyone ranked higher than you, boss. Boss is fine, but so is Sika or just Rae. Anything but ma'am."

Footsteps thundered from the east tunnels, Veck's hood displaced from his head. The Hawk leaned over, huffing. "Soldiers. They're coming. In the tunnels." He winced, holding his side and sucking in another breath. "I don't know how, but—"

"Fuck." Rae grabbed the maps and with a surge of will, pulled flame from her lantern and set them aflame. Chucking them in the stone corner to disintegrate to ash, she looked at

Meeka. "Get back out there, now. Spread your crew out to different districts to make sure the rest of the Hawks know the tunnels are compromised."

Braka, still chewing, hoisted the table on its side to block the east tunnel Veck had emerged from.

The five other Hawks who'd stayed in the tunnels took up positions near the hallways, looking to Rae.

"Join Meeka's crew in getting the word out." Rae nodded her chin in the direction they should go. "I don't want anyone returning here."

Braka watched the others scramble to gather their things and follow their instructions. "I'm not leaving you, boss."

Rae clenched her jaw. "I'm not staying here, either. Let's go." She took the south tunnel, hoping to escape the original way they'd entered.

As they navigated the tunnels by memory, the air grew suffocatingly thick with smoke.

Rae coughed, holding a cloth over her face. She couldn't risk using her power to blow the smoke off, as the air could feed the fire. "Why is the smoke getting into the tunnels? All the entrances should be blocked off."

"Unless the soldiers who found it are trying to smoke us out. Or parts of the south district are collapsing." Braka scowled, pulling Rae to a halt. "If they found the cave exit, we're walking into a trap."

"You're right." She shook her head. "We need to—"

In the shadows of the tunnel ahead, a pair of figures appeared amid the smoke. Maroon scarves wrapped around their faces. Their swords already drawn, one pointed at Rae and gave a muffled shout.

The Mira'wyld opened her palm, inviting the fire from the sconces into her grasp. She flung it at the soldiers, the ball of fire plummeting like a stone down the narrow tunnels. One soldier shoved the other out of the way, and they parted just in time for the orb to sail past them into the curtain of smoke.

From the darkness where the smoke swirled, a projectile hurtled outward, and Braka stepped in front of Rae to catch the crossbow bolt on a wooden plank he'd plucked from the tunnel floor.

Rae's left forearm shocked with tingling, and she looked down.

The blackened tattoo Damien had made for her brightened with power.

How...? Damien?

Implications whirled in her mind, but she lifted her left hand.

May as well test it out.

She clenched her hand into a fist, channeling energy into the silver rings. Her blue recurve bow burst from her grip, and she grinned. "Gods, I missed this thing." She sidestepped around Braka and drew back on the bowstring. An arrow materialized in a pulse of blue light and she let it loose, sending another right after at the soldier charging down the tunnel.

"Nymaera's breath, what is *that*?" Braka gaped at the weapon as Rae loosed another arrow into the plumes of smoke.

"A gift from my husband." Rae watched her targets fall and turned. "But if I have it, something's happened. Something might be wrong. We need to get to the castle. The safest place is with them now, anyway."

Chapter 35

THE NERVES IN CORIN'S GUT tightened with each step as they grew closer.

This is almost all over.

They paused outside the door to one of Iedrus's private chambers at a wave from Damien. With another gesture, they all backed away, retreating into the hall.

"Definitely more guards in there," Damien whispered. He narrowed his eyes as he stared blankly at the decorated oak door. "But I can't get a clear picture of how many. Something is blocking me."

Corin scowled, but was relieved Damien had the power to sense it rather than the group relying on him. "What'd block it?"

"Another Art user, potentially." Damien shrugged, turning to Jarrod. "This could be the last door between us and Iedrus."

"If it were me, I'd have my chief vizier in there with me." Jarrod side-eyed Damien. "You're the only one who has a chance at challenging her if she's in there. No offense meant to *my* chief vizier."

Maith shrugged. "I'm a scholar, not specialized in destruction. I'm content in my role, especially when you have such a skilled practitioner already." He motioned to Damien, a smirk lingering on his lips.

Corin glanced both ways down the open hallway. Rich mahogany wood gleamed in the lantern light, the extravagant location hardly the place for the coming battle. "There must be other entrances into this chamber. Can you tell where in the room the guards are?"

Damien shook his head. "But I'd assume they'd be posted and ready close to every doorway. Better not to split up."

"Agreed. Better to keep our strength focused." Jarrod patted Neco's head. "But we need a plan of attack. Damien can focus on the vizier. The rest of us need to take out the guards. Iedrus himself isn't much of a threat."

"Are we giving him another chance to back down?" Corin watched Jarrod, resisting the temptation to grasp his hand. The familiar anxiety of combat rose in his chest like a swarm of bees.

"He won't take it, but I'll offer if the opportunity arises."

Damien turned back to the door, his spear clenched at his side. "I'll go in first to pull any crossbow fire to me. But I won't be able to protect us from a second volley since I'll have the vizier to deal with. So don't dillydally."

"Dillydally." Corin choked on a laugh. "I'll be sure not to shilly-shally either, then. Or lollygag. You got any colly wobbles?"

"Fuck you." Damien started towards the door.

Jarrod's jaw flexed, his eyes dancing with humor. "You sound a little ornery." He looked at Corin. "Maybe we should skedaddle before Damien gets namby-pamby."

"And fuck you, too." Damien's lips pursed to hide the smile as he turned to Jarrod. "Ready, your highness?"

Jarrod nodded. "I've been ready for months."

Face growing more serious, Damien nodded. He rolled his shoulders as he faced the door, sucking in a slow breath.

Corin tightened his grip on his sword, the weight rocking comfortingly with his subtle movement.

Maith walked after Damien, steps silent on the thick carpet.

Jarrod looked at his husband and shrugged. "This is it, Captain. Ready to no longer be a rebel?" He touched Corin's chin.

The touch banished the nerves at the pit of his stomach, bringing Corin a sense of calm that should have been impossible. He pulled Jarrod in for a quick kiss. "I love you."

"And I love you."

"Ready?" Damien tensed, glancing at them.

Jarrod lifted his sword and nodded, releasing Corin to follow the Rahn'ka. "Let's do this."

The door ahead exploded with a brilliant flash of Damien's power, a domed field rupturing the wood and cracking the frame. Light jolted on the barrier's surface as opposing projectiles collided with it, the crossbow bolts clattering to the ground at Damien's feet as he and Maith stepped through the doorway.

The room beyond came into focus through the waves of light. The far wall boasted large windows overlooking the east, the sky split with orange and pink as the sun peeked over the distant hills. The curtains continued around the room, the side walls painted with murals depicting historical Helgathian battles both on land and sea. Four steps led to the raised portion of the room in front of the windows, a line of six guards with crossbows standing on the bottom step. Each reached to the quiver at their side to reload.

A decorated officer stood behind them, his silver hair shining amber in the sunrise. He lifted a fist, and the guards froze, crossbows lowered. At least a dozen more guards stood on the floor in front of the stairs at either side, swords in hand.

"Well, well, well. Congratulations on making it this far."

The power shivered, dropping from the air as Damien sidestepped to the left and Corin followed his gaze back to the platform in front of the windows.

Jarrod stopped between Corin and Damien, Neco at his side.

Twenty feet behind the guards, Leorithin Iedrus sat on an ostentatious chair meant to resemble the throne in the main castle courts. A gold crown rested on his bald head, like the painting, but a smirk twitched his features. He tapped a finger on his armrest, several gaudy rings on his hand. "It's a shame the rest of Helgath can't witness the death of their beloved rebel leader." He looked at Maithalik. "Cute trick with the barrier, but you're no match for my chief vizier, auer or not."

A woman stood at Iedrus's right, her arms crossed inside a maroon robe that matched her short red hair. Her squared shoulders radiated a confidence that matched her smug smirk. However, her gaze tracked left, following Damien instead of Maith.

"Time's up for your treachery, Iedrus. Helgath isn't yours to rule, anymore. You're a traitor under your own laws." Jarrod lifted his chin. "Step down and you'll receive a fair trial like the rest of your men."

"Ha!" Iedrus slapped the wooden armrest. "Step down? You think because you showed up, I'm just going to *give* you the throne? I'd much rather provide a family reunion. I'm sure Reznik would love to see his renegade son."

A growl reverberated in Corin's chest, and he eyed the reloaded crossbows, still lowered while Iedrus spoke. He glanced at Maith, who'd moved left with Damien to challenge the collection of guards on that side of the platform.

Six guards each. No problem. And Damien just gets the one...

Jarrod gazed at the man, amber eyes jarringly calm. "I don't believe in mercy for the honorless, but for you, I will make an exception and ask you again once all your guards are dead."

Neco snarled and launched forward, barreling into one crossbow guard, Jarrod right behind him.

Corin lunged, finally able to focus without the constant need to control an unseen barrier. As the room devolved into clashing steel, his spelled sword cut through the guards' armor without resistance. Each blow flowed into the next, his sword holding strong against the attacks.

His muscles ached as he withdrew his blade from the chest of the last soldier on his side.

Maith struck down the last of the standing guards, and Jarrod threw one of the two remaining crossbow-armed guards into the stone wall. Neco pinned the other with a snarl.

Iedrus's master of war, the silver-haired officer, had backed to be at his side, a gold-hilted sword in his hand.

Iedrus glared to his right, and Corin followed his attentions to the man's chief vizier.

The woman focused on Damien, and even without the power, Corin felt the tension building in the air between them. She'd removed her robe, revealing a pair of black leather breeches and a long blood-red tunic. It hung to her knees, split on both sides up to her hips.

The Rahn'ka paced away, drawing her attention down the room from Jarrod. His eyes narrowed, already slightly unfocused in the way that enabled him to draw on the ká around him. But everything else seemed perfectly in place.

Have they even thrown a single attack yet?

"Mina!" Iedrus snapped.

The chief vizier twitched. Without another warning, she threw her hands forward and an explosion of flames erupted from her palms. It lashed, rising in the air like a whip as she twisted her hand. The room heated, but the tongues of flame collided with Damien's barrier. The pale blue runes of the Rahn'ka swirled, taking hold of the living flame. The length of it wriggled like a snake, pinned between two points.

With a quick gesture from the chief vizier, the end still attached to her broke off and shot towards Damien. It struck like lightning, but not at him. It tore into the floorboards at his feet.

Damien spread his stance, and where his boot touched, the embers crackling through the marble turned steel blue. His body dropped an inch as part of the floor collapsed, but it ceased as he stepped forward, whirling his spear. It cut through the fire like it was a living thing, and the whip vanished. Swinging the butt of his spear up as he approached the vizier, she leapt back, avoiding the blow.

She clapped her hands together, and as she drew them apart, the air between her palms turned to a bruised-purple color. Reaching into the shadow, she gripped the handle of a weapon, large curved blades on either end of the handle. With a swing, it caught the bottom of Damien's spear, forcing him to spin it again.

Purple mist coiled around the shining black metal of her weapon, and she swung it at Damien's chest.

He jumped back, lifting his arm just in time to catch the next blow. Sparks flew from the diamond-shaped shield that protected his forearm.

Holding his spear parallel to the ground and slightly behind him, energy gathered in its shaft. Corin recognized the excited pulsing of the runes as they reacted to the channel opening. Damien didn't strike, despite the chief vizier exposing her right side to try another blow he defended against. She pushed him back one small step at a time, physical blows coupling with bursts of the Art which Damien narrowly avoided.

The vizier stepped back, sweat pouring from her brow. She grimaced, thrusting her hand to her side as she gathered a white-hot orb of fire.

Damien stood straighter from the hunched position she'd beat him down to, his spear vibrating in his hand.

Mina let out a roar of anger as she hurled the ball, larger than her head, at Damien. It soared at the speed of an arrow, and Damien was too close to get out of the way. As he lifted his shield, the ball exploded against it. Raging fire curled around the Rahn'ka's shield, licking at his skin, and Damien cried out.

But instead of collapsing like he looked ready to, Damien lunged. He swung the entire weight of his body with the throw of his arm. The spear left his hand in a flash of pale light, and despite his aim appearing off from Corin's perspective, it curved.

The vizier, wide-eyed, jumped to the side, but the spear turned itself in the air. It slowed for a moment as the head met whatever feeble shield the vizier had attempted before it shoved through.

Pale light flickered through her ká, all focused towards where the spearhead protruded from her sternum. She collapsed to her knees, blood pooling from her lips as the spear pushed deeper into her with a gesture from Damien's hand, even though he stood ten feet away. As the vizier's body crumpled to the floor, the spear tugged free, soaring through the air to Damien's waiting grip. His body sagged with exhaustion, eyes wearily watching the vizier's body.

Corin tried to steady his breathing, but movement behind his brother drew his attention.

A guard, clutching his sliced-open side, rose with his sword pointed at the Rahn'ka.

Jarrod stepped forward. "Behind you!"

Neco raced forward, but the wolf was too far away.

As Damien spun, a blue blur split the air. The Art-laden arrow sank into the guard's head, dropping him to a heap on the floor at Damien's feet.

Corin followed the trajectory, eyes landing on Rae.

Braka stood behind her, a pair of daggers drawn.

The Rahn'ka moved fast, placing himself between Rae and the rest of the room as he whispered to her, too low for Corin to hear, but his eyes were angry.

Together, Corin and Jarrod turned to face Iedrus, Maith coming to stand next to them.

Neco growled.

Iedrus glanced at the wolf and huffed, rising from his seat. His master of war whispered something in his ear and he shook his head, glaring at Jarrod. "You plan to kill an old man in his own home?" He crossed his arms, hands inside his coat.

"Planned to, if given no other option. I promised you a last chance to step down, so here it is. Concede the throne, Leorithin, it's over."

Iedrus lifted his chin with a sneer. "I will not give over what is rightfully mine to an upstart criminal. It is my duty to protect the throne."

Jarrod stepped forward. "Even if it means your death?"

"Perhaps. But even better if it's yours." Iedrus lunged, surprisingly fast for his appearance, withdrawing a knife from inside his coat. He stabbed the weapon towards Jarrod's middle, its surface shining in the sunlight.

Before Corin could intervene, Iedrus's master of war leapt at him, forcing him to raise his sword to deflect the attack. Whatever warrior the old war master had been before disappeared as Corin's enchanted blade tore across his chest. He collapsed as Iedrus cried out.

The corrupt king's wrist snapped as Jarrod squeezed and twisted it.

"Stabbing me, really? Can you be more original?" Jarrod jerked his wrist harder, and the weapon clattered to the floor.

Iedrus wriggled like a snake, reaching behind him for a second dagger. It cut a thin line across Jarrod's hand before the king snatched his wrist again.

"I gave you a chance to step down." Jarrod growled as he seized Iedrus's blade. Spinning it, he slammed it into the tyrant's chest.

The fallen king cried out, clenching the front of Jarrod's tunic. Blood bubbled from a sinister smirk as he pulled himself closer to the king. "I'll give Reznik your regards."

Yanking the blade free, Jarrod drove it in again, breathing hard.

Iedrus choked, his eyes glazing over. He slumped forward as his smirk faded, dripping crimson on the floor.

The room stood in absolute stillness, everyone staring at the body as it collapsed to the floor. The crown clinked down the stairs.

Corin listened to his own deep breaths, meeting Jarrod's eyes as he stepped forward. He entwined his fingers with Jarrod's. "You all right?"

"Aye." Jarrod squeezed Corin's hand, still breathing fast.

Braka grunted. "So, what's next, boss... es."

Jarrod looked past him at Rae. "Why are you two here?"

"Iedrus's men discovered the tunnels and blocked the exit to the forest." Rae glanced at Damien. "We figured with you was the safest place."

Neco leaned against Jarrod's legs.

The king stroked the wolf's head. "Someone needs to blow the horn to announce the end of all this."

"I'll do it." Rae hurried to the stairs to get to the previous floor where the gigantic horn was built into the stone wall.

"I'll go with her." Maith patted Damien's shoulder before running after Rae.

The Rahn'ka looked like he was about to fall over as he approached Jarrod.

Corin glanced after Rae. "The pregnant woman has more energy than me, fantastic."

Jarrod's brow furrowed as he looked at Iedrus's body. "It doesn't feel over, somehow."

The windows and walls behind them vibrated with the low rumble of the horn as it rose to its throaty pitch. Three long blasts sent the surrender message to the troops below. Silence settled before it started again.

Corin squeezed Jarrod's hand harder. "We better get you changed for your formal address to the people."

"Gods, when do I need to do that?"

"Sooner the better." Damien leaned against the wall. "Everything is going to be in chaos until you do. Even if not many show up, word will spread through the city. Then the country."

"No pressure, then." Jarrod ran a hand over his face.

"You're king, now." Damien glanced up at them. "Technically, both of you, but Jarrod's the one that matters."

Corin rolled his eyes and thumbed the scar on Jarrod's chin. "I'll be at your side."

The horn stopped, and the castle hung in silence.

Iedrus's body lay across the steps of the room, his master of war to his left. Both stared blankly at the ceiling, and the smell of blood overtook the room

Corin's eyes roamed, finding the gold crown that'd tumbled from Iedrus's head. He picked it up, examining the hammered metal and inlaid stones. Crossing to Jarrod, he held out the crown.

Jarrod took it, turning it over. "It's not as heavy as I expected." He kept it in his left hand and took Corin's with his right.

"Let's go find a place to get cleaned up." Corin tugged Jarrod towards the room's entrance. "You mind playing bodyguard, Braka?"

The big man picked up his daggers from the ground. "You got it, your majesty."

That's going to sound weird for a while.

As they exited the room, Rae rounded the corner with Maith. She smiled and walked to Damien, who wrapped his arm around her.

He kissed her temple and shook hands with the auer. "How's it look outside?"

"As soon as the horn sounded, there appeared to be a shift. But it's hard to tell from here. We'll have to formally send out soldiers to regain control of the city. Arrest and imprison those still acting in loyalty to Iedrus." Maith's eyes flitted to the crown in Jarrod's hand. "A speech is in order. Gather all the military still left in the castle and surrounding city. If they see the crown... they'll obey."

"Hope so. That's a lot of trials, otherwise. I'll get changed and head to the balcony to address the military if you can work on getting everyone there. I'll address the civilians after."

Maith nodded and hurried off.

"Does anyone know where Iedrus's family might be?" Rae looked at Jarrod.

The king shook his head. "His wife wasn't here, and I don't know what happened to his sons. They could have fled."

"Maybe they saw how crazy their father was acting and didn't want to be part of it." Corin encouraged them all towards the stairs. They started down them slowly, each too tired to take them any faster. "I need a nap. You think there will be time before the speeches?"

"I'm sure we all feel like we could sleep for weeks." Damien smirked before they finished the descent in silence.

"We should find that nice cook again. Corise. Maybe she'll be helpful in pointing me towards a bed." He groaned. "But the kitchens are so far away."

"She's not in the pantry anymore, where you *imprisoned* her." Rae tilted her head at Corin. "I let her go. You're lucky that lock was easy to pick."

"*Now* who is going to direct me to a bed?" Corin whined.

The Mira'wyld scowled. "Well, I'm sure you don't want to sleep in the royal quarters until all the madness has been scrubbed from them." She sighed. "Besides, I don't think there's time for a nap."

Corin hummed a loud whine. "No one understands how exhausting it is to overthrow a king."

Chapter 36

JARROD STARED AT HIS REFLECTION in the tall mirror as the tailor worked, fitting and measuring.

Curled in the corner, Neco's side rose with each sleeping breath, his paws twitching.

Afternoon light streamed in from the large windows overlooking the city. The southern district still smoldered, but the flames had all been extinguished shortly after the surrender horn. The outer wall of the city had a new line of flags erected. The Helgathian maroon stitched with silver representing House Martox whipped in the wind.

Below, people lined the streets with vibrant flowers, both in celebration and memorial of those who'd fallen.

A small regiment marched from the east barracks towards the castle, making their way to the courtyard intended for

Jarrod's announcement. He couldn't tell if they were Martox guards, rebels, or Helgathian military.

But I suppose they're all mine now.

The tailor smoothed the fabric at Jarrod's back, touching where it needed to fit his shoulders.

The king's gaze trailed to the crown he'd yet to wear, sitting on a table near the window. Footsteps outside the room brought his eyes back to the mirror, watching the door behind him as it opened.

There's only a few people who wouldn't bother knocking.

"Starting to look like a proper king." Corin carried a pair of mugs, steaming with the aroma of coffee. He exaggerated the movement of his gaze as he studied Jarrod up and down. "And I am still a very lucky man to call you husband."

Jarrod chuckled, taking the mug Corin offered. "Considering you're bringing me coffee, I'd say I'm the lucky one, here."

The tailor's gaze flitted between the two of them, tension lingering in his shoulders.

Why is he so nervous?

"I figured we both could use something to keep us going for the afternoon." Corin glanced out the windows before he turned and leaned against the stone wall between them. He'd already been 'accosted' by the tailor, though his uniform didn't contain nearly as many intricate layers. The silver insignia of House Martox gleamed beneath the decorative pauldron on his left shoulder. Someone had even attempted to comb his golden hair, but as he ran a hand back over it, it was clear what'd messed it up again.

Corin's attention shifted to the crown, and he gestured with his chin to it. "Try it on yet?"

"No." Jarrod sighed. "Figured I had time."

The tailor moved to his pant cuffs, folding them where they'd need to be hemmed.

Corin sipped his coffee, still watching Jarrod. He looked tired, but concern etched his face, too.

Jarrod looked at the tailor. "What is your name, sir?"

The man looked up at him and hesitated before speaking. "Soren, your majesty. Soren Kenner."

"Soren. I'm sure you're used to a different kind of leadership, but I hope as time progresses, you become more comfortable in our presence. There is no need to be wary of myself or my husband."

The tailor bowed his head. "Of course, your highness."

Jarrod nodded. "Would you give us a moment, please?"

"Yes, your highness." Soren straightened and hurried from the room, shutting the door behind him.

Letting out a breath, Jarrod lifted his hands in defeat. "Everyone is terrified of me, no matter how nice I am."

Corin gave him a small sideways smile as he set his mug on the windowsill. "People don't know what to expect. They've been serving under Iedrus their entire lives, potentially, and he was a tyrant. It'll take time, but they'll realize the kind of man you are."

"How is the rest of the staff adjusting to the change in leadership? Are you seeing any resistance from them or the military?"

"Here and there, but nothing to worry about. It appears most of the military in the city were just following orders. They're perfectly willing to lay down arms and pick them back up in the name of House Martox. We'll have to keep an eye on them, of course, to see if they're loyalists, but for the most part the military is falling in line. I've appointed my grand generals and now it's up to them to put procedures in place."

Jarrod rolled his shoulders. "There's so much work to do with this country."

Corin crossed to him, taking his hand. "And we'll take care of it all, one day at a time."

Squeezing his husband's hand, Jarrod nodded. "I wish my father could see this."

"Me too." Corin rubbed his thumb against Jarrod's. "He'd be so proud of you."

"I hope so." The king looked at the crown again. "It all feels so surreal."

Corin slid his arm around Jarrod's waist and met his lips in a gentle kiss. "Want me to pinch you?" He smiled as he traced his thumb over Jarrod's scar on his chin. "You will be the greatest king Helgath has seen in millennia."

A grin spread over Jarrod's face. "And yet, the best part is having you next to me, *not* pinching me." He kissed Corin, drawing out the affection.

Corin hummed against his lips before a knock at the door broke the kiss, but he didn't pull away entirely.

Neco lifted his head, ears pricked towards the door.

"My king, the troops are assembled and awaiting your word." Auster stood in the doorway, his own attire polished and pressed for the occasion. His beard had thickened with more white than it'd had when he was first assigned to Jarrod.

Gods, that was only a year ago.

Jarrod looked down at his pinned pant cuffs. "Soren can finish this later."

"They won't see your pant cuffs through the balcony, anyway." Corin tugged on the front of Jarrod's coat, straightening it. He glanced at the crown and smiled. "And that gets to wait until coronation."

"When did Damien say that will be? A celebration will help the city heal." Jarrod touched Corin's face and stepped down from the raised platform the tailor had him on. He headed for the door, nerves fluttering in his stomach.

At least I'm getting better at giving speeches.

The big black wolf rose and trotted after them, staying close to Jarrod's side.

"In a few days. Gives you time to prepare *that* speech, too." Corin closed the door as they left the room, following Auster.

When they arrived at the balcony, Jarrod didn't let himself hesitate before striding out into the warm summer air. As he crossed to the center of the curved balcony, the soldiers below banged their weapons and shields, their voices rising in scattered shouts.

At the back of the balcony, Damien, Rae, Maith, and Vinoria stood with his highest ranking Martox guards, rebels and Hawks. Their fists clapped to their chests, and the crowd of soldiers mimicked the action.

Jarrod faced the courtyard, Neco on one side and Corin on the other.

The open stone area served as the front entrance to the castle. One hundred yards across, intricate statues of Helgath's old kings decorated the boundary, a view of the city's stone buildings beyond. The troops stood in their ranks, forced to leave space between for the row of three multi-tiered fountains.

The king put his fist to his chest and then raised his hand.

The mass of soldiers quieted.

Jarrod let the silence reign for several breaths before he spoke. "Brave men and women, you have fought valiantly. Regardless of where each of you stood yesterday... This day, we unite. This day, we all fight for the same side and we will honor our fallen comrades by not repeating the mistakes of the past. Things are going to change in this beautiful country. It will take time... and I ask for your patience as we form new traditions. New laws. As we do away with ruthless tactics and make way for equality and integrity.

"I have the privilege of leading the way, but I cannot do it alone. Together, we will rise and overcome the injustices that prevail in our cities. Together, we will move forward and uproot corruption. I need every one of you to seek abuse of power and destroy it as you would an enemy at our gates."

The soldiers banged their weapons again, shouting a cry of support.

Jarrod swallowed, gripping the railing in front of him. "You are the force behind ridding us of the evil that lurks in the streets. You have the *strength* to defend the helpless and with your loyalty, we can absolve the sins of yesterday and restore our country's might!"

The crowd burst into cheers, abandoning the stoicism. The roar rose, thundering through the air in victorious jubilance.

Three days later...

People packed the courtyard, throwing flower petals and rice as they cheered. Trumpets blared in the distance, repeating the glorious notes of the coronation ceremony.

Jarrod resisted the urge to adjust the gold crown on his head, the formal regalia less suffocating than when he'd worn it days prior.

At least my pants are hemmed, now.

The king turned from the crowd, giving his council a subtle smile as he returned inside, a weight he didn't know was there lifting off his chest.

When the door to the balcony closed, diminishing the roar of cheers that continued outside, Jarrod looked at Corin and admired the simpler gold crown his husband wore. "That went well, I'd say."

"Very well." Corin stepped close, placing a gentle kiss on the king's lips. "Just like I expected, you're settling into your new role with grace."

"I don't know, the speech could have used a bit more refinement." Damien grinned in his teasing, patting Jarrod roughly on the back. "We'll finally have some time to relax. At least until the formal celebration ball in a month."

Rae hugged Jarrod, leaning forward to accommodate her belly. "You were wonderful."

The king released her and grinned, shaking his head. "I can't believe it's all over. We all need a bit of downtime."

"Going to enjoy it while I can. Before Bellamy makes his appearance." Damien wrapped his arms around Rae from behind, kissing her braided hair.

As the officers dispersed to return to their duties, Corin took Jarrod's hand. "There is *one* more thing."

He led Jarrod through the halls they'd rushed down during their assault on Iedrus. Now, Martox guards stood at the positions around the stairs and doorways. They gave a salute to the king the moment he was in eyesight, not releasing it until he'd passed.

"Are the royal chambers ready?" Jarrod tilted his head as they started up the last set of stairs. He glanced back at Rae and Damien, who walked hand in hand behind them.

Damien had a knowing smile on his lips and shrugged at Jarrod.

"Yes. I already asked for our things to be moved into them, but there's something else, too." Corin turned to walk backwards once they reached the top of the stairs, tugging Jarrod with both hands into the massive room that marked the entrance into the royal chambers.

Jarrod narrowed his eyes at his husband. "You've got that look on your face like you've accomplished something sneaky."

"I've definitely earned my position as an honorary Ashen Hawk."

"What did you do?" Jarrod looked around the space, admiring the freshly painted walls and new furniture. The battle that'd ravaged the space felt like a distant memory instead of mere days ago.

Corin led him to the wall that used to don a mural of Iedrus, now covered in light-grey tempera paint. He released Jarrod and strode to a large painting at the center, grabbing the corner of the drape covering it. "We all worked with the artist to make sure it was perfect."

"This was your idea, though." Damien motioned to his brother.

Corin looked back at Jarrod, meeting his eyes. "I really hope you like it." He tugged on the curtain, and it cascaded to the ground to reveal the painting.

Jarrod's breath caught.

Depicted in formal attire, Reznik stood behind a teenage version of Jarrod. He sat in a chair in front of his father, dressed in black with his vest hanging open as it always had when he was a Hawk. Reznik's hands rested on his shoulders, gazing out at the viewer. He looked as strong as Jarrod always remembered him, his stern face softened with pride.

Jarrod's throat constricted, and he touched his face, swallowing through the emotion misting his eyes. He drew in a shaky breath. "Wow..." He approached the painting, wrapping his arms around his husband. "It's perfect. I don't know what to say. Thank you. So fucking much. I love it."

Corin held him tight, smiling against his neck. "I know you miss him, and I hope this will help you remember how proud I know he is of you." He pulled back, touching Jarrod's cheek to brush away the tear that'd escaped. "I have plans for the rest of the day, too. And it begins with enjoying our private chambers with a nice, long bath."

Chapter 37

One month later...

DAMIEN PACED THE ROOM, CHEWING on his nails. "I can't believe she kicked me out."

"I don't blame her. You wouldn't stop doing... that." Corin waved at Damien, pouring liquor into a glass. The sitting room at the front of Damien and Rae's chambers provided plenty of places to rest, but the Rahn'ka couldn't bring himself to sit.

"Sit," Corin prompted for the fourth time, holding out the glass.

Damien's eyes darted to their bedroom door as Rae cried out, the energies inside a storm his ká struggled to comprehend. His body tensed, and he resisted the urge to charge back inside. The burly midwife would only kick him out again.

A knock echoed at the other door before it swung open, Jarrod stepping through. He looked more himself, though his black vest was definitely crafted of finer leather. "I came as soon as I could. How's she doing?" Jarrod held the door open for Neco and the big wolf slunk to the closed bedroom door, whining.

The king looked at Damien, then to the closed door. "Why aren't you in—"

"She kicked him out." Corin poured another glass.

Jarrod smirked. "I'll check on her." He opened the bedroom door, only getting it a foot open before Rae shouted.

"Get out!"

The midwife slammed the door, and Jarrod made a face. "Nevermind. Apparently my power has limits, even in my own castle." He smiled, joining Corin in the seat next to him.

Damien groaned, running his hands through both sides of his hair. "This is all fine. It's all going to be fine. Women give birth... all the time." He stalked over to the table, snatching one of the glasses Corin had poured, and downed its contents.

"All the time. And Rae is tough, she'll be fine."

Rae yelled again, and it lasted longer than the previous time.

Jarrod cringed and chuckled at Damien. "You couldn't hear it, but she cursed at you under her breath."

"Me?" Damien held out the empty glass to Corin, and his brother poured more. "I guess that's fair. I technically did this to her." He looked nervously back to the door as he drank. He crept forward to put his ear against the wood.

All the power of the Rahn'ka and I can't do anything to help with childbirth.

"It's only been a few hours since the contractions got bad. Labor can last much longer." Corin held up a glass to Jarrod. "Might as well sit down. You too, Neco."

Neco gave Damien's hand a lick before he abandoned his post at the bedroom door. He rubbed up against Jarrod's legs and plopped onto the floor.

The king stroked his ears. "I cleared my schedule for the rest of the day, and tomorrow, too, so let me know if you need anything." Jarrod eyed Corin. "I hope this doesn't change her mind about doing this again."

Another scream echoed from inside the bedroom, pitched higher than the rest. A second followed it, then the wail of a newborn.

Damien straightened away from the door, his heart leaping into his throat. Before anyone could tell him otherwise, he turned the doorknob and rushed into their bedroom.

Rae laid with her head back against the stacked pillows keeping her in an upright position, a silk sheet covering her bent legs.

The midwife and two other women stood in the corner, fussing over the baby who continued to wail at the top of his lungs.

Panting, Rae opened her eyes and focused on Damien as he crossed the room to her. Sweat beaded her brow, her hair sticking to her face, but she looked gorgeous.

She smiled and looked at the midwife. "Is he healthy?"

The greying woman bundled Bellamy in a cloth and brought him over, settling him into Rae's waiting arms.

Damien sat on the bed beside her, awe overtaking all the nerves. He curled his leg beneath so he could get close and kissed Rae's hair as he peered down at the little face within the blanket.

Bellamy squeaked, gurgling as he stopped crying.

The midwife rounded to the other side of the bed. "Best to nurse right away." She unbuckled the shoulder strap of Rae's dress and guided the baby to the breast.

When Bellamy latched, Rae gasped. "Wow, that feels weird."

"Oh, he's a natural. Little champ." The midwife grinned and shuffled away.

Damien chuckled and kissed her hair again. "He's perfect." He put a hand on top of Rae's, tangling his fingers with hers.

"He's beautiful." Rae stared at her son, eyes glistening. "Gods, he's here. Our son is here."

Damien tightened his hold around Rae. "Good work, Mama."

After only a brief amount of time with his wife, the midwife ushered Damien out of the room again to let Rae rest.

He carried the bundled baby to where Jarrod and Corin still sat, and both men rose to their feet.

Damien glanced up, struggling to take his eyes away from the rounded cheeks of the baby. He smiled as he touched his soft skin, and his entire body lightened. "Time to meet your uncles, Bellamy," he cooed as he approached them. The baby felt so delicate in his arms, he hardly knew how to move without jostling him.

Neco reached Damien before either of the men, but slowed before he barreled into the new father's legs. He whined and lifted his nose to sniff the baby's feet.

"All right, buddy, but no licking." Damien leaned over just enough for Neco to get a good look and sniff. The baby squirmed, little hands escaping from the folds of the blanket.

Neco whined, then licked Damien's hand.

"My turn." Corin held out his hands and Damien frowned, hesitant to let his son go. "Oh, come on. I won't drop him, little brother."

Damien shook his head as he transferred Bellamy into Corin's arms. "Careful with his head."

"I know, I know," Corin grumbled, his hand already in place to support. He grinned down at the baby, playing with one of his balled fists with his finger.

Jarrod stood next to Corin, stroking the child's dark wispy hair. "He's so little." With his other hand, he clapped Damien on the shoulder. "How you feeling, Dada?"

Damien sighed, smiling. "Happy he's perfect, and Rae's just resting." He watched as Bellamy yawned in Corin's arms and the soldier made a ridiculously high-pitched sound. "Time to give him back."

Corin frowned. "Jarrod hasn't gotten to hold him yet." His brother transferred Bellamy into Jarrod's arms, and the king cradled the baby.

"Aren't you just the sweetest." Jarrod tilted his head. "I'm gonna teach you to throw knives like the best little thief in the world."

"All right, all right, give him back." Damien beckoned his hands. "We can stop planning for his future now."

Jarrod sighed and relinquished the child back to his father's arms. "Is there anything you need at all?"

Damien looked down at Bellamy's sleeping face, running a hand over his hair. A wisp of his ká danced from his touch, and the baby's responded with familiarity. "No. I have everything I ever needed."

Epilogue

One year later...
Autumn, 2613 R.T.

RAE GLARED AT THE ROASTED quail on her plate and wrinkled her nose.

Nope, not gonna happen.

Bellamy, sitting on Damien's lap, squealed and chucked his food onto the floor. His dark baby hair had fallen out months ago, replaced gradually with golden locks that matched his father's.

"I get you, kid. I don't think I can eat it, either." The Mira'wyld rose from her seat, her stomach turning over. "Bread it is." She took a loaf from the platter in the middle of the table and tore off a chunk, giving some to her son.

"No quail, either, huh?" Damien frowned. "You can't just eat bread." He leaned to pick up Bellamy's food, putting it back on the table before pushing the baby's half-empty plate away.

"I don't just eat bread. I eat fruit, too."

"Was it like this with Bellamy?" Damien bounced the one-year-old on his knee, making Bellamy giggle.

Rae shrugged. "Yes, and no. I couldn't eat certain things while I was pregnant with him in the beginning, but this child is pickier." She touched her flat stomach, the life within not yet showing.

Damien frowned. "But it still feels normal? Like before?"

Does he have to ask me every day?

"I'm sorry." Damien responded before she had to protest out loud. "I'm just worried."

"If it ever feels off, I will tell you immediately." Rae smiled at him, sitting again. "And if you stop asking, that means I only need to field daily inquiries from Jarrod and Corin."

After months of research, the Rahn'ka had painstakingly taken parts of the kings' ká to form new life growing in his wife's womb.

"When are we supposed to meet with the royals from Isalica today?" Rae chewed on a bite of bread. "We need to treat this with care. Our peace treaty with Ziona is still rocky."

"Jarrod and Corin are entertaining them for dinner. We're to join after Bellamy has gone to bed. Figured it was better than introducing more chaos into the situation."

The child squirmed wildly in his father's arms, giving a protesting screech as he forced Damien to lower him to the floor. His little hands thumped as he crawled towards Rae, pulling on her legs to stand upright and grab at her tunic.

Rae nodded, taking Bellamy's hands to help him keep his balance while standing. "Probably best. Corise will let me know if he wakes up and needs me."

The cook had expressed interest in babies after Jarrod took the throne and ended up making an excellent nanny.

"Anything to give you a chance to breathe. While I know Bellamy misses you, you can have some time apart from him, too."

"Almost bedtime." Rae smiled at the little one, who laughed.

The child lowered himself to the rug, pulling away from his mother to crawl towards the chest of toys at the edge of their sitting room. He pulled himself up, tossing toys out onto the floor.

Damien reached across the table and took Rae's hand. "I'm sorry I haven't been around as much as I should. This personal advisor stuff is complicated. And Sindré insisted I need to go back to the sanctum in Jacoby to study more soon. Might have given them the wrong idea when I was there to figure out how to make this happen." He gestured towards the baby inside her.

"You'll need to take a leave while you deal with Kin, too. It's almost time to wake him up. Unless you want to leave him longer?" Rae squeezed his hand.

Damien chewed his bottom lip. "He and Amarie are both better off in slumber right now. We still don't know enough to even start making plans for Uriel."

"They're safe, at least." Rae stood and went to their bedroom, leaving the door open to talk to Damien. After arranging the blankets, she drew the curtains closed. "We have time."

"You say that, but the only reason we have time is because Uriel hasn't made another appearance. It's been quiet. We haven't seen any Shades either, when I would have expected them to weasel into the court while a new king was getting settled."

When she turned, Damien stood leaning in the doorway looking at her. "I can't help thinking we've just been lucky. That something's coming and we just don't know it yet."

Rae shrugged. "Perhaps. Or perhaps you're not used to peace." She approached him, draping her arms over his shoulders. "Andi is coming to visit next week and see Bellamy again."

"She still talking like she's going to kidnap her grandson to raise him to be a proper sailor?"

Laughing, Rae looked at Bellamy while the boy bashed two wooden toys together. "It's cute that you think she might stop."

"He *is* freakishly adorable." Damien wrapped his arms around her waist. "Takes after his mother."

"He'll be the best little Ashen Hawk you've ever seen."

"Best little *Rahn'ka*." Damien smiled, but then sighed. "But I like this. Just us, living peacefully in the castle. Without all the Art stuff sometimes." His face grew serious. "I don't want to have to worry about the fate of all Pantracia and Uriel."

"Right now, you don't have to. C'mon. Help me put Bell to bed and then we can go join the others."

Walking into the ballroom decorated with long banners around its vaulted ceiling, Rae fidgeted with the layers of the red satin dress she'd put on.

The room could host hundreds, but they had invited only a handful.

She scanned the few faces, locating Damien talking with Vinoria and Maith. His uniform coat buttoned close to his neck, hiding his Rahn'ka tattoos from the visitors to the castle. He'd cleaned up far faster than her, and, at her insistence, had gone ahead to join the small gathering while she got dressed after putting Bellamy to bed.

Corin appeared in front of her, eyeing her outfit. "That isn't cinched too tight, is it?" He wore his usual kingly attire, including the thin gold crown that sat naturally against his forehead now. He handed her a small cup of guaritho, which she'd started drinking again.

Rae frowned and hugged Damien's brother. "The baby is fine, it's not that tight. Where is Jarrod?"

"He got called away to deal with something, but he should be back soon. Just some paperwork to sign off on regarding the new policies for the academies and their recruitment procedures."

Rae gave Corin a droll look. "Riveting."

"Important." Corin tapped her nose playfully. "Every day, even a year later, there's still work to be done. Including playing the humble host to visiting royals. I never imagined meeting a single king, let alone being one and meeting all of them."

The Mira'wyld shook her head. "It's still strange for me, too. Where is the Isalican king?"

Corin turned, searching for a moment before gesturing to his brother. "Damien is meeting him now."

Rae followed his gaze to the man Damien shook hands with. Her chest seized, stopping her breath.

The Isalican king grinned, releasing the Rahn'ka's hand and smoothing his mid-length windswept chestnut hair. His chin sported a perfectly trimmed beard of a slightly darker brown. He looked comfortably dressed, the blue vest tunic shaped to his fit form. The turbulent sea of his eyes focused on Damien as they spoke.

Impossible.

Adrenaline spiked into her veins and she tore her gaze away, turning her back to keep him from seeing her face.

And Damien is right there with him.

Corin's brow furrowed and he touched Rae's arm. "You all right?"

"No." Rae shook her head, breathing faster. "I don't feel well. I need to leave." Without giving Corin an opportunity to question her, she walked calmly from the room, her hands shaking as she turned the doorknob and exited into the hallway.

Fear riddled her insides as she put a hand on her stomach, pressing her back against the wall.

Closing her eyes, her mind showed her an image of the shadow beast chasing her and Amarie across the strait. The boom of his roar and snap of fangs in his canine muzzle.

She fought to control her breath, rushing in and out of her lungs.

The door next to her clicked open and she jumped, whirling away from it.

Her gaze met Damien's.

"Corin said you were feeling sick again." Damien took her hand. "You want to go upstairs and I can help with the nausea a little so you can come back and enjoy the night?"

Rae shook her head rapidly back and forth. "It's not that. I don't feel sick. I just—"

A staff person somewhere in the hall dropped an empty serving tray and it clattered to the floor, making her jump again.

Damien's grip tightened. "Dice, what's wrong?"

"That man you were just talking to. He's the king of Isalica?" Dread piled in her stomach, mind spinning with the implications. "That's Matthias Rayeht?"

"Yes, I was hoping we'd meet him together, but he caught me before I saw you. He looks younger than I expected, considering he's been king fourteen years already."

"No, no. Damien. You don't understand. I know his face." Rae squeezed Damien's hand. "He can't see me."

"Rae, slow down." Damien glanced at the door into the ballroom and down the long empty hallway. "What's going on? Why can't he see you?" He took her other hand. "You're shaking."

She'd never forget that face. "That's *him*. That's *Uriel*."

The series continues with...

SISTERS OF THE
FROZEN VEIL

www.Pantracia.com

THEY ARE SISTERS... NOT BY BLOOD, BUT BY MAGIC, AND THEY WILL CHANGE THE TIDES OF WAR.

With the unexpected company of a temple acolyte, Isalican Crown Prince Matthias Rayeht arrives at the contested border of Feyor while posing as one of his own guards. An assassination attempt interrupts their first night, which escalates into a full-blown battle. And Feyor sent more than just their dire wolves.

Katrin thought she understood war. But when she's thrown into the chaos, she gains a whole new vision of the bloodshed. A vision so unlike the one that led her to follow a handsome royal guard. Danger thrusts her into the woods alone, where she finds an enemy in the frozen night.

Dani is a warrior. A Dtrüa. A shapeshifter created by Feyor. But with the battle underway... her leash may snap.

Desperate to avoid war, enemies must overcome their prejudice to see the truth. And the truth, hiding behind a veil of lies, could change everything.

Sisters of the Frozen Veil is Part 1 of *Shadowed Kings* and Book 8 in the *Pantracia Chronicles*.

Made in the USA
Monee, IL
12 March 2024

54373242R00256